MY GUN
SHOOTS
BULLETS

MY GUN SHOOTS BULLETS

A MacCoole & Boone Western

WILLIAM W. JOHNSTONE

and J.A. JOHNSTONE

PINNACLE BOOKS
Kensington Publishing Corp.
www.kensingtonbooks.com

PINNACLE BOOKS are published by

Kensington Publishing Corp.
119 West 40th Street
New York, NY 10018

First Printing: February 2024
ISBN-13: 978-0-7860-4951-6
ISBN-13: 978-0-7860-4952-3 (eBook)

10 9 8 7 6 5 4 3 2 1

Printed in the United States of America

CHAPTER 1

"Seems to me you ought to pay closer attention when I share a sweet memory of my cherished youth." Hokum Boone picked the lint from a knob of chaw he found in his possibles bag and stuffed it in his cheek.

His business pard and best friend, Keller "Mac" MacCoole suppressed a smile and glanced to his right, well aware that the longer he refrained from responding, the more worked up ol' Hoke was liable to get. It worked every time. Mac took his time tugging out a black, finger-length cigarillo that looked less like a cigar and more like something a sick dog might have left behind in an alleyway. He licked the end, then popped it between his lips and scratched a match head with his thumbnail.

It flared, and as soon as he set fire to the end of the cigarillo, Hoke did what Mac expected. He set to moaning and clucking and growling as if Mac were working him over with a cudgel.

"You all right over there, Hoke?"

"No, I ain't all right, and you dang well know it! Every time you set fire to one of those god-awful stinkers, I'm liable to expire from a case of the agonizing tremors I feel deep down in my innards!"

"You're certain it's not that hunk of old, used chaw you found in your pocket that's making you feel awkward?"

"No, I tell you! I hardly ever save my chaws for later."

"I know," said Mac, snapping his big fingers. "It just may have something to do with the fact that you are wrapped in a suit of greasy buckskins that haven't seen a good scrubbing, and neither has the varmint trapped in them, for many, many moons. Hmm?"

"No again! And I'll tell you a thing or three, Mr. Thinks He Knows Everything! It just so happens that buckskins have natural smell-deadening qualities. You ever wonder why you are likely surrounded by deer and elk and such most all the time, but you hardly ever smell them?"

"Except when they're in rut." Mac plumed a cloud of blue smoke over toward Hoke, who gigged his paint, Chummy, ahead a step to avoid the noxious cloud.

"Rut, my foot! You are in rare form today, MacCoole, and toying with danger! And besides, I happen to know you only smoke those stinkers to annoy me." Hoke almost grinned. Almost. The rangy woodsman knew he had to keep his ornery demeanor from slipping, lest he appear weak.

Mac wrinkled his own nose at the rank smoke he was generating and puffed again. They were not like any of his finer cigars, that was for certain. "You know, Hoke, I do believe that was the first true thing you've said all day."

"You mean to tell me you don't believe what I told you about Cousin Merd and the half-woman, half-tree creature? Why, everybody in Hoddy's Gulch knows it for a fact, but then again, I'd expect doubts from someone such as yourself, who hasn't had the good fortune or good sense to spend time in Hoddy's." Boone smiled at the memory of the place. "I ever tell you that the Gulch was named for my great-grandpappy?"

Mac nodded. "I do believe that earthshaking revelation has passed from your lips a time or three, yes."

"And you're a better man for hearing it, Mac MacCoole. Let me tell you."

"I can't disagree, Hoke, that at the end of my days I will look back on this life and I will say to myself, 'Mac, you have had a vast assortment of fascinating experiences, seen a host and a half of astounding sights, and heard sounds the likes of which you will recall far into the afterlife.'"

"Uh-huh, that's the truth," said Hoke, nodding.

"But none of those vivid, sweet recollections," continued Mac, trying not to grin because he knew Hoke would glance at him soon, "will ever compare with Hokum Boone's assortment of windy tales."

"Windy tales? That's what you think these are? Why, they are pure fact! Gold, I tell you! Why, people hear them and shake their heads! I don't doubt but they are thanking the Almighty for allowing them to hear such astounding truths!"

For a spell, neither man spoke as they plodded along, riding from the northwest back to their home base in Denver City. They were fresh off a mild town-taming job for a wealthy widow woman who owned an entire mining town in a valley in Oregon.

Other than her trusted manservant, who Mac and Hoke suspected was also her longtime lover, Madame Steiner claimed she could trust no one. And if what had been happening to her at a steady and alarming clip was an indication, she was correct. It seemed the old girl's inherited fortune had been set up such that she had, up to then, little reason to root into her finances.

But it turned out she had been the long-term victim of unscrupulous, unsavory characters, namely a mine foreman, Eddie Tinkerson, and his rapacious wife, "Sweet."

And then, when Madame Steiner's townsfolk, all of whom had been living a meager existence, beholden to her and her business, noticed they were being shorted on their weekly rations of flour and fatback bacon and sacks of beans, trouble had begun. There were other supplies they were being shortchanged on as well, discovered as Madame Steiner investigated further. She finally had cause to look deeply into the earnings of her many local mines, and what she found appalled her.

Steiner was at her wit's end when an acquaintance wrote, telling of a couple of men who roved the West, taking on jobs considered too unlawful for the law and too dangerous for most other mercenaries. But Mac and Boone were hardly ordinary men.

They received a missive from Madame Steiner, explaining the situation and requesting their assistance. It seemed money would not yet be a concern, though if the situation kept up, it might well become a worry.

As the men had had little going on at that time, a month and a half prior, and had grown restless and, for Boone, at least, increasingly financially strapped, they wrote back to Steiner forthwith and accepted the work.

They rode to Steiner's Mountain, naturally, and made good time. Within a week, they found themselves gracing the front steps of Madame Steiner's mansion.

It had then taken them the better part of a month to infiltrate the inner group of Eddie and Sweet Tinkerson. The mine foreman had initially regarded them with suspicion, but as the days wore on, they proved indifferent and then useful to Tinkerson's larcenous ways.

One night, they plied Eddie with the last of Mac's decent bottles of whiskey he'd brought along. The thief had become a bit loose with his tongue, enough so that they learned more in one evening than they would have in a month of further snooping about his nefarious deeds.

It turned out that Tinkerson had been raking Steiner over the coals for years. At first he'd only dared to filch a little at a time, and always covered his tracks with the utmost care.

Then he began sending wagons loaded with ore down the backside of the mountain they mined.

And as time progressed, he realized no one was going to harangue him about his loosely kept books of accounting. So the greedy rat grew greedier. And then Mac and Boone ground Eddie and Sweet's operation to a skidding halt.

Now, back on the trail and making for home, each man was mired in his own thoughts. Sometimes those thoughts overlapped, as with an old married couple. After a few long days on the trail, usually Boone would circle back, say something about how they met all those years ago in the war, in a battle to the death, in the midst of a dank, dark swamp.

They had been surrounded with slithering, snapping creatures. And in the wet, fetid heart of that swamp, the two men had savaged each other, delivering a thousand nicks and cuts and gashes. None alone had been fatal, but if they had continued, each surely would have laid the other low given a few more hours.

But in one of their mutual halts to catch breath and wet lips, the blood adversaries—Hokum Boone as a grayback and Mac MacCoole as a bluebelly—heard shouts—dare they guess?—some sort of distant yells of "hoorah" from beyond, up the long hill and back into the light of afternoon, on the battlefield above.

They then were beckoned, heralded by officers of each side, standing side by side and shouting to them to cease their battling because the war had come to a halt; Lee had called it a day. It was over.

That's when those two men, one in blue, the other in gray, and each oozing red, had officially met. From then on, they became fast friends, then business partners, then best of friends, confidants, and foils for each other's foibles and jokes and follies.

And their trail banter, as had been exchanged on that day, was of the ribald and humorous, rubbing, ribbing quality.

They were, after all, flush with cash, following yet another successful mission during which their shared thirst for derring-do and adventure and excitement had been slaked. Plus, there was the bonus of them being able to help deserving parties to overcome forces seeking to do them harm.

Madame Steiner had smiled and waved and wept as they rode off, so grateful had she become to them. Her man-servant, Willard, had even cracked a smile on his normally stoic face.

They'd stocked up on trail goods at the nearest noncompany town, on down the valley a ways, with bacon and flour and cornmeal and apples and dried fruits and tobacco and whiskey and various other items they would enjoy on their slow journey back to Denver City.

The weather was fine, no storms on the horizon that they could discern. Their horses, Mac's big Appaloosa, Lincoln, and Hoke's smaller but steady paint, Chummy, were in fine form, and they were on no man's clock save their own. And theirs, for the time being, had ceased to tick. Late starts and early camps were the order of the week. And that suited each man right down to the ground.

And then they met the women. After a fashion . . .

CHAPTER 2

Five months earlier

The portly gentleman in Highland tweeds puffed on a large meerschaum pipe, a commissioned piece, its ornate surface carved to resemble the man himself, complete with waxed mustache, muttonchops, and trim beard.

Pipes and fine tobaccos were an indulgence Winterson Blaswell could well afford. He was, after all, one of the wealthiest men in America, a shipping magnate with primary offices in both Boston and Providence, where his mansion dominated a sizable wedge of premium real estate overlooking the busy port.

As he gazed out on the bustle and ebb and flow of commerce in the harbor, much of the trade of which his business accounted for, Blaswell smiled and grunted in satisfaction. He ruminated as he sent forth clouds of blue smoke into the high-ceilinged office with its richly carved paneling and thick imported rugs.

He had done rather well for himself since coming to America as a young immigrant from Latvia. He'd recognized various needs in life, needs others also recognized, but for which most people merely yearned.

He, on the other hand, had an innate skill—he'd heard

others call it a gift, though he never said this of himself, no, no—for finding solutions to problems, finding ways of turning needs into wants and then supplying them.

Take ice, for instance, commencing a worn tale he had often told his daughter, Philomena, at dinner of an evening. Oh, he knew the poor girl had heard the story of his rise to fortune a thousand and one times, but once he'd tucked into a third glass of red wine during their meal, he could not help himself, he simply had to boast, even a little.

And Philly, named for the birthplace of her dear, departed mother, always listened with a half smile, so like her mother's that made Blaswell felt as if she really were hearing it for the first time and not merely indulging his bragging whimsies.

If there was one thing he could wish for, the one thing money with all its wonders simply could not buy, it was to spend another day, another hour, a single minute, with Philly's mother, Edna. Dear Edna, gone from their lives these last four years now, taken by a case of creeping, chronic pleurisy.

"Trade it all," he whispered to his reflection in the window. "Trade it all . . ."

From behind him, a voice cleared.

Blaswell spun to see his right-hand man, the young Thurston Kane, standing with the inevitable sheaf of papers held before him, no doubt requiring his signature.

Kane was a decent young fellow, dapper, tending in his wardrobe selection toward the outdated but serviceable. This was also reflected in the man's speech and mannerisms. Despite this, or perhaps because of it, Blaswell liked the young man. He somehow reminded the portly businessman of himself some years ago. From poor stock, Kane had worked his way up and out of the bonds of poverty. He was shrewd and keen to learn. *Eager,* thought Blaswell, *and hungry.*

And best of all, it appeared as if Thurston Kane was fond of his Philly, too.

And as Philly was no longer a child, but creeping into the first years where the word "spinster" might well be muttered in the salons and drawing rooms of Blaswell's wealthy if snide acquaintances, Winterson thought perhaps it was time the girl married.

The one impediment he noticed, at any rate, had been and continued to be her looks. The poor thing was not what anyone might consider attractive to the opposite gender. Not that Philly was homely, but neither were Winterson nor dear Edna possessed of facial appeal.

This trait, unfortunately, was passed on to their one and only offspring. But he most decidedly could say that what she lacked in looks, Philly made up for in mental acumen. Had she only been born a male, he might be inclined to allow her what she always pestered him for—to help run his burgeoning empire.

Thankfully, Thurston Kane had come along. That might well solve both problems—the marrying off of Philly and the future of his empire. For Winterson Blaswell knew he would not be around forever. His attacks of gout had flared with more frequency of late, and the thumping of his heart, like a locomotive on an uphill grade, woke him now and again in the night.

Of this latter, he told no one. The former, he knew from his doctor's advice, could be solved by reducing his intake of sweet meats and whiskey and wine, even tobacco. *Perish the thought*, he would say. He did not work so hard for so long to abandon the rewards of such a life now!

Then he would smile and light up his pipe. Or a fine cigar. And hoist another after-dinner snifter.

"Sir?"

"Kane, yes, a good morning to you, son."

They both seemed to like this ritual, though it was well

into late morning. Blaswell had grown accustomed to having Kane around, and in the short ten months or so since the young man had arrived and shown such promise, Blaswell had gradually loaded down the lad with more and more duties, telling himself that the more he was able to do that, the more time he would be able to devote to important matters, such as establishing the new rail line, which would allow him to breach, develop, explore, and unfold untold new markets. Already his efforts, moving from planning to implementation with the recent establishment of an office in San Francisco, were making national headlines.

With all this exciting new momentum bristling in the air of the opulent office that morning, Blaswell and Kane surveyed the big map spread out yet again upon the central table.

"This will be the first and most important section of the new rail line, Kane. The bedrock, the very foundation spur that will eventually run from Chicolo, north of Sacramento, over the Sierra Nevada range, north to Oregon and Idaho.

"Why, not only will it reach into the newest and most promising agricultural lands and goldfields in all of North America, it will crack them wide open! And then, why, then, it's all a matter of speculation, my dear boy. In short order, I daresay nobody in these burgeoning United States and beyond will be unfamiliar with the name Winterson Blaswell!"

The portly gent smiled broadly, rocking on his heels as if he were about to tumble right over backward. He set down his prize pipe, lest he swing a waving arm and smack the gentle creation into a bookcase.

"Yes sir," said Thurston Kane, doing his best to maintain his serious demeanor. "Though I am hardly a judge of such matters, I will posit a notion that you must have already entertained yourself."

"And that is, my boy?"

"Well, that perhaps you should run for office."

"Do you mean mayor of Providence or some such?" Blaswell chuckled.

"Well, no sir, I meant on the statewide level. Or perhaps, dare I say it, at the national level. Why, a man of your vision could easily hold the highest office in the land."

"Kane, Kane, you are a clever young man, that much is certain. But the office of president is not open to one such as I—I was born in Latvia, lest you forget—"

"Sir," said Kane, "pardon me for interrupting, but such laws are changeable. What is America if not a place of change?"

"Well, yes, that is true. But look, enough of that now, my boy. You have certainly given me food for thought. Yes, yes, of course I had entertained notions of perhaps one day sharing my, dare I say, *expertise* in building and shaping an enterprise into more civic-minded duties. But the time is not yet ripe. But what it is time for is to plan the next steps in the rail line.

"What I need now is someone on the ground out there. We'll set up an office, a base of operations in San Francisco, of course, but this person will have to arrive well ahead of time and meet those contracted firms we have lined up. There will be much to do, much to do. And once they are in situ, as it were, this person will need to meet the ships bringing the first loads of immigrant labor forces we have sent for from China."

Blaswell rubbed his pink hands together and smiled. "I tell you, Kane, being able to give all those families this opportunity! It's something I never had, arriving here as a penniless youth. Oh, think of the leg up we'll give them."

"Indeed," said Kane, thumbing through the papers on the table before him.

"Yes, yes! We shall establish encampments for them in which they will be able to work, live, cook—oh, the lot of

it. Living, daily living. Only they will no longer be scrabbling for a meager livelihood in their natal lands! No, they
will be in the United States of America, my boy. Working
for a living, earning lucre to give their offspring the very
best this bounteous land can offer!"

He thumbed his lapels and looked out the window. "And
we will be there at the outset to guide them. Why, jobs
building a railroad is just the start. I envision entire towns
all along the routes. And one day those modest villages will
become booming centers of progress and commerce. And
populated with the very people we helped to bring here.
Think of it, Kane, all of them contributing to this American
dream!"

"Yes sir," said Kane. "And all of them beholden to
Winterson Blaswell and Company." As Kane said this, his
eyes shone, and he nodded in agreement with himself.

But his boss was not smiling. "Well, that may well be a
by-product of our efforts, surely, but it is not the primary
motivation. You see that, don't you, Kane?"

"Oh, oh, of course, sir. I only meant that . . ."

But Blaswell was off, roaming the room again, setting
fire to his damnable pipe, thought Kane, and about to
embark on another windy discourse about the wonders of
his life.

Kane made to head him off before it was too late. "Sir, if
I may . . . we need to discuss the applicants. I believe I left
you the stack of applications listing their qualifications."

"Applicants, Kane?"

"For the manager's job, sir. In California."

"Oh, yes, well . . ." Blaswell waved a hand at the papers
on his desk. "They are all fine men, I'm certain. But I have
another idea in mind that I would like to discuss with you,
Kane."

"Oh?"

"Yes. You see, it involves you, personally. It's no good

having our enterprise being commandeered by a stranger. I need someone I can trust out there, man! This is the largest undertaking in our yearslong, methodical plan to broaden beyond the East. Whoever that is will represent the name Blaswell clear across the country. It is of the utmost importance that this person be eminently trusted and trustworthy. Do you understand?"

"Of course, sir, that's why—" He held the papers up, but Blaswell interrupted him.

"No, no, Kane, I'm not speaking plainly enough for you, I see that now. What I need, what the company needs, is you, Kane. We need you out there. Don't you see? You're the only one I can trust such an undertaking to."

"Me, sir?"

Kane suppressed a wide, wide smile. Doing so was the single most difficult thing he'd had to do since beginning work for Winterson Blaswell.

"Yes, Thurston. You." Blaswell stood behind his desk and leaned forward, his pudgy fists resting atop the blotter. "I suppose I don't have to mention how close you and Philomena have become in recent months. I may be her father, son, but I have eyes. The one thing I have hoped for some time now was that she should find a suitor who might be worthy of her, and of what she will . . . not to put too fine a point on it, but what she will one day come in to."

Blaswell bowed his head and waved his hands wide, to take in the room. It was a gestured attempt at humility, one Kane had seen before, one he knew was intended to encompass the entirety of Blaswell's massive holdings. And Thurston Kane did not take it lightly. He was suitably impressed.

Kane was not born into wealth. Far from it; in that regard, he and Winterson Blaswell were much alike. But where Blaswell grew up believing in the innate goodness of his fellow humans, Thurston Kane grew up believing in the innate worthiness of himself and in the innate worthlessness of most others he met.

He felt that he and he alone deserved everything life could offer, nothing less than all of it. And if he was not to become heir to a fortune, he could, by God, marry one.

That he had found such a person was no surprise to Kane. Finding Philomena Blaswell and then courting her was all part of his personal business plan. That she had a face like a mud fence—well, that could be tolerated and dealt with for as long as was necessary. And then provisions could be made to clear that fence from the landscape. Time, he told himself. All in good time.

By the time he had worked for Blaswell for a month, Thurston Kane felt he knew how the old man thought, how he went about things. Oh, sure, his employer could still surprise him, but for the most part he was confident he could land a solid guess as to Blaswell's next move in most any situation.

In fact, Kane often played a little game with himself, just for fun. He would predict what Blaswell's response was going to be before he consulted him on a topic, be it a new business venture or plans for the rail line project, or one of the many various shipping issues that invariably cropped up in a day's time.

Kane reckoned he was at a 90 percent success rate. And then Blaswell would lob in a skewed response that would throw off Kane's average. But that made it all the more fun.

And so, Thurston Kane was extremely gratified in the days following Blaswell's revelation that he wished Kane to head up the Blaswell Railway expansion enterprise on the West Coast. It was a decision Kane was not in the least surprised by, though in the days leading up to the announcement, he had been increasingly worried lest he do something to perturb his portly employer before the offer could be made.

He was also certain that this would be a test, in Blaswell's eyes, to see if Kane was indeed worthy of marrying his beloved daughter, the horse-faced Philomena. *Ha*, thought Kane. Blaswell had on several whiskey-fueled occasions all but hoisted the slight woman into the air and handed her to Kane with his best wishes and kind regards.

Nonetheless, Kane decided he would work as hard on this project as he ever had on any project, perhaps harder. And more to the point, he would make darn certain the immense task was completed ahead of schedule and, most important of all, so far under the projected budget there would be no doubt that Kane was the very match for Philomena.

And that, in turn, would secure his future as all but heir to the Blaswell empire. He supposed he must also speed up the wooing of Philomena if she, also, were to take him seriously as a suitor.

She was less predictable than her father and had surprised him at times with her frankness and opinions about matters she should not have concerned herself with. That annoyed Kane, as he felt, as did Blaswell, that a woman's place was at home, fretting and wringing her hands lest her man, the breadwinner, the patriarch, come home late from the office.

Ah, time enough for such concerns, Thurston, said Kane to himself as he beckoned a hansom cab on the eve of his departure. One last meal at the Blaswell residence, one last opportunity to kiss the hand of Philomena. It certainly beat kissing her face.

CHAPTER 3

Mac had been the one to hunt up fresh meat the afternoon before, so now it was Hoke's turn. And Mac didn't mind a bit. He was fonder of setting up camp and getting the cookfire crackling.

He'd done just that, and had been assessing whether he should go fetch more wood when Boone showed up with a brace of rabbits. *Good*, thought Mac. *I'll dress the critters and get them frying and he can fetch more wood.*

He smirked because he knew how that suggestion was likely to go over with Hoke. His buckskin-clad pard was likely to grouse and carry on until Mac said fine, he'd fetch more wood, and Boone could tend to the meal preparation.

Faced with that choice, Hokum Boone would nearly always choose the wood gathering. He wasn't much of a cook beyond biscuits and beans and bacon frying, but he liked to hunt and tend fires and natter on about any topic at all. And that, mused Mac, was what made them decent friends and trail pards.

Boone had just gone through the very ritual Mac envisioned, much to the big man's amusement, and had wandered off in search of more firewood when Mac heard voices.

They belonged to folks taking no pains to keep themselves quiet. They drifted to him from the west, accompanied by the squeak and squawk of dusty wagon wheels begging for lubrication. Whoever it was remained too far away for Mac to see, given the clusters of sizable boulders, the sparse growths of pine, and the hilled terrain.

Before long, Boone reappeared from the northeast, with an armload of decent wood, enough to carry them through, and maybe even to get the coffee on the boil in the morning. Good enough.

He slowed up when he saw Mac standing with his gun hand at the ready, the keeper on his hammer unthonged and an ear cocked to the west. Mac glanced at him, then nodded once in that direction. Boone set down the wood and accompanied his pard, also taking the usual precautions when strangers were about.

They spread apart from each other a dozen feet and squared off, just in case.

The squawking and the talking increased in volume; then the noses of an overworked team of horses slowly appeared, working into view from around a massive boulder twice the size of a miner's cabin.

Then the wagon they were dragging appeared, the seat before which was filled with two men. The entire affair, from horses to the odd, tall wagon, was a grimy, dust-caked affair.

One man was fat and looked uncomfortable, his thick head painfully red from the sun where it bulged out from beneath the black or brown bowler—it was tricky for Boone to tell the actual color for all the grime.

The other man was thinner, equally grubby, and looked to have come out on the short end of the stick in a dalliance with some disease that left his countenance pocked and pitted.

They rolled to a stop, and as the dust clouds continued on, dissipating into the east, they looked down from the seat and the thin man nodded toward Mac and Boone.

"Smelled your smoke, figured we'd give us a look-see."

"And what would it be you're looking for, mister?" said Boone.

"Huh?" The thin, pock-faced man squinted hard, drawing his brows together tight, accentuating the grime in the sweaty crevices and divots of his hard face. "Huh?"

"You said that already," said Boone, smirking.

"What my pard is wondering," said Mac, "is why you figured we'd be up for a 'look-see,' as you call it."

"Oh, well, never know who you might run into out in these parts, ain't that right, Clem?"

The big, sweaty, stubble-faced fellow in the wagon seat next to him nodded, but his scowl and fat, wet, pooched lips didn't alter from their pucker.

"I'm Leonard Wilkes, by the way," said the thin man.

"Pleased to meet you, Wilkes. Your man Clem there ain't much of a talker, now, is he?"

Mac could tell Hoke was on the slow boil, working himself up to something, because his skinny, buckskin-clad pard had tugged out his corncob pipe some time before. Even though he hadn't yet filled or lit it, he held it between his teeth and got that squint that told Mac Hoke was in a ruminative mood.

"You gents mind if we light on down and set up camp nearby? Respectful distance, of course."

Mac and Hoke exchanged looks, slight shrugs, then Mac said, "Nothing we can do to prevent it, though I will caution you that my pard here is one hellacious snorer."

Boone nodded. "True enough. Why, it's been said I began the practice as a wet-nose bairn. Even in the cradle, I could rouse the hounds at Uncle Pa-Paw's cabin—he'd be our nearest neighbor, some ways down the lane in the Gulch, where I was raised—to set up a howling ruckus.

"Why, when it was safe enough to do so, come spring, seeing as how I was birthed in the midst of a howling blizzard, my dear sainted mammy set me in the henhouse for the nights. Figured I was old enough to earn my keep. And it worked, too, in some ways. Kept the foxes from raiding the eggs. But the hens suffered terrible." He shook his head, as if this lamentable situation had happened just the day before.

Leonard Wilkes nodded as if he'd just been told a sage truth, then a slow grin spread over his face. "I see that you are a leg puller of the first order, sir. I commend you for that. It's been a long ol' time since I came across a man capable of holding his face set serious like yours whilst sharin' a great windy. Yes sir, I commend you. And to prove my gratefulness, I will share something with you gents, something we're bringing with us, you might say."

The first thing Boone thought of was that these men, with their big, rambling wagon, might well be ferrying whiskey from the coast. That notion held promise. He had been about to tell that rascal where he could find the bear in the buckwheat for insulting his childhood story, one of which Mac knew Hoke was proud. But there was promise in what the stranger was offering, so Hoke kept his mouth shut. For now.

It would be another forty minutes or so before Mack and Boone were to find out just what it was this man was talking about. And when they did, they were more surprised than they had been in all their long years together on the trail.

The two strangers had angled their team off away from them, down a gully and behind a jumble of boulders and trees to set up their own camp. Some minutes later, Mac and Boone exchanged looks as they tidied up their campsite, something they always did once they'd finished their meal.

They had heard the sliding rattle of chain being pulled through steel and dragged along wood. Then the squawk of unoiled, dust-caked steel, thirsty for lubrication, as a door of some sort was swung. Then a slamming sound as that door crashed to the earth.

"What in the . . ."

Mac sipped his coffee. "The wagon, I reckon."

"I reckon," said Boone, looking toward the top of the rock jumble a hundred or so feet away, beyond which and down a bit, sat their new neighbors.

"Hey! Hey now, fellas." They heard Leonard Wilkes's voice before they saw his head slowly bob up around the far right edge of the rocky jumble.

He smiled their way. "You fellas want a treat, you come on over. Camp's all set up now. I think you'll like what you see."

With that, his smiling face turned and he disappeared again. They heard his boots crunch gravel as he walked.

"What do you make of that?" said Boone.

Mac sipped his coffee again. "I don't know. They're an odd pair, to be sure. But then again"—Mac stood and tossed the coffee dregs from his cup—"maybe they think the same of us."

"Never!" said Boone. "I'm not so sure about them fellas."

"Same here. But it would be downright unneighborly of us to not take a peek, now wouldn't it?"

"That's a fact," said Boone. He checked the horses, checked that the picket lines were secure, while Mac cleaned out the coffeepot. "We have daylight on our side, see what we're up against."

"Could be they're innocent as newborns and just behaving kindly."

"Yeah," said Mac. "Or it could be otherwise." He checked his revolver and hip knife, and Boone did the same.

They strode on over, keeping a sharp eye out and without any verbal agreement. They knew what the other was thinking—namely, that they were going to keep tight, make certain nobody got behind them to sneak back to their site and pilfer their goods and horses.

They weren't certain what to expect; likely a couple of

drummers with a wagonload of goods, perhaps liquor, given the man's sneaky smile and hints.

But they were not expecting to see five women, shackled, seated before the side of the wagon, its sides, which had been previously fully upright and enclosing the space within, boxlike.

The women, they saw right away, in addition to being shackled, were quite haggard looking. They also appeared to be Chinese. They were pretty, slight, and slim, with dark hair, but unkempt and grimy, as if they had not had the opportunity to bathe in many days. They looked so tired that keeping their eyes open was a labor.

"My word," muttered Boone.

"You said it," said Mac.

They assumed the women had been in the wagon the entire time the two men had rolled up and talked to them nearly an hour before. No wonder they looked tired. It was August, a month that wasn't known for offering creatures, be they man or beast, a cool, pleasant time of it.

Mac rested his hands on his waist. He and Boone stood a good twenty feet from the new, barely flickering campfire. "Did you keep those women chained up and riding in that dank wagon all day?"

"Well, now," said Leonard. "I was hoping you would accept our kindly intended invite without passing judgment on us."

"Oh, not judging," said Mac. "Just surprised to see what it is we're seeing."

"Oh?"

"And what is it, exactly," said Boone, "that we are seeing, if you don't mind telling, that is?"

"Don't mind?" Leonard smiled his broadest smile yet. "Why, come on over, gents, and at least share in a libation and all will be revealed. I know, I know, you're wary of us. And that's a good thing, because we are wary of you as well."

"What about the ladies? Don't they get to partake of the fire, and some food? You are feeding them, ain't you?" said Boone, his voice clicking up a pinch.

"No worries about them. They're fine. And of course we feed them. They are, after all, our livelihood, if you get my meaning." He winked.

Mac and Boone exchanged glances. Boone nodded, and that meant Mac would be the one to speak. They both knew what was happening here, and they knew it was not right. Their gut reactions to these men had been on. But they were going to go with their standard approach in such odd situations: be honey-tongued and catch the flies.

"Not sure I follow you fully, Mr. Wilkes," said Mac. "But we will take you up on your kind offer of a drink."

"Sure!" said Boone, winking at Leonard. "If we had known, we would have drug along a bottle of our own."

"The night is young, gents. I'm sure we can host you and then, if you care to later, you can reciprocate."

Mac and Boone ambled over to the fire, their backs to a stone slab, and accepted the two freshly wiped out tin cups with a liberal dose of whiskey in each. The bottle wore no label and while that was not necessarily a sign of poor quality whiskey, it did not fill the men with confidence. They would be pretending to sip, they both knew. And would have to be on their toes while whatever this situation was played out.

"Ain't you folks going to eat?" said Boone after a long moment of silence.

"Oh, yes, we have some bread and cheese. But just now," said Leonard, "as is our custom, we like to enjoy a drink after a long day on the trail."

Mac glanced at the ladies. "And the women? Aren't they thirsty as well? Seems like being cooped up in that wagon all day, bouncing over a rocky trail, would be a wearying ordeal."

"I know I'd be looking for a drink of cool water, myself," said Boone, glancing at the women.

"I see that you men cannot avert your eyes from our passengers." Leonard smiled, his eyes half lidded. "Well, now, let me fill you in on a little secret."

He leaned forward, his elbows on his knees. "We are businessmen, me and Clem. These women—ladies as you call them, ha—are a commodity, plain and simple. No more, no less."

"Might be they'd disagree with you on that score."

"Might be," said Leonard, shrugging. "Not really my concern. And they are in no position to disagree, as you see. Besides, there's no way of telling, seeing as how they don't none of them speak a lick of English."

He looked over at them. "Do you, you Oriental savages?" He and Clem both found this highly humorous. Leonard's laugh was a high, whinnying sound and Clem was soundless, merely bouncing where he sat.

"How do you know?" said Boone.

"How do I know what?" said Leonard.

"If they can speak English or not? You tried to talk with them?"

"First off, they ain't for talking, they're for . . . well, I think you get the idea. And second off, they are spoken for, escaped women who owe money to folks who paid for their passage to California. We're doing them a favor."

"How do you figure that?"

"Why, without folks such as Clem and myself, such fallen women would become victims to bad folks. We're protecting them, you see. But seeing as how their business is of the romantic sort," he winked again, "we are prepared to allow you two men to partake of a . . . what's the word?"

Leonard snapped his finger and pointed at Mac and

Boone, nodding. "Yes sir, that's the word! A dalliance. A dalliance, that's the very word for it. And all for only a slight fee, drastically reduced from the usual rate, you see, because, after all, we are neighbors and all."

"Well, you never did answer my question, Leonard," said Mac, wetting his mustache with the whiskey. He barely tasted it, but not to his surprise, it was not a quality liquor. It would not matter, as he and Hoke would not be sampling of it deeply. There was something in the air that told each man to keep his guard up and his senses and wits sharp. And junk booze would not help that endeavor.

"And what question was that, now?" Leonard's smile was strained, his eyes wearing no pretense of kindness, for he guessed what was coming.

"Why are those women chained, man?" said Boone.

"Ah, yes, well, that's simple." Leonard waved a hand toward the five women, who still sat or leaned or squatted along the side of the wagon, glancing occasionally toward the men, then looking away. Their emotions were not discernible on their faces.

"For their own protection, of course," said Leonard, winking at Mac and Boone. "And I will mention again, since we are neighbors of a sort, at least for the evening, that we are prepared to offer you two fine gentlemen a dalliance with your pick of the ladies. For a fee, naturally. Can't go around in life giving away things; otherwise we'd be out of business in no time at all."

For some reason this set Leonard to giggling.

Finally, Mac said, "Might be we're interested. Might be, might be. No way of knowing for certain unless we go on over and take ourselves a look, now, is there?"

At this Leonard and Clem both stood. The skinny, chatty one kept his false smile pasted on his face. "By all means, fellows, be our guests. But one of us will have to go over there with you. You understand, it's nothing to take personal offense to, but those Chinese beauties are our property, after all, you see."

"Understood," said Mac. "Boone, you stay here and keep an eye on the fire, and I'll inspect the goods, as it were."

"Sounds fair," said Boone. "Then we'll trade off."

"Oh, you can both go on over together. That's not a problem, gentlemen."

Mac smiled. "We appreciate the offer, but no. One of us at a time is about all these ladies could handle seeing." He'd meant it as a joke, and while it worked on Leonard, the skinny man's false smile seemed to falter.

As Mac approached the women, with Leonard a couple of steps behind and to his left, Mac took note of the entire setup. The wagon's goods were as they had seen, piled in crates. And soft, poorly tied bundles, likely bedding, sat in the midst of the floor of the wagon.

The chain the women were bound with was looped twice through an iron ring, the steel of which looked to be as thick around as a man's thumb, and likely well bolted where it emerged from a hole in the lumber from the front corner of the wagon.

The chain, a thick, half-rusted affair, ran from one woman to the next. It ran only to their ankle manacles. Their wrists, while not bound, bore harsh signs in the form of welts and scarlet rings. They had been bound recently with hemp rope or steel cuffs.

The chain ran from one woman to the next, before ending much as it began, looped twice and thickly through a ring at the back corner of the wagon. Mac got the impression they all had been traveling for quite some time.

He wanted to inspect the shackles closer to look for a way to free the women.

As if reading his thoughts, Leonard said, "Me and Clem know what we're doing. Ain't no way these women are going to make a run for it." Leonard leaned forward, as if to offer Mac a confidence.

He lowered his voice. "They may be delicate flowers of the Orient back home and over California way, but here, they're little more than playthings." He straightened, nodded, and smiled, as if he'd just shared a great truth. "Ain't that right, ladies?"

The women, noting the man's harsh tone, looked at him. Again, Mac noticed no emotion on their faces.

Mac walked along before the women, all of them now hunkered or seated on the ground. They would glance at him, then look away. One of them, the last along the line, looked up at him and stared hard straight at him. Nothing but her eyes indicated any sort of emotion, but in that instant he would swear they had an entire conversation.

He knew, of course, and had known as soon as they had seen the bound women, that these two reprobate men were human slavers, but exchanging the glance with the woman helped Mac decide to stop dithering and deal with the situation.

He turned to the man. "I tell you what, Leonard. I tell you what, me and my pard there have been riding hard for some time now, and it would be a fine thing if we could work the kinks out of our ropes, if you know what I mean." They had walked back to the fire while Mac spoke.

Each man settled down again.

"Now," said Mac, "what sort of fee are you considering? Me and Boone here, we're not rich men by any means."

"Oh, now, now, I said we was neighbors and all, didn't I?"

"Yes. Yes, you did."

And then, right in the middle of these protracted negotiations, Boone tensed, and his hand slid from where it rested on his lap, quick as a snake strike, to his revolver's butt. His rawhide thong had already been thumbed free.

"You keep moving like that, Fat Boy, and you best get down to it and skin that smoke wagon."

Boone's voice was low and clear and his eyes bored steady and true, right at the nonspeaking Clem, who Mac saw had shifted his fat-fingered right hand close to his own gun, a dainty-looking little six-shot.

In fact, the fat man had been worming his hand down that way, closer and closer, for a couple of minutes, all the while looking elsewhere, mostly gazing down at the fire.

"Hey now!" Leonard jumped up to his feet, hands high. "What is this situation, gents?"

"You tell us," said Mac. "Here we are, guests of your invitation, in your campsite, and it looks as if your fat friend there is trying to surprise us. Can you explain that?"

Mac kept his hands resting light and easy at his waist. He watched Leonard's hands, still held up by his head. They seemed to relax and slump down toward his shoulders.

"Don't do it, Lenny," said Mac, shucking his own gun. It appeared in his big ham of a hand, cocked and ready, as if he'd conjured it in a stage performance.

"Whatever is going on here?" said Leonard, holding his hands still, but too damn close to the back of his neck for Mac's liking.

"Keep your hands still, boy. Or you're done."

While this played out, Boone had gotten the drop on Clem, who had indeed managed to get his fat fingers curled about the walnut grip of his gun. But that was as far as he got.

Boone had stood and palmed his own gun and, as with Mac, he'd shucked it ready for play in eye-blink speed.

Mac stood a dozen feet from Leonard and did not dare shift his eyes from the man.

Leonard's left arm flexed and Mac ducked low, thumbing back the hammer to full cock. "Don't do it!"

But it was as if the man had grown deaf and filled to

brimming with more confidence, all at once. He kept reaching with his fingertips, all the while not taking his eyes from Mac's.

"You jackass," growled Mac. The big man waited the skinny man out a few quick moments longer. The man had not slacked off one bit in his pursuit of whatever weapon was nested between his shoulder blades.

Mac had seen such shenanigans before, and he did not appreciate the fact that he'd likely have to kill the dumbest man in the world. Mac growled another oath even as he stole forward to engage the idiot in close-in work.

Leonard, once again, did not look Mac in the eye or even drop his own smarmy smile at all as he flexed even farther and drew out from betwixt his shoulder blades a long, thin-bladed knife that looked more suited to slitting open the belly of a fresh-caught trout than in savaging a hand-to-hand opponent in combat trailside.

Mac caught sight of the fat Clem making his own bold move but knew Hoke would have that in hand. He could not afford to look askance at Leonard. It amazed Mac that somehow, in that blink of time all this was happening, Leonard actually seemed to believe he might come out victorious in this silly little devolving mess of a situation.

And yet . . .

Leonard kept his bloodshot eyes on Mac's and fully tugged free the knife in a swift, clean movement, zinging the stiletto in a smooth, whipping motion right at the bulk of Mac's big form.

But Mac's bullet was quicker and found its way to the skinny slaver's neck, where it drove like an angry, gray fist into Leonard's Adam's apple, coring its way in and blooming out the rear of the center of the man's neck stalk.

It blew a hole as large as a child's fist, spraying meat and white bone, leaving the ragged, bloody hole, and a still-smiling Leonard's head, to stare, then wobble, then flop to one side.

The women screamed and did their best to skedaddle, the chain preventing them from going anywhere farther than a foot to two in any direction.

As Mac's shot boomed out, Boone leapt, clearing the distance between him and the fat man in a single, blurring jump of buckskin-clad wrath. He led with his revolver and managed to deliver a quick rap to the man's head, knocking both of them to the ground.

They rolled, but Mac glanced quickly and saw that Boone was on top and delivering another quick clubbing to the fat man's head. Then, straddling the portly fellow, he held the business end of the gun to the man's pate, dimpling his thick forehead.

"I told you, Fat Boy! I told you that you ought not to creep those pudgy fingers of yours down toward that gun, didn't I?"

All the while, fat Clem, though he did grunt and wheeze, made no other sounds.

"What? Tree rat ate your tongue?" Boone cackled as he flipped the man's little gun to the ground a yard away.

Then the fat man opened his pudgy lips as if to speak, but he just sat there, showing Boone that he had a near-full contingent of teeth, a bit stained. *So whose weren't?* thought Boone. But there was no pink tongue in there. Just a scarred nub of gristle where the meat of the tongue should be.

"Dang, son! Why didn't you say so? I would have refrained from saying such a mean-spirited thing."

The man, his eyes blinking hard, was clearly dazed and addled from Boone's blows to his head. Clem sagged back against the earth and his big head slumped to the side.

"Huh," said Boone, feeling around in the thick flesh of the man's fat neck. "Still alive. I expect I was too fearsome for him to look upon much longer. He'll come to, though."

Boone looked at Mac. "Another tongueless snake, just like that batch of religious freaks some time back; you recall them?"

Mac nodded, but said nothing as he leaned over the sprawled figure of Leonard. He toed the slaver's shoulder, but the man was well and truly dead.

"What was he thinking?" said Mac in little more than a whisper.

To his right, chains slid and rattled. He looked over and saw the women all struggling to their feet. They looked from Leonard to Mac, then over at Boone. They held back, and the one at the end, who had made bold eye contact with Mac, held her arms as wide as she could before the others, as if to shield them.

Again, she stared hard at Mac, though this time there was defiance in the look, as if she was daring him to approach them. But there was fear there, too. And for good reason, he knew. They were still chained, and the brutes who had treated them as—what had Leonard called them? Playthings? Well, they were now dead and subdued. And these two new men, men who were in the midst of perpetrating brute violence, were likely their new masters.

"Ma'am, I suspect you can't understand what I'm saying, but you have nothing to fear from us. We're . . . not here to cause you harm."

"That's right!" said Boone, smiling as he shoved up and away from the fat man. "We didn't start this fracas, but by gum, whenever somebody does, you can bet we'll end 'er, right enough."

He stepped off, away from Clem, and slid his revolver back into its holster.

Then one of the women shrieked and pointed, her chains dragging tight against them all as she shoved backward against the side of the wagon.

Both men spun to look toward where she was pointing, just beyond Boone.

That was when the fat man struck out with his near arm and snagged Boone's ankle, muckling onto where his moccasin laced up over his trousers.

The wiry woodsman had enough time to shout, "No!" before he was upended.

Luck was not with Boone then, for the fat man rolled hard toward him and, faster than any of them could have imagined, lay atop Boone, clawing for his revolver at the same time Boone did.

The gun was out of the holster and somehow ended up in the fat man's palm. He thumbed back the hammer just as Mac thumbed back his gun's hammer and sent a lead bee buzzing into Clem's homely, bald head.

The fat man slopped flat against the squirming Boone, who shouted and wheezed and flailed to no avail until Mac leapt to them and shoved the dead man from him.

Boone didn't stop moving until he had crabwalked backward nearly into the smoking fire.

"What in the hell is with these two brutes?"

Mac stood over the fat man, lifeless and the back of his head a blasted mess where the bullet had clawed its way out of the fleshy skull.

"I don't know," said Mac, staring down at the two dead men, his shoulders slumped and his revolver hanging limply from his hand.

The taking of a life was never something a man sought, nor should he take pleasure in it—any man worth his salt in life, anyway. Be the victim man or beast, for self-defense or for food, the taking of a life weighed hard on both Boone and Mac, and the silence of the moment showed this hard feeling only too well.

Neither had killed another man before the war, and though in the years since that brute time of death, they had done their best to avoid taking the lives of others, nonetheless it happened, it seemed, all too often.

Then Boone stood, brushing the dirt from his buckskins and smacking them down. He retrieved his revolver, checked it, and once more slid it into the holster. Then he fixed eyes on the women, and settled on one in particular. He walked over to her, grim faced, stood before her, and regarded her for a long moment.

They all looked back at him, and then all but one, she of the defiant gaze, looked away, anywhere but at this man of violence standing before them.

Boone swept his old, green felt topper off his head, the 'coon tail wagging. He held it before his lean belly and bent low in a bow. "I thank you most sincerely, ma'am, for saving my sorry skin. Truly. I owe you a mighty debt and I don't know how to repay you. But I would like to be given the opportunity to try."

The woman who had pointed was one of the ones now looking away, but the defiant one at the other end of the string stepped forward a half step. "Free us," she said. "Then . . . no debt."

Mac and Boone exchanged glances of surprise, then looked at the woman. "You speak English," said Boone.

She nodded. "Yes."

Mac strode over to Clem and rummaged in the fat man's pockets.

"What are you doing?" said Boone.

"Check Leonard's pockets for the key."

Boone stared at him a moment.

"The key! To their shackles, man," said Mac.

"Oh!" Boone slapped and patted the skinny dead man's pockets. "Yeah, of course, that was the plan all along," he said, looking up at the woman. "We . . . we aren't like them, ma'am. Not at all. I hope you believe that."

She said nothing but did nod slightly once.

Boone smiled, his hand deep in the man's front right trouser pocket, and tugged out a small steel ring with two keys swinging from it. "Got it!" he said. "At least I hope that's the one."

"Yes," she said. "Both have one."

And as soon as she said it, Mac pulled out a similar key ring from the fat man's inner coat pocket. "Yep," he said.

"One'll be for the shackles," said Boone, approaching the talkative woman. "And the other likely for the chain itself."

Mack approached the end of the chain, fastened through the wagon and back to itself with a steel padlock. Boone made to squat before the first woman to undo the shackles binding her feet. Then, halfway down, in a squat, he looked at her. "No offense, ma'am, but you ain't gonna kick me or some such, are you?"

"Why would I?" she said. And though her tone was level and serious, as was her steely gaze, Mac thought he saw a slight smile on her face. *That,* he thought, *was a good sign.*

Boone nodded and bent to his task. Soon the manacles were unlocked.

He helped Mac with the last of the chain and drizzled it onto the bed of the wagon in a steely, snaky pile.

The women moved off a ways from them, and then, at Mac's suggestion, moved over to the fire. He poked the embers and refreshed the blaze with a couple of snapped lengths of wood.

"What do you think, Hoke? Bury those two here or load them up and take them to the nearest town?"

Boone scratched his chin. "They're a mess."

Mac nodded. "And we don't know how far we'll have to take them, nor how long it'll take us."

"I reckon that decides it, then. We should bury these two, then report their names and the situation to the law.

Wherever that may be," said Boone. "They weren't the sort of men I'd mix with, but there's no call to leave them out for the night critters to molest."

"I wish we had brought a shovel," said Mac, half smiling at the absurdity of lugging such a thing around with them.

"Yeah." Boone sighed. "A shovel sure would make the job easier."

"There is a shovel," said the woman. She pointed to the front of the wagon.

"Really?" Boone smiled and rubbed his hands together. "Well, now, ain't we the lucky ones." He climbed up inside the wagon and found a wide crate, built in, spanning the width of the wagon, nested beneath the seat.

The front was wedged shut with an oak peg holding a hasp in place. He nudged it out and flipped over the crate's door with a squawk and a thud.

There, amid a jumble of tarps and rope and more chains and manacles, was a shovel, about three feet long. The handle had snapped off halfway up the shaft.

The end was well chewed and rounded from hard use. It was also dull as an old tooth. But it was, by God, a shovel. Boone dragged it out of there, smiling as he hopped to the earth and looked about for a place to dig.

"We will help," said the woman.

"Oh, no, ma'am. That's all right."

"No," she said, shaking her head. "They hit us with that very much," she said.

"Whatever for?" said Boone.

She no doubt understood, but made no more comment.

Mac and Boone selected a patch of level earth a few yards from the campsite proper and set to digging. Soon the women moved over and stood nearby in silence. The bold, chatty one moved to Mac, who had the shovel, and nodded. He handed her the shovel.

Soon they all were trading turns, but Mac and Boone worked double time when it was their turns with the shovel, aware that it was tricky going for the women, as their footwear was little more than flat-soled, thin shoes made of ratty cloth.

In less than a half hour they had dug out a single hole, three to four feet wide and six feet long and most of three feet deep.

"Good enough for them," said Boone.

"We'll mound rocks atop," said Mac. "Then they're on their own."

"Hope they like each other," said Boone. "Because they're about to spend a whole lot of time close up and personal." He smiled, but the women still wore their somber faces. He guessed he couldn't blame them, but it had always pained him to see sad folks, especially women, for some reason. And children. And old-timers.

Mac laid a hand on his shoulder. "Let's carry them over."

They did so, and Boone stood straddling the fat man once more. Then he looked at the women. "We should go through their pockets for personal effects and such, something to tell us who they were. We can tell the law when we get to the next town."

Again the women did not respond.

He proceeded, and Mac did the same with Leonard. They found little more than the usual array of trifles in men's pockets: folding knives, matches, chaw, sacks of tobacco. It was eerie work going through the pockets of dead men. "You don't happen to know their names, do you, ladies?"

The woman shook her head. "Only what you know."

One of the other silent women spoke in a low voice to the chatty one. She listened, then said, "She says she heard them say 'Saint Loo-ee' sometimes."

"Oh, St. Louis? Missouri?" said Boone. "Why, that's something useful. Sure, good work, then. We'll be sure to tell the law that, and whatever else we can find out in the wagon. Might be they have some letters or some such in the wagon."

CHAPTER 4

Later, Mac and Boone decided they needed to make one camp out of the two. Though it would have been easier to bring their gear and Chummy and Lincoln over to the slavers' camp, Mac and Boone's site was higher up and broader, with more space for stretching out. And considering there were five women and a two-horse team in their charge now, choosing the other site made good enough sense.

The change in site seemed to have a beneficial effect on the women, too. Or perhaps it was just the fact that they were now free, or away from the two dead slavers who did who knows what to them, but Mac sensed the women were a little less guarded.

He even saw two of them exchange slight smiles, and perhaps a giggle behind a raised hand. It made him feel good.

And the women were all eager to keep busy, it seemed.

Finally, with everybody all resettled, including the horses, which were fed and watered, they turned their attention to food. The women looked painfully thin, and Mac and Boone laid out their own provisions so the women might be able to tuck into anything that was already prepared.

They chose leftover corn cakes and small bits of jerky, and declined hot coffee when it was offered.

It turned out the chatty woman was more fluent in English than they had suspected. And not only that, but the other four women all comprehended English to some extent, for they nodded and proceeded to do whatever it was Mac and Boone suggested needed doing.

"You ever heard of such a thing?" whispered Boone to Mac. "Why, not liking coffee? It's, it's . . . downright sad." He shook his head, as if he'd just heard about someone's favorite dog dying.

"I think they'd prefer tea, Hoke. You still have some of that licorice root that old woman at the mine camp gave you?"

"Yeah, course I do. She said you could chew it and make a paste for a cut or some such."

"Didn't she also say you could make a tincture of it and drink it?"

"By gaw." Boone snapped a finger. "Might be you're right! Let me find it. You put water on the boil."

Mac nodded. If ever there was a fellow who could make tea out of an old root, it was Boone. Soon they had a small pot of water with a handful of slivered shavings floating in the pot, from the root. The smell, both men had to admit, was quite nice.

"Almost makes a fella want to give up coffee!" Hoke slapped his trouser leg, and dust rose up. The ladies appeared a tad startled but smiled indulgently and sipped their make-do tea. They seemed to like the flavor, judging from their nods and raised eyebrows. *Or,* thought Mac, *they were awfully good at being polite.*

"Say, whilst we're waiting for that big goober to cook up vittles for us, maybe you'd want to hear a bit about where I hail from. Hoddy's Gulch is the name of that sacred place. . . ."

"Hoke?" Mac looked at his pard over the cookfire.

"Yeah, Mac?"

"Perhaps the ladies would care to share the particulars of their journey with us."

"Oh, right, yes, I was just gonna ask them that. Ladies?"

The chatty woman looked at Boone a moment, then at Mac. She looked at her fellow travelers, and they all nodded slightly, so she folded her hands in her lap and eyed Mac.

"I am Wan Li." And for the next twenty minutes she told them the story of how she and her four friends came to be in the clutches of the slavers.

"It begins with the railroad, I think," she said.

"The railroad?" said Boone. He looked at Mac, who gave him a hard stare, and Boone shut his yap and settled in, sipping his coffee, which he laced with a drop or three of whiskey.

"Please, Wan Li," said Mac. "Continue."

She nodded and proceeded.

"My husband and son, and all of us, we are all," she moved her hand toward her fellows, "from China. We all have families and we all come here on a ship with promise of work in America. For the Blaswell empire, a new line of railroad. They tell us we will have a house and, most important of all, work. We want our son to grow up in America; in China there is no . . ." She looked at her hand, searching for the word.

"Opportunity?" said Mac.

"Yes, that is it. Opportunity. But here, we think this would be so good for us." She smiled at a memory. "So we sell everything we own, which was not much, but we wanted as much money and as few things, only what we need. Then we ride the boat, long time, so crowded. There was much sickness. Our son, he was so sick. We worry for his life. But we get to California. San Francisco, they say, and we think it's going to be okay. And for some time it was as we were told. We were nervous but so happy. So strange to be here, but so happy."

She sipped from her cup. "Then we get to the place, the place we will work. It was not what we were told. There were no homes, but we had no choice, they pay for our journey, we must do the work, they tell us, or we would go to prison."

"What was wrong with the place once you got there?"

"Oh, it was pretty country, yes, but they put us in tents. Okay, only short time, they tell us. Then they take the men from us. Okay, say the men do the hardest work, needed somewhere else. When do we see them again? One week, they say. Okay, so the women and children and even many old people, we begin to do work, too, cutting trees and shaving bark, clearing land, they tell us. Okay. Then we cook and do laundry for the other men."

"What other men would they be?" asked Mac.

"The . . . men with guns who watch us."

"Guards?" said Boone, leaning forward.

"Yes, guards. They say for our own safety. But they don't let us leave anywhere. Some of the women . . ." Again she indicated her friends. "They have troubles with them. Because the men are not there, it is easy for the guards to . . ." She looked away from them, and her eyes welled with tears.

Mac nodded. "I see."

Wan Li was silent for some time. Boone cleared his throat, and in a softer voice said, "Ma'am, I am beginning to get an idea of what has happened to you all at this railroad camp. But how did you come to be with those men? The ones we found you with?"

"They . . . take us from our children, and the old ones. But not all the old ones. Old women, they are taken, too. Then our children!" She looked at them both, emotion showing plainly on her face for the first time. "They sell us!

Sell us all! The children for slaves, we think, and the women for . . ."

"To be used by men." Boone looked at his big-knuckled hands as he said this.

"Yes, that is right. We were taken from our families. Never see our husbands, brothers, sons, daughters . . ."

"And all of you ladies had this happen?" Mac looked at the other women, whose eyes were also tearing.

Wan Li said something to them in their own language and they all nodded, looking at Mac and Boone directly and long, for the first time.

That look was what Mac could only later describe to Boone and to himself as one of extreme desperation. The most extreme he had ever encountered.

Later, alongside the fire, Mac and Boone spoke together in soft voices about this odd new situation in which they found themselves.

"Mac, you don't suppose this is the big, new rail line we read about in the papers back home in Denver City, do you?"

"I do think it is, yes. If the rumors and news stories are correct, this Blaswell is richer than rich. And with that usually comes great power, influence, and all its trappings."

"You mean he's probably greased wheels to look the other way so he can build this rail line."

Mac shrugged. "Maybe, maybe not. But if I were a betting man—"

"Which you ain't."

"No," said Mac. "I work too hard for my money to toss it away on games of chance."

Boone snorted. It was the same old story. He knew Mac wasn't scolding him for his frequent gambling runs, but he did have a point. They worked hard. And yet Boone thought such endeavors as hard work deserved to be balanced with equal amounts of play. It was a topic on which they never would agree.

"Oh, but this is a rum deal," said Boone finally.

"For whom?" said Mac.

"For them poor folks, all around! Who'd you think I meant?"

"Hoping it wasn't for us," said Mac.

"Oh, man, you cut me to the bone with that remark, MacCoole. And here I thought you knew me."

"Take it easy, Hoke. I am funning you, as you like to call it. I know you pretty well, I expect." Mac sipped his spiked coffee. "You know this wasn't our fight, but—"

"But it is now," said Boone.

"Yes. Yes, it is. And we need to investigate it, at the very least. But these women, they need to be brought to safety first. We can't risk bringing them back there."

"No, too risky for them by half. What do you reckon, then?"

Mac scratched his stubbled chin and gazed at the dying fire. Boone knew not to interrupt him when he had that deep look. He called it "rumination," but Boone had no use for two-dollar words for a common task, in this case, thinking.

"We'll need to take them to the nearest town, of course. I imagine we can find a marshal or some such who isn't already roped and tied by Blaswell."

"You think they'll go for it?" asked Boone, looking to their side at the still forms of the five women. They'd doled out what blankets they could and made the women as comfortable as possible. As for themselves, they figured they'd sit up part of the night tending the fire. They had a whole lot to discuss and plan.

And a couple of hours later, over coffee laced with whiskey and much low, close conversation, they devised the best plan they could, given they didn't truly know what they would be facing.

It wasn't likely that Wan Li and the others were lying, but in Mac and Boone's experience, each story had at least two sides. The women had their side and Blaswell's outfit had theirs. No matter who ended up being the most truthful party, the situation bore investigation.

It would mean riding westward in the morning. It was too late to pore over their meager maps now, by firelight, so they turned in to catch a few hours of sleep.

As was their custom, they tossed a coin, and one of them would keep watch, then the other would spell the first.

It was common sense practice they employed on the trail whenever they felt they needed to keep alert at all hours. There was a feeling in the air this night that told them to take no chances. It also told them that from here to California and beyond, they were on another job. This time without pay.

And neither man minded in the least.

CHAPTER 5

Shaky Driscoll was so named because he had spent years stewing himself into a stupor each night and then spent the better part of each day shaking and trembling, trying to moderate his intake of rye whiskey from discreet pulls on his flask.

The only thing that saved him was the fact that he was, much to his surprise, still a solid shot with a revolver or a long gun. Though he had to admit his aim had been suspect of late. Still, his reputation as a fierce gun hand wafted about him almost as much as the odd, boozy stink he carried.

He'd been hired on to ride point on his own handpicked team of tough men for the back East dude, Thurston Kane, who himself was overseeing the construction of that fancy new rail line running from California all the way inland to who knew where. Shaky didn't much care, as long as the promised cash came through regular as a clock. And so far it had.

Specifically, Shaky and his men had to keep the coolies, those fresh-off-the-boat workers from China, in line. For the money the man was paying, Shaky and the boys could do any damn thing the man asked them to.

Heck, he reckoned they'd done just about everything for money anyway. What was a few months of prison camp work? And if anyone got out of line, why, Kane did that thing with his eyebrows and head nod that all the money men did that were supposed to tell you without telling you just what it was they expected but didn't want to know about.

Lucky for Kane, Shaky had been down that trail before. Runaways? Nothing a bullet or rope wouldn't fix. And anyone fixing to shirk their duties? Same deal, though Kane said to be careful with the women; no injuries that were visible, lest the slavers who bought them wouldn't pay top dollar. And their menfolk? Don't break too many fingers, and no legs or arms, lest the work suffer.

Okay, then, thought Shaky after his first meeting with Kane. *We know where we stand with this fella, and Kane knows that in order to pull it off, he best not be tight with the purse strings.*

That had been some months before. And Thurston Kane was true to his word, even more so, because he was so tickled with the progress that had been made. That was thanks, Shaky reckoned, to the fact that he and the boys bested every deadline Kane set, so the dude paid them bonus money.

That was a first for Shaky, and he knew he was being manipulated, for he felt a loyalty increasing toward Kane, but who cared? The money was plentiful and the work was not anything he'd popped a sweat over yet. Good pay easily earned—wasn't that the way everyone wanted to live?

"Boss!"

Shaky roused himself from his reverie. "What?"

The man who'd called to him was his second-in-command, Reginald Conley. He was a ruthless animal, enough so that sometimes he even put a quick stab of fear in Shaky's gut. But Shaky knew how to best the weasel and still keep him employed. He knew Reg was a fiend for the women. And as Kane promised, there were plenty of them around.

And that meant there was plenty to keep Reg occupied and happy. And Shaky had learned that a happy Reg was a loyal Reg.

All this had been agreed on with Kane and Reg and the boys months earlier. And Shaky had had little cause to regret signing on. Until now.

"Boss, them men are refusing to work again. More every day. They say—well, the few who can talk English, they say they want to see their women, then they'll get back to work. They also want better food and a day off each week. Can you imagine?"

Thing was, Shaky *could* imagine that. He understood all the complaints the Chinese men had were legitimate. He understood all that. But it didn't mean he was going to go all soft. And it damn sure didn't mean he was going to give in to any demands.

"As it happens," said Shaky, popping a quick nip from his flask. He dragged the back of his hand across his lips. "I got me a telegram from Kane."

He let that settle in the air before Reg. It seemed to impress the oaf, as Shaky knew it would. Actually, it was those pencil-headed fools, the engineers and the foremen of the construction, who got most of the dispatches, every few days, from Kane. The boss man only visited the site once every week and a half or so from his office in San Francisco. But in the latest batch of dispatches, Shaky got himself a pinned-on note from Kane, telling him there was going to be a fresh batch of workers at the beginning of next week. A whole new crew.

"And you know what that means," Shaky told Reg after he mentioned the contents of the note.

Reg stared at him like he knew he would.

Shaky sighed. "You worry me, Reg. What the women find interesting about you has to be on the outside, 'cause inside there's just a rattling sound." Shaky tapped his temple.

Reg narrowed his eyes. "If you wasn't my boss, Shaky, I'd be liable to take offense to that."

"But I smiled when I said it," said Shaky.

"Yeah, I reckon."

"Anyways, what I'm on about is that we don't have to put up with those whiners on the line." He left their cabin and began walking to his horse. "Come on."

"What we gonna do, Boss?"

"We're going to give them what they want."

"How we gonna do that when we done sold their women-folk and kids already?"

Shaky sighed again. *No wonder I drink so much. The Good Lord put me on this earth to test me, I see that now. I do believe I'm passing, though.* To Reg he said, "Just follow me and you'll see what I'm talking about. Keep up if you can."

"Dang hell, Boss," said Reg. "You know I can ride faster than you any day of the week."

"That's not what I meant, Reg. Just do me a favor; when we get to the line, point out who all are the troublemakers and I'll take it from there."

"You bet, Boss."

Again, Shaky sighed. But he smiled, too, for he was about to do one of his favorite things—he was about to make an example out of malcontents. Did his heart good to take the rowdies down a few pegs.

CHAPTER 6

Morning came earlier than Boone liked. It always did. Though he swore he slept like a cat and kept one eye nearly open at all times, in truth he snored like a ripsaw stuttering on a knob of rooty oak. He knew it, but he'd be damned if he was going to admit it to Mac. That big goober would never let him forget it.

This time, Mac was toeing him in the ribs. Then on the arm. Boone reacted as he always did, by swinging his revolver up out of the crevice he kept it nested in on his right side, between his arm and his ribs.

"Easy, pard," said Mac.

"What you go kicking a man when he's asleep? Besides," said Boone, "I'm like a coiled rattler. Why, it was said in the Gulch and talked about to this day, no doubt, that as a child I had more in common with rattlers than . . ."

"Hoke, no time for windies this morning."

"Windies! That there is a true story."

"I know; I recognize it."

Boone sat up. Even in the predawn light, he could tell something was amiss with his pard. "What's wrong?"

"The women," said Mac, glancing toward where they'd left them the night before.

"What about them?" said Hoke quietly, sitting up.

"They're gone."

"What?" Boone sprang to his feet. He slept fully dressed in his buckskins and moccasins in order to be, as he said, "ready for what the day brings."

"I don't know how they did it, but they slipped away in the night."

"Slipped away," said Boone, toeing the blankets the women had used and then folded up neatly and left in a stack. "Or were they swiped?"

"Not likely," said Mac. "I can't imagine they'd take the time to fold their bedrolls or any such thing if someone had made off with them in the night, do you?"

"No, I guess you're right about that." He looked around. It was still mostly dark, with the sky purpling toward the east and glints of the coming day's sunlight lifting the veil of night already.

"What about the horses?"

"That's the thing," said Mac. "They're all there. Ours and the two horses from the wagon team."

"What is their game?" said Boone, looking about the campsite with his hands on his hips. "You check all around?"

"I did," said Mac. "No sign. They light-footed out. I can't imagine they'll get far. It was still fully dark when I got up. I'd begun reviving the fire when I noticed they were gone."

Despite the situation, Boone smiled. "I see you set the coffee on while you were at it."

"I did. No reason not to be civilized."

Boone nodded agreement. "It's as if I said it myself."

And within minutes, their coffee was bubbling and Mac poured a cup for each of them.

A few minutes after that, Boone drained his second cup and shook out the grounds. "We best get after them."

It took him a few minutes to saddle Chummy.

"Since you're the better tracker," said Mac, "you should

see what you can turn up within a mile or so. I'll finish breaking camp. If you don't have luck, we'll split up and give it a wider look."

Boone nodded, ready to go.

"West will be the most likely direction."

"Why west?"

"Because they want one thing—to get back to their families. Remember, they're not fancy ladies by trade or choice. They're mothers and sisters and nieces and wives, all of it."

Boone nodded. "Well, now that it's light I should be able to track them easy enough. I can't imagine it'll take long. We'll meet back here."

"Right. Good luck."

Boone merely nodded and bent low, eyeing the ground.

Mac knew it wouldn't be difficult for Hoke to find the women, a simple job for the best tracker Mac had ever worked with.

And the big man was right. It didn't take but twenty minutes for Hoke's piercing whistle to reach Mac.

Hoke rode back at a gallop. By then Mac had the camp fully broken and Lincoln saddled. The two other horses and the wagon were a different story and a potential headache. Mac figured he'd wait to hear what Hoke had to say before he made a decision about them.

"You were right," said Boone, sliding from the saddle. He tucked into a cold biscuit and the last of the coffee. "They beelined westward. Just the five of them, no other tracks. All still afoot. Looked like they were in a hurry, but out here, they won't get far. I figured I'd fetch you instead of tackling them on my own. I have no idea if they'll be ornery or not. And I can't imagine having to tangle with five women at once. I don't doubt they'd overpower me!"

Mac saw that Boone was serious.

"I mean it! Why, I don't know them from Adam. They're all worked up to get back to their men, ain't they? Seems to me they'd be liable to do most anything. No, you and me both should be there. We'll brace them."

"Right," said Mac. "Now help me with those two wagon horses."

"We ain't going to take the wagon, are we?"

"No, they'll ride the horses. We'll just need to lead them. They'll slow us a little, but they're not in bad condition. Should be all right."

With that, they rigged up serviceable bridles and reins and tied lead ropes, one to each. Mac wrangled them, riding behind Boone. "Okay," he said. "Let's move."

Boone rode point. "We'll reach them well before lunchtime. Then maybe we can fix us a proper feed. I feel robbed if I ain't started my day with a full gut."

And true to his prediction, they saw the five women, all walking in a line and making slow progress westward. They stopped and looked back when Mac and Boone approached.

"What did you think you were going to do for food, ma'am?" said Boone, clucking his horse forward as he addressed Wan Li.

"We must go to our families."

"I understand that, ma'am," said Mac. "But this is not the way. We can take you to the next lawful town, and there will be folks there who will help you."

The women said nothing but looked at the ground before them. Even Wan Li, it seemed, had lost some of her brazen edge.

In a low voice, half turned from them, Boone said to Mac, "I'm getting the feeling they're thinking about us the same way they thought about those slavers."

"How do you mean?"

"Look, Mac, you're a good soul, but sometimes you like to do things so tight to the law that you don't see what's happening right in front of you. You know what I'm saying?"

"Not really, no."

Boone sighed. "Look, we take them women to a town, you know what's going to happen to them? They're going to be hated by everybody there. You know how they treat the Chinese back in Denver City, right?"

Mac looked into the distance, but he wasn't seeing the mountains. He was picturing the kind face of Mr. Chin, who ran the bathhouse and laundry. The local toughs were always threatening to cut off the man's hair, always making fun of how he spoke.

Mac had had to point out more than once, and usually with a half-drunk man's shirt balled in his fist, that Mr. Chin was an accomplished musician, a calligrapher, and that his command of the English language was second only to his command of his native Mandarin.

Most of those words never made it far into the offending drunk's mind, but the fact that Big Mac MacCoole was holding them off the floor and telling them this through gritted teeth, that Big Mac MacCoole was a friend of Mr. Chin's, was enough to keep the idiots from further threats.

Some of them, of course, were hard learners.

"Yeah, I guess you're right. What do you propose we do, then?"

"Well, I don't see as we have much choice," said Boone. "Have to take them with us."

Mac looked at the ladies. "It would make it simpler for us to find the camp. But what about when we get there? We can't lead them back into the lion's den."

"Didn't think of that," said Boone. "Dang it, Mac, I can't think of everything!"

Wan Li must have overheard, because she said, "We will be no trouble. But we will find our families."

"Ma'am, we aren't worried about you causing trouble, but we don't want trouble for you."

"If you cannot help us, let us go. We will find our families."

"Now hold on," said Mac. "We didn't say we weren't

going to help you. We just need to rethink part of our plan."
Mac rubbed his chin a moment, then said, "Okay, what if we
set up a camp well away from the site? You ladies can stay
there, but keep low and safe until we come back for you."

The woman talked with her friends, then she asked,
"How long?"

"It might well take a few days."

"Yes." She nodded. "We can do this."

"You have to promise us, though, that if we don't return
in, say, four, maybe five days, that means we came upon
trouble."

"And that means," said Boone, picking up on Mac's
thought, "that you all had better skedaddle to a safe place.
Go to a town, tell them what's happening, and use our
names. Everybody knows us."

Mac smiled. "Boone might be overstating our influence,
but he's right, it can't hurt. But that's only if we fail to turn
up evidence enough to prove there's something off about
their business."

Again, the women conferred in low tones. Some minutes
later, Wan Li turned back to them and bowed with low, thin
grace. "Yes, this will be . . . acceptable," said Wan Li. Then
she smiled and nodded.

With that settled, at least for the time being, they helped
the women up onto the backs of the two wagon horses and
the entire odd party moved westward at an increasing rate
the farther west they ventured. But that was where they
needed to be. And quick, in hopes of preventing other lives
lost or ripped apart.

The journey took them three days. Along the way, they
got to know the women much better, and were able to learn
their individual stories, each one as painful to hear as the
last.

All the misery they had endured and that their families
were enduring—and all the other people still there, and no

doubt more to come—strengthened Mac and Boone's urge to assist them from a position of sympathy to that of necessity.

After three days, they traveled along a well-used roadway, one that Wan Li told them had been the very road they had been taken eastward by the slavers.

She knew this because the slavers had unlocked the wagon and forced them to take care of the domestic chores of the camp before dark several times. The road was familiar, particularly as the distant hills and rocky, mountainous outcroppings were memorable.

Wan Li said each of the women had tried to keep the journey in mind so if they ever found the opportunity to return, they would know how to get there.

On the afternoon of the third day, Wan Li told them that they were getting close. She pointed northwestward. "That mountain," she said. "The railroad camp is on the far side."

"You're certain?" said Mac.

She nodded. "Yes."

Several times her confidence had steered them, so Mac saw no reason to doubt her now. By his own map they were certainly in the region in which he suspected the rail line was being built.

He called a halt to their day earlier than usual, and they camped well off the roadway. Several times they had done so in recent days, as Boone, who had frequently scouted the road ahead, had trotted back to tell them that folks were approaching.

Only once did they fail to detect signs of someone, and that had been days before, when a lone rider had come upon them from behind, also making his way westward. He was a dispatch rider carrying letters of import, and had little time to chat. But the ladies were agitated and afraid he might tell someone he'd seen them on the road.

Bu as Mac said, it couldn't be helped. So they went ahead

with their plans and would deal with whatever trouble might poke out at them in due course.

That night, Mac and Boone firmed up their plans once more, refining them to whatever extent they were able. They spent the rest of the time readying the women in their concealed campsite well off the roadway.

They had taken what supplies they had determined would be necessary from the slavers' wagon, and those, coupled with their own waning stores, would have to keep the women until they could come back.

"Well, it's a good thing you all are light eaters," said Boone. "Way you all pick at your food, you could survive a month out here on this." He waved an arm to indicate the modest inventory. "I never could figure out how women—well, the skinny ones, anyway—could not tuck into a meal with gusto. My word, if I ate what you all eat, I'd weigh about what the hind leg of a skeeter does. And that's the truth of it!"

By then the women all merely smiled at him and went about their chores, preparing tasty food for Mac and Boone, and for themselves, of course. But they seemed to like the fact that Boone was a big eater, and Mac, too, as a large man, really put away the food, as Boone said.

Though each man tried to go easy on the provisions in case they had to last the women longer than they hoped it would.

In the morning, the men ate lightly, then saddled up Lincoln and Chummy. Before climbing into the saddle, Mac said, "Now, Wan Li and ladies, you promise us you'll stay put. We can't get to the bottom of this if we're worried about you as well."

"We will stay in this camp," she said, nodding.

Mac and Boone nodded, and after an awkward few moments, they mounted up and rode toward the distant mountain, on the far side of which they trusted they would find the rail line camp.

"You believe her?" asked Boone once they were out of earshot of the camp.

"No," said Mac. "But what can we do? They're not slaves, at least not to us. That's the entire point of this adventure."

"It is an adventure, ain't it?" said Boone. "Just like all our other ones." He smiled. "I prefer to think of them that way myself. Makes life more exciting."

Mac smiled and pulled out a smelly cigarillo.

"Aw, now, I thought maybe we'd seen the last of them things!"

"No," said Mac. "I kept them safe right here." Mac patted his vest pocket. "Didn't want to offend the ladies."

"Well, what about me?" said Boone, a tinge of desperation nipping at his words.

"You? Oh, you're different."

"How so?"

"For one, you're always telling me one thing and then saying or doing the opposite. So I figure what you're really telling me is that you like these cigarillos, even though you claim not to."

"That don't make no sense! I hate them; how much plainer can I say it? They smell like something a diseased dog hacked up in an alley behind a bar."

Mac set fire to the little black cigar. "Oh, that's interesting."

"Look here," said Boone, nibbling on a knob of lint-covered chaw he'd fished from his possibles sack. "By your logic, I ought to say I love those things. Love the smell, the whole works."

"Do you?"

"No! And I ain't gonna lie!"

Mac shrugged and puffed up a glowing tip on the thing, then pushed out a big cloud of blue smoke. Right over in Boone's direction.

And so they rode, making their way slowly around the base of the substantial mountain for the next few hours.

By midafternoon they found themselves overlooking a narrow plain with a whole lot of dust being raised. It was being kicked up by a whole lot of workers making their way in and out of several rocky roadways spidering out from the work area. They were making for the mountain itself.

"You think they're gonna blast on through the mountain?"

"Seems likely," said Mac. "It's a fair bit of work, but it's a whole lot shorter than going around or up and over. I think. I've never built a railroad, myself, so I am no expert."

"I worked on a fair few blasting jobs in my day, mainly in the war. But that was mostly ruining things to slow up you bluebellies. A hole in a mountain's a different piece of work."

"That it is," said Mac. "Well, what say we get on down there and see if they buy our story?"

"Sounds good to me," said Boone. "I hope it's lunchtime down there, 'cause I'm fixing to gnaw off my own hands."

CHAPTER 7

"Who be you?"

Boone looked about himself in a grand, exaggerated way, then back to the man who'd spoken to him. "You talking to us, fella?"

"Yeah, I'm talking to you!" The man was short and not overly muscled, but he had one of the largest heads Mac or Boone had ever seen on a person. It was difficult not to take note of it; then it was equally difficult to not stare at him. But looking away was tough, too.

"Yes, ah"—Mac concentrated on the man's red plaid shirt—"we heard there might be paying work hereabouts."

Big Head spat a stream of brown chaw juice and dragged a cuff across his stubbled mouth. "Might be you heard right." He shrugged. "Then again, might not."

"Well, which is it?" said Boone, not impressed at all with the large-headed man or his response.

"Take it easy," said Mac in a soft voice. "Remember why we're here."

Boone replied with a low growl, "All right, then. You do the talking before I hop down and take a round or three out of this odd fella."

"Who you calling odd?" The man stepped forward, his

shotgun swinging from cradled position before his chest around and was about to raise it up to bear on them.

Mac and Boone were used to this sort of person, all bluster and no play, and they conjured their revolvers even faster.

The man's mouth sagged into a frown. "Aw, now, fellas, I can see you didn't take kindly to my funnin'. I do believe the boss man, that'd be Shaky, he might could use another couple of men such as yourselves somewheres around here. I . . . I could get him for you."

"That would be most civilized of you, Mr. . . . ." said Mac. "I don't believe I heard your name."

"Aw, hell no. My name don't matter at all. I'm here, and that's enough."

There was a long pause when none of the three men moved, save for Big Head's eyes.

Finally, Mac said, "Well, will this Shaky fellow be along soon? Should we wait here for him?"

"With me?" Big Head looked left, then right, as if he were being surrounded.

"Why?" said Boone. "You ain't hiding something, are you?"

"No, no, it's just that . . . I don't expect Shaky anytime soon and he's a busy man and I'd have to go fetch him."

"Oh," said Mac, relaxing a little, to show the man he wasn't going to shoot him. At least not yet. But he did not move his revolver from pointing at the skittish fellow. "Well, if that's all, me and my pard, we're happy to wait right here for you."

Still, Big Head did not move.

"Well?" said Boone.

"It's just that nobody has ever come along this way looking for work. Or anything. It's why I like it here. Keep an eye on things, but they ain't too busy, if you know what I mean."

"Not really," said Mac.

"The other road. Yonder." The man moved his large head back to indicate a direction somewhat behind him. "That's the big way in and out, for now, anyway. Supplies and slaves and such."

"Slaves?" said Boone. "Ain't that illegal now?"

"Well, yeah," said Big Head, leaning forward a little. "But you'd never know it the way them Chinese get treated. If it was up to me, they'd go easier on them."

"But they don't?" said Mac.

"Don't what?"

Boone sighed. "Go easy on them. The Chinese."

"Oh no, no, they're rough on them. But I reckon they got a right to be a little harsh. After all, the big boss, Kane, he paid their fare and all. Shipped 'em on over for free, drug their whole families along, too. Even the old, toothless ones."

"Oh, well, it sounds like you're all filled up with workers, then."

"Nah, them are the laborers. The ones who do all the lugging and digging and pounding."

"The hard work," said Boone.

"Sure," said Big Head. "Hey, wait a minute. You saying I don't work hard?"

"I never said such a thing!" Boone shook his head. "But I can tell you do like a good chin-wag."

Mac cut in with a glance to Boone. The last thing they needed was for Boone to keep this goober from talking. They'd already learned more than they expected. But they were rapidly getting nowhere at all.

"Look, mister," said Mac, "we'll make you a promise, Nobody goes in or out while we wait for you to fetch Shaky. Or else you can take us to him."

"Oh no, that would never do. He's a busy man, is Shaky.

And Reg, he would surely pin my ears back and roast me whole if I brought somebody in unannounced."

"Who's Reg?" said Boone.

"Only Shaky's right-hand man." Big Head leaned forward once more and in his lowered tone said, "And a meaner man when he ain't spent time with a lady of an evening."

"Oh, I see," said Boone, who really did not see much at all. "Well, look, if you won't go fetch this Shaky character, I will," and with that, Boone thumbed his heels against Chummy's barrel and moved forward.

"Oh no, no!" Big Head gained his initial obstinance and stepped to his left and into the trail in front of Boone and Chummy. "I'll go. Never said I wouldn't. But you fellas made a solemn promise to wait here and not let anyone in, right?"

"You bet," said Mac, nodding with a grave, somber look on his face. "Absolutely. We will be right here when you return."

"Okay, then. Now, what was it you was looking for?"

Boone sighed long and loud. "Tell this Shaky we want work. Now git to it!"

An hour later, they found themselves in the presence of the mighty Shaky, who was grilling them in a rather haphazard way.

"You got a problem doling out beatings on laggards and dubs?"

"What sort of beating?" said Mac.

"Oh." Shaky slipped a battered silver flask from his inside jacket pocket and unscrewed the top. He upended it and guzzled back a couple of glugs. "Something you'd give a dog who stole your supper right off the table while you watched."

"Why would you watch a dog do that?" said Boone.

"Huh?"

"A dog, stealing your food right in front of you. Just chase them off."

"That's not the point. Now, do you men have what it takes to work here? We have need of a couple of men to ride hard on these lazy ones from the Orient."

"I got no problem with that," said Boone. "They're here on your dollar, ain't they? Stands to reason you should get a full day's work out of them, then!"

He strutted back and forth in the small, dingy cabin that served as Shaky's office. Or, as the man himself called it, "the base of operations." Mac eyed Boone and shook his head. His pard was laying it on thick.

"So, Shaky, are you in charge of the entire project, then?" asked Mac.

"Naw, but what me and Reg do is the most important thing going on here."

"How do you figure that?" said Boone.

That seemed to bristle Shaky, for he said, "You know, I'm the one who should be asking questions here, not you. You two are almighty nosy. But I'll take you on, seeing as how I could use two more men. The workers are getting uppity and I need enough folks in charge to keep them in line so we make all our deadlines."

Mac followed Reg to what Shaky called "the Line." It was where all the noise was coming from, for as they rounded a great jut of stone, the enormity of the project was finally revealed to Mac up close. He'd seen much of it from above, back on the trail, but now, on this slight rise, he saw what must have been one hundred men, most of them in grimy, loose-fitting clothes that had once been white, and some wore odd, woven hats, all brim and ending in a point atop the head, to keep the sun off.

It was a grim scene, but impressive nonetheless. Men moved forward lugging steel rails in cradling straps and setting them in place. Before them, other workers swung picks and great mallets and steel sledgehammers and shovels.

Other men were down there as well, white men in clothing that showed sweat down the backs and under the arms and down the fronts. But they were white, and were not engaged in lugging or pounding or anything other than overseeing the laying of the rails.

They held long poles and communicated with waving hands to one another over long distances. Others walked with what looked to Mac to be surveyor's chains. They were measuring distances.

Far to the left, toward where the rails were headed, the intended roadway ended in a slight gouged divot in the mountain. Everything that wasn't raw rock had been cleared away, and scaffolding was being built up on either side of this spot in the rock face.

"Is that going to be a tunnel?" said Mac.

Reg looked at him with a sneer. "What's it to you? You aren't here to do anything but make sure those workers down there stay busy. If you see even one of them slowing down, you crank off a shot."

"You don't mean shoot them?"

"No, not right off. First, second time, just fire warnings shots. Most of the time they get the idea and pick up their pace. Sometimes we have to drag one off for a little persuading, if you know what I mean." He grinned at that, as if he relished those moments.

"And if they still don't keep up?"

"You seem like a smart fella; you figure it out."

"Shaky said the company paid to have these men brought here from China, but they also brought their families."

"Yeah. So?" said Reg, scanning the activity below with a spyglass.

"So I'm just wondering where all the kids and women and old-timers are."

"They're around. Back at the base camp. You see those tents?" Reg pointed with the extended spyglass westward toward a cluster of what looked to be sixty or so tents, canvas affairs all clustered too close to one another. Mac guessed they were a good half mile or more away, and he saw tiny forms moving about there, though very few of them.

"Yeah, I see it."

"Well, that ain't even the base camp." Reg said this with a tinge of pride, as if he'd come up with the idea for this rail line all by himself.

"No?"

"Nope," said Reg. "Base camp is way the heck up thataway, toward where we're headed. Not far from Devil Gorge. That's where the women and kids are kept. Locked up tight, sort of what Shaky said the head boss, Kane, told him was his secret way to keep the men, here, working hard. It's clever, really. See, it's a way to make sure they do the job they was hired to do. And let's just say that mostly they do, because we have all them others locked up over to the base camp. The ones still with us, that is."

"What does that mean?"

"It means, mister, you ask too many fool questions, and I told you more than you need to know just now. I will tell you, though, that if you like the women, you could do worse than to root around and turn up a Chinese woman before they're gone."

"Gone?"

"Never mind. Now, last thing I'll tell you is we got

another crew working from the northeast coming west, going to meet us at the gorge. They'll get there soon, in fact. We'll meet up with them and then help them finish building the big trestle. I hear tell it may be the biggest one ever built." He nodded.

"That sounds impressive," said Mac.

"You ain't kidding. But it ain't gonna happen if the likes of you and me stand here yammering away."

"What about the women?" said Mac, pulling a half grin he hoped looked sufficiently wolfish.

"Oh, I see," said Reg. "You are tempted by what I told you, huh? Well, you cool your heels and it'll work out for you, that's all I can tell you. If you don't . . ."

"Yeah?"

Reg shifted the rifle cradled in his arms as he collapsed the spyglass against his chest and slid it back into a leather holster on his belt. Then he patted his rifle. "Then you get what I give them Orientals who make too many mistakes. And I got no problem doing it, neither."

Mac nodded. "Understood."

"You best hope you understand. I know you're a big fella and all, but that don't make no difference to me. And I can darn sure tell you that it makes no never mind to Shaky. He'll gut you as soon as look at you."

"If you're trying to put some sort of fear into me, you'd better work harder at it, Reg."

Reginald glared at Mac for a few moments; then a slow slight smile spread over his face. "Okay, I'd say we understand each other."

He began to walk away, then said, "I'll still kill you deader than dead if need comes to that."

"I understand," said Mac. "And I'll do the same for you."

"Good. That's what we want to hear. Now, you see that rocky knob over there?" Reg pointed across the wide draw toward a promontory of pink-tinged rock the size of a buckboard.

"Sure."

"That's where you'll be for your first shift."

"When does that begin?"

"Ten minutes ago. Get over there and don't do a thing except keep an eye on the Chinese and such."

Again, the big man merely nodded his head. Then he surprised Reg once more by striking out to make a beeline for the spot. He was soon sliding down the scree-riddled embankment.

"Hey! You can't just walk on over there from here! You got to make for the eastern end and go on down that way!"

"Nope. This is the quickest route. I intend to work for my wage, not wander around inspecting the place."

With that, Mac was gone, down over the side, sliding on scree and raising a cloud. As he intended, he also raised more than a few glances up from the laborers. He wanted to make his presence known, for good or ill. It worked.

A whole lot of Chinese laborers looked his way, and as he walked through their work he looked them over, doing his best to memorize their faces. He didn't have a clear notion of why, but he felt it was important. He also tried to appear not unfriendly toward them, for all the good it would do. Here he was, a white man carrying a rifle, but he couldn't change that perception of him. Yet.

As he walked none too quickly, he took in all he saw. It was a habit more than anything. And he knew Boone was doing the same. Make a mind picture of each face, each gun, animals, anything at all. You never knew what was going to prove useful later on. Frequently the most innocent or boring details proved helpful down the road.

* * *

Back at Shaky's shack, Boone employed his best casual, no-nonsense attitude, and did all he could to appear ornery and not overly chatty. Not an easy task for him, as it rubbed his fur the wrong way, but he had taken a measure of this Shaky fella and saw him to be a drunk, jittering through his day with frequent stabilizing nips on the bottle.

He knew with men such as this that the drunker they got, the meaner they got. And he wanted to keep that particular trait at bay for a while, at least. He figured he could do that by appearing mean. That often put strangers ill at ease. If Shaky didn't know just where he stood with this newly hired fellow, he was likely to play it cool himself.

In such instances, Boone liked to pretend he was a great actor of the stage, one of those big, fancy folk from one of those windy books Mac always had his nose stuffed into when they were back home in Denver City, resting up between jobs.

Boone pictured himself as a hard man with a long history of killing. A man who had a whole lot of hidden skills he didn't much talk about. He would nod when folks asked a question, or maybe shake his head, but that was about it. And he would not quite scowl, but he would not smile either. And he wasn't the sort to talk about himself.

Boone reckoned that other than the lack of chatty bits, this playacting he was getting up to wasn't all that much different from who he really was.

So when Shaky told them he had need of someone on the small side, thin and mean, maybe even a little cruel, to "work the encampment," as he said, Boone knew he was just the man. Thing was, Boone didn't feel small nor mean nor cruel.

He'd been about to take the drunk to task when he realized he must be one hell of an actor to have convinced him he was all those things. So Boone grunted and glowered instead. It had worked.

They rode northwest for the better part of a mile to a wooded valley that no doubt had once been a pretty place. Until Shaky and his men, on the orders of this mysterious Kane fellow, the big boss, had set up shop there.

As they rode closer, he saw that the trees, which appeared to be somewhat numerous, had indeed been far more numerous at one time, judging from the preponderance of stumps, ragged and gnawed away like teeth in an old-timer's mouth.

The wood had been used to build a hard-looking, knobby palisade. The closer they rode, the more sound he heard. Human sounds. And they weren't pleasant sounds. There was much crying of children. But no laughter of kids, one of the sounds Boone most enjoyed hearing in life.

"As you can see by now"—Shaky had paused his horse atop a small rise overlooking the camp—"these folks are prone to be layabouts. What you and them other men there, there, and over there"—he gestured with his flask— "are paid to do is two things: make certain none of them slows down. I want them all to be up to something of use. The thinking behind that, as Mr. Kane told me—and I will allow as how that is clever thinking—is that a well-worked slave is a tired slave. And yeah, I used the word 'slave.' Because until these devils pay off their debt to Mr. Kane and his boss, they are our property. And if they are our property, I own their mangy backsides. And if I own them, they are slaves. My slaves."

"You said two things."

"Oh, yeah. Well, the other one is the most important of all. You got to see that they don't escape. As you can see, the walls around this place ain't what you'd call something you couldn't climb if you had a mind to. But knowing that there's a gun aimed at your sorry head, you for sure will think twice or three times before you commence a plan to escape."

Boone nodded and spat a stream of chaw juice. He didn't chew much, but when he did, it tasted so rank that after a spell all he wanted was to get rid of it.

"You get what I am telling you?"

Boone nodded once, slowly, and continued to eye the encampment. All he could see were sorry souls, mostly old folks, a few cripples—some old and some younger—and children. He did not see, nor did he expect to see, many women. Most of the ones he saw that were still on the younger side were crippled. That held true to what the women told them—that most of them were being sold off as prostitutes and dragged on out of there before anybody with any power could get wind of it.

Did Kane and his boss folks, whoever they were, actually think they could get away with this and nobody would ever know?

The only way that might work out for Kane was if . . . if he killed off anyone who ever knew these women were here. Sure, that had to be their plan all along. The poor children and old, feeble folks in the encampment were never going to see freedom in America. They were being worked like rented mules down there.

Boone saw children and old folks hewing crossties and cobbling together small, poorly constructed shanties, and smithing steel over hot fires. Here and there he saw small, smoky fires with black pots hung over them. One fire, off to the side, held two larger cauldrons. They steamed away while a woman stirred one, then the other, then back again, with a large wooden spoon type of implement. Had to be the camp laundry she was tending to.

He bet himself a gold piece that once these people grew too weak to work, and thus were no longer useful, they would be killed off. Same with the men preparing the rail beds and laying the rails.

It was far too brutal to think about. The mind someone had to have to even think this was acceptable was . . . well, it didn't bear thinking about. And yet, here he was, Boone, having to think about that and nothing else. And pretend he liked it, too.

"You will notice there ain't much in the way of women down there. Which is a damn pity, if you ask me, though it's even worse for a man such as Reginald, who is fond of the ladies, if you understand me."

Shaky shook his head. "I don't know how he does it, but he insists on making certain all the women we ship on out of here are up to the task, if you know what I am saying. The caravans have dried up for now, not too many females of useful age to sell to them.

"But I just got word that we're expecting Mr. Kane to bring in a fresh load of Chinese in a few days, which is why I hired you two fellas on. So that'll be something. I know Reg will be happy to see them new women. It's been a dry patch for him."

Shaky seemed to think this was humorous because he chuckled and sipped. Boone got a dose of cold comfort, knowing he was keeping Shaky in somewhat good humor. But he wasn't certain he'd be able to keep up this act for long. He and Mac had to make things happen, and soon. Trouble was, how?

They were split up, which they figured might happen, but that meant they might not see each other often, if at all, and so would not have the chance to chat about a plan of attack.

It had happened before, but it was always a pain in the backside. *Well*, thought Bone, *just have to do as I see fit.* The big task was to free everyone, bust up the place, get the law in there, and hopefully do it all before the new folks arrived and got themselves tortured or worse. And do it all without getting anybody of value hurt.

Just like that, thought Boone to himself, wincing inside. He looked around himself once more, tamping down the wad of panic rising in his gorge, and spat. "Best let me get to it," he said, eyeing Shaky with what he hoped was a hard stare.

He didn't want to be in the man's presence any longer than he needed to. He had to get some time alone to think this thing through.

First thing he was going to ask himself was: What would Mac do? His big pard was always a level thinker, knew his way around a thorny situation, and then came up with a solid way out of it.

As Shaky nodded and rode off, Boone let out a long, slow breath and gazed back down at the camp below. He let his eyes wander along the rim above, almost even with him but on the far end and distant side of the camp. He saw four other men such as himself, all standing, with two seated on horseback. All of them held rifles, and all were looking back at him. And they all looked like genuine hard characters, not play actors.

CHAPTER 8

Wan Li wasn't certain how long to wait for the two odd men. She also was not fully convinced they could or should trust them. Certainly they were far less evil than those who sold them to the slavers. How much less, time would tell.

Perhaps she had guessed wrong about the two men and they would return as they said. They'd certainly helped them. But there was a chance they were going to go to the camp and bring guards back from there, then claim a reward for turning them back over to that vile man, Shaky.

It was confusing, but all the women discussed the matter shortly after the men departed. Two of them decided the men could not be trusted. After all, they were the same sort of men who had lured them to America. And then imprisoned them. And beat their families. And separated them. And then sold them. And then bought them and abused them. A life among such men could not be tolerated.

Two other women felt as though the men should be trusted. They reminded the others that they had been kind and had not tried to do the things that most men wanted to do to them.

And so it was up to Wan Li, as she had become the leader of the small group of women, to decide what it was they would do.

"I do not believe they are bad men. We will wait here for them for two days. If they have not returned by then, we will go to the camp on our own. I believe those men, Mac and Boone, are bothered by what is happening to our people. But I am afraid they do not understand what they will find there."

She let this proclamation hang in the air, for they all knew to what she referred. The beatings, the losses of their children, their husbands, their parents. Their meager possessions all taken from them and burned. The poor food and awful conditions in which they were told they must live—tents with holes, rats, and snakes. No heat, and what blankets there were had stains and holes.

It was bad enough that everyone they had traveled to America with wished they could go back to China. Even those who had left there with some sort of trouble hanging over them.

Still, Wan Li had to believe that not all people who lived in America were bad. Not all of them wished them harm, surely. But would any of them survive long enough to find the good ones?

Perhaps they had in these two men, the ones who called themselves Mac and Boone.

"Come, pack what we will need, and be ready. We will leave after two days."

"What if they come back before then?"

"Yes, what if they come in the night before then?"

Wan Li considered this. "This is a good point. We will move our camp, and when the time for their return draws near, we will be watchful of this place, in silence. If the men return alone, and not with the guards, we will know they mean us no harm."

"And perhaps they will be successful by then."

"Yes." Wan Li nodded. "Perhaps." But she secretly doubted that. The camp was a bad place and the worksite they could only guess, would be far from there and much worse. Her thoughts turned once more to her husband and their son, Wing, who had a bad leg that prevented him from walking well and from playing with the other children. She hoped they were somehow all right. Somehow.

CHAPTER 9

The rifle shot snapped Mac from the slight reverie he found himself in. It had been a long day, and this work was not what he had in mind—overseeing men who were being worked to death. He wondered what sort of day Hoke was having. Then the rifle shot cracked the air, pausing all sounds of dragging, crashing, pounding, and shouting of the guards.

Mac's trained eyes quickly located the drift of blue smoke from the rifle of a guard across the ravine from him. The man had lowered the rifle quickly after the shot, as if he were afraid to be seen as the shooter. But it was plain enough. And it was also plain enough to see where the bullet had gone, and what it had done.

A clot of enslaved workers had gathered about the form of the fallen man, but then, as quickly, had dispersed as one of the guards, down on the level work field with them, began berating them and threatening them with his rifle. He even jammed the snout of the rifle into the temple of the one man who remained with the fallen man, who lay still, unmoving.

The shot had likely done its job in full measure, leaving the man dead.

But the smaller one stayed bent low over the fallen man. At first, he did not budge from hugging the fallen man. He appeared to be rocking back and forth, hugging the unmoving body.

Even from his distance, Mac could see the spreading stain on the chest of the man's grimy white tunic. The man had been shot in the upper back and the bullet had ripped its way through his body and out his chest.

The guard jammed the rifle's barrel harder against the small man's temple, shoving him over on his side. Still, the small one clawed his way back to the shot man's chest. Clearly he was fond of the man, perhaps a relation.

The man with the rifle appeared to enjoy the act of shoving the smaller man away, for Mac heard him whoop and do it again.

Mac did not like this one bit, but if he raised his rifle to send a warning shot down at the man, it would likely be misconstrued. And then the man clubbed the younger, crying man and knocked him cold. He pointed toward another slave and gestured for the man to drag the dead man and the clubbed man off to the side.

Mac's eyes were wide, his breath stoppered in his throat. He was just too new and too far to do a damned thing. He'd rarely felt this helpless.

Separately, after their shifts, Mac and Boone were each instructed to make their way to a long row of tents, army style but with taller sides. They were erected atop a rise, as befitting everything about guards, overlooking the rabble of slaves. Each man saw the other from a distance and exchanged a nod.

They approached each other, lugging their gear, and ended up standing before a tent third from the eastern end of the line.

Other tents they passed were already occupied, many with the flaps thrown wide for airing, with tidy or untidy bunches of gear atop folding cots, one to a side. There was room enough in each tent for a walkway between the cots.

The tent they ended up standing before contained only two empty cots.

"Man told me to find a bunk that's empty." Boone eyed Mac, then the tent.

"Me too," said Mac.

"Looks like we'll bunk together," said Boone. "That'll be a change."

There was less than four feet between tents, so they knew there would be great call for them to be as discreet as possible when discussing this new, bizarre situation.

"You have a good first day?" said Boone, doing his best not to dump everything he gleaned on Mac's ears all at once.

"Yep," said Mac, dropping his gear bag on one of the bunks. He wondered idly if it was going to be long enough. He was north of six feet and he'd rarely found a bed that was comfortable in life. He'd had to modify the bed in the room he rented in old Mr. Pritchard's boardinghouse to make it a pinch longer.

"They tell you where to find grub in this place?"

Mac smiled. It was good to hear the old Boone, already whining about food. "Cook shack and mess tent are down at the far end."

Boone grunted and eyed a clot of men walking by outside, looking rested and in no hurry to take on their shift as guards. He noted a smaller group of men across the way, puffing pipes and talking to one another in low tones. They stood about a table with great rolls of paper, perhaps four feet in length, eyeing whatever it was atop the table.

"Engineers, surveyors, likely," said Mac, answering Boone's unasked question.

"Ah," said Boone. In a lower voice, he said, "Wonder how they stomach what they're seeing."

"Paid off handsomely," said Mac. "Very much so, in fact, according to another guard I talked with earlier."

"Brutes all," growled Boone in a low voice. "Them women was right as rain. We got to put a stop to all this, Mac. I can't go through another day and not do something."

"I know. Me too. I'm on what they call 'the line,' where they lay the tracks, blasting, digging, pounding rock. It's a whole lot like a prison camp, but these folks aren't prisoners. They've done nothing wrong."

He crossed his arms and gazed out the front of the tent. In an even lower voice, he continued, "I saw them kill a man today, and beat another into submission. Found out later the one they beat unconscious was just a kid." Mac's voice grew tight in the telling.

Boone glanced at him. Seeing such injustice was hard on a man, but for a big fellow, Mac had always taken it deep, as if he was the one who'd been stomped on. Boone felt much the same way.

"I was too dang far to prevent it," said Mac. He looked at Boone. "But no more."

"Right," said Boone. "Pretty much the same where I'm at. All old folks and kids. It's bad, Mac. They're treated like less than slaves, worked hard and fed little, their tents are hardly worth using. Forced to do all the laundry and firewood and hew beams, smithing, stables, the works. Mac, we need a plan."

"I think we can subvert from within while trying to find this Kane fellow."

"I heard tell he's coming in soon with another batch of Chinese. But he ain't here just now. Still back at his offices in San Francisco."

"Okay, but maybe we can each do something to take the guards down a few pegs."

"We need to free the slaves, get them on out of here."

"Yeah. One good thing is that they aren't chained, not even where I'm at."

"No matter," said Mac. "The guards are the chains and the locks. Without the guards, and with weapons, the workers stand a chance."

"Of what?" asked Boone. "Do you think they're just going to walk on out of here? Half of them ain't had a decent meal in Lord knows how long. They're weak, which I am sure is all part of the plan of that Shaky fella."

Mac nodded. "Good point. But we have to try. Maybe we can subdue all the guards at once."

"Any ideas?"

Mac shrugged. "Poison them enough to make them ill? Surround them and disarm them? I don't know."

"One of us should ride for the law."

Mac nodded. "That should be you. Be easier for one of us to get away from here than to get all the slaves freed and away at once. We need lawful numbers."

"Why me?" said Boone. "I'd rather stay here and dole out some justice of our own."

"I know that, but trust me, this will be far more effective. I'll do what I can to keep them from killing anybody else while you ride hard for the nearest town. You're a faster rider, anyway."

"You're right on that point, mister." Boone grinned. "But the nearest town will likely be all bought and paid for by this vicious Kane fella."

"Good point. Then a city. Sacramento. Anywhere you can send a telegram. Or several. We are owed a few favors. Time to call them in."

"Yeah, that fat politician from back Ohio way; he's due to pay up. Think on it some more while we go for grub. I can't hold out much longer."

Mac nodded. "No sense all of us starving. We should keep our strength up even if they can't."

He nodded toward the ragtag mess of tents below where a few cookfires smoked low and meager. The folks who were moving about down there moved slowly, as if they were a hundred years old and had sore bones. Which they surely did.

CHAPTER 10

Thurston Kane realized he was whistling, actually whistling, as he went about his morning ablutions. He paused and smiled, eyeing himself in the mirror, straightening his cravat and admiring his clean-shaven jaw, his jaunty, thin waxed mustache and chin beard. It was a look he'd recently taken on and quite liked.

It grew in well, and he suspected it lent his otherwise—if he must admit it—plain face a devilish, rakish edge he felt certain the ladies here in San Francisco found attractive, perhaps even a little dangerous.

Most of all, however, Kane had to congratulate himself on everything he'd made of his life. Why, think of it! It had been less than a year and he'd gone from a young man with few prospects in life to one with more prospects than most any man in the history of the world!

He chuckled at himself in the mirror. Perhaps all of the world was a slight exaggeration. "Ah, well," he said, mentally thumbing through the random thoughts making their way in, then out again.

The biggest impediment to his plans he foresaw was the gun-crazy ways of some of the guards, and the way they'd been handling the prisoners. Not that they were really doing much Kane didn't want, but that they had a tendency to be heavy-handed and kill when he really could not afford to lose any more laborers at present.

But that was all about to change. Glancing at his pocket watch, a fine gold piece he'd indulged in when he learned that fat boss of his, Blaswell, had invited him to the family mansion one evening. It had not been merely to discuss the day's labors, but to meet his daughter, the, as it turned out, not-so-lovely-to-look-upon Philomena.

Still, it was the opening Kane had pushed for, hoped for, any way to marry into a wealthy, empire-building family was everything he had wanted, worked for, waited for.

And now here he was, in San Francisco, in a rented, modest brick building he had insisted he would need as a base of operations to oversee the job.

And if he didn't get a move on, he would miss the ship's arrival.

He had a special contingent of men and wagons to haul the fresh wave of Chinese laborers—the men, the women, the children, the old ones—overland to the camp they had spent a month, many months ago, erecting.

They'd had a few tense times in those early days, when the engineers and the head of the construction crew were threatened. And then a camp-wide brawl had broken out because one of Shaky's men—a young, green hellion—had felt slighted because of his handling of the prisoners. Shaky, on Kane's orders, had subdued the youth and given him an ultimatum that was clear: toe the mark or die himself. It was what Kane wished.

"No one," Kane had told Shaky, "leaves my employ easily. It's either in a pine box or many, many months from now, paid well and smiling and tight-lipped. Is that clear?"

It had been clear enough to Shaky, who Kane knew shared some of his own outlook on life—namely that the weak lost and the strong, the persistent, won all.

Kane and Shaky were such men. And Kane was stronger

than Shaky. Kane was not uncertain just how, at the end of this phase of the job, he was going to make certain Shaky ended up in a pine box, but it would happen. Oh, it would happen.

Kane's carriage arrived at the dock as the stevedores began unloading the nonhuman cargo from the hold. His own cargo, dozens of haggard, confused, frightened Chinese, stood huddled in a large mass on the dock, corralled by a half dozen of Kane's guards.

Thurston Kane bit back a curse. He had dawdled too long at home over a breakfast he hoped would suffice for the long trip to the job site. He sighed as he walked toward the new arrivals.

He was still months from fulfilling this first and most important leg of the rail line. Once that was in place, he could relegate the on-site logistics fully to the engineers and construction foremen. Until then, Blaswell wanted Kane very much on site. And that was understandable to Kane, though regrettably so. But it was all part of his plan for success.

Blaswell could not live forever, particularly if he kept stuffing himself with all manner of fat-soaked meats and cheeses and wines and pastries. Kane had, of course, poo-pooed the doctors' advice, and told Blaswell what he wanted to hear, which was that he was a robust man from the old country, descended from a long line of robust people who outlived all doctors, was he not?

Well, yes, in fact that was somewhat correct, Blaswell had agreed. What went unsaid, Kane knew, was that Blaswell's forebears had all lived long lives because they worked hard and ate peasant food, not fatty, butter-soaked concoctions.

No matter; it was all working according to Kane's plan. His sigh turned into a smile as he approached the latest batch of Chinese folks. There was the fellow from Chinatown who he employed as a translator for the new arrivals. Kane knew him only as Wing.

"Master Kane," said Wing, bowing low. "Good to see you today. I did as you wished and told the new arrivals only that they have been expected."

"Good, Wing. Thank you. Now, tell them, please, that we are excited to have them working for us and we will begin our journey, without delay, to their new homes."

Wing did so, and Kane noted slight though genuine relief on a number of the faces before him. He really wished these fools no ill will, but to him they were a mere means to an end. An end that consisted of him running the Blaswell empire, though in a renamed capacity.

Kane was a solid name and would serve him well then. But to get there, he had to endure the monotony of the trip before them, trailing behind the Chinese in the commodious wagons he had rented for this purpose.

"Master Kane?"

"Yes, Wing." Kane liked it that Wing called him "master," but he disliked what Wing was about to ask him, which was something they both knew he was going to ask, just as they both knew what Kane's answer would be.

"Master Kane, these newcomers would like to know if I shall accompany them on their journey. May I tell them yes?"

Kane sighed through his smile. "Unfortunately for you, Wing, there is no room for two translators. And I have one at the camp already. Which I believe I have told you in the past."

Kane maintained his smile, but he wanted to bellow in the man's face. Too pushy. He also detected something, perhaps, on Wing's face that told him the ambitious Chinaman might be trouble on down the road.

For now, he would serve his purpose.

"Master Kane?"

"Yes, Wing." *Really,* thought Kane, *this was going too far.*

"They are wondering, as am I, why you have armed men holding them here."

"Ah, yes. Tell them that is for their own good. Tell them that San Francisco, particularly along the waterfront, is a dangerous place. It is for their protection."

Wing bowed and related the information. At least Kane hoped he had. It was annoying that he never knew quite what was being told his newly bought laborers.

"Tell them for me who I am, what I do, and that if they have any troubles, they should seek me out. Tell them that a translator will be awaiting them at the other end, once we reach the camps."

"Camps?" said Wing.

"Ah," said Kane. "The place we are headed. I sometimes refer to it as that instead of any town name because it is easier that way. Ultimately, I wish to let the Chinese name their own town. And while the camps are not the final location of the towns Blaswell has promised to help them settle, it will be a fine starting point." Kane smacked his hands together. "All right, then?"

He turned to the guards. "Gentlemen, please help escort our newly arrived guests and their goods to the wagons we have at the ready."

The men nodded in silence and made a show, as Kane had instructed them, of being smiley and solicitous. So far, so good. He wanted only to get the hell out of Frisco with his people, and away from the law.

Up to now, with previous shipments of workers, he had avoided paying the exorbitant taxes levied on honest, industrious business concerns such as his, or rather Blaswell's, notably those importing goods, of which the Chinese laborers qualified under the law.

But he'd been able to lay silver across the palms of the six men who most needed such midnight barroom attentions, and this method had thus far paid off.

His laborers came in on time, or nearly so, and as he already bore the necessary completed forms and stamped paperwork, some with wax stamps, and all marked "Paid," there was little anyone could do. He still had an abiding fear that one of these money grubbers had somehow double-crossed him. But no, it appeared they all liked the cash more than the idea of sleeping guilt free.

With this shipment of fresh laborers, Kane was confident he could make it to the great trestle, and then he would breathe much easier.

And now a child was crying. Kane looked at the slowly moving mass of Chinese. Why couldn't they trot when he wanted them to? *My word.* They'd been given free passage all the way to America, and they were now on dry land instead of wallowing on a roiling sea for weeks, months on end. And they had employment ahead of them, and they were about to be ferried in large, open-air wagons to the site of their temporary homes, along the rail lines. And yet they seemed dull, as if they were reluctant to get a move on.

"Wing, whatever is the matter with them? Tell them that my time and my money are being wasted. We have many miles to go before we stop. So we had better get moving." Kane smacked his hands together in a light, hopefully playful manner. He capped the movement with a reenergized smile. "Let's get to it, people!" He waved a hand at the sky. "Daylight waits for no man!"

The young translator regarded him for a moment, then nodded once and addressed the people, who had once more petered en masse to a halt. Kane's guards looked close to losing their patience as well. Two that he could see were grinding their teeth and not doing very well at keeping their smiles stretched wide.

Presently, Wing turned back to him. "On their journey here on the ship, there was a powerful storm. The ship felt as though it was going to turn over and dump them all in the great ocean."

"Yes, yes," said Kane. "What of it?"

"An old woman on board, one of them here, warned them that this was a bad sign, that they would have no luck unless they could make proper prayers once they arrived here."

"Ah," said Kane. "I see. Well, we don't have time for this, but I tell you what." He smiled again, nodding at the people. "We have to stop halfway to the rail camp, to rest for the night. It is much prettier there, where we will camp, than it is here."

Kane waved an arm and shook his head, frowning, as if this place, the docks, all of it, was indeed most foul.

"I believe the place where we will camp will be so much more suitable a place for them to pray and give praise to their good fortune. And if we reach it early enough, they will have extra time to rest as well."

Wing related this information, but an old woman in the midst of them raised her voice and peppered words at Wing. He returned back to Kane once she was done, and he shook his head. "It is no good. She is an elder, a sage among them, and she tells them that this is no good. They must pray here."

Kane strode to Wing, wrapped an arm about the shorter man's shoulders, and spun him around, walking from the crowd of haggard Chinese travelers.

As soon as Kane's back was turned, he lost his smile and gritted his teeth. He bent low and growled in Wing's ear. "Now you listen to me, Wing. I don't give a fig what that batty old woman has or hasn't said to them. They are going to get in those wagons and do it right now, or I am going to personally see to it that they are all arrested and held in prison on charges of breach of contract until the next ship is ready to depart for China.

"I don't care what you tell them, but you have five

minutes to get those people loaded up on those wagons, or my men there"—he nodded toward the guards—"will do so. And they will not be as gentle as I am. We are wasting time, and that means we are wasting money. And that is unacceptable. Do you understand me, boy?"

Again, Wing stared at Kane. This time, though, Kane saw a twitch of fear on the young man's face.

Good, he thought. Exactly what he wanted to see on the face of every person, no matter how small and insignificant they were to his daily life.

Prayer indeed, thought Kane. The old heathen would be among the first to go. If she was too old to be found attractive by a slaver who knew of a love-starved mine camp somewhere, she would be worked hard and, as the ranch hands said, put up wet.

CHAPTER 11

Early the following morning, Mac and Boone found themselves called upon to do the same thing they had done the day before, stand guard over the unfortunate laborers.

Mac saw an old man fall to his knees. Twice he was sent sprawling to the graveled earth as he rose on shaky legs.

As soon as the guard kicked the man in the backside for a second time, Mac was in motion, bolting for the pair, the old man groaning and exhausted though his day had just begun, and the guard, braying like a witless donkey.

"Hey, you!" growled Mac, barreling forward. The young guard turned his toothy grin on Mac, expecting to see a smiling comrade about to praise him for his skillful way with the workers.

Instead, he saw a large, broad-shouldered man closing in on him fast. The youth recognized Mac as one of the new fellows, and his grin slipped from his face. "What you doing?"

"I could ask you the same, you little whelp!" Mac strode right up to him and landed a kick on the kid's half-turned body.

The big boot connected with the kid's backside and sent him flailing and sprawling into the dusty earth a few feet from the old Chinaman. The kid's rifle had flown from his grasp and clattered against some rocks.

"How do you like it, boy?"

"Hey, man—they ain't like us!" said the kid, scrambling backward to escape the flare-nostriled, stalking Mac.

"They're animals! Even Shaky said so!"

"So Shaky's the sole arbiter of intelligent thought and proper behavior here?"

"Huh?"

By that time, other guards had closed in.

"What's the matter with you, new guy? You some sort of Chinese lover?"

"Maybe I don't like to see a bully have his way with an unarmed person."

"Give the Chinaman a gun and see how he does!" shouted another guard who'd wandered over but stood twenty feet away and still kept his eye on the workers. Mac told himself to pay attention to that man; he had shown himself not to be distracted from his duty of guarding the workers.

"Enough of this foolishness!" It was Reg, the second-in-command beneath Shaky. He looked properly riled. Despite the hubbub, Mac saw that the old Chinaman who had been kicked down by the young guard had limped off. Other workers risked looking their way, and Mac thought he saw a boldness, perhaps a welling of hope on their faces, however brief, replacing their usual hunch-shouldered, hangdog look.

Come what may to him, he had been unable to stand witnessing any more of the brutality inflicted on the workers without doing something. It had been too little, too late, and he knew that an unintended result of his horning in on the guard's treatment of the old man would likely result in the riled guard targeting the old-timer and plaguing him until he expired. Mac also knew he could not, would not let that happen.

"You big brute!" growled Reg, stalking right up to Mac, a rigid finger pointed up at his face. "You pull that crap again and I'll shoot you myself, you hear me?"

He didn't wait for Mac, who stood his ground and glared down at him, to answer.

"Any hard wording of the guards got to be done, I'm the man for it, not some pathetic little guard, no matter how big he is!"

Reg spun and pointed that finger at the young guard, still scrabbling on the ground. "Get up off your backside, you idiot! Now!"

Mac knew he had to make a decision—take a stand and risk the entire wobbly operation he and Boone were in the midst of or back down and humble himself and, in so doing, likely be of more use to the Chinese laborers. He sighed and nodded and endured the glares of the other guards. One went so far as to spit a stream of tobacco juice just before his boots as he walked back to his station.

But Mac reckoned he'd done the decent thing, and that would have to be good enough for him for now. Until the next time, and he did not doubt that would happen soon.

Mac glanced at the old man, who by then had resumed his place on the line, shuffling over between two younger men who closed ranks around him. Mac could tell they were asking him questions, likely if he was all right. Few words were exchanged, though, because Mac knew they were all forbidden to talk with one another.

The sounds of steel hammers plinking steel rails and pins and pounding rock filled the air once more, now that the hubbub had dwindled.

Mac held his rifle cradled in his arm, ready to swing in a moment.

To his right, he saw Reg stomping toward him. *Here we go*, he thought.

"You walked off before I was finished, man!"

Mac kept his cool gaze on the man, noting that Reg was unlike a lot of men he'd met, who wilted under his glare. It amused Mac, but he did not grin. That would only inflame the foreman's ire.

"You do your job and keep your nose out of other folks' business, or else!" With that, Reg stomped off, muttering about having to mother hen a bunch of fool kids.

Mac didn't care; he let it roll off his back and wondered just what he was going to do to subvert this operation. It wouldn't be easy as there were so many guards. Then again, he and Hoke had never chosen the easy path.

As for Boone, he was back at his own post, above the camp, deep in thought because he found a way, or so he hoped, to maybe free some folks.

Not but an hour after breakfast, he'd seen one of the guards, a fat fellow with an outthrust bottom jaw and a broad, single black eyebrow across his forehead, receive a jangling ring of keys from Shaky.

Then he'd seen the fat man take his time walking about the place, unlocking gates and the chains that held a few folks tethered to their work stations—such as the crippled older woman who tended the big, steaming laundry pots.

Boone wasn't certain how she could even lift her leg to drag that chain around the spot where she labored all day, walking from the stack of soiled clothes over to the cauldron on the fire over to a second cauldron on a second fire. Then over to the woodpile to fetch more splits of wood to keep her water hot, then to the washboard.

Boone was curious to know why the man was unlocking the gates and all, so he walked over toward another guard not too far away. The fellow pretended not to see him. *Some guard*, thought Boone.

"Hey, fella!"

The man looked away.

"I know you heard me, you goober!"

That got the fellow to look his way. "You best not be calling me such a name."

"Oh, don't get your knickers in a knot. I just wanted to ask you a question, is all. You being an old hand here and me being new." He wasn't averse to stroking feathers if it would provide answers. And it usually worked. Just like now.

"Well, all right, then. What is it you want to know? And be quick about the asking—Shaky don't like us yammering to each other."

As he said this in a lowered voice, the man, easily a head taller and a shoulder wider than Shaky, bent his head like a kicked dog and looked around himself.

"What I want to know is why that fat fella yonder"—Boone nodded toward the man who was still waddling about the enclosure below, jangling the key ring—"is doing unlocking the gates."

"Oh, well, we usually unlock a few of them so the workers can get out there and saw trees and fetch water. But today, there's another reason."

Boone waited, but the man did not offer more.

"And what's the other reason?"

Again the man glanced left and right. "New shipment."

"New shipment? Of what? Steel rails? Supplies? What?"

Again, the man ducked his head and in his lowered voice said, "Slaves. A whole new batch of Chinamen!"

"Oh," said Boone. He'd been counting on trying to sneak out and make for the coast and the law. He figured he'd be followed, but it would be easy enough to lie and say the work wasn't what he had in mind, should he be caught.

"They coming in today?" he asked.

The man shrugged. "Might be today, maybe tomorrow. Don't know."

Boone nodded but didn't reply. He had some thinking to do, so he moseyed back to his spot to think.

CHAPTER 12

At his post at midday on what all the guards referred to as "the line," overseeing the workers, Mac saw a number of riders trotting in toward camp from the southeast.

They rounded a scraggly outcropping and three were in his sight, perhaps a half mile off, maybe less. And then another couple rode into view. Before they finally stopped appearing from behind the rock, he counted at least six riders.

It was obvious they were making for the railroad camp. He sent out a short, close whistle that was heard by the one man he hoped would hear it—the guard closest to him, about twenty yards to his right.

The man looked at him and nodded. "What you want?" He seemed to be annoyed instead of grateful for the interruption in the hours-long task of doing very little.

Mac nodded toward the line of riders.

The other guard looked and said, "Yeah, okay. I see 'em." He walked closer so they wouldn't have to shout to each other, and stopped when he was about a dozen feet away.

"They're what we all call the fetchers." Then he leaned forward and spoke in a low tone, as if sharing a secret. "That's the choice job, I tell you. I hear the pay is double what we earn, and you get to ride on out for days at a time, free on the trail." He smiled at the thought.

Mac wondered, if such a prospect was so enticing to the man, why he didn't just ride on out of here and take to the trail.

He didn't say any more, so Mac asked the obvious. "Why 'fetchers'?"

The guard snorted and shook his head, as if Mac should have known the answer to so inane a question. "'Cause they go after them who run off from here!" He shook his head and walked back to his spot along the rim.

Mac looked back toward the line of riders. There were seven, and they were making slow but steady progress. More importantly, he saw them with more clarity now and realized that one horse in the middle carried not one but two riders: one upright, the other draped behind the rider.

And that rider was not holding a long gun as the others were before and aft.

So, these men were guards, too, but they fetched runaways. One of them appeared to be dead, and that other one with him, Mac now saw, was also a man, and he rode with his hands bound behind his back.

They trotted closer and closer and were within twenty yards of him when Reg thundered up on a brown mount. Mac noticed that for all the man's bluster and bravado, he rode poorly, slopping this way and that in the saddle.

The line of riders saw him, and the man in the lead held up a hand that halted those behind him.

Reg closed in on them and jerked the reins back, forcing the horse to halt hard, dust clouds plumed upward from where it stood, splayfooted and confused. Reg leapt from the saddle, shouting as soon as his feet hit the dusty earth.

He nearly ran the few yards over to the lead rider, waving his arms and bellowing. The slight breeze carried toward

Mac, who was able to hear much of what Reg shouted: "Why are you bringing him back? What in hell ails you?"

The man in the lead, apparently the head fetcher, said something softly, because Reg cupped a hand around an ear and cocked his head, as if to mimic someone hard of hearing.

"I said," shouted the man, "the other one ran and this one didn't. We cornered him in a little box canyon and drew down on him, all six of us. He didn't stand a chance and he knew it."

"You didn't answer my question! I asked why did you bring him back like that? And you know darn well what I mean, you lippy brute!"

"Oh, you mean alive? Hell, Reg, we can't go killing a man for such reasons! You know that, elsewise everybody about this place would be dead. And then who'd do the killing?"

Mac's brow puckered at the notion. This man's logic sounded a whole lot like Boone's—certainly no dafter. The notion amused Mac enough that he let slip with a light smile. But back to the game at hand, he thought, and he watched, knowing this might not end well for the middle rider.

Reg strode over to the right side of the lead guard and looked up. "Who hired you?"

"You did, Reg."

Mac noticed the man was not smiling now.

"And I dang sure don't like to be talked down to like that, you hear me, boy?"

"Yes sir. Reg, I—"

Reg held up a hand.

Mac could see the man was shaking with rage. What on earth was he all worked up for?

Reg strode back along the line and paused beside the rider in the center. Mac saw that the man was another

Chinese laborer, and his hands were bound behind his back. His shirt was half torn away and his exposed skin was filthy with grime and layered with fresh cuts, as if he'd run through a gauntlet of knives.

Reg, his chest working hard and his hands hanging limp by his sides, looked up at the man for a moment. "Somebody get him down off that horse. I don't feel like waving my hands around to get him to understand me."

None of the riders moved to accommodate Reg's request quick enough for his liking. He shouted, "Do it now!"

Three of the fetchers jumped down awkwardly, still holding their rifles, and ran for the center horse. One came up beside Reg, the other two worked that way from the horses' left sides.

All of a sudden the Chinese man, whose face Mac hadn't seen clearly until then given the angle of shadow from a nearby rocky cornice, shifted in the saddle and gave out a startled, sharp cry in a hoarse voice.

Mac saw the man's face was swollen and bruised all about the eyes. His cheeks were puffed as if he was a chipmunk with a mouth full of seeds.

And he pitched off the right side of the horse, his swollen eyes wide, a shout jerking out of his equally puffy mouth.

His slight form flailed and twisted, as if he was fighting the shove he'd obviously received from one of the men on the other side of the horse, but to no avail. Then he collapsed right down on Reg, who was not prepared for the unintentional attack.

The two men flopped hard to the earth, dust rising from their writhing, collapsed forms. Reg was the first to gain his feet, and the Chinaman tried to rise but only got one leg up beneath himself and swayed on the other knee.

Reg, shouting unintelligible words and redder in the face than ever, whipped his revolver free of his holster, and in one quick movement planted the snout of the barrel against the woozy, confused prisoner's bruised, battered forehead. And then Reg pulled the trigger.

The muffled, cracking sound shocked everyone. The horse that had carried the two prisoners, now just the one flopped form, skittered and bolted, and two of the other men ran after it.

Reg screamed at the collapsed mess at his feet that seconds before had been a man with hopes and dreams and ambitions and family.

He kicked at the form once, twice, before stepping back and pointed with the revolver at the dead man and then at the others. "He attacked me! You all saw it! The SOB attacked me! Ungrateful Chinese! This is what you get when you try to do them a favor!"

The draw and shot had happened so quickly that Mac had little time to act beforehand. Now he stood with his rifle aimed right at the foul back of Reg. "No call for that!" he shouted, knowing he was endangering his life and ruining any chance he and Boone might have had at working to crack this nut from the inside.

Reg's reaction to Mac's words was immediate and bold. He turned and aimed his revolver dead-on at Mac. "You dare to tell me what in the hell I'm supposed to do and not do with my prisoners?" His tight laugh was short and grim. It ended with a sound that was bitten off and spat out.

"I thought they were hired workers, Reg. Now they're your prisoners?"

The average person would not have noted the quick change that flashed over Reg's features, but even at the distance separating them, Mac noticed. And he knew in that instant that the man had him marked, no doubt, for a troublemaker, for someone who would, if Reg had any say in the matter, end up as had the poor Chinaman at Reg's feet.

The look from Reg also told Mac that he'd poked and jangled a mighty raw nerve. And he was glad of it. This entire place looked and seemed to be run by a small clump of men who had become so consumed by making money, either as employees of the man at the top, Kane, and higher, or as Kane himself, who apparently ran the place like a mad tyrant.

Either way, they were operating by large payoffs that they felt they could get away with anything. And their experiences thus far had proved them correct.

Mac could stomach this no longer. He kept the rifle snugged to his shoulder and felt rather collected and cool.

It was possible he was going to die in the next few moments, something that, as they spent more time at this vile encampment, he felt was more likely with each passing hour.

Mac realized with a stab of keen urgency that he looked forward to the life he'd imagined for himself one of these fine years, once he and Boone decided to hang up their trail duds.

He pictured that little place in the mountains, beside a clear, cold stream. The idea of one day sipping water from that spring freshet was something that kept him going. And if he shot Reg now, which would be that easy, as simple as touching his fingertip to the trigger, he would be taking away one evil man from the number of them who seemed to grow all about him in society, more and more with each passing day.

But that would be all he would accomplish. They would dump him in a shallow grave and run a railroad track over him and no one would be the wiser. Boone might never even know.

And the women they had vowed to help—they would receive no vindication, no answers about their families. And Kane and Shaky would have won.

No, this was not the way, Mac, he told himself. But what was the way?

All this and more flashed through Mac's mind in the brief seconds he and Reg stared each other down.

"Lower that rifle, or a half dozen of my men will drill holes into your new boy hide. You got me, man?"

Mac did not lower his rifle. That would be all but pulling the trigger on himself. "What's the assurance?"

Then a curious thing happened. Reg lowered his revolver, slid it into his holster, unbuckled his gun belt, and laid the thing on the earth at his feet, beside the newly dead man.

"There," he said, smiling. "And now I'll tell my men to knock it off and get back to work. You, man, will take that gun off cock, hold it down by your side, and come on down here. We got some talking to do."

"Why should I believe you?"

"Because I'm the darn boss and I can have hell rain lead down on your head in seconds." He shrugged and kept smiling. "Or you can take me up on my offer. See what's what. I like your style, man. Ain't a one of these other fools, except maybe for him over there"—he jerked a thumb to indicate the leader of the fetchers—"got backbone enough to tell me what to do and what not to do."

Reg's words hung in the air for a few moments. Then he continued, "Up to you, mister. Stay employed and have a future, or stay ornery and die right now."

They stared at each other a few moments; then Reg whistled and shouted, "All you all, get back to work and do not, *do not* shoot this man! And I mean it! We got things to discuss, him and me."

He looked back at Mac. "Now come on already. I got things to do."

Mac nodded and lowered the rifle, once he was certain the other guards had gone back to their boring posts.

Mac approached Reg with as much caution as he had ever used when scouting in the war. Usually that was while on patrol at night, setting the perimeter and training the knock-kneed youngsters, rawboned farm boys whose only experience with guns had been in taking deer for the family table.

Making meat and making death in war were two different things, and because they were stuck with him and he them, he did his best to harden them to the indifferent ways of warfare.

He thought all this as he approached Reg, with his gun lowered and with the possibility that each footfall could well be his last, for he trusted this rascal to keep his word as much as he trusted a hydrophobic dog not to bite.

He made it down the slope and was halfway to Reg. Everybody seemed to be going back to their places and tasks. The fetchers had calmed their mounts and were fidgeting, uncertain of what to do next. It was obvious to Mac that they were used to Reg's outbursts.

Shouts rose up from the west, farther back along the line where rails were stacked and being dragged into place. There were one, two voices, then a third, shouting down the others, followed by a gunshot that cracked the air and stopped the shouting, but not for long.

The first two voices began again.

Mac, Reg, the nearby workers, who had been keeping their heads down like kicked curs, and the fetchers all halted and looked toward the ruckus.

Up the line, halfway back to where the supplies were stacked and distributed, two Chinese men huddled together, but stood tall, staring at the guard who'd fired the shot into the air above their heads. As the sound of the gunshot faded into the blue sky, and though they clung to each other, haggard and bent from their labors, they resumed speaking loudly, in near shouts, at the guard, then pointing toward Reg. Mac knew just what they were worked up over—the vicious killing by Reg of their fellow homesman.

Their spirit and defiance was one of the most admirable, brave acts he'd ever witnessed.

Reg's voice whipped through the air, killing the noble moment, as the guard lowered his rifle at the two men.

"No!" shouted Reg. "Don't you shoot them! We need them."

"What about the man you just killed?" said Mac.

Reg spun and stared at him with that near-lunatic look once more on his face. He pointed a shaking finger at Mac. "Not that it's your affair, but he was a bad seed. He bolted once; he'd go for it again. Had to be done. And besides, he lunged at me."

"Or was pushed," said Mac.

Reg shook his head and strode toward the two men who had caused the commotion. "Here, now. Let me deal with them. You, Jake, go on and see to those others. No slacking. We have a pile of work to get through before Mr. Kane gets here!"

He covered the ground separating them in a few short moments, kicking at a slow-moving Chinaman and sending him sprawling on his back in a flurry of tired limbs and a shout of surprise. It may well have been rage the man was expressing, rage that quickly clipped off when Reg stopped and glared down at the man on the ground. "You got something to tell me, curse your hide?"

The man was immobile, fear dawning on him faster than if he'd slipped into a river of it. He stared back up at Reg, who stood over him, his hands on his hips. "That's what I thought," said Reg. "Yellow skin, yellow heart. I tell you, if we didn't have no need to keep you around a while longer, you would be kissing your sorry self goodbye. Lucky for you," he said. "I have other matters to attend to."

With that, Reg resumed his hard walk to the scene of the incident.

Mac walked farther down the slope, halting between the

dead Chinaman and the two men Reg was making for, muttering about the genuine hardships of his job and how nobody seemed to understand his daily struggles.

Mac could have found this diatribe humorous—it reminded him a little of Boone—but then he looked down at the headshot man on the ground. Dead for no reason other than he was being ill-used and sought freedom.

The other man hanging over the horse had been equally abused; his face, in death, was also a fleshy, pummeled lump where he'd been beaten by more than one man. And likely when he'd been tied up and unable to defend himself, if he had had the strength to do so.

Reg reached the two defiant men and held up his hand in a halting gesture to the guard, who still stood with his rifle half raised, ready to shoot at any second. Without breaking his stride, the fiery little foreman slapped the nearest of the two men across the face, followed through and, swinging again, backhanded the other man.

He kept this up, the two men staggering, then falling backward. As they fell, Reg leaned into and leapt atop them, his fists leading the way. The two men, weakened from work and hunger, fatigued by lack of water and too much heat, tried weakly, feebly to resist.

But Reg was well fed, underworked, and desperate for the money he felt these men were costing him. But he didn't dare kill them. The thing he most wanted was that money, and if he lost any more workers than he already had, they were going to be in trouble. Already they were down about two dozen men, not to mention all those women.

Reg kept thinking about all those women and the promise they had had; not all, but a good many of them. But Shaky had sold them off before he'd been able to make certain for himself they were worth selling.

And then there were the kids. Damn if that boss man Kane and Shaky weren't more concerned with making a buck off the kids and women than they were in getting the rail line done. Reg had had it figured right from the start. You keep the rail line rolling forward and then you had the right to concentrate a little on the side action. Not the other way around.

But the problem with his way of doing things was, as he was beginning to learn, he'd been too free in giving his guards—his men, as he called them—the opportunity to dole out hard justice when they saw fit. Most of them were solid seeming, so there wasn't a problem with that so much as with himself, if he had to admit it.

They saw him lash out and deal what he called "corrections" to the shirking workers, and they felt obliged to do the same. Pretty soon, with regularity they'd had Chinamen laid out, moaning and bruised and kicked up, men with busted limbs from beatings. And then, of course, they had to do for them with a bullet just so they could get some peace from all the moaning and screaming and bleeding.

Then, of course, they had Chinamen stacked up like cordwood. Couldn't bury them fast enough. And the ones left had to do the burying, of course, and they were near useless, carrying on as they did.

You'd think they'd never seen a dead Chinaman before!

All this flashed through Reg's mind as he laid into those two shirkers. The idea that they felt as if they had the right to stop working and talk back to the guard! As if they were their equals. The thought of it boiled up inside him and he couldn't seem to stop laying into them.

He pummeled and kept right on, hearing their fool whining and crying beneath his bleeding fists. Their pale, bony bodies felt like sticks in a burlap sack, crumbling beneath his blows. He kept right on with the beating until he felt a big, strong hand smack down on his shoulder, snatch his shirt, and yank him backward hard.

Even then, Reg wasn't certain what was happening, and

he kept right on windmilling those shots at whatever he could land on, then his fists hit nothing but air.

"What in the hell?" he screamed. His vision, which was blurred by sweat and rage and now the raw sun soaking down on him, began to clear as he lay on his back with a boot on his chest.

He grabbed at it and it pushed down harder. As he looked up, shifting his head from side to side, he saw a large, silhouetted man looking down at him. The man also had a rifle pointed at him. Then he recognized the man. It was that lousy, big fella again. He'd barely finished his previous run-in with him and now this!

Why Shaky hired him, along with that other one who looked like a woodsman in that rank buckskin garb, Reg had no idea.

The big man spoke again: "I just can't seem to leave you alone for five minutes, can I?" Then, to the two workers, Mac said, "You two okay?"

The Chinese men who lay gasping on the earth on their backs, bloody-faced and wheezing, did not respond.

Why did I ask them that? thought Mac. *What an idiot I can be.* Of course they weren't all right. They are as close to death as a person could be without actually, as Boone would say, giving up the ghost.

"Reg. You are an asshole. I was going to see what you had to say, and I'm certain I'm going to regret turning my back on those other fools you have working for you, but what in the hell is wrong with you? You have everything going for you. It seems to me you could work up a sliver of kindness somewhere within your mangy hide and treat these men better than you do.

"If you feed them well, they'll be able to work better, faster, more efficiently. If you allow them to have breaks for water during the day, especially in this heat, you'll get more work from them. But no, you can't seem to see the logic of that." Mac shook his head.

"So you attack them and wear them down and abuse them without mercy, and then you're angry when they pathetically try to stand up to you because you are killing them. What in the heck ails you? Where is the logic in anything that you or Shaky or, for that matter, this Thurston Kane, do? You all ought to be put through the same pool of muck you're putting these men through. See how you like it."

Mac knew his diatribe fell on deaf ears. He didn't care. He also didn't care that there were a dozen rifles trained on him once more. That he held a rifle on the boss of the guards was the only thing saving his neck. But as it happened five minutes before, it wasn't going to last.

Here I go again, thought Mac. *Courting death and not coming off as much of a suitor.*

CHAPTER 13

It wasn't in Boone's makeup to dither on a thing. Once he decided, he went for it, full bore. As he liked to imagine it, he was a steam train, stoker's elbows flying, barreling up one grade and down the next, and by gum, it felt good to see the scenery whip by in a freakish blur.

And so when he thought on the situation and saw the awful mess these folks down in the stockade were in, he knew Mac was right. He had to go for the law and soon. No waiting.

The trick was how to get on out of here without Shaky and his band of fools stopping him.

Then a thought came to him and he acted on it, not wanting to repeat the hemming and hawing of earlier.

"Hey!"

No response.

"Hey, you! Fella!"

The man sighed and glanced at him. "What is it now?"

"No need to take that tone, you youngster. Look, I need to make for the latrine. Breakfast is sitting hard with me. My gut's working up a case of the nervy drizzles, if you understand me."

"I don't want to hear what all your gut is up to, man. Just go do what you need to."

"Okay, then, but I'm telling you so if Shaky comes around, he won't think I'm shirking my duties! Never was a man alive who could claim that of Hokum Boone!"

At that the man nodded, then stiffened, not quite looking at Boone. And Boone knew he'd made a grave error in revealing his true name.

Boone thought quick and said, "Yeah, my friends say, 'Rokum Goone, you're a real worker. Ol' Rokum Goone's a worker and a half.'"

But the man to whom he'd spoken made no move to look back toward him. He remained ramrod straight. Not a good sign. He knew who Boone was, and if he knew of Boone, he likely had heard of Mac. Because together they were known far and wide.

They'd been having that trouble now and again these past couple of years, ever since they'd made names for themselves saving the bacon—and wallets—of a few famous folks who insisted on telling their stories to newspapers. Soon, the whole of the West wouldn't be fit for them to live in!

Boone spun away and made for the general direction of the guards' latrines, mumbling all the way. "Too blamed chatty for my own good, that's what I am. Mac was right, blast it! I'm too blamed chatty. . . ."

When he made it to the latrines, he saw that one of them was unoccupied, its door hung open, an unspoken rule most folks knew of—leave the doors open in decent weather to let the stink drift off.

But the door of the second outhouse was closed. Occupied? Then he had his answer: A boot scraped, and he heard a suppressed groan from within.

Nothing for it, he told himself. *I'll have to climb in and wait out the groaner*. And so, with care, he crept in, as quietly as he might, just in case the occupant of the other one was hard of hearing.

It took a while longer than Boone would have liked, perhaps ten minutes, but then he heard the usual stomping and cussing and rattling of the door, and finally boots ground gravel on out of there. He peeked through cracks in the planking and saw that the retreating man was none other than Shaky his own self.

Boone waited a minute more, just until he knew the man would be out of sight. He didn't want to risk them seeing each other. Next up, he had to get to the stable where he and Mac had been instructed to house Lincoln and Chummy. It was northeast of the latrines by a good eighth of a mile or so.

He slipped out of the latrine door, letting it close softly behind him, then with near-constant looks over his left shoulder, he hotfooted up the winding trail toward the barns.

It was a dangerous route because men and beasts made frequent use of it in ferrying goods from the larger, lay-down yards that also resided up there. And within a couple of hundred yards, he saw a wide fellow ambling toward him. The man carried something on his shoulder and leaned with it, compensating for its dead weight.

As they approached each other, Boone recognized the fellow as the camp cook. Boone smiled and nodded as they came up alongside. The man slowed and looked at Boone. "Sack of flour, huh? Hope it's for the Chinese folk. They're looking mighty peaked."

The man's expression never changed from taciturn, but he spit a gobbet of brown juice. "Mind your own affairs." He ambled onward.

"Too chatty, Boone, too chatty. . . ." he mumbled as he hurried along.

He'd almost made it to the last bend in the rocky, winding road right before the barns when another fellow, this time one on horseback, trotted around the bouldered cornice.

The man slowed up, halted. "Where you headed?"

"Oh, errand for Shaky."

"Huh," said the man. "Not like him to entrust a new man to anything more than guard duty."

"Well, ah, I reckon I got that trustworthy face, is all."

"Uh-huh." The man made to ride on, then held. "What's your name anyway?"

Boone gave him a hard stare. "I never said."

"I know, that's why I asked." Then he smiled. "I'm Grady." He nodded in greeting.

Boone sighed inside. Had to be a friendly, chatty one he came across, didn't it? "Gomez," said Boone, squinting off toward the barns.

"Huh, you don't look like a Mexican."

"Not all of us do," said Boone and walked on.

Behind him, he heard the man say, "What in the hell does that mean?"

Boone kept walking, feeling his face heat up.

This wasn't going to plan at all, at all. But he had to keep on, or all was lost. Those folks were desperate for help, and soon the new ones would be, too. Best to fetch the law, as impartial as he could find, before the womenfolk were sold off to slavers. Those thoughts spurred his footsteps and carried him with conviction to the stable.

It took him a few frantic minutes to locate Chummy. He was outside in the second corral of three. And he wasn't but a few yards from Mac's big mount, Lincoln.

Boone knew the hostler would be lurking about, and for good reason, because he'd heard they'd had trouble with a small party of Indians, no one knew just what flavor, a week or two before. They'd made off with a couple of beeves and two horses.

It was with some trepidation that Mac and Boone had left Chummy and Lincoln there. But the stableman had a couple of armed men helping him, so that eased their minds. *Until now*, thought Boone.

He didn't relish the thought of getting shot while tending to his own horse.

"Hey, now!" said a nasal voice behind him. "What's this here?"

Boone patted Chummy but turned his head slightly. It was the head stableman.

"You can't be talking to me, can you?"

"You bet I am!"

"Good, then. Good to know you're not afraid of tending to the stock. I kind of thought you might be good at what you do when I met you the other day."

"What you doing in there?"

"Why, what's it look like? I'm rounding up my horse!"

"Why?"

"Why what?"

"Why you need your horse?" The man stood just outside the corral, a shotgun cradled in his arms, but his eyes were narrowed and he looked bristly all around.

"Whyever does a man need a horse? I'm fixing to ride on out and I aim to use my own mount to do it."

The hostler shook his head. "Nah, nah, that can't be right."

"Why?"

"'Cause Shaky don't allow nobody out nor in save for the men who do the bringing of the goods in and out, that's why!"

"Who said anything about Shaky?" Boone tried to keep his gaze hard and level, and not show any of the gut flivvers he was feeling.

He patted Chummy's rump and walked around him, back toward the stable, shifting his rifle to his other hand as he climbed the corral rail.

"Where you think you're going?"

Now on the same side of the rail from the hostler, Boone sighed. "Look, man, I've about had enough of your nosing around in my official business. Let me remind you that Shaky ain't the top boss of this here job, is he?"

That rattled the hostler, for he'd turned pink faced and stammered, "You mean . . . Mr. Kane?"

Boone nodded, wondering what it was about this Kane fellow that had everybody acting as if they were walking on a field of newly hatched eggs. "Now you're understanding me."

Boone leaned his head forward, and in a low tone said, "Can't let that get out, though. There'd be the devil his own self to pay if word got back to Mr. Kane that he was being second-guessed. You understand me?" Boone tapped the end of his nose and eyed the man.

"Yes sir, you bet." The hostler backed up, right into the rail fence.

"Now, I need to get my saddle and all. Where'd they get stowed?"

"Come on inside. I take care of the tack. Just back here."

Boone followed the man into the dim but cooler stable. The smells were familiar and warm, and somehow, no matter the time of year—could be high summer—a warm, well-tended stable reminded him of Christmastime. And that was one of his favorite times of the year, mostly because of all the good cheer folks seemed to feel toward one another. It was a fine time.

"Yours is there, beside that one the big fella used. He your friend?"

"Maybe so," said Boone, then tapped his nose again and gave the man a slight nod with squinted eyes.

"Oh," said the hostler, confused.

Boone wasn't certain what the gesture he'd been making was supposed to convey, other than to keep the hostler nervous. But it seemed to do the trick.

He grabbed his saddle and bridle and blanket and legged

them back outside. Then he whistled low for Chummy and led the horse outside the corral.

He was halfway through saddling Chummy when he heard one, two horses clop-clopping up from the direction of the encampment.

He worked his way around to the far side of Chummy and cursed himself for not saddling quicker. He looked over the horse and saw no one, reasoning they were hidden behind the stable.

"Got to make tracks, Chummy," he said, tightening the cinch. With no more thought than that, he snatched up the hanging reins and swung aboard. He heeled the feisty paint into a lope, making for the roadway that circled wide north of the camp and various lay-down yards, barns, and workshops.

He was not quite ready to let out a sigh of relief but was on the verge of drumming heels to urge Chummy into a gallop when he heard a voice that sounded familiar shout, "Hey you! Get yourself back here! Now!

Then he heard thundering hoofbeats, the sounds of one horse trailing, and all the while the rider shouted. And then a second horse joined the first.

Boone bent low and hugged the pommel, drumming his heels and all but holding his breath. "We got to make tracks, Chummy. I do believe I am in it up to my neck this time!"

CHAPTER 14

"I'll be jiggered if that wasn't Shaky himself," muttered Boone, his cheek low and brushing Chummy's mane. All manner of conundrums and possibilities pulsed through the rangy woodsman's mind. None of them ended with him or Mac coming out on the good end of any of this.

Nothing for it now, he thought, and urged his little steed on to a faster clip.

The terrain was new to him as they'd come in from southeast of here, but so far it was forgiving. It was bordered with bold juts of sandstone and random stands of scraggly trees, and it wound between them in a curved manner, once switchbacking nearly upon itself to get around an otherwise unpassable ledge.

Boone began to feel as though he might get away with his skin, though this did nothing to shine the fact that he'd ruined the fib he'd concocted for himself, and Mac, too, because they'd ridden in together. They had shown it was plain they knew each other and were on friendly terms.

They rounded a huge knob of rock and he reined up to give Chummy a quick breather while he cocked an ear to his back trail. And he heard hoofbeats, coming from more than one horse. In fact, it sounded like three. And they weren't slowing.

"Come on, Chum, time to really make tracks!"

They churned dust down a steep section, and Boone began to see a vista open up before him. And the sight of it increasing ahead did not fill him with hope. It meant they were heading down to a flat, and that meant he would be a sitting bird he was damn certain they were going to pick him off.

The only thing he could think of doing was to angle to his right, hard, and make northward, hoping there was a trail, or at least land he could make into a trail. Barring that, he was stuck with either turning and confronting them or making for the open ground, which he now saw was as he feared, low and wide. And the trail he was on clearly led to it and through it. And in a straight run.

"North it is," he growled and eased Chummy to his right. But any hope Boone had of that direction paying off with a forgiving landscape was, it soon became apparent, not to be. The way also dropped off leading not to a flat but farther north along the spine of this sizable ridge.

Before him, though, lay a wide declivity composed of boulders the diameter of a wagon wheel, and nothing a horse could pass over or through even with any luck at all.

He slowed up and considered, in a glance, what he faced. The only possibility for escape lay to his left now, down the slope and across the open plain below.

And so down they went, switchbacking wherever he could, cutting around boulders and below crags, taking advantage of clots of stunty pines where he could.

In another minute or so, while moving as quickly as he could and still keep hidden from eyes coming from above, Boone reached the midpoint of his descent. He glanced upward and saw one rider, then a second emerge from behind the big cornice rock.

They looked about them, swiveling their gaze, rifles drawn and laid across the saddle horns.

"Nothing for it," said Boone, knowing that at any moment they might see him. And they did.

"There!" one shouted.

Boon didn't wait to figure out which it was. Likely Shaky, and they were going to draw down on him, too.

He kept descending, hugging what cover he found. If he could make it to the bottom, he might buy himself time by hugging the base and cutting south. North would land him at the feet of that boulder field.

By the time he skirted that, he'd be picked off. But south, along the ridge, he might hold out longer; long enough anyway, he reasoned, guiding Chummy tight to huge, tumble-down boulders, to discover some new possibility.

A bullet spanged off a rock to his left, pluming dust. The sound of the shot reached him a second later. Distance like that was even deadlier. He'd feel it before he heard it, not that he was ever fast enough to react in time once a shot was heard in closer range.

Chummy was beginning to flag, his breathing coming harder. "Easy now, boy," said Boone. "Easy. Not worth getting a bullet for."

The solid little horse was always like that, keen in a fight, as if he knew just what Boone was hoping for and anticipating it, giving his all without Boone asking.

A second bullet nibbled earth to his right. They had his location marked, for certain. Not difficult when you had the high ground.

Boone slid from the saddle and led Chummy back slightly upslope, beneath a massive overhang that looked far in, as if it might be home to snakes and such. He'd deal with that as he had to, but right now they needed the protection the gifted jut of stone might offer.

There was enough cover that they might be able to catch their breath and figure out a next move. He'd backed himself into a tight spot with few ways out. But so far in life he'd always made it out. So what was one more such instance?

The grim question wasn't one to dwell on. He made certain they were tucked in as far as they were able to go under that slab of shade-giving, cooler rock. Then he checked his rifle and his gun belt, felt the revolver and the hip knife there. And on his saddle, his tomahawk.

He'd taken to wearing it on his horse of late and strapping on the hip iron instead, because the weasels and rascals they'd been dealing with the last year or so were increasingly overweaponed with things that threw lead. Boone knew the value, much as he detested it, of matching or exceeding a rogue's abilities with superior weapons.

Tethered loosely to a jag of rock, Chummy stood hipshot and resting from the thus far arduous journey. Boone stood closer to the outer edge, glancing left and right, uncertain from which direction his pursuers might choose to descend on him.

Surely they had seen him work his way over and then beneath this great drape of stone, hidden from their sight. It was possible they could find a way to split up and surround him. It was also possible they could wait him out.

Boone took stock of his scant provisions—only a goatskin of water the reluctantly obliging stableman had furnished him with, and a couple of old apples as a treat for Chummy in his side bag, which always rode on the saddle.

He also had three or four strips of jerky, prone to greening, riding in the depths of his buckskin tunic. They were for emergency purposes, but somehow he never remembered to toss the old ones to the rats and refresh the supply with newer, less-rank strips.

Presently, Boone heard shod hooves ringing on stone, but it was an intermittent sound and not useful in telling him how many pursuers there were. He groaned and cursed his impulsive self. *Too hasty this time, Hokum, old boy.* Pappy would be shaking his head and Ma would be clucking in the kitchen, slamming pans and muttering about how she couldn't figure where he went wrong.

That led him to thoughts of his childhood in Hoddy's Gulch, rousting about with Cousin Merd. And that led him to smile as he remembered how they used to whittle and practice working knobby old nubs of chaw filched from their pappys' pouches.

It tasted awful, but it sure was fun, spitting and marking off the distance covered. Hoke won most of the time. Then, before they knew it, it'd be near dark and they'd have to trail on back home under cover of the night sky. It never bothered him, but sometimes Merd would let out a whimper. But the thought at that moment was a good one, for it told Boone what he needed to do.

He'd wait them out, by gum, and take off on out of there once full dark came.

And he knew they weren't anywhere near the full moon, which could foil his plans for certain. That was a rare but welcome lucky break.

He almost smiled; then he heard horse shoes on stone once again. This time it was coming from a whole lot closer. And it sounded like from his right. The way he'd come.

He pivoted, eyeing that direction, noting that Chummy, too, had turned and faced that direction.

That horse had to be half dog, he thought, and not for the first time in their long association. While he looked to his right, he failed to notice that Chummy had shifted his gaze to the left edge of the great slab of rock.

Then he heard a slight scuffing sound, and a man he recognized stumbled and slid a few feet down the slope and struggled, with a clawing free arm, while the other whipped high, holding a rifle.

Chummy skittered in place and whickered low, and Boone backed a few steps, bending so he wouldn't knock his head on the uneven, sloped stone ceiling. At the same time, a slight tumble of pea-size gravel dribbled down the slope.

Boone decided the man to his left was the immediate threat, and he drew down on him. The man, alarmed that he had accidentally slid into harm's way, stared over at Boone, half nested in the shade, fear widening his eyes.

And then Boone recognized him—it was that one he'd seen on horseback, riding away from the stable toward the encampment. Must be he tipped off Shaky that Boone was making for the stables. Though it didn't much matter right now.

His footing somewhat stabilized, the man raised his rifle, far too slowly, as if he were underwater, his eyes blooming wide and his stubble-ringed mouth parted and drawn wide. He raised his rifle a bit higher, higher, and swung it the last half foot to aim at Boone.

"Don't!" growled Boone, his rifle snugged to his shoulder and ready to bark.

The man slowly shook his head, as if to say he was unable to comply with the directive, though perhaps he wanted to.

That was all Boone could allow, and he touched the trigger. His rifle spat death, and the bullet cored the dead center of the man's forehead, traveled through the man's skull and brain, then his skull again, and bloomed outward, spraying the close-by rocks behind with his life juices.

The man stood, jerked into an upright pose for a second or so, his eyes wider than ever and his mouth now a big, drawn, gaping hollow of surprise. His rifle slipped from his weakening grasp and clattered on the rocks.

He seemed to be staring dead ahead, right at Boone, and the buckskin-clad man swallowed back a lump. He never liked to kill, though he had done it plenty of times in his life, no matter what sort of animals, be it a chicken for Sunday supper or a man bent on doing him the same sort of damage. It never sat well with him.

And he had reasoned plenty of times in his life that any man who was comfortable with taking the life of another creature, no matter its size, was no man, but a cowardly bootlicker more suited to quivering in the shadows.

He swung back to his rifle after the few seconds' interlude, expecting to see another man leering at him, already twitching a finger on the trigger. What Boone saw instead was the same thing he'd seen before—a graveled slope bereft of anything but rocks.

But then he leaned forward and looked beyond the big stone slab's far edge and saw a shadow that shifted slightly. Rock shadows didn't move. And there wasn't any vegetation to speak of up here, he recalled from his descent.

Okay, he'd wait them out. Maybe whoever it was didn't know their compadre was dead. Maybe he thought it was Boone. That confusion might buy him a couple of seconds.

CHAPTER 15

Mac sensed rather than felt the danger his pard, Hoke, was in. Somehow, he knew Boone was hard against it— "it" being some sort of trouble.

But knowing Hoke, he would not go easy on the mind or the body. Likely he'd been caught in the act of doing something he shouldn't, or he was on his way to that very thing. Mac sighed, knowing some of that was true. He needed to do something, and soon. Trouble was, he wasn't exactly certain how far to go with this subversion business, not until he knew what Boone was up to.

This was one of the few times in their years working together when they went into a job with only half-formed notions of what to do. They'd been swayed by the women and their stories of abuse, of torture at the hands of the guards. And once they arrived here, and gained access to the place, then been taken in as guards themselves, they saw for certain—not that they doubted the women—they had been wholly correct about the conditions.

He wondered, too, what the women were up to. Were they keeping still at the campsite as Mac and Boone had told them to?

And then he looked across the shallow valley toward the

berm where the guards came to the site from the off-hours encampment and saw three men, two of whom he recognized as guards and the third as Reg, the man in direct charge of the guards. And they were all looking his way.

When they saw Mac eyeing them, they looked down, back at one another, anywhere but at him, though they kept in their tight cluster, chewing the fat over something that, if Mac were a betting man, would bet was not going to bode well for him.

He had already distinguished himself as someone reticent to dole out the sort of foolish punishment unearned and undeserved the other guards were only too happy to deliver to the heads, backs, limbs, and minds of the workers. Was he next? And what of Boone?

To Mac's surprise, though he double-checked his weapons and kept himself on high alert, nothing unusual happened. At midday, a replacement was sent so he might join the other guards on his shift to partake in the brief repast they called their noon meal.

Mac regarded the haggard, sweating men below, working at a sliver of their ability, and all because whatever genius who ran the job failed to supply them with adequate food and water. They needed, yet were not receiving, at least enough to keep them from moving at a snail's pace, struggling just to stay upright, let alone function as the employer wished them to.

And here he and the other guards were, ushered to a tent where they might enjoy food and drink out of the baking sun. They were men who had done nothing at all to earn a meal that day. And once again, Mac knew he had to act, had to do something, anything at all to rattle this foolish operation hard enough to halt it.

Mac saw that the other guards had leaned their rifles on a wooden rack built for just such a purpose inside the chow tent's open doorway. Then they made for large glass jugs containing cool water afloat with lemon slices.

He sipped a glass of it himself and tried not to think about the haggard laborers collapsing not but a few hundred yards away.

He noticed Reg enter the tent and stand in the open entryway behind him. The surly little subforeman faced the interior of the tent, a shadowed spot still lit well enough from the open sides, which Mac noted all seemed to host lingering guards in and out.

He made quick assessments, saw the number of men— more than a dozen—and sensed a coming fight, one in which he would be alone. Alone against them all.

Now a few of them looked at him. Reg smiled, and it was not something the man was used to doing, for it looked painful to him.

"Reg, boys, what's this all about?" said Mac, backing up to the table. Behind it were stacked crates and bundles of food. But to either side of him, beyond the ends of the tables, men all glared at him.

Mac tensed.

"You and your friend . . ." Reg let the words hang.

"Which friend would that be?" said Mac, his hands hanging loose, ready to bring into play his revolver and his hip knife, one on each side of his belt.

"Don't game me, mister," said Reg, his false smile already sliding away as if it were a rat only too happy to flee the unwelcoming presence of Reg's face.

Mac saw that while Reg hadn't advanced on him, the game was evident: He would hold still where he was, keeping Mac's attention by yammering at him even as the rest of the men shambled toward him. There was no sign they were going to draw down on him. So this was going to be a silent beating, then. And he didn't doubt that if they killed him, they would not shed tears.

"Your friend—he was caught in the act of stealing a horse from the stable. Now that's a serious fine; that there's a serious charge. And he's paying it up just now."

"Yes, yes, that does sound serious. But what's that got to do with me? We both happened to ride in at the same time, but we're not acquainted beyond that."

"So you say. We know different. Don't we, boys?" Reg glanced at the other men slowly tightening the noose about Mac. They mumbled agreement and leered and kept advancing, none of them, Mac noted, looking eager to be the first to reach him.

"And what's more, we know you and him to be other than who you say."

"Oh?" said Mac, feeling the edge of the table against the backs of his thighs. "And just who do you think we are?" But he knew what the answer would be. Their reputation was growing these past few years, and it was logical that seedy fellows such as Reg and Shaky knew who he and Boone really were and what they did for a living—cleaning up after law-free folks such as Reg and Shaky.

"Yeah, man," said Reg. "Shaky knows who you are, and so do a couple other of the boys. And I damn sure do. Oh yes, you see, me and a fellow I used to work for some months ago—now that I think on it, it's been the best part of a couple of years since then. But we knew a man who had himself a run-in with you and that rascal you work with. Am I right, Mac MacCoole and Hokum Boone?"

Mac shrugged. "You're telling this story."

"Damn right I am! Enough of this foolishness. Boys? Do it up."

Before any of the other guards could advance a step closer, Mac shucked his six-gun and had it palmed, cocked, and aimed at Reg's head. "Go ahead, boys," said Mac. "And what little sense Reg has will leak out of the hole I am about to give him."

"Uhhh . . ." said Reg.

"Yep," said Mac.

"Don't nobody move!" said Reg.

"Yep," said Mac.

Then, from behind him, on the other side of the table, where all those crates and bundles resided, where he'd counted on no person being located, Mac heard a sliding, scuffing sound. He saw a brief flare of surprise on Reg's face as the man's eyebrows rose a pinch.

Mac was caught in that finger snap of time between deciding to pull the trigger or spinning to face a new threat. He had hoped to get out of this without drawing blood, but he knew his foes didn't feel the same way; it was a safe bet they felt the opposite.

He half spun to see who was coming at him from behind, bending at the same time, knowing Reg and the others were already on the move, barreling toward him.

His gun swung and he triggered a round into the silent, leaping form of a small, wiry black man with tight-set teeth and eyes blazing with anger. His outstretched arms ended in hands grasping in age. And the bullet that tore into his gut, high up just beneath the breadbasket, did not slow the man's descent toward Mac, but it did wreck the fool's intention.

Mac jerked to his right, and the wiry man dropped like a sack of wet cornmeal, hitting the dry earth with a smack.

Oddly, the little man offered up pitiful mewling, gagging sounds as he wriggled and writhed. He landed facedown, his nut-brown arms and hands snatching and clawing at earth, clawing, releasing, finding nothing pleasing in the spasmodic task of dying.

But Mac saw none of this as he had already spun, keeping

low, his back to the table, to level his gun once more on whoever might be closest. There were too many of them, all on him at once. He triggered one, two more shots before he collapsed, bucking and punching and kicking and snarling beneath the fury of a dozen men.

CHAPTER 16

It had been two days since the two men left, and Wan Li knew she and the other women had a big decision to make, and they had to make it soon. If they ventured back to the railroad camp, they risked capture by the brutal guards.

But there was one in particular Wan Li had decided that, no matter how much he frightened her, she had to see again. He was named Reg and he was one of the big bosses. As such, he told her it was part of his job to make certain all the goods they sold were in proper working order.

And that was the excuse he used to do what he did. To all of the women, as far as Wan Li could tell. And, it seemed, especially to her. She had resisted him, at first merely shaking her head and saying, "No." Then, "No!"

And then, when he grabbed her and tried to kiss her, she struggled and fought back. And for this resistance he slapped her hard across the face, and she felt a harsh buzzing in her head.

She had not cried since giving birth to her son years before, because it was so difficult and painful, yes, but also because she was so happy. But after Reg slapped her face and stunned her, he began ripping off her clothes, and even then, when she resisted him, shoving back and punching at him with her small fists, she did not cry.

It was not until he punched her—never on the face, though—and had doubled her over in pain had she begun to cry a little. Because he did things to her that only a husband should be allowed to do.

It was then that she knew, finally knew, what was going to happen to her, to her husband, to their son, to all the families who had come here on behalf of the big Blaswell company to work on the railway line. She knew what was really going to happen to them.

They were ruining families, they were working men to death, they were taking children from their mothers, husbands from wives, old ones from their adult children and grandchildren.

Families were peeled apart, the members of which might never see one another again in this life. They might not live long. And there was nothing she could do about it. Nothing any of them could do about it.

And Wan Li had believed this until that day, just days before, when those two strange men had saved them from the two slave masters who were going to sell them to someone else, someone who would work them as prostitutes until they became diseased and died.

But those two men had come along and changed everything. And now, for the first time in a very long time, Wan Li felt something she had not felt since they had lived in China. She felt a dim flicker of hopefulness come to life within her.

And though she knew she had no real reason to hope for what she most wanted—to see her husband and son alive again—she knew, if only for the sake of the other women, who were as mired in loss and hopelessness as was she, that she had to lead this group of women. And to where? Back into the place the Christians called Hell.

And the one person she wanted most to see, other than her beloved husband and son, was Reg. And she would kill him with her own bare hands. And then she would kill any of the men who allowed him to do this thing to them all. Any of the men who told him to do this, any of the men she could find.

This desire she did not share with anyone else, but she guessed that if she did, the other women might feel the same way. And so that feeling gave her more strength.

They had departed from the campsite, riding on the horses taken from the slavers, two women to a horse and one woman walking, a job they all took turns at. But they agreed they would only get so close, and then they would live on the edge, in quiet, and spy on the camp, looking for signs of their loved ones, looking for the two men who saved them. Hoping for so much and expecting so little.

It was a feeble plan at best, and Wan Li knew this, but it was what they had and it was better than the life they had had before. They also knew the risk they were all taking was large. But what choice did they have? This was their fight far more than it was the fight of the two men who had saved them.

They only knew they had to try. And none of the women was afraid any longer of dying. They were only afraid of dying without knowing if their families lived or died.

And so the five women moved slowly back toward the despised railroad camp. They made their meager rations last, stretching them out to last for a long time, how long they did not yet know.

The two kind men had been generous in sharing their rations—Wan Li knew they had given the women most of everything they had. And it was far more food than they had been given at the camp or with the slavers.

But the women had to save their meager strength, for none of them was well and they moved as old women might, though none of them were old.

How they were going to fight once the time came for them to do so, none of them knew. But fight they must and fight they would. Until they succeeded or died in the attempt.

CHAPTER 17

The shadow on the gravel slope moved left, then right, then slipped backward, upslope, and disappeared. Along with it, Boone heard slight crunching sounds, as if someone was walking. *Which was,* he thought, *exactly what was happening.*

There were at least two others in addition to the man he shot.

"Come on out of there, you useless liar!"

Boone grinned. It was Shaky. And he sounded good and riled. Wonder how long he can hold out before he needs to head back to his quarters at the camp and knock back a few swallows? Probably a while yet, as the man always seemed to have a flask on his person.

And what was this business of calling him a liar? *Heck,* thought Boone, *I've been called so many things in my life, it'd be easier to list off the things I ain't been accused of being.*

"Come on, now! I ain't got all day!"

Boone was about to shout back that he'd best get along without him, then, but he thought better of it. It occurred to him that the soak of a boss man didn't rightly know if he was alive or dead.

And because Boone knew Shaky was not about to make for camp without knowing or, more to the point, without making damned sure Boone was sucking gravel, that meant Shaky was flummoxed, not knowing who had fired that shot.

He surely had a good idea, though, because his man hadn't whooped it up to tell Shaky he'd killed Boone. No, this game wouldn't go on for much longer.

And he was right. Because Chummy whickered low once again and Boone, crouching, crabwalked slowly, taking care not to make much sound as his moccasins touched gravel, over toward the horse.

He still kept each side of the overhang in view, swiveling his eyes to each side constantly. The horse must have seen something, smelled something closing in on the left side once more.

But Boone failed to notice the paint's gaze wasn't on the edge of the opening, where the other man had come from, but closer in, farther in beneath the overhang. Something had moved back there in the dark crevice where the slab rested on raw mountain face, as it had for thousands of years.

Something had made a home back in there and did not take kindly to strangers camping on its doorstep.

And so it would do as it always did when this occurred— it would drive them off. And it would drive them off the only way it knew how, with fangs.

Too late, Boone heard the slow, shaking, dry, scattery, clicking sound. And then he did. For the first few seconds, as the sound built in intensity and speed and volume, it echoed lightly, filling the air the way cool, running water will splash and echo in a grotto.

But this was no grotto and it was no cool, cleansing rivulet making that sound. It was a king-size, bull-of-the-rocks diamondback, its girth as thick as a healthy man's forearm, its fangs long . . . long enough to do what they were meant to do, and then some.

And that's all Chummy needed to know. Instinct stomped roughshod over loyalty, and he bolted fast and hard on, out of that otherwise cool, pleasant place.

"Chum!" growled Boone, clipping off anything else he might want to shout because he'd be heard by the others. "Damn horse," he whispered, eyeing the spot back in there where the deadly sounds bloomed.

He detested snakes, particularly rattlers, and did his best in life to give them ample room. As this one emerged from black shadow, Boone knew two things: It was the biggest rattler he'd ever seen and it was distracting him from the sure approach of Shaky and whoever else was out there with him.

As sickened as Boone was by the emerging sight of the monster viper, he also knew it didn't get that way by being young and stupid. No sir, this snake was a savvy old man or woman, and it didn't really deserve to die with a bullet in its head—if Boone's shot was lucky enough.

But neither did Boone feel he deserved to die this day or any other day by snakebite. So the choice was simple. He aimed his gun and waited for it to slide nearly soundless, closer, closer . . . and then it paused, though its rattling continued and, if anything, grew louder.

The snake, Boone realized, had paused because there was a sound to Boone's right, which was also the mouth of the overhang. He glanced that way and saw no one, but he knew one or two or more men were closing in. The horse bolting had emboldened them.

Any second now and I'm going to have it from both sides. And as if to prove this thought, the viper resumed its sliding stalking of him, quicker than before.

For a brief moment, Boone was mesmerized by the thing. It kept coming and coming, emerging from out of the ink-black shadows, and still it didn't seem to want to narrow up and end it.

He guessed the thing was easily more than six feet in length. It was still a dozen feet from him when Boone heard the sounds outside again, boots on gravel, closer. He glanced to the wide, daylit mouth of the space, but again saw no one moving.

Boone had room behind him, back toward the far end of the rocky room. He stepped slowly, but quick enough to keep pace with the snake.

It didn't matter. The thing sped up. Hissing now, its head wider than Mac's sizable fist, its mouth open, tongue flicking, and within that flexing maw, Boone saw hard, pink knobs of flesh. He envisioned himself in there, being chomped and punctured and needled and stabbed by those glistening white fangs, curved like a wild boar's tusks.

"Good Lord almighty," he whispered through sweat-stippled lips.

Then, to his right, a rush of sliding boots on rocks and a voice cracked the dead stillness. "Don't move!"

And for a sliver of a second, Boone, uncharacteristically for him, did not move. Except his eyes. He flicked them to the new threat but saw the mighty bull of the snake took the new intrusion caused by the closest invader to him. It shot across that smooth rock slope, straight for Boone.

The buckskin-clad woodsman opened fire, triggering once, twice, stepping backward the whole while. Smoke filled the rocky den and the stink of gunpowder singed the very air. Boone's hearing felt sizzled and his head rang. He could see nothing but trusted, if he kept low, still facing the snake and crouching, he could scamper backward, hidden by the smoke.

Had he hit it? He thought perhaps he had, but he had no way of knowing—and then he knew. For he felt something slam into his forward leg, the right, and he jerked away from it, and fell backward to his rump, hard on the stone floor.

He was beginning to see now, but he couldn't hear a lick, including the other gunshots cracking the gloom. Instinct kept him jerking back and crabwalking away from snakes and the other gunman. And then his head smacked into rock. He'd reached the tight-cornered crevice of the far side of the declivity.

The smoke slowly parted, wafting in and out as if fanned from the mouth of the space. He glimpsed the snake roiling and flailing, and then out of the black gloom from whence it had come, before he could react and jerk away, its thick body smacked hard across his face. It sent him sprawling, knocking him to his right.

Had it sunk fang? He felt all right, but he knew it could be a few moments before the venom seeped in enough to lay him low, a twitching, swelling, purpling mess of agony. He'd seen it before, and only stood helpless as others tried and failed to help the victim with futile, feeble efforts. Once snakebit, once dead. He knew this to be true.

Then he'd, by gum, deal with the rascals who caused all this—and he looked with more intensity to his right, toward where the other man—or men—were. There was someone there, skylined at the opening.

Was it Shaky? And why wasn't he shooting anymore?

Boone didn't much care. He swung his gun, intending to take one of them out before the venom worked its way into him.

The man, whoever it was, appeared to be looking for him. Maybe Boone was back in the dark far enough that he couldn't be seen. But within moments, as more of the smoke cleared, he knew he would be seen.

And as the smoke cleared, Boone saw what was facing him was a single man who stood about fifteen feet away at the mouth of the rocky overhang. Boone's gun held true on the man, but he had his own rifle half raised. He appeared to be staring toward Boone. But not really at him.

Boone didn't think he was fully hidden in the dark and smoke, but then a flashing movement to his left caused him to glance that way—and he saw what the man was looking at. It was the snake, a massive, roiling, boiling beast that moved like a bullwhip, coiling and uncoiling, writhing and jerking and whipping, rolling like a wheel one way, then another. And not five feet from Boone.

The tip of the rattler's big tail, which held more buttons than he'd ever thought possible for a rattlesnake, now pulsed and shook, emitting its freakish sounds spasmodically.

Boone's shots, it seemed, had done damage, and he caught sight of the huge, wide, flat head, the jaws snapping and snapping out of reflex. It was too dark to see if its eyes were fixed on him, but he knew that even in death, or near death, a rattler can kill a man twice over and have venom to spare.

He had to get away from that flailing beast.

"Oh my word!" groaned the man outside. Boone wanted to tell him to shut the heck up and move out of the way. He was tempted to shoot the fool just to clear a path, but somehow at that instant it didn't seem sporting.

So he kept his gun trained on the fool and shouted, "Hey! Get outta there!" If the man didn't snap to and move, Boone would darn well let him have a taste of a bullet, in the leg or some such.

The man shook his head, as if he'd been slapped, and glanced toward Boone. "You alive?"

"Darn right I'm alive, no thanks to you! Now get away so I can get out of here!"

Then the man forced a laugh. "Not on your life!" And tried to swing his gun over to aim at Boone.

"No sir!" Boone's gun barked once and delivered a bloody punch to the man's left leg. He saw the black trousers shudder, and jelly blew out of the side as the man screamed and toppled, his rifle whipping from his grasp.

He writhed and rolled, almost as much as the cursed snake Boone was already scrabbling to get away from. He scampered out the front of the cave's mouth, and as he did, he saw that the man was not Shaky.

"Where's . . ." Even as Boone said it, he spun to his right.

"You mean me?"

Too late, Boone saw that he was leveled down on by Shaky, whose rifle aimed squarely on Boone's chest. His own gun was only halfway raised.

"Drop it now or you will die sooner than you are going to."

"That's an odd thing to say," said Boone, taking his time in following the directive.

"Odd how?" said Shaky, a sneer pulling his face wide. "And shut up!" he growled, not at Boone but at the writhing man Boone had shot in the leg.

"Man's in a bad way, Shaky. Like to think you have a drop of kindness in your veins. At least tourniquet the wound, give him a shot of your whiskey."

"And you shut up, too!"

Boone shut up but could not help the half grin that crept up on his face.

Behind and off to the left of him he heard the still flapping, flopping snake. He kept an eye on the menacing viper with quick side glances.

"Don't you never mind about that snake. Looks to me like you shot it all to heck. Just reflex."

"You don't say?" said Boone, giving in to his lifelong habit of becoming annoyed at having anyone tell him something obvious.

"You know," said Shaky, shifting his grip slightly on his rifle stock and adjusting his uphill boot, "for a fella who's about to die, gutshot, out here in this snake-infested hell on earth, you sure are a lippy one. Kind of a shame to do away with a man with such sand as you got."

"I'll take that as a compliment."

"Take it any way you like, fool."

"You been talking to my pard—" Then, once again, Boone knew he'd spoken too much.

"Ha! You mean that big goober you traveled in with?"

"No, I never did nothing of the sort. I only run into him when we showed up at the same time for work."

"You expect me to believe that . . . Hokum Boone? And yeah, I know his name, too, one Mac MacCoole. This was pointed out to me by others. Was going to deal with you two today anyhow, but your little wander has beat me to it."

"You seem to know all manner of things you think you know, but what you don't know is a whole lot." Boone nodded, as if that had explained every single thing the man might have cause to question. Ever.

Shaky nodded. "I see you still haven't dropped away that gun of yours."

"Oh." Boone looked down. "This old thing?"

"Yep. Drop it now." Shaky cranked off a shot that whistled the air close by Boone's left arm.

Boone yelped and hopped to his right, letting his gun clatter to the earth. He thought maybe the buckskin fringe hanging off the sleeve had parted from the breeze of the shot.

"Hey now!" said Boone, but he realized the shot was intended for more than getting him to comply. The moaning and mewling sounds behind him ceased.

He glanced over his left shoulder and saw that the shot had done what Boone had chosen not to do. It had bored a hole in the wounded man's forehead and he lay still, facing them, his eyes gaping wide and his mouth wider, as if he'd been told news of the most shocking sort. *It never would be as shocking as that to you*, thought Boone. *Poor rascal.*

"Hey now, yourself. I never could tolerate a whiner, nor someone who didn't take what was doled out to them and keep shut about it, even if it wasn't something they particularly wanted."

"You're a hard man, Shaky."

The drunk shrugged. "I reckon along about now that pard of yours, MacCoole, is dead or on his way. Maybe you two can ride the glory trail together. 'Cause you darn sure ain't going to ride the trails together any longer in this life. Got me?" He raised the rifle and snugged the butt to his shoulder, laying his cheek along the stock.

Given the accuracy of the shot he'd dealt the now-dead man behind him, Boone thought Shaky was toying with him. Boone raised his hands to shoulder height, palms toward Shaky. "I don't suppose you want to know how I can make you rich, and quick."

"Sounds to me like a ploy to buy yourself time!"

"Course it is, you fool! Would you do any different? Don't mean it ain't true!"

"Which part?"

"Which part what?" said Boone.

Shaky sighed. "True? Which part is true?"

Boone narrowed his eyes. "You calling me a liar? Every word I ever spoke in my life has the sweet ring of truth in it to one degree or another!"

"Enough," said Shaky, looking to Boone as if he suddenly couldn't bear any more of this chatter.

He appeared to be weary to the bone; his eyebrows drooped and his tongue kept flicking out, licking at his parched lips. He looked, in the span of a few breaths, to be exhausted. And much to Boone's satisfaction, Shaky's grasp on the rifle began to tremble—slight at first, then more pronounced.

"Darn," growled Shaky. "Darn."

"Now look, Shaky. We can work this thing out. Killing me won't help you a bit. But me and Mac, see, we got pards like you wouldn't believe. I mean big ol' players, like politicians and such." He nodded.

"Big deal," said Shaky, shakier now than ever. "Only thing I need is for you to be dead and for me to have at that flask in my coat pocket."

"Well, the first doesn't sound too good to me, but that second, why, that's a fine idea."

"I bet you'd like that, yeah. But I got enough for me and me alone. 'Never share your whiskey,' that's what the old-timer who visited the cooper said." Shaky smiled at a joke known only to him.

"Got me two things to say, then," said Boone. "One, you'd do well to consider my offer. Sure, I'm trying to save my skin, but who wouldn't?"

"What would I want with politicians?"

Boone sighed. "You got to think of your future, Shaky. Why, you get in good with politicians and such, you can introduce your boss man—what's his name? Kane?—to them. That sort of thing never goes unrewarded, don't you know."

For a moment, given the squinty, furrowed-brow look on Shaky's face, Boone thought he'd made a dent in the man's intention of killing him. Then Shaky shook his head.

It was then that two things happened at once: The still-roiling, headshot serpent managed to coil, then unwind a mighty last fling of its writhing mass, sending a great rope of itself arcing between the two men. Shaky touched off his trigger and his rifle snarled out a shot.

But Boone was already on the move, dropping to his left and rolling on his shoulder, ducking beyond the whipping snake. He landed awkwardly, sprawling to his side, his moccasin sliding on a spray of gravel kicked up by the snake.

The big, bullet-blasted-but-still-dangerous head, the jaws snapping slower now but still deadly in reflex, was close and unpredictable in its movement.

The snake had taken the bullet Shaky sent Boone's way, and even though the thing was dead, or nearly there, it seemed to rile it all over again.

Shaky cursed and hopped back, away from the new slide of the tail, which whipped in a slow curl right where he'd been standing.

"Your life is charmed, Hokum Boone!" he said, his footing bumbled by loose stones.

"It's a sign!" growled Boone, regaining his knee and leveling off on the man.

"You kidding me? Ain't no sign, except that you're a demon of some sort!"

Just then, the other man Shaky had brought with him slid down the slope to Boone's left and, rifle snout guiding him, decided to join the fray.

"Where in heck you been?" growled Shaky, his rifle drawn on Boone, and Boone's gun leveled on him. Neither combatant looked up from his intended victim.

"What happened to Merle?"

"What in heck you think happened to him?" growled Shaky. "That son of a gun shot him dead!"

"Not true and you know it, you lying drunkard!" said Boone, never taking his eyes from the man. "I shot his pin out from under him, but you doled out that eternal headache for the poor fool."

"That true, Shaky?" said the newcomer.

"What do you think?" said Shaky. "You know me, what do you think?"

"Yeah . . . I know you."

The man's sudden, cold tone was enough to shift Boone's gaze from Shaky for a sliver of time to see what the man meant by how he said it. It was all the time Shaky needed.

He squeezed his trigger again, but his still-sliding footing got the better of the situation, and the shot sizzled a furrow in Boone's upper right arm, parting the buckskin and the flesh beneath it as a tiny plow might the soil in a field.

But instead of earth, this yielded an immediate spray of blood and flecks of flesh that forced Boone to howl and drop his rifle, his left hand snatching to cover and squeeze the hot wound.

He knew he was soon to die, unarmed and wounded. *Like that cursed snake,* he thought.

"That's enough!" shouted the newcomer. He held his revolver steady on Shaky.

"You talking to me?"

"Yeah, I reckon."

Then Shaky sighed and lowered his gun. "All right, all right. I guess you're right and all. This day has been a bust. We keep on like this and that rail line won't never get done. And I don't trust Reg to run things in my absence." He shifted his gaze to Boone, who was gritting his teeth and bent over, his hand still clamped on the nick he'd received.

"Besides, I got to get this fool back there."

"You going to let me live, then?" asked Boone, trying to sound normal. He knew he wasn't likely to die from the wound, but it sure throbbed the dickens. And it wasn't set to feel better any time soon.

"Yeah, I had a change of heart. You are worth more to me alive than dead. Not that there ain't a court in the world would convince me of any misdeed, should I lay you low. But I have a feeling if you are alive, you'll be a prize catch to show to Mr. Kane. He's always looking for proof that we're doing what we are paid to. Ain't that right?"

The man who'd stood up to Shaky nodded. Appeased by his boss's change in tone and demeanor, he lowered his gun. Joining Shaky's employ as a guard was his first truly big mistake in life. Lowering his revolver was his last.

Shaky's smile slipped, and he whipped up his rifle once more, drilling the poor fool in the chest. "That's for the sass you gave me, boy."

He let the man's wide eyes stare a moment, then the man's knees bent and he began to waver on his feet.

Shaky drove another bullet into the man's forehead, slamming him backward, as if yanked by a rope from behind. He dropped to the earth, dead, dust rising from his fall.

"And that's for trusting me."

Boone said nothing. It had happened too fast for him to snatch up his own gun.

Shaky turned to him. "You going to flap that big mouth of yours at me, or can I have a moment or three of peace?"

Boone glared and said nothing.

"Good." With his rifle still aimed at Boone, Shaky strode up the slight rocky rise and toed Boone's gun out of the way. "Turn," he said, jerking the rifle's muzzle. "And drop down to your knees."

Boone did as he was told, expecting a bullet in the back of the head. All the man's talk about Boone being useful didn't amount to a hill of beans.

But in that he was mistaken.

"Arms behind your back."

"You shot my arm."

"Too bad."

Boone sighed and let go of the still-seeping furrow at the top of his right arm. He felt immediate blood begin oozing again. Still, it wasn't too deep a wound, so he was counting on the bleeding slowing up and scabbing over. Couldn't happen soon enough for his taste.

He complied with Shaky's demand and soon felt rawhide strapping being cinched tight about his wrists. He winced, knowing to keep his mouth shut, otherwise Shaky would derive even greater pleasure from causing him more grief.

"Stand."

Boone struggled a moment, and Shaky snatched his collar from behind and yarned him upright. *He was stronger than he looked,* thought Boone, keeping that fact in mind for the future.

"Now walk to your right. Up the slope."

"My gun—"

"You won't need it."

"Still. It's a nice piece."

Shaky sighed, and Boone heard him snatch it up. Boone glanced over his throbbing, burning right shoulder at the barely twitching, massive snake.

"Now walk."

They made it to the top of the slope, and Boone saw three horses standing hipshot up there, where he'd departed from the crude trail. "My horse," he said.

"We got horses, darn it. Now walk."

"At least let me call him. He won't have gone far. Like the gun, he's a good horse."

"Call him?"

Boone nodded and cut loose with three whistles—two short and a higher-pitched long. He followed that with a shout: "Chum! Chum! Come on, boy!" Then he whistled again.

"Stop this foolishness and get over to that brown there."

Just behind them, they heard hooves on stone and there came Chummy, switchbacking up the slope to their right.

"Told you. He's one of a kind."

"Huh. All right, then. But no more games."

"What about them other fellas?" said Boone.

"What about them?"

"You going to leave them here?"

"Yep. Just meat now. Not a one is of my concern."

"You cruel brute."

Shaky laughed. "There's that annoying Boone I have come to know in so brief a time. Now, load up . . . before I change my mind!"

Boone whistled low for Chummy once more and the horse came alongside, head down as if he were about to be berated by the man who brushed him and fed him apple slices.

"Rascal," murmured Boone. He leaned against the horse's left side and raised his left moccasin up to the stirrup. Without his hands free, dragging himself up into the saddle was going to be a trick.

"Shaky."

The surly drunkard had already mounted and was taking long pulls on a short bottle stashed in his saddlebag. He worked up a sound of disgust, stuffed in the cork, and rode over to the right side of Chummy. The paint barely flinched.

"Lean over," said Shaky.

Boone complied, knowing what the man was up to.

Shaky reached over the saddle, grasped the back of Boone's collar once again and, without warning, dragged him upward.

Boone lessened the discomfort by shoving upward with his stirruped left foot. It worked, but it was rough on Boone's wounded shoulder. He gritted his teeth and forced himself back, barking an oath as he situated himself.

"Smarts, don't it?" Shaky brayed at his amazing wit.

"It'd smart a darn sight more if I'd hit you where I wanted."

He looked at Boone and poked a long, ramrod-stiff digit between his own eyes and brayed some more.

"You're a mess of fun, Shaky. Anyone ever tell you that?"

"Just women." Again, Shaky cut loose with his whiskey-tinged laughter. "Now," he said, calming himself, "ride on ahead of me. And don't get any notions about thundering off. I got my gun cocked and aimed right dead betwixt your wing bones. In fact, if I look close, I can almost see your lungs bleeding dry from here."

Boone didn't respond. He wanted to, but he was trying to conserve his waning strength. He'd lost a bit of blood, and between that and the day's sun frying downward, he was feeling all done in.

And so they rode eastward, back toward the railroad encampment. This day had not gone the way Boone had hoped. He admitted to himself that it had gone in one direction he'd known was possible but had hoped to avoid.

But if what Shaky had said about Mac was true, Boone was getting off easier. At least for now. Still, Boone had a difficult time believing Mac had been killed by this idiot's men.

But even a big ol' grizz like Mac MacCoole can get himself killed. The thought knotted Boone's guts and left him feeling even worse.

"Why do you treat the Chinese workers so poorly, Shaky? What did they ever do to you to deserve such treatment?"

A few long moments passed, and Boone was tempted to turn around and look at the man. Then he heard a bottle swishing. He thought a few swallows of whiskey might go down fine right about now.

Much to his surprise, Shaky rode up on his left side and held out the bottle. He saw his mistake, as Boone looked from the bottle to him and laughed. "Open up, Hokum Boone!" and he held the bottle to Boone's mouth.

Boone had no choice but to swallow fast; the upended bottle was not waiting around. Somehow he managed to get most of what was offered into him before Shaky pulled it away.

"Enough of that. I'm no charity." The mean drunk reined in a bit and drifted back to the hind position.

"As to your question, it ain't a matter of what they done or ain't done to ol' Shaky. It's what Mr. Thurston Kane wants. And a man as powerful as that, why, he gets what he wants. Now think on that," said Shaky, swallowing back another few glugs.

Boone realized the booze was making the foreman chatty, so he kept his own yapper closed. Also, the few swallows of liquor he'd gotten helped to relieve the throbbing in his arm, something that renewed with each jostling step Chummy took.

"Now, just think on that, will you? As wealthy and as powerful as Kane is, why, he has a boss man, that Blaswell fella, who is even more powerful, and has a whole lot more money! Why, a man like myself—and even a fella like you, Hokum Boone—if you wasn't so bent on riding down the do-good trail, we could do all right not rubbing their fur the wrong way, if you know what I mean.

"All it takes is a few months of 'yes sir, no sir' and do whatever the hell they want done to those animals they drug over here on boats, and I get a nice, fat coin purse of gold. And maybe come the next job that needs doing, they'll think to themselves, 'You know, we got need of some hard tasks that need doing, and that fella Shaky, he did it up right on that railway. Might be he'd like some more such work.

"And before you know it, there I be, hat in hand, coin purse out, ready for more." He brayed like a mule, and within a few moments, Boone heard the dull thunk of an emptied bottle hit the dirt some yards away.

They still had a piece to travel, so he hoped either Shaky

was a quiet drunk on the downhill side of a bellyful of whiskey, which wasn't all that likely; few men were. Or maybe he had another bottle he could nibble on for the rest of the trip.

Soon enough, Boone heard the punk! sound of a cork being worked out of a fresh bottle. Yes sir, it was going to be an interesting ride.

CHAPTER 18

Mac crawled out of unconsciousness, and though he ached all over, as if he were a big thumb that had been hammer struck over and over again, he was pleased to note he was, indeed, still among the living. For how long remained to be seen.

"'Bout time you woke up, you big slug."

The voice was familiar, but other than a slight groan, Mac had not done much more than shift his head slightly and had yet to crack an eye.

"I said—"

"Heard ya," said Mac, though it came out as a hoarse whisper. What had happened? And then it came back to him. The voice was Reg's and the beating he'd taken was inflicted by a dozen of Reg's men, or Shaky's, or maybe that was Kane's. Who really cared at this point?

Mac scrunched his eyes slightly, and then smiled. "What's the reason you kept me alive, then, Reg?"

There was a pause long enough to let Mac know he'd probed a nerve somehow with the second-in-command, or was that the third? Or the fourth?

"What makes you think I intend to keep you alive, MacCoole?"

While he flexed his arms and legs and fingers and toes

and worked to open up his half-buttoned-up eyes—he'd bet he was a puffy, homely-looking thing about now—Mac decided not to answer Reg's question but to ask one himself instead.

"Just who is in charge of this mess you've created, Reg? Huh? Is it Winterson Blaswell? Or Thurston Kane? Or Shaky? You? Nah, can't be you or Shaky. You two are just lackeys. Simps without much of a clue, isn't that about right, Reg?"

Mac heard a low, growling sound and then quick boot-steps across planking. Closer, closer, and a boot stopped, but the second didn't, not until it landed a hard, driving kick into Mac's ribs on his left side.

He wheezed from the blow but snatched with his left arm, popping his eyes wide at the same time. The fingers of his big left hand closed vise tight around the shaft of Reg's boot. Mac yanked and rolled to his right. It worked.

Reg yowled, an undignified, girlish sound, and flipped over backward. Mac was on him, though moving slower than he would like. The beating had taken the wind from his sails, though he had been playing up the resulting ailments a pinch to get the upper hand on Reg. Still, he felt he had strength and size enough to subdue the flailing Reg.

Mac was in the act of grabbing Reg's revolver from its holster when the shack's door slammed inward, bouncing against the wall and spasming on its hinges. "What's going on in here?" bellowed a voice.

Mac glanced up briefly but did not like what he saw.

"Don't you shoot him!" barked the still-flailing Reg. "He's mine!"

A fat man stood in the doorway, gun drawn and pointed at Mac, and two more men were right behind him, their weapons also pulled. They stood and stared.

"Doesn't mean . . ." Reg fought some more. "You have

to stand there"—he bucked and shoved at the big man atop him—"and do nothing!"

It took another moment before the fat man slopped into the room, followed by the others. They attacked Mac just as he was sliding the revolver from Reg's gun belt.

A couple of choice kicks and punches rendered Mac, much to his dismay, all but immobile once more.

Reg shoved backward away from Mac before trying to get to his feet. He used the sprung door as a guide to help him stand. The entire time he glared down at Mac as if he were looking at a three-headed snake.

The attackers paused in their attentions and backed up a step or so. Mac scooched backward himself against the plank wall and rested there, touching his tender face and not liking what he felt. "If your men get any dumber, Reg, I'll have you next time."

Instead of flying off the handle as he'd proven was his easy preference, Reg surprised Mac by snorting.

"You sure take a heap of killing, Mac MacCoole."

To that, Mac had nothing to offer other than to grin. And then he coughed and winced, doubling over. He'd felt that sharp, lancing pain before. Broken ribs. He'd have to keep from agitating his bones for a few days. But something told him that was not likely in his near future.

CHAPTER 19

He had to admit the Chinese women were, on the whole, quite attractive. Then again, he reminded himself, he had been courting a woman who was, at best, the exemplar of plain.

Philomena Blaswell was as staid and common looking as her father was extraordinary and uncommon. But the big deciding factor in courting the young woman was that she was the one and only heir to her daddy's massive fortune. And any man who married into that, Thurston Kane once more reminded himself, was a lucky devil indeed.

"No, no," he murmured as he walked across the campsite to his tent. It is not luck, not luck, not luck, but hard work and long-term planning that got him where he was now. Lined up to be the very man to wed the wonderful Philomena.

Kane smirked. *Steady on, Thurston. Don't go throwing about the superlatives just yet.* Blaswell had made it plain that he had to succeed at leading this massive venture for the big man's empire. And in Blaswell parlance, that meant Kane had better bring in the project ahead of schedule and under budget.

"Mr. Kane, sir."

He paused and closed his eyes. "This had better be good, Ralston." He turned to face the mousy little assistant. "I am, as should be apparent to you, on my way to my tent. And I trust my tent is set up per my instructions."

"Ah, yes sir, Mr. Kane. Your tent is perfect."

"That I will judge. Now, what is it, Ralston?"

"Ah, it's . . . ahh . . ."

"Good lord, man, spit it out or you're through."

"Yes sir. There's a man—a man rode up while you were talking with the . . . ah, the Chinese women, the Chinese workers, sir."

"I talked with all of them, damn you."

"Yes sir."

"The man."

"Yes sir. He is, ah, from the camp, the works, the camp, sir."

"What? Why? Why didn't you tell me earlier?"

"I tried to, sir, just now."

"Where is he?" Kane looked about him but saw no one unfamiliar. "Is he one of the guards from the camp? What's going on there?"

"Sir." Ralston held up his shaking hands. His twitching eyelids matched them twitch for twitch. "He's still here, getting coffee at the cook fire."

Kane shoved past Ralston and made for the fire without hearing what the man had to tell him. The sputtering assistant trailed along in his wake. "Sir, sir, it's good news, sir. I promise you."

"I'll be the judge of that, Ralston. And if it isn't," Kane turned, holding up a long finger between them, then resting its tip on Ralston's sweaty nose tip, "I will not be held responsible for what I will do. Do you understand me?"

"Yes, yes sir." The small assistant nodded as if his head was on a spring.

Kane spun and made once more for the cook's part of the camp.

"Oh, Mr. Kane!" The rider stood and smacked trail dust

from his faded blue trousers, then coughed. "Sorry, was a long ol' ride. I didn't expect to see you. I . . . I just rode in to deliver the news that Reg sent me to bring, and then I was fixing to ride on back out again. On account of the fact that Reg told me I should."

As the man spluttered and yammered, Thurston Kane regarded him with head lowered, through unblinking eyes. It was a habit he had perfected since he realized it unnerved people.

He had noticed, particularly in negotiation, people tended to talk too much for too long and were far too nervous. And when he did not reply, but merely stared at them without expression, or with an expression that could be construed as mildly annoyed, they yammered on even more. And that made them even more nervous.

And this, as it turned out, was always good for business in the end, because they shared far too much about their stance in whatever negotiation might be playing out. It was in part responsible for how he was able to procure leases to so much land on behalf of Mr. Blaswell for this massive railroad project.

He did it now with this rider. The man did not take the hint that Kane's lack of response should be a sign for him to shut up. The fool kept blathering on and on. Finally, he spent himself, like a clockwork toy wound down to the last click and ping.

Kane let the silence settle on them all like a wet wool blanket. Even the cook and the other few guards lingering too near the fire, too eager for coffee, had drifted away because the scene was truly uncomfortable. Then Kane pulled in air through his nose and spoke: "I want to know two things: Who are you? And why are you here?"

The man pulled in breath to prepare to talk.

Kane held up that long finger. "Be brief."

The rider nodded slowly, as if he were thumbing through

a dictionary in his mind, looking up the definition of the word "brief." Finally he nodded and half smiled. "My name is Gary Numark. And I am here because Reg sent me." He nodded again, smiling at his accomplishment.

"And?" said Kane, indulgently suppressing a sigh.

"I . . . I told you why I was here, didn't I?"

Now Kane sighed. "Good God, man," he said in a tired voice barely above a whisper. "Why did Reginald and not Shaky send you here?"

"Oh. Um, I told that little feller yonder." The rider nodded past Kane toward Ralston, who Kane saw was some yards behind him, looking as if he was about to mewl out some pathetic excuse to justify his existence.

"And now you will tell me. Or I will have you clubbed to death."

The rider's self-assured grin slipped and any rosy redness perched high on his cheeks leeched away as the weight of the words settled on him. "Them two fellas, newly hired? They weren't who they was supposed to be. Turns out they are famous lawmen or some such. It ain't good."

Numark felt confidence seep from the ground up through his boots and back into him, as it had just dawned on him that he had the information the boss man required. It crossed his mind at that moment, too, that he should have parlayed this little venture into something a little more rewarding. And after all, hadn't Pap always told him to be the one to toot your own horn?

He stood a little straighter and folded his arms over his chest. "Now, sir, Mr. Kane, ah, I was wondering, what sort of vittles might you be serving up hereabouts tonight?"

Kane regarded the man for another long moment. He still had little idea what the oaf was yammering on about and he needed to find out more, but perhaps Ralston could do it. Talking with Numark was like shouting into a tin bucket and expecting the universe to answer.

Kane suddenly felt very tired. In a weary voice, he said, "Cook will see to your wishes, Mr. Numark."

Kane turned. "Ralston?" He walked toward his tent.

"Yes sir?" The small, bald man scurried to catch up.

"Have him clubbed or drowned or something. I am weary of this game. I must rest. And then I demand the full story, do you understand? And from you. Not that yammering buffoon."

"Yes sir," said Ralston.

As Kane entered his tent, he heard Ralston say, "I did try to tell you myself, sir."

Kane paused. "So you did. Next time, try harder. Save me from that ever again happening." He entered the tent, the flap flopping closed behind him.

"Yes sir," said Ralston, smiling because that, if anything, was the closest he knew he would ever get to feeling as if Mr. Kane was considering keeping him employed into the future. He smiled as he strode toward the campfire, wondering how much of Kane's directive toward the rider he should carry out.

Some minutes later, Kane, sipping a glass of whiskey while seated in a folding chair under a shade canopy before his tent, looked up at his approaching assistant. "Ah, Ralston. Did you tend to that confusing man?"

"Yes sir," said Ralston, relieved that Mr. Kane was calm and cool, as he usually was at the end of the day, once he'd been served his whiskey. He was also wondering if by that, Kane meant he'd made certain that Cook fed Gary Numark. Ralston decided not to say anything more about the odd rider.

"Excellent. Now, what is this business about newly hired men not being who they purported to be?"

"In truth, sir, I don't know much more than what he mentioned to you. Apparently, Shaky hired two new men who, as it turns out, are some sort of officers of the law, but even on that, the matter is as clear as mud, sir."

Kane steepled his fingers and considered the situation. Then he shifted his eyes upward. "I'll have to deal with this myself when we arrive in that forsaken wilderness camp. Shaky knows my standing order—all lawmen are to be persuaded with cash to leave us be. Perhaps they did not give these men enough money."

"Or," said Ralston, emboldened by the lack of admonitions from his employer, "perhaps they are working under cover of disguise. Or they cannot be bribed."

Within moments, Ralston knew these were thoughts he should have kept to himself. Kane regarded him through half-lidded eyes. "You know how I feel about that last word, Ralston. They are not bribes when the recipient has a choice."

Ralston wasn't so certain that was strictly true, nor was he certain that many of—perhaps all of—the lawmen receiving money from Kane to look the other way about so many things ever had much of a choice.

Kane sipped his drink and crossed his legs. "How are the new workers settling in?"

Ralston pasted on his good-news smile. "They are as happy as they might be, sir. The children are playing, the older folks are resting after today's journey, and women are preparing food over their fires."

Ralston wondered if any of them had an inkling as to how truly horrible their lives were about to become.

"Good. That's good to hear. Soon enough, they will know the true cost of signing an agreement with Blaswell, by way of me, ha! But for now, this one night, they will hopefully enjoy themselves to the full. For tomorrow, we reach the diggings. And then the fun begins."

"Fun for whom, sir?"

"Ralston, you are fast outgrowing your boots in my employ. See to it that you are not too tasked. I have need of someone of your abilities and your discretion and capabilities in playing fast and loose, shall we say, with whatever it is I require to be played with in such a way."

"Yes sir," said Ralston, bowing as though he were in the presence of a sultan. He wasn't quite certain what all that might imply, but he could hazard a pretty good guess, and he liked what he heard.

Several hundred yards away, under the watchful gaze of a dozen guards, the Chinese, haggard and confused, were doing their best to take in all they were experiencing. Not much of it made sense to them, but they had faith that it would in time. They felt a hopefulness they had not in many months.

The travel had been grueling, with lives lost on board the ship. The crew and the captain were not pleasant people and they had felt unhappy with their choice, doubting themselves with each day that dawned aboard, and with no land in sight.

Then, when the coast of California was spotted, many of them refused the cramped quarters belowdecks and instead chose to take their chances on deck, as if keeping the land in sight might result in a hastening of the ship somehow. But they had been caught in a doldrums, as someone explained the lack of significant movement, a place of low and then no wind.

It lasted for a day and a night, and then the winds resumed, and suddenly, within hours, there they were, approaching the city docks. And now? Now, here they were, after spending the day bouncing in a wagon over rocky terrain and through pretty but dry country, here they were, encamped in that same terrain.

Someone had mentioned serpents and large bugs that

would strike and eat children, so they all knew to be watchful.

They felt wary of Mr. Kane but were unable to ask him questions. He seemed not to want to be near them, for once he had addressed them at the docks, he kept to himself. But they knew he was a very busy man, a very rich man. And he was not even the man who had sent for them!

They would one day meet Mr. Winterson Blaswell, this had been promised. On that day, they had agreed, they would all wear their finest silks, and honor him with a feast and with songs from their homeland. And gifts, for he was truly a great man to provide them all with such a rare and wonderful opportunity to begin a new life in this bold new place.

Yes, they all agreed, "lucky" was the one word to describe them all.

CHAPTER 20

"You did what?" Shaky trembled as he shouted the question, spittle flecking from his mouth.

Reg had never seen him so angry. "I . . . I sent a rider off to intercept Mr. Kane's caravan. Tell him about MacCoole and Boone. I . . . I figured he'd want to know. I figured it was what you would have done. And you did say I was in charge while you were away."

"Fool!" Shaky upended his flask and guzzled down a few hits of rye. "Who'd you send?"

"That Gary Numark. He's a hell of a rider."

"He might be able to ride a horse fast, but he's an idiot. Bested in that only by you, Reg. Now Mr. Kane will think just because we sent a cursed rider to find him, we can't handle a thing at this end. My word, what were you thinking? No, no, never mind. I don't want to hear any more. Mr. Kane will be here and I'll have to explain all this to him and I need to figure it out. I need to think of something to tell him. God, this is all I need."

Reg stood there by the door to Shaky's shanty, his hand on the handle.

Shaky looked up. "You still here? Why?"

"Well, Boss, I was wondering, what are we going to do with MacCoole and Boone?"

"What are we going to do? Why, I've half a mind to kill them and be done with it."

"Then why don't we?"

"Because, you idiot, they're famous folk. If whoever sent them came snooping around, they'd be sure to find sign of them, or folks who'd seen them, or some such. Or worse, sign of all the other stuff we've gotten up to hereabouts. No, it's took risky. Best to keep them close, shackled."

Reg's eyes widened, and he nodded. "I get you. Make an example of them. Put them to work beside them Chinese men, huh?"

"Oh yeah, yeah, that's what I was getting at, yeah." Shaky swigged again and glanced at Reg around the bottle. "Why, they're tailor-made examples for them in the new batch the boss man is bringing in. Show them we won't tolerate unruly behavior. We're so serious we'll deal with white men the same as we would a Chinaman!"

He replaced the cork on the bottle. "Now, go fit them out with shackles on their legs, with chain enough just so they can shuffle. But keep their hands free so they can work. We got rock needs bustin' and rails needs shifting and ties needs dragging."

"You bet, Boss. I'm on it."

"Yeah, well, make mess of it like you did with Numark and you'll be the one in shackles."

Reg managed to keep his humble smile on his face until he closed the shack door behind him. It slipped away quickly and he sneered as he walked off. "Next time you threaten me, Shaky, will be the last time you do."

He rode his horse up to the stable, where the two men, MacCoole and Boone, were tied up and under guard. With those two, it didn't mean much. But shackled, they would be far easier to handle. "Shackled and beaten as regular as clockwork," he said, jouncing in the saddle. Frequent beatings were Reg's preference for keeping peace and punishing any worker who even thought of stepping out of line.

He rode on up to the stable and saw the six men he appointed to watch over the two bumped-up, bruise-faced men. They were lashed to corral posts, hats gone, shirts ripped to shreds; they'd had to peel that buckskin off Boone. He was fit to be tied over that, as if he never took the damn thing off. And from what the fellas said, Boone smelled about like that, too; he was one rank chicken.

Just as well they were going to keep MacCoole subdued with beatings; he was one big fellow. Muscles and scars and muscles and scars: That's about what they saw when they ripped off his shirt.

Them and those two eyes; no matter how buttoned up with bruises they were, somehow that big cur managed to glare at them, as if marking each one of them for a future beating he was going to dole out.

Reg had to laugh at him, right to his face. But he secretly felt chills from the man. Downright frightening fellow was that MacCoole.

Boone, on the other hand, was lippy and annoying. Both of them were about to receive another round of beatings with Reg's favorite hardwood chair-leg club. Bruised up a man's muscles nicely and, depending on where he used it, it rarely resulted in a complete crippling. He didn't particularly want to lose any workers. Not when they were so close to meeting the other crew at that trestle.

And then, they had been promised, there would be ample money doled out to them all, bonuses and a party of some sort. That's what Kane had said, and so far his promises had proved up.

Reg could practically taste the liquor and fancified foods as he strode on over to the two sagged men at the corral posts, about a dozen feet apart.

"Well, did you two miss me? I had some business to

attend to, but I promised I'd be back, and Reg always keeps his promises. Just ask any of them Chinese workers who crossed me. Oh, too late, you can't. Why's that? Because they're all dead!" He brayed like a donkey.

The guards joined in, nodding and smiling. Anything Reg found funny, they darn sure were going to as well.

It wasn't lost on Boone or Mac that this might well be one of the most dangerous spots they'd been in in all the years they'd been doing this sort of work. Mostly because they'd managed, usually through intention, to avoid being caught in dire spots together. That way there had always been one of them free to help the other out of the sticky mess he found himself in.

But now, oh boy, this outfit was ruthless, rotten from the top down. And because it was known that Mac and Boone both had seen behind the veil Shaky and Kane and whoever else had draped over the entire crooked affair, they were likely to be killed for this discovery.

They were going to be; both men knew that as sure as he knew his own name. There was no way Shaky and Reg, and so Kane, would ever let them go and risk them revealing the truth of the operation to the world.

So far, Mac and Boone knew that Blaswell's new rail line was the toast of the town back East in Washington, and lauded in newspapers from here to there and back again.

Reg grabbed hold of the chair leg and gave it a few quick swings. Boone and Mac both gritted their teeth. The man approached Mac from behind and spread his legs slightly, as if he was about to split wood at the chopping block.

"Hey, jackass!" growled Boone.

The man jerked his gaze around to Boone, who was tied to his left, along the corral.

"You can't be talking to me," said Reg, low and hard.

Boone made a show, as much as he was able, of looking disgusted with Reg. He shook his head and grinned through his puffy face. "Shoot, son, you are about as pathetic a man as I have ever seen. Honestly, you swing that foolish stick any weaker, I'd swear you was half child."

"Boone, shut up," said Mac, who had taken advantage of the distraction to readjust his stance. He had his shoulders, stressed and stretched, upright. He knew Boone was only acting up to distract Reg. And what's more, he knew Reg was too crafty not to see through it, too.

So where did that leave them?

They were soon to find out. For Shaky came thundering up on a fresh mount, though he, for the most part, looked shaggy and haggard, too. It had been a long ol' day so far, with too much happening, too much liquor, no food in his gut, and too little sleep. And to come back to mess like this was annoying as hell.

"Don't go whompin' on them anymore, Reg! We need them to be able to work so when Mr. Kane gets here and dumps the new batch of workers off on us, we'll be able to use these two as examples. Want to start them new ones off on the right foot. We will need the Chinamen more than we'll need these two troublemakers. You got me?"

Reg let the chair leg swing by his side. "Yeah, Boss. Okay." He nodded to one of the guards. "Shackle their legs and wrists, too, but the wrist shackles will come off once we get to the line."

"Rails or rocks?" said the guard, a wispy, ferret-faced fellow who could not hide his toothless grin.

Reg scratched his chin and looked skyward, as if in deep consideration. "Make it one on each. Yeah, that'll do to start."

The journey to the line, not but a mile or so from the stables, was made easier for them, not out of any concern

Reg felt for their welfare, but for the sake of the job. They wanted the men there and in place before Kane arrived.

He would, as Reg and Shaky knew, first inspect the progress. If he was pleased, he would merely nod and then confer with the engineers and other construction men for a time, then make for his cabin.

It was a sumptuous affair that both Shaky and Reg wished they were allowed to use when Kane wasn't there. They considered a finely appointed small cabin such as that, sitting empty most of the time, to be a terrible waste.

But though Shaky had the key to the place—it was fitted out with a steel lock on the front door—he was forbidden to enter it, save for official business. That did not include him raiding the boss's liquor bottles.

Even Shaky knew this would be a bad idea; Kane was a mild man on the outside, but one with notions such as his was not one to be trifled with.

After all, much of what they all got up to at the camp was his idea. And that alone should tell a body something about Thurston Kane. He was also the one who told Shaky what they were going to do with the Chinese womenfolk.

Shaky was fine with carrying out the man's orders, as long as Kane didn't turn on him. He had to keep an eye on that fellow, back East businessman or no; he was as wily as a rock rattler.

CHAPTER 21

"Is it that bad?" Boone tried to grin through the split lip and loose teeth from his latest round of beatings.

"You've been prettier, Hokum Boone," said Mac. He ached all over, but despite that, he found Hoke's never-give-up attitude a balm, and he grinned in return.

"Well, then, let's us just see what all we can do on the line, as that fool Reg put it, to get their attention."

"I'm not certain it's their attention we want. You know those guards will be eyeballing us more closely than they will be any of the others. No, we'd do best to subvert from within the ranks."

"Sub who?"

"Subvert. Ruin it from inside. If we can convince the others to help, we'd be better off."

"How?" said Boone. "They all look like they've given up."

"Yes, because they've been here for a long time. Everything that could be done to them has been done. Well, almost."

"You mean death."

"Yeah." Mac nodded.

"So how do we subvert?"

"I don't know yet," said Mac. "But I'm thinking."

"Don't think too long," said Boone, nodding beyond his pard. "Yonder's the diggings."

"You two enjoy your chatting," said the big, sloppy-butted guard driving the wagon. "'Cause it's the last one you're likely ever to get." He sent a rope of thick chaw spittle sluicing to the ground. Grinning, he dragged a fat, grimy hand across his mouth.

"He's right," said Boone in a low voice. "We have to act fast, whatever we do, because the way these fellas feel, we won't last long."

"That's true," said Mac. "But they're going to wait until Kane arrives with the new workers. That's when we start to worry."

"That doesn't leave us much of a sliver to work in, but we can do it."

"Have to get the new men to see reason."

"Shouldn't be too difficult, if they get a look at the folks who have been here for a spell. They look like hell."

"So do we, Boone." Mac grinned again, but this time it was a grim look, and he meant it as such. "First things first. We need to—"

"Shut your mouths now," said the fat driver. "I'd be no better off than you two fools if they was to learn I let you two yammer on and on. Couldn't make out a word of your whining, but the way you two carry on, you'd think you was married."

"Married?" said Boone, loud enough for the driver to hear him. "Them's fightin' words, mister!" But he winked at Mac.

The big man knew how Boone felt about settling down with one woman. The word "married" was enough to send Hoke into a sputtering tirade, saying it wasn't natural. He believed that man was meant to rove and ramble, to spread his seed, as Boone put it, far and wide, so he could be sure he'd leave the legacy on the earth that nature intended.

Mac wholly disagreed, intending, hoping, that at some point he would find a woman with whom he could share a long, quiet life, tucked off into the mountains somewhere beside a river, somewhere he could hunt and fish and garden a little, a place for him to read books and think.

"Think?" Boone would say. "Good God, man, there comes a time in life when a fella should do all he can not to put too much thought into his affairs. I for one would prefer to act and skip the thinking part."

Yes sir, thought Mac. *They were as different in so many ways as night was from day.* And yet they were pards for life, that much he knew. Even if he wanted to dunk Boone in an icy stream now and again.

The wagon rolled to a stop, grinding gravel beneath its steel-banded wheels. "Get your backsides out of that wagon, you two."

"Can't," said Boone, jangling his shackles and jerking the chain that was looped through the rails on the sides of the wagon.

The fat man looked at Boone's arms, then at Mac's. They both were locked in. He grunted and tugged out a big ring and thumbed through the odd, heavy assortment of keys. He saw Boone eyeing him, so he half turned away.

Boone exchanged a knowing glance with Mac. This fat one was a fellow they had to keep in mind. They could take him down fairly easily. He already proved himself to be a soft fellow, one with a big mouth but who seemed to have little stomach, a funny thought at that, for anything requiring effort.

He produced a key with a grunt, held it up, and looked at it through a squinty, fat brow, then nodded at Boone. "Scoot on over this way. And don't try nothing! I am a dangerous fella."

Boone thought perhaps the man was joshing with him, but no, the fat man's face was pulled into what he no doubt intended to be a menacing glare. Boone kept his snicker to himself and did as he was bade.

Mac and Boone eyed the key ring and took note of which one worked the shackles. It appeared to them that the wrist and the ankle shackles were identical, so it stood to reason there would be but one key that would work on them all. And it was as luck would have it: a distinctive key with a double loop, decorative grip atop, finely forged.

As the fat man worked the key in Boone's shackles, a guard walked over, his rifle cradled in one arm. With the other, he smoked a cigarette, raising it to puff, squinting through the brief haze of smoke as he exhaled. "Don't neither of you men think of making a move. I'll shoot you both down sure as looking at you."

They looked at him and saw that he wore a squint not only because of the smoke but because he had been beaten about the face.

"Believe me," said the man, looking at Mac, "I'd as soon shoot you as look at you. You're the one what did this to my face, you savage."

Mac returned the look. "Just as well you had help," he said. "Otherwise, I would have finished you off."

"Oh, you just wait your turn, big fella. I'll do for you, no mistake. Me and the boys won't forget you. And him, too." He nodded at Boone. "Just because he's your friend." He smiled and showed blackened teeth, and his giggle was a ragged thing, as if he was gargling wet gravel.

When both men were unshackled about the wrists, they were shoved off the tailgate of the open-ended wagon, and though they tried to maintain their footing, they each stumbled a bit.

Mac regained his footing first, with the help of the wagon. Then the man with the rifle shoved Mac's hands away from their grip on the wagon.

Mac made a lunge for the man's rifle, but his injuries

slowed him and he grasped at air, and received a swing with the rifle butt, which connected with his upper arm and knocked him off-balance once more.

Boone by then had hauled himself to his feet and also lunged toward the guard, but the fat wagon driver jostled himself between Boone and the guard.

"Best pick your battles, you little buckskin rat." His voice was hard, but when he leered down at Boone, he saw not the hatred that all guards seemed to carry toward their captives but more than anything a warning in the fat man's eyes. A glaring of caution. Boone replied in kind, his nod of understanding barely perceptible.

The guard wasn't looking anyway. He had his squinty eye fixed on Mac. He did his best to sidestep around the other guard, who was eager for a repeated round of butting the big prisoner with the rifle stock.

But the fat man appeared to be clumsy and staggered sideways, oddly enough ending up between the seething guard and Mac, just long enough for Mac to regain his footing.

"Get outta the way, you fat fool!" growled the guard.

"Hey now," said the fat man, scowling. "Ain't no way to talk to me. I ain't no different than you, you scurvy goat!"

Mac and Boone took advantage of the interruption in the guard's attentions to shuffle away from the wagon a few paces.

"Hey! Where in hell do you think you two are headed?" The hard guard was not an easy one to shed.

"Don't make me beat you . . . yet. Ha! It'll happen soon enough. I get first crack at you, big fella. Then the other boys will have a go. I expect you won't survive the beating. You neither, you little weasel."

It was all Boone could do to keep from replying. He didn't mind being called a weasel so much as the man threatening them, and especially Mac, with so much lopsided revenge.

"You sure must have riled those boys to get such a passel of them rippin' mad at you like he is." Boone whispered this to Mac, who merely grinned and nodded.

"Now march, you fools." The guard planted a boot sole against Mac's backside and shoved. Mac was not expecting that and pitched forward, nearly ending up on his knees again. But he remained upright and did not let his building anger take him over.

He and Boone both knew they had to pick their battles. This was not the time or place to put up a fight. They had to work hard to stay alive and somewhat free of injury, at least until the new workers arrived. It should be any day, according to the paltry scraps of information they'd managed to piece together.

They were being herded toward the line, and they saw several of the workers already there, looking toward them with surprise on their sweaty faces.

"Any chance we can get our hats back?" asked Boone. "I work better when my head ain't baking in the sun."

"Shut up. Where you're headed, you won't need a hat for long anyway."

"Now that's just dumb," said Boone.

Mac glanced at him and under his breath said, "Hoke."

But it was too late. As they shuffled forward, the guard herding them shoved Boone with his boot much the same as he'd done with Mac. Mac groaned as Boone, on feeling the boot begin to shove him, lurched to his right and spun, his freed hands already grasping.

He caught nothing but set himself in a low stance, his legs spread as wide as the chain would allow and said, "Come on then, mister. You man enough to come at me without your gun, or are you a fearful little beast?"

By then another guard had bounded over and stood next to the first. They both looked a little shocked.

It was about then that Mac saw the method to Boone's madness and he, too, faced the guards and hunkered low and squared off.

He sensed that Boone was using the moment to show the other workers, and they were but ten yards from a whole lot of them, that two obviously beaten-up and much-abused white prisoners were still able and capable of defending themselves, of putting up a bit of resistance to their tormentors.

They had to begin showing the workers there was value in standing up for oneself.

Of course, Mac knew, as Boone was well aware, too, that this entire display could go the other way and sink them before they even got to working shoulder to shoulder with the Chinese laborers. But it was worth the risk.

And it looked, for the moment at least, like it might well work, too. "What's the matter?" said Mac. "You know you are only able to take us on if you're armed, isn't that right? Not man enough to fight me, huh?"

For a brief moment, Mac thought for certain they were going to convince the guards to lay down their guns and brawl. But then another guard across the small canyon rim cracked off a shot into the air, and that brought a sense of reality back to the scene, as if they'd all been slapped across the face.

The two guards—the original squinty man and the newcomer—exchanged a quick glance, as if to verify they were both reading from the same book, and then the look of confidence gained from their grip on their guns once more took over their faces.

"Get yourself turned around or I will part your hair low with a bullet. You got me, you big ape?"

Mac shook his head low and slowly turned around once more, his back to the guards. Boone followed suit. It was not a comfortable position to be in—armed men behind you with nothing but hatred for you. And one of them was a fellow you'd already beaten the crap out of.

That last few yards to the cluster of workers was a long walk for Mac and Boone.

"Now what?" said Boone, keeping the guards in sight, not allowing himself to be spun around and treated like a boot rest again.

Mac had been working side by side with a thin but wiry young Chinaman who looked away every time Mac met his eye. They were lugging rails, along with a dozen other men, but the weight was such that they had to pause in their staggering lift by rope and strap every twenty feet or so.

The guards evidently knew the weight was too much to bear all in one go, even for such a force of men, and so they did not lay the business end of the bullwhip on the backs of the rail luggers. But neither did they tolerate them pausing for more than fifteen seconds at a time. It was not sufficient time for them to regain their wind, but it was all they were given.

At one point there was trouble at the far end of the rail. An older man had staggered and fallen to one knee while they were still lugging the rail.

"For mercy's sake! Give the man a minute to rest! All of them—you'll get far more work out of men who aren't treated like rented mules, you fools!"

Mac closed his sweat-stung eyes for a brief moment. It was Hoke, telling the guards what they should and shouldn't be doing. If his pard kept on like that, he was going to be killed before the day was out.

Surprisingly, it appeared to work. The entire group paused for a longer break, while Mac saw Boone help the fallen older man to his feet. He rubbed the old-timer's calf muscles and nodded, talking. The guard watched and shook his head, as if he'd never seen anything quite so odd.

Mac smiled. That was Boone all over, hard on the outside but as soft as a kitten when it came to his fellows.

"You stand against . . . ?"

Mac looked at the man to his side. The young Chinaman glanced at him, then looked away.

Mac said, "You asking me something?"

They both spoke out of the side of their mouths because they'd been threatened that talking amongst themselves would not be tolerated.

"You stand against . . . men with guns."

Oh, so that was it. The Chinaman was impressed by him and Boone standing up to the guards. *Good thinking, Boone,* thought Mac.

"Yes. We are not afraid of them." He closed his mouth then; a guard was glancing their way.

"You strong," said the man, suddenly looking as if he was the very opposite of what he was accusing Mac of.

"No, but together," said Mac, "we can all defeat them. Do you understand?"

"No." The man shook his head, looking around him at the workers spread out, as if the very sight of all his fellow countrymen suffering was far too disheartening for him to endure.

"We must fight back," said Mac. "I will show you. And my friend, too. Be strong for a little while longer." He smiled and nodded.

It was then that a guard saw him and strode over. "What were you told about talking to one another?"

Mac looked at him through his still-swollen eyes but said nothing.

The guard was unnerved by this and looked away for a moment; then, without warning, he swung his rifle butt up hard, connecting it with the young Chinaman's cheekbone.

The man staggered under the blow and slammed into Mac, who held him up and at the same time took half a step and angled his right shoulder before the man. "You want to repeat that, you'll have to club the both of us. He didn't say a thing, I did. Why didn't you hit me with your little gun, huh?"

Mac knew he was skating on thin ice, and he felt a whole lot weaker than he was letting on. If that man took such a swing at him, he'd likely flop sideways, too. How were they going to last until the new folks arrived? And then how long were he and Boone going to be kept alive once the newcomers were brought in? Like they said earlier, it was a narrow sliver of time they had to work with.

No, there was no time for him to be weak-kneed about any of this. He had to show strength and resistance for these already much-abused, weakened men. He knew Boone was feeling the same way. *But dang,* thought Mac, *he'd give a whole lot of money for a long nap on a bed of soft spruce boughs in the high country.* He promised himself a nice, long, relaxing trip, alone, to the timberline country once they made it through this ordeal.

If they did.

He'd called that guard's bluff. The man had backed down. Mac sighed inside, knowing he'd come close to receiving another thrashing, and this one he wasn't certain he'd make it through.

One more minute. That's all you have to do: Endure it for one more minute. He told himself this over and over, keeping his eyes on the work, and on the young Chinaman he was paired with. He had taken quite a hit and was already weakened.

Despite the beatings they had received, Mac didn't doubt he and Boone were still in overall healthier condition than these workers. Had to be. At least he and Boone had been eating regular meals up until they'd been found out.

These poor saps had been here for weeks now, some of them months, mistreated and starved and denied proper water during grueling days. What was the point of treating people like that?

Cool it down, Mac, he told himself. *One minute, then you get through fifteen of them, then thirty, then before you know it, you've knocked off another hour. Then two, then the day has dwindled.*

He hated to wish his time away like that, but there was nothing for it; he had to endure for the sake of himself and Boone, certainly, but more for the Chinese enslaved here. And for those about to arrive. And for those five women. He'd nearly forgotten about them and now hoped they had stayed put where he and Boone had left them.

Even that would not be a good idea, though, because they only had enough food for so many days—perhaps a week and a half at best if they rationed their servings. Fortunately, they were used to living on little.

But it bothered Mac, and annoyed him, too, because he enjoyed eating, likely more than most people he knew, save for Boone, who had what his own grandmother used to call "hollow legs." And now they'd put those women in a situation in which they had little choice but to comply.

A whip crack sounded not far behind him and made him jerk around quick.

"Tighten up, boy!" snarled a guard who was looking at Mac. "You ain't paid to doze off whilst you work!"

His immediate response, of course, was to reply with something along the lines of *I didn't realize I was being paid at all.* But he knew that would not go over well.

The guard walked on down the line as Mac and the young Chinaman and the rest began their next round of heaving the rail on down the long, dusty trail from where it had been hauled in by teams of oxen. The beasts of burden could only get them so close to where they were needed, and so the men must do the rest.

"You awake attention," said the young man to him without looking at Mac.

"Yes," replied Mac. "Thank you."

He knew the young man meant he needed to pay attention. And the man was correct, or he would risk getting others in trouble once again for his own meandering thoughts.

CHAPTER 22

The hours passed slowly, as if Boone were wading in waist-high mud, thicker than any he'd squelched through in the war. And that was saying something. He'd been having much the same experience as Mac, of that he was pretty certain, because he could see his pard setting to the work same as him, with that quiet, grim, doggedness Mac MacCoole always put into things.

Boone wanted to lie down and curl up more times than he could count all that day. He didn't have a pocket watch; didn't need one and never had. He could tell close enough what the time was by the position of the sun. But on this day he could barely bring himself to look where the blasted, vicious thing was.

The task he had been set to was not like Mac's, however, from what he could see. Mac was ganged with the rail luggers, and Boone was set swinging at a ledge, mostly at pesky jags of rock that were in the way of whatever the engineer fellas figured was the best place for a railroad line.

Boone thought he might never get up the nerve to ride on a train again. He hadn't been on one since the end of the war, when he was sent across a couple of states in a boxcar with a passel of other "Confederate combatants" to rattle their way back into the south to be dumped off.

It had been an unpleasant experience, yet the only thing that made it tolerable was that he was accompanied by Mac MacCoole, a steadfast pard even then, just weeks after they'd done their level best to kill each other in that swamp. Mac had insisted on accompanying Boone back on the train.

He'd lied, of course, and volunteered as a Yankee guard to make certain the Rebs made it home and did not do anything they shouldn't. Mac had had to keep his distance from the Rebs because most of them were still of the mind that the Yanks were a mangy lot and deserved gutting should the opportunity arise.

But, eventually, they got to the end of the line, all the way to Tawny Pass, and were once again checked on through. Then they were finally discharged from the annoying, watchful eyes of the bluebellies at Camp Chester.

Mac and Boone had a fine luncheon together, and Mac said that as an officer, he'd been called down to the camp to help close up shop. And that because Boone had mentioned he had little left to go back to—his family had dispersed and suffered grievous damage in the war—he'd likely not linger beyond a week or so.

Besides, Boone mentioned having an urge himself to see what lay out there on the frontier of the "union." He'd said that last word with a sneer, as if the word left a rank taste on his tongue.

Mac nodded, said he was figuring on doing much the same. They both mulled this thought as it hung there betwixt them while they sipped their coffee—not chicory either, but genuine coffee.

Then they'd both said, at about the same time, too, that neither man would be averse to letting a stranger tag along, if only so he could save him from all the dangers the trail offered.

Boone, as he recalled, had been emphatic that it was Mac who was likely going to need a whole lot of saving from dangers. As MacCoole was a big man, he would be prone to all manner of hazards and ills, also on account of him being a Yankee and all.

Boone also recalled that Mac had allowed as how Boone would be a surefire victim of all the ills the wilderness beyond the Appalachians could lob at a man.

Such good-natured but hard digs hadn't let up in all the years since taking to the trail together, first as two men merely exploring what lay beyond the next rise, the next range, the next river, the next bend in the trail. Frequently, there was no trail.

And then—Boone wasn't so certain exactly when it came about, but one day they were being paid to escort the families of miners on up to their husbands at their diggings. The menfolk of the town had sent for their families, bidding them to come to a little place called Opaline or some such, far up in the hills in the cold reaches of Oregon.

The trouble was that these women and children, and an older man and two strapping lads no more than thirteen or so, had arrived late in the season, in October, in the nearest downcountry town. From there, it was still roughly four days' hard journeying northward to get to Opaline.

Mac and Boone were drifting from ranch job to timber job, and at that time had a little jingle in their coin purses and were looking forward to resting up and figuring out their next moves.

That was when this small train of wagons arrived. There were three of them, plus the family of some crazy person amongst the miners who insisted his family—a woman and a boy and a girl, plus chickens and a cat of all things, and various other worldly goods—must use a hand cart so as not to abuse God's burdened beasts. He was some sort of devout German.

Boone recalled the entire group of them were already ragged when they arrived in that frozen town. They were in no condition to travel north, at least not unless there was a break in the weather. And two days later, a spell of unseasonable warmth moved in.

A wise old man who worked part-time at the mercantile but who had been an instructor of planetary circumspection—Boone never forgot that phrase, even all these years later—had told them without a doubt the warm weather would last for four days. But early on the fifth day, a storm would move into the region.

He peppered his reasoning with enough two-dollar words that Mac was impressed. And Boone knew that as Mac was a big thinker and reader of books himself, if the old gent had impressed him, there was something to it.

As to the haggard travelers, they were still tired but game to move on. Nobody in that little muddy town down on the flats below the mountains would give them any help beyond pointing in the general direction of Opaline and saying, "Good luck."

Well, Mac and Boone had not liked from the start the fact that these people, though ill prepared, were eager to see the patriarchs of their families. In their excitement, they were going to make for the high trails without any clear sense of how to get there.

Between cursing the men snug up in the hills with their horde of gold or whatever it was they were having success at digging up, and fretting over these poor folks when no one else would tend to them, Mac and Boone decided they had to lend a hand.

At first, some members of the group did not want their help.

"Why forever not?" said Boone, rubbing his worn, green felt topper back and forth on his head. "You daft or something? Got you an urge to get lost and freeze to death in them mountains?"

Fortunately, Mac had stepped in right about then and

smiled and explained that he and his pard were professionals in this field and would be happy to act as escorts and guides to Opaline. Boone knew it was the fact that the womenfolks, even the married ones—maybe especially the married ones—all seemed to get swoony and silly whenever Mac showed up.

So they finally agreed to allow Mac and Boone to lead the way. Good thing, too, as it turned out, for the old man's weather predictions had been a little off.

As Mac said later, it was likely because the old man was used to living down in town, and though every day he looked out his windows and measured the breezes and did all manner of odd things and wrote lots of tiny marks in his books, nonetheless, he only took into account the town.

Mac and Boone sniffed snow on the air in the afternoon of their second day, and they traded off: One rode out to shoot game—a large deer or two to feed such a sizable group—and the other to oversee the setting up of a proper camp. Something in which they and their beasts would all be able to keep from dying in the coming blow.

In a couple of days, the group made it to the little mine camp snugged up high in the mills, but not before they had to endure two lashings of a brutal duo of quick storms, another on the heels of the first.

They stayed hunkered in at that camp until the storm blew itself out, though they complained about not making tracks for Opaline on emerging from their snowy grotto that morning following the initial storm.

But Mac shook his head. "It's no good, folks. There's going to be no turning back to find this spot again."

"What makes you so all-fired uppity where our matters are concerned?"

Mac regarded the youth for a long moment, then said, "I understand your suspicions of us. I do. Seems to me you could have done better on your own, sure, if you were lucky.

But boy, I'm here to tell you there's another storm coming in, maybe tonight, and you still don't have a clear idea how to get to where you want to be, do you?"

All that day in the hot sun at the Blaswell rail site, Boone traced through that early adventure with Mac in his mind as he and the other men pounded stone. Somehow it did him good.

He recognized this but did not dwell on it too deeply. In his opinion, folks spent far too much time mired in their own heads and far too little time getting out and about and making things happen for themselves in their lives.

At any rate, he thought, *all this thinking about the past was fine and well, as long as he didn't fall behind or get strapped or whipped or clubbed by one of those idiot guards.*

So far, he'd managed to keep swinging the sledge and hitting rock enough that they left him alone. Boone wasn't certain how he was going to live through this mess today, let alone a second day, or more. And then he remembered the new batch of folks from China were due any time now.

And as if his thoughts had somehow conjured that notion into being, a ripple—that was the only way Boone could describe it—worked its way through the slaves. Murmurs began, the slightest of pauses in their labors. They had heard something, perhaps, or heard other slaves and their shackles make sounds that were different than those of still others. They had altered somehow, and that told them all they needed to know—a change was coming.

Even the guards had slipped a mite in their ministration of shouts and whip cracks and turned to see what the commotion was. There, northwest of the worksite, close by the camp where the laboring men were held, one wagon rolled into view, then another. They were open topped and packed with people. A third rumbled into view, followed by more of what had also preceded them: armed riders.

The wagons were packed with people standing, holding the side rails.

A covered black barouche followed the entire affair, driven by a thin, bald man.

"That'll be Mr. Kane," said the guard nearest Boone, as if they had been conversing and he had asked the obvious question.

Boone, for the moment, also forgot the master-and-servant relationship and asked, "And the wagons?"

The man's gaze lingered on the barouche topping the rise, skylined, then shifted his gaze back to Boone. His serene, almost smiling face, reassembled into its customary mask of sneering anger.

"Them'll be the new Chinese! Now, get back to work! White or no, you ain't fit to ask questions nohow!" The man raised his whip high and let it unfurl, a looping, long snake of a curl that ended in a cracking sound that sizzled the air beside Boone's sunbaked head.

"Now, you listen here, fella! That sort of behavior might get you big chuckles from your pals in the guards' mess tent but not with me! I'm old enough to dang near be your pap and you got no call to treat me that a way! Nor anyone else here! You wet-nosed whelp. I wasn't chained, I'd hang your ass on a tree limb and let the critters have at you!"

In the midst of what Boone knew Mac called one of his "tirades," Boone noticed behind the man, up on the slight ridge, that the barouche had slowed and then stopped. Whoever was in it had now leaned forward enough that Boone could see the face and bowler of a white man in a dark suit, leaning out the open top door of the buggy.

They were watching what was going on here. Boone figured if he drew attention to the guard he was shouting at, he might be able to buy himself time enough to back on out of this fit he hadn't been able to stop.

The entire time the guard regarded Boone with puzzlement, as if he couldn't quite understand the words being shouted at him. Boone reckoned that was because nobody in the camp had ever talked to him that way before. Nobody had ever dared.

Boone halted and said, "Looks like your fancy admirer has taken an interest in you. Or me." He forced a chuckle, though he was so weak and tired, it was all he could do to catch his breath after shouting like that.

The guard turned his head enough to see the barouche once more, and he saw what Boone did—the same staring man.

"Oh my word" said the man. "That there's Mr. Kane himself! I don't know how he's going to take what he's seeing here." The fear in the man's voice was evident in the quaking, stage-play whisper in which he spoke.

"Only one way to take it, if this Kane is a man at all!" shouted Boone, loud enough that he hoped the man in the wagon could hear. "And not some spineless fool!"

The guard gasped. "Shut up that talk, now!"

"No, I won't!" Boone shouted. "You all are abusing folks, and I am one of them. It's wrong and I ain't the only one who knows it! Slavery is illegal, don't you know! I fought long and hard in a war that decided it, by gum, among a pile of other things."

Then an interesting thing happened. As Boone watched and the Chinese men resumed their tasks behind and all around him, the little half door of the barouche swung outward and the man stepped out.

The driver hustled down from his seat and the horse walked forward slowly. Words were exchanged between the two men. The driver threw up his hands as if he were so confused, he didn't know whatever to do next. He scrambled back up into the seat and set the brake, then looped the lines and hustled back down again.

By then the man, shaking his head, watched the wagons loaded with new arrivals recede farther eastward. Boone knew they were following the main route from this moving camp, then looping around to the permanent encampment he'd originally been stationed at. Where the woman and kiddies and old folks were forced to worry and work away their time.

The man—it had to be, as the guard said, Mr. Thurston Kane—swung his gaze back on the diggings. With an ebony cane, a silver ball atop it, swinging in his black-gloved hand, he beckoned the man who'd driven him. The skinny little driver dashed forward, and Kane followed.

Boone narrowed his eyes and swung his sledge again. "Looks to me like you're in for it," he said, half eyeing the guard. The man was most definitely rattled.

Boone was not certain if he was in for it, in fact, or if the guard was. Or any of them. But it would be good to see this Kane up close.

The bald, skinny driver in front of Kane bustled up to within three feet of the guard, his face red and his eyes wide. Boone got the impression all this was highly unusual behavior.

Then, before the little man, whose mouth worked like that of a beached fish, could speak, Kane strode on up and shoved the little man aside.

That action alone would verify within a few short moments all that Boone needed to know about Thurston Kane.

"What is the meaning of all this hullabaloo? I heard that creature there," he pointed his black cane squarely at Boone, "from inside my buggy. Is this the way you allow your workers to treat you, man?"

It was the guard getting his ear filled with Kane's venom.

Boone figured he had little to lose, so he laid the sledge over his shoulder in an effort to look a pinch more menacing.

"Now see here, Kane. I know who you are and I sure bet you know who I am by now. I ain't one of your bought-and-paid-for slaves you can just work to death and then dispose of, however you do that. No sir, I am a certified free man come here looking for work and was hoodwinked and nabbed by your men. Before I knew it, I had the stuffing beat out of me and chucked on over here, swinging this sledge all day!"

He paused and eyed the man.

Boone had to hand it to Kane. He was a cool character. Up close, he was younger than he expected him to be, but in most other ways he was about what Boone thought he'd be. He was a dapper dresser, one of those fellows who did his best to look as if he was always in control.

He glared back at Boone. No, glaring wasn't quite right.

"Shut up, you," snarled the guard, but his bite was gone. He sounded like a schoolmarm cowed by the big farm boys in the back row.

"No, I don't believe I will," said Boone.

Kane pulled in a big, deep breath through his nose, then, without taking his eyes from Boone's face, he half smiled. "Ralston."

"Yes sir," said the little bald, skinny driver of the barouche.

"Have that man dealt with." Kane raised his cane and pointed it square at Boone, then lowered it.

The little bald man said, "Yes sir, right away, sir."

Then Kane said, "And that one." He swung his cane to point at the guard.

"Oh, oh Lord no, Mr. Kane. I got me a wife and two kiddies back in Missourah. I only come out here for the work. I swear, it was all working just fine until this lippy fool—I mean that lippy fella there"—he nodded toward Boone—"oh, I'll see to it that it don't never happen again, sir. I swear it."

Kane finally swiveled his eyes to rest on the guard. He sighed. "I must be exhausted. It is the only thing that could account for the fact that I am feeling this charitable just now. But yes, you may retain your position. But one more, and I mean one more incident, and I'll see to you personally. Do you understand me, you?"

The guard nodded his head, as if he was being paid by the nod to do so. "Sir, uh, yes sir. I uh, I'll do you proud, sir, Mr. Kane."

"Yes, yes. Now, back to it." He shooed the man away and turned. "Ralston?"

"Yes sir."

"Ralston, while I am here and have gone to all this trouble to walk over here, we may as well acquaint ourselves with the level of incompetence we are saddled with at present. For I fear we may miss the deadline for our rendezvous with others at the trestle."

"Sir," said the thin man, "surely it can't all be as bad as that. We have yet to see the entire camp. Perhaps we will encounter surprises that will help you change your mind."

Kane again breathed in through his nose and made for his right, westward, along the rim of the berm that enclosed the massive, sprawling, busy worksite.

CHAPTER 23

There was a line in front of the latrines. Two lines, in fact, and each was occupied.

"Whoever heard of a camp this size having two one-holers!" The man who said this was a short, squat fella with normally flushed cheeks that were now a pale ash color sheened with sweat.

He shared this pallor with most of the other men, nearly a dozen, in the lines. Some of them fidgeted from foot to foot, several stood bent with their hands gently rubbing their bellies, others squatted, their arms on their knees, their heads bowed as if they were in fervent prayer.

One man broke ranks and, trailing a moaning noise, rushed for a nearby jut of craggy rock. As he rushed, taking somewhat ginger steps, he worked his braces down off his shoulders and fumbled at the buttons on his trousers. They weren't complying, and he shrieked, "Come on, come on!" filling the air with the sounds of his desperation.

He made it around to the backside of the rock and squatted, his torso still quite visible to the others, some twenty feet away. He howled and groaned. The embarrassment felt by the other men quickly diminished, and several of them broke from the lines and sought nearby cover as well.

One man, seeing everything close by already occupied,

bolted across the plain toward nothing at all. His panic increased, and at the same time his steps grew shorter and shorter until he came to a halt and hugged his belly and dropped to his knees, moaning and groaning. He pitched to his side and fouled himself.

The other men looked away, pity and revulsion warring on their grimy, drawn faces. The ones at the front of the lines banged on the outhouse doors and cursed the current occupants in desperate, blue language.

Soon, the rest scattered and sought relief elsewhere, most not making it too far before succumbing to their gastric ailments.

"What in the hell is this?" shouted Shaky, loping up on his horse. He was finishing up eating a handful of cold corn cakes. He'd just left the mess tent by the encampment and had polished off two bowls of Cook's oddly tasty chili.

"Hey, you, Butz, what's happening here? I ain't paying you fools to stand around the outhouse!"

The man to whom he spoke, Butz, a tall bean of a man, shook his head. "Can't talk now, Boss. Got to go . . ."

He hustled past Shaky, who sat his horse, glaring down at the man who'd just dared to disobey him, waved him off as if he was a slave himself! The nerve of these overpaid, underworked guards . . .

Shaky slid down out of the saddle, and as his boots hit the gravel, his guts offered up a bubbling, growling sound, the likes of which he hadn't heard from himself in some time. Not since the morning after that last big, ripping drunk he'd finally tailed off some weeks before. That had been a horrible few days. So much so that he'd almost, *almost* sworn off the drink. But no, that wasn't a possibility, he'd determined the very next day.

But this? What was this all about? He'd barely had half a bottle today.

"You didn't eat that chili, did you, Boss?" Butz tossed

that question back over his shoulder as he bustled off, making for the low shrubs yonder. "That meat was off!"

"You get yourself back here, Butz! Tell me what you mean!"

But Butz was not slowing down. Shaky shook his head and made for the latrine. A lengthy sit-down session might do him some good.

"Get out of my way, you fools! Git!" He shoved his way to the front of the line and snatched the door handle, a leather loop tacked onto the warped planking. The stink wafting from behind the door made him pull a tight face. "Who is in here? He die or what?"

None of the other men said a thing. Two more gave up on the line and bolted elsewhere.

"Get out of there now! I got things to do, and they are more important than anything you got going on in here!"

From within, a sobbing groan sounded.

It was enough to stifle Shaky. Then his gut began roiling once more and he felt twinges down deep in there. *Uh-oh*, he thought. *What is happening here?*

As he held a hand tenderly to his gut and pounded on the door with the other fist, Butz's words came back to him. The chili . . .

Damn that cook.

CHAPTER 24

Less than an hour after Boone's encounter with Thurston Kane, they were all allowed a dipper full of water from a leaking wooden bucket.

"Would have been able to give you all more water," said the guard lugging the pail and smiling. "But she's a leaker!" His guffaws were impressive only to himself.

Boone resumed his place smacking rock beside the Chinese fella from earlier. Boone kept looking around, more desperate with each passing moment, knowing he had to find a way to break free and help liberate the Chinese laborers, before they were all killed by fools with guns and no sense. And he had to do it before he became a worn-to-the-nub worker like all the rest.

"Hey," said a voice to his right.

Boone glanced up. There was a Chinese face, sweaty and yet smiling.

"Hey yourself!" whispered Boone. And then he looked harder at the smiling man. "Wait a minute," he whispered. "You ain't the same fellow as before."

"Yes, yes, you are right." He kept his voice low and glanced out from beneath his wide-brimmed hat.

"Where's the other fella?"

"I tell him go back some." The man moved his head

slightly, as if to indicate the vague but busy direction behind him. "Too much worry on his mind."

"Good of you. Say . . ." Boone had an idea he wanted to spring on the smiler.

But instead, he was genuinely surprised when the man spoke once again. "You go from here? I help. We get all men out."

"Are you serious?" said Boone. "That's music to my ears. You got a plan?"

"Plan?" said the man. "I not know."

"Ah, okay, then you want I should muckle onto this problem, see where it takes us, eh? Well, okay, look . . ."

That was when the guard, who not long before was berated by both Boone and Kane, decided to walk back slowly toward them. He was still looking up the line at others in his charge, however. That gave Boone an idea and the opportunity to share a few more words with the smiler.

"Got me a plan, as it happens. But I need you to set up a distraction whilst I pull it off."

The man looked at Boone as if he had just explained that apples grew on pine trees.

"Never mind. You just need to act like something's wrong so I can do what I need to. Okay?"

"Ah," the man spoke softly out of the side of his mouth and did not look at Boone, "I see. Okay, okay . . ."

And then the guard happened on them. "I am watching you, Boone. And don't you forget it neither."

"Good," said Boone. "'Cause I got to find a latrine and quick, elsewise I am going to commence to making a mess of this very spot where we have to work and you have to stand. You got me?"

The guard narrowed his eyes and shook his head. "You already had your break."

"First off, you call that a break? Tease a man in the grip of a serious thirst and then you tell him that's all he gets for the rest of the day?" Boone wrapped up the small tirade with a hand rubbing the belly of his greasy buckskin tunic. "I'm telling you, mister, I got a powerful gut ache."

"Not my problem!"

"Oh, it will be. Come on, lead me on over there and I'll do the rest."

For long minutes, the man deliberated, uncertain of what to do. Finally, he called over to the nearest guard, a skinny fellow a long way off. "You look after my men here. This fool's got to use the latrine!"

"No way. Tell him to hold it!"

Boone's guard groaned. "He said no way."

That's when Boone looked upslope and saw the big fellow with the key ring who'd driven him and Mac over to the line in the wagon.

"Tell you what." He grimaced and rubbed his belly harder. "Fatty up yonder ain't doing a thing. Let him tend me and you can do what you need to here. I'll be a good boy. But I got to go, man!"

The guard looked upslope and caught sight of the big guard, who appeared to be doing little more than loafing near the wagon and trying to make it look as if he was busy.

"Okay, I'll take you up to him, but I got to get back here right off or I'm in trouble!"

"I know it, I know it! You got yourself a wife and kiddies in Missouri. I heard you before. Now let's go!"

Before Boone turned, he bent low, set down the sledge, and winked on the sly to the smiler beside him. The Chinese man nodded almost imperceptibly.

Then the guard prodded Boone on the arm with his rifle barrel. "Move! Get up there!"

For the sake of the maneuver he was about to attempt, Boone kept his temper in check, but having a man nudge him like that set his molars to grinding. He settled for a sneer as they climbed the slight rise.

"Hey!" shouted his guard. "Hey!"

The fat man looked at them.

"Tend to this one! I got to get back down there!"

"Yeah, all right, all right." The fat man made it seem as if he was doing the Missouri guard a whale of a favor and sighed and dragged himself on over. "What is it now?"

"He's feeling poorly and I am busy."

"Uh-huh, okay." The fat man shucked his revolver and wagged it at Boone. "No games. I don't play no games."

You're about to, thought Boone. *Because I do*. But he kept his mouth shut and kept on instead with the belly rubbing and the pained-face look.

His first guard loped back down the slope and the fat man nodded Boone ahead toward a drop-off with a knotty log wedged crosswise between two boulders.

An open-pit dumper, thought Boone. *Why would I expect any less?*

When they reached the thing, Boone looked back downslope and saw that they were out of sight of the others. He bent low, groaning, and the fat man, feeling as if his prisoner was truly incapacitated, relaxed a pinch. Just as Boone expected.

That gave him a sliver of an edge. With both of his bony, hard-as-rock fists locked together, Boone swung them upward like a cudgel, right beneath the fat man's sweaty chin.

He heard the man's teeth come together hard, like river rocks slamming in a raging spring freshet. As he half expected, the big, sloppy man was an easy drop. He wheezed and groaned, his eyes rolled white in his head, and he bent at the knees.

Boone had to dance sideways to avoid having the big sop flop down on top of him.

"Damn," said Boone, surveying what he'd done. He realized as he bent into action that he should have somehow kept the man conscious, so he could lure the other guard back up here.

No matter; he'd make do. It came as second nature, in fact, to both him and Mac. Adapting to the unforeseen was what they did best.

It wasn't but the work of a minute or so to find the key ring swaying deep in the fat man's trouser pocket, a creepy, sticky, sweaty experience Boone did not want to repeat. It gave him the shudders, but it was worth it to have his ankle manacles undone. He quickly slapped them on the fat man and then tugged off the man's gun belt.

He pulled it on and had to use the point of his hidden Barlow folder's blade to make a quick, crude hole so the big belt fit him.

The fat man still lay there, unconscious. Boone reckoned two minutes had passed since they'd come up here. The hidden freedom would not last. Time to act. First, he cocked an ear. He heard no sounds that might indicate a distraction caused by the smiling Chinaman. He didn't think the man had understood him, but you never knew.

Boone could not wait. He checked the fat man's revolver, then cleared his throat and shouted downslope toward the first guard in as close a voice as he could come to the fat man's. As he shouted, he realized it wasn't very convincing. But it would have to do.

"Hey, need some help up here with this prisoner!"

A few moments passed, and Boone was about to shout again when he heard the guard from Missouri say, "What? You deal with him!"

"No!" said Boone. "You get up here!" He shrugged, hoping that might annoy the other guard enough to get him to drag on up the slope once again.

"I can't! I'm busy!"

Boone sighed. For the plan to really work, he needed to have that man on up here and out of the picture down below.

"Get up here now!" he shouted in his best fat man voice. It still didn't sound much like the unconscious man, but Boone was beyond caring.

Another few moments and he would have to make a break for it and figure out how to free the men on the line later. And then he heard a low, grumbling cursing and boots on gravel, striding up the slope. *Here it was,* he thought, doing his best to position himself where the unsuspecting guard would turn and be caught with Boone staring him down, gun in hand.

And that was just about how it happened. The guard from Missouri saw the fat man prone on the ground, but he'd already walked too far forward toward the latrine pit, giving Boone enough space to get the drop on him but still remain somewhat hidden from eager eyes from below.

"That's far enough." Boone smiled as the man turned and saw that the tables had been turned. "Drop that rifle, and unbuckle the gun belt, too."

"I'm . . ." The guard swallowed and licked his lips. "Ah, I'm . . ."

"Yeah," said Boone, still smiling. "Me too." He wagged the fat man's revolver. "Get to it, sonny."

The guard complied and soon was on his knees beside the fat man. Boone stepped up behind him, and he brought the butt of the revolver down alongside the guard's head, above the ear on his right side. It did the trick. The man dropped forward, neat as you please, beside his fellow guard.

"That was for calling me a fool."

Boone rummaged on the man's belt, taking the revolver and bullets, then checked his vest pocket, yielding a handful of shells for the man's rifle. That reminded Boone that the fat guard had had a rifle earlier as well. He'd try to locate it before he left the scene of his latest crime.

The next thing Boone did was snatch off the skinnier guard's vest and hat, which he donned.

"Now for the big finale," he muttered and, stuffing rags in each man's mouth, he tied their hands behind their backs and rolled them, one at a time, into the slops pit.

"And that was for shoving me along with your gun. A Boone don't take kindly to being handled."

He looked down at the tangle of two men and was relieved to see they were both face up and not about to drown in the mess.

"Beats dying," he said. Then he got a whiff of the pungent fumes that rose up from the roiled funk below. "Or maybe not," he said, pinching his nose and making for the slope.

"Time to see how good an actor I really am," he muttered, and spied the fat man's rifle, leaning against a boulder at the top of the slope. He grabbed it up, then walked back down to the line. He had to act fast, before the other guards got a good look at him and raised rifles on him.

He nodded to the smiler, who was still working, head bent, but looking sideways at Boone. And smiling. Boone unlocked the man's ankle manacles and then handed him the keys. "Free the others," he hissed. "Now! And hurry!"

He turned and resumed a stance that gave him the best chance to pick off the guards as they noticed something was amiss.

It didn't take long. The smiling Chinaman had freed four of his fellows when the first shout, far to Boone's left, rose up. "Hey! What's going on over there?"

Boone waited a moment, feigning ignorance, and shrugged. It bought him a few seconds. Then another shout rose up from the same direction, off to Boone's left.

"Time to play," he muttered and brought his rifle up. He hit two guards with the first two shots. By then, another two guards had delivered lead over at him, but their shots were hurried and sloppy.

Boone doled out three more shots and hit two more guards. He was pleased, but now the lid was off and the place was a shambles, with folks howling, Chinamen and guards alike. People ran in no detectable pattern or direction, reminding Boone of headless chickens on slaughtering day, a grim thought.

There was a boulder to his right and behind, perhaps a dozen feet, and he made for that, lugging both rifles. He hoped like heck he'd popped off enough covering shots that they didn't nail him in the back on his way to the relative safety of the boulder.

He made it and glanced behind, along the line, and saw a guard about to draw down on the escaping Chinese workers.

Boone whipped a rifle up to his shoulder, snugged the stock to his cheek, and let loose. The guard had waited a moment too long to do the same, and now he lay flat on his back, an oozing bullet hole between his eyes.

"Hey!" shouted a voice down lower. Boone sneaked a peek; it was the smiling Chinaman. He'd freed a pile of folks and they were swamping westward along the tracks, taking cover and leeching outward, snatching weapons from the fallen guards.

Boone waved and shouted, "Keep on!"

Then he resumed looking for guards dumb enough to stay put. He found three. They still held their posts and looked angry that they were being bested. "Idiots," snarled Boone and, gauging distance and windage, he sighted on them, one at a time.

It bothered him to snipe them like that, but they had all proven to him, and to everyone else there, especially the Chinese workers, that they, to a man, had no desire to be anything less than the brute oppressors they were. So Boone let them have it.

One by one, each of the men fell. Boone did indeed feel twinges of guilt with each shot dealt, but the owlhoots had asked for it, behaving as they had.

And then Boone saw no other guards about, neither up nor down the line. The only people moving were the retreating forms of the Chinamen, raiding the fallen guards for weapons.

A brief flare of pride welled in him. He hoped it could continue, but he knew Reg and Shaky had a whole lot of other gun hands about the place.

It was high time to find Mac and really open the ball.

CHAPTER 25

"I see no further reason to keep those two spying men about the place," said Thurston Kane in a low, steady, cold voice. "We must, we must, we must dedicate our efforts, all of them"—he glared at Shaky from beneath lowered brows—"to making it to the trestle. I'll be visiting there soon to see what progress the other crews have made.

"I will tell you, Shaky, that overall, I am unimpressed with how this camp has been run in my absence. I told you this was a most crucial period of time, did I not?" Without waiting for a response, Kane continued on, "That we could not, under any circumstances, afford to lose any more workers. And yet here I am, seeing markedly fewer men laboring to bring the rail line forward.

"So why is it that our crew has all of a sudden gained two white men? Famed lawmen, if you will, operating outside the law? Hmm?"

"Mr. Kane, sir, it's simple, really. They just showed up, and since we was down a few men, only 'cause I was following your orders and not tolerating anybody who lipped off nor refused to do their work, why, I thought we should hire them boys on."

"Oh, I see. So you hired them on as laborers?"

"Well, no sir, no. I hired them on account of the fact that

they needed work and we needed guards. Didn't have no idea who they were nor that they wanted to cause the outfit here such harm."

"But they have!" shouted Kane, slamming a fist on the tabletop before him.

No one said a thing. When Thurston Kane shouted, they all knew from hard experience it was a warning that everyone should shut the hell up.

They might have argued that way for many minutes more, back and forth, with Kane becoming increasingly agitated, but a rifle shot cracked through the tense air in the shack and Shaky bolted for the door.

It came from a distance, down toward one of the guard shacks, not far from the mess tent. Before he could give it more thought, even more shots rang out. Volleys of them.

Kane hung back, eyes wide. He was, as it turned out, and well known to them all, absolutely fine with doling out punishment and dire grim circumstance to others, particularly when measured against business and the need to make money.

The safety and happiness and health of others was never a consideration from the start of this project, though he realized that in order to satisfy most other people, he had to feign kindness. It had not been easy for him.

As soon as Shaky exited the shack, another bullet zipped, this one intended for them, chunking into the wood of the right side of the doorframe, driving him back inside. He slammed the door and hunkered low, slicking his revolver from its holster.

"What's going on out there?" said Kane. He had already crouched down, partially behind the table. It was an awkward pose, and he was wondering if there really was need for such caution. Might he not continue with his work at the table? He had so much to do, all the paperwork he had not gotten around to attending to before leaving San Francisco.

He glanced to his left and saw Ralston crouched in the corner, his spindly arms over his bald head.

"Your weak limbs will not stop a bullet, Ralston. It can easily pierce your arm and enter your head. Best to use your time wisely. Especially given the fact that Mr. Shaky, here, is paid to deal with this sort of thing. Also, I am paying you to assist me, and not, I must reiterate, to crouch on the floor and whine like a witless child."

"Yes sir," said Ralston, and yet he did not move.

"Well?"

"Yes sir. But it's gunfire, sir."

"Yes, I'm well aware of that, Ralston. Mr. Shaky? What is the verdict? Will we be killed before teatime or can you and your men stop this—"

Before he could finish the sentence, another shot, then a fourth drilled into the cabin. One snapped right through the window, shattering the glass on an upper pane and lodging in the back wall several feet above Kane's lowered head.

Ralston screamed and curled into an even tighter ball. Kane glanced at him again and, despite thinking that perhaps the little fool had some good sense after all, he sneered. "Get up, Ralston. You disgust me. Get up or you are fired."

The man peeked at him.

"Get up, Ralston, or you will work the line."

Knowing that Ralston was a weakling and a soft-bellied thing, no matter that he was overall a most effective assistant, Kane nonetheless was disgusted by the man's spineless tendencies. Enough so that he would risk leaving the dolt here to perish while working on the rails.

Shaky catwalked over to the door and nudged it open. "Hey!" he shouted. "What in the hell is going on out there?"

He received no response save for a whistling gust of wind. This was followed after a long, quiet moment, by another bullet. This one smacked high on the outside of the cabin.

"Darn it," he growled, pulling his head back in. "I can't see any of my men and certainly none of whoever is sending these lead bees at us!"

Ralston whimpered but continued to make his way over to the table where Kane sat alternately glaring at him and his meager progress, and at Shaky.

"Well?" said Kane.

Shaky looked at him. "Well, what?"

"Aren't you going to go out there and see who has done this thing? I don't have all the time in the world here, you know. This silly little episode is preventing me from assessing the remainder of the work. And after all, Shaky, this sort of thing is what you were hired for. If you are not up to the task, I suspect Reg will most certainly be interested in the post. Hmm?"

Shaky growled and crabwalked over to a window farther back on the east wall and glancing out the glass, then quickly nudged it open from the bottom. He paused, waiting for shots. None came.

"Oh, for heaven's sake, man," said Kane. "Get out there and do your job. And don't think I won't remember this when it comes time for that promised end-of-job cash bonus to be paid. Don't think I won't remember this!"

Shaky growled low in his throat once more, then, with a shrug, he hoisted a knee up onto the window's sill. Clenching his entire body, it seemed to him, he worked the rest of himself up onto the sill.

Behind him, he heard Kane berating that pathetic little man, Ralston, that they needed to get to Kane's cabin, and quick.

"And you, Shaky, will meet us there. Is that understood?"

"Yeah," he grunted from the window.

So far, no bullet sought out Shaky's projecting kneecap. Emboldened by this, he continued until he dropped out of the window and landed half on his feet, revolver wagging and waving, to arrange himself up out of the dust. He kept low and glanced along the side of the plank-sided building toward the front, where the bullets had come from.

Then he began a slow, low skulk toward this odd and unexpected new danger.

CHAPTER 26

Mac heard gunshots and knew Boone had managed to free himself. Mac had, too, merely by overpowering the nearest guard. The ease of it had surprised him, but was welcome, especially as he felt, as Boone often said after a night of carousing, like a "hot batch of homemade sin."

Now Mac was on the move, after laying waste to a couple of other guards and freeing a handful of Chinese laborers. They were now armed and scattering, and so was Mac.

As he hustled from cover to cover, he thought about Boone and wished him success, though he knew his pard didn't much need it. He envied Hoke's ability to seemingly heal up after a beating of some sort, enough that he could function as the situation demanded.

They were evenly matched, age wise. If anything, Boone was a year or two older than Mac. He never quite knew his pard's true age, as the wiry woodsman claimed his folks never told him when he was born, because they, as he claimed, could not quite recall themselves, what with a dozen or so kids floating around the homeplace in Hoddy's Gulch.

On this particular day, arguably one of the most crucial he and Hoke had experienced in all their years on the trail together, Mac was feeling at his most poorly. They'd taken some mighty thrashings in their time, and they each bore the scars and cold-weather aches to prove it. But this latest, from a pile of men under Reg's command, had been one heck of a beating, and it had taken a mighty toll on Mac, inside and out.

His vision still joggled when he ran and his head pounded, his ribs felt to be a snapped pile of sticks floating in his chest, and his right leg felt as though it was about to buckle under him any moment, his knee being a staved-in mess. And he thought the little finger on his right hand was broken. Damn thing was surely broken, in fact, as no normal finger would swell to twice its normal size, not bend, and turn the colors of a stormy sky.

Yes, he'd all but decided this was going to be his last adventure in a professional capacity with Boone. He had been squirreling away his earnings for years and had more than enough to buy that slab of land somewhere in the high country.

It would be a place where he could build a comfortable cabin, a barn, a workshop, and fish in the high mountain streams when the whim took him, which he knew was bound to be often.

And when it grew to be too damn cold outside and his bones ached from war wounds and those sustained in work with Boone through the years, after the war, why, he'd head on into the cabin and light a fire in the fireplace and brew a pot of coffee. And then, by gaw, as Hoke would say, he'd sit down with a pipe and a good book. Yes sir, there was enough promise and goodness in such a plan for any right-thinking man.

And if he should one day meet a woman who appreciated the things in life he did, and who maybe could introduce him to other things he might come to enjoy, too, why, all the better. Time would take care of that. And speaking of time, yes sir, it was time to call it a day. But not just yet. He had to make it through this last mess first.

Mac sighed and figured he'd best get at it. He had to get this ball rolling so Hoke could do his part. Just like anything else in life, one thing depended on another.

His part of the plan called for quicker action than he was giving it. Mac checked his borrowed rifle and revolver and made for the encampment.

He had surprise on his side, that and the two guns he liberated from a drowsy guard were his upper hand. He had to dole out some hard justice to as many guards as he could, and quick. Or Boone would find himself in even more danger than he was walking into.

Neither man kidded himself; they knew when they parted that this situation had the makings of a trash heap bonfire that neither of them might escape. But that didn't mean they weren't going to do all they could to free those poor Chinese folks.

As Mac scooted in a limping fashion toward the nearest cabin, he forced himself to recall the gut-deep sadness on the faces of those Chinese women they'd helped to get free of those slavers. And the brute killings he'd seen Reg commit since he and Hoke had arrived at this awful place. Mac still cursed himself, and knew he would for the rest of his days, for not being able to do a damned thing to stop them.

But the feelings of rage he'd conjured within himself at these unjust atrocities helped drive him onward.

He knew there were at least three men in the cabin ahead, one of whom might be Reg. He wasn't the snake's head, nor was Shaky, but they were surely its rattle, and Mac sorely wanted to cut them off. Make the snake writhe a bit.

The one he really wanted was that vicious head of this snake, Thurston Kane, who he'd seen or heard precious little of since he arrived here with the new batch of Chinese workers fresh from the ship.

He didn't think the man had left the area yet, as he'd overheard two of the guards saying that Kane usually kicked around for a week or so once he arrived. But until he could track down that rogue, Mac resolved to dole out a few tough lumps of brutality of his own to anyone who wasn't an enslaved worker.

The sun was not playing nicely today, he thought. Hatless and squinting away sweat, Mac inched around the edges of the last boulder between him and the shack. He already heard sounds from inside—a quick snort of laughter, as if one of the men had told a risqué joke, and then the others had simmered again, waiting for a fresh voice to chime in.

The closer Mac drew to the shack, the more assured he became, This was where he belonged, in situations such as this. Even his aches and pains ebbed a bit. Enough to let him concentrate on what needed to happen.

He knew he was going to kill men today. He would provoke them to aim for him and then it would be fair, or as fair as killing another ever might be. At any rate, it would provide him with the excuse he needed to lay them low. He did not like to think like that, but as Hoke would say, in for a penny, in for a pound.

After a couple more moments of dithering, Mac pulled in a deep draught of hot, dry air, felt the brute heat sizzle and scald his parched throat, and was thankful for it. For now, he was well and truly wide-awake and alert, as much so as he was going to get on this day anyway.

He wormed his way around the back side of the shack, looking for a window, and was rewarded with the sight of one on the far side. He crept closer to it, carefully placing his boots one heel at a time so as not to instigate any sound that might perk an ear inside. The planks sheathing the shack's walls were puckered and gappy, but battens covered most of the vertical seams.

The sun's angle was such that on this side of the shack,

anyway, he wouldn't cast flickering shadows through the gaps as he walked. Still, he moved slowly toward the window. He had to know how many men were inside before he commenced.

Two steps more and he reached the window. There had been no interruption in the unintelligible murmurs from within, so he didn't think they were on alert. He eased up slowly, in case one of them happened to be looking toward the window, and then he was able to see in. The glass was begrimed, but even so, he could see well enough to the inside. It was dark but not so much that he couldn't make out the two shapes. There might well be a third on a bunk or chair tucked in a corner, but he'd have to deal with that as the play unfolded.

He eased himself down again, low walked past the window, snagged a fist-size rock from the ground at his feet, and angled away from the shack about a dozen feet. His aim was good enough that he could hit the glass from there. He was partially hidden and thus protected by a boulder.

Of even more importance was the clear trail he had behind him, which would lead him to a spot from which he might spy much of this end of the camp.

He lobbed the stone, and it arced just as he hoped, low and easy, right into and through the glass. The window burst apart, spraying glass inside.

As he expected, shouts and the scraping of chairs and a general clatter of noise rose up from within. It wasn't enough sound that the rest of the camp might come bolting on over. Yet. But wait until the shooting commenced.

Mac knew this simple little ploy would work because he'd used it at least twice before. Men the world over were a jumpy lot, especially guilty men such as these, and they would do as he expected.

And they did.

They slammed out of that stuffy, hot shack, braces

flapping and boots half tugged on, sweat-stained shirts stuck to their backs and guns being checked for cartridges as they ran in an awkward dance.

They split up, three of them—two took one side, one the other—on the far side from Mac. They made their way around the side with the window.

He wanted to laugh at them, Big, tough men riled by a tossed rock. But he had the advantage of having the drop on them, having his rifle drawn and snugged to his shoulder and cheek, and as yet they were a trio of skittish prairie dogs, swiveling their fool heads left, then right, then left again. And seeing nothing.

Any moment, though, and they'd see Mac, hunkered beside the boulder. And the fun would commence. He would not shoot until they readied themselves to shoot him. And the first one did just that, after wasting breath and a motion by shouting and pointing "There!" at Mac.

"Yep, here," said the big man, and touched off his trigger a breath faster than the speaker.

Mac's first shot caught the man square in the chest of his sweaty longhandles and the guard slammed backward, whipping to his left side before he flopped to the earth, his fingers clawing gravel and his heels drumming in a senseless last rhythm.

Mac swung to his left a few inches, lining up his second shot before the first man completely toppled to the earth. The second man also lined up a shot, and though Mac's bullet punched a hole above his left eye, his shot peppered the boulder a foot from Mac's head, causing him to jerk back below the rock, wincing from the sting of countless shards of stone fragments.

He wiped a hand down his sweaty face and looked at his palm, seeing flecks of blood smeared with dust and grime. He blinked rapidly but still could see just fine. No harm, then.

By then, the third man had retreated back around the cabin.

The man surprised him, for instead of holing up, Mac heard his boots slapping the hard-packed gravel trail away from the cabin toward the camp proper. Or so Mac assumed. He glanced about to make doubly certain, then he retrieved the weapons from the two shot men.

Given the fact that the three men had been in the cabin and not roving the property with guns at the ready, Mac felt safe in assuming word had not spread very far that Mac and Boone were on the loose. But the sounds of the fresh gunshots would obviously alert other guards and Shaky and Reg for certain, as well as the surveyors, the engineers, and other contractors who were all folded into Kane's moneyed fist.

They would all be out gunning for Mac and Boone. It was Mac's task to create as many distractions and disturbances as he could, all the while leading as many of the men to their ends with well-placed bullets. Or, at the very least, away from the direction Boone would hopefully soon be busy—the slaves' camp on the rail line.

The second part of Mac's task was to make his way, in roundabout fashion, toward the quarters of the rest of the enslaved folks: namely the women, children, and old folks.

Anyone who wasn't up for brutal work on the line, hauling rails and ties, clearing gravel and shifting rocks, banging away at other rocks too large to shift was fair game for Mac and his rescue run.

He and Boone had spread the word among the few men on the line who comprehended English. There were precious few of them, but they seemed to get the word out quickly. Though many of them appeared to doubt the possibility of escape, Mac was heartened by the fact that they looked agreeable and keen eyed.

The proof was in the result, though. Would they find the men willing to take the risk, or were the majority of them too downtrodden and beaten down to make a go of it? Again, time would tell.

Mac didn't worry about the third man who'd escaped, but roved as quickly as he could up the slope toward the rise that led to the cook and mess tents. That was a gathering point for the guards, a place where Reg issued his orders and Shaky could often be found, nursing a cup of whiskey-laced coffee and grousing about how nobody was moving fast enough for his liking.

Mac wasn't certain what he could do to intimidate an entire tent full of guards, but he had to try. From a distance.

As he catwalked closer, he heard before he saw the commotion the shots had created. Men were pounding their boots seemingly in all directions. He heard shouts—it sounded like Reg—for men to get the hell out there and quit lingering over their coffee.

It was time for Mac to unleash a few more rounds of distraction. He scurried upslope behind the tents and managed to do so by a judicious choice of boulders. He climbed about thirty feet in elevation and figured that was suitable enough to begin.

He wedged himself behind a boulder and waited until the bulk of the men—or so he assumed—had exited the two side-by-side tents and were well away from it; then he began firing.

He sent his first shot high, not considering sniping of an unaware man to be sporting in the least, even though these heartless snakes had never given quarter to the enslaved men in their care.

The effect was immediate and wild. Men scattered like hay chaff in a stiff breeze, making for anything that might provide cover. Most were too far to hotfoot it back to the tent effectively, so they kept on running.

But a number of them, perhaps six to eight, held where they stood, dropping low to a knee and returning fire. They

were the ones Mac was most concerned with, for they were
the ones with obvious experience, unafraid to hold in place
and give what they were getting.

Mac emptied one rifle and snatched out his revolver,
squeezing off shots that were meeting with surprising success.

By then, they had marked his location, and though the
men could not see him, they knew where he was by the quick
bursts of smoke rising from his shots. He was not concerned
with them sniping him . . . yet. While he still had the sliver
of the element of surprise he had bought himself left, Mac
delivered lead in hot, smoking doses in a steady rhythm.
Howls from his clueless victims filled the air.

The lucky ones came to the realization sooner rather than
later that being out in the open as they were would not end
well for them. But they fired and hustled to the nearest
cover, which in the case of most of them, appeared to be
boulders. A rare few scurried back into the tents.

Mac had hoped he'd be able to set fire to the tents and
really drive them out, but the scene had unfolded quicker
than he expected. Had he not been overtired and sore as hell,
he suspected he would have known beforehand there was no
way he was going to pull off that coup.

Mac had dropped three men who were now not even
twitching, and another two that had continued to move. One
was shot in the upper thigh, and that rascal still managed to
drag that useless limb to safety behind a jumble of broken
boulder shards. The thigh-shot man hunkered low and
waited for the sniper to show himself.

He didn't have long to wait. Mac raised his head and
squeezed off another shot. The thigh-shot man would do no
more hobbling. The bullet caught him betwixt the eyes, as
Boone had seen Mac do many times before.

And then he topped off the shot with a smack to his own
thigh, as if he were waking a dozing old man. He didn't

want to get cocky, but he had begun to feel as if a ray of hope was blooming in this otherwise dour day.

Boone and Mac had worked as much as they dared on their meager plans before moving forward, each knowing these were the thinnest odds they'd faced in a long ol' while. But they also knew that unless they acted, and soon, they were doomed to die because Kane was intolerant of any impediments. And the veteran Chinese workers were getting more fatigued by the minute, while the new ones were quickly buckling under the savagery that was to become their constant foe.

Two of the beleaguered guards tried to make an end run to Mac's left side, presumably to climb up around him and then put the squeeze on him, if the one man coming up on his right side was an indication of their intent. Mac held the high ground for a bit longer, but if they succeeded, he would lose that, and likely his life.

He picked off one of the two on his left, a solid shot that slid into the side of the man's rib cage, high up, as the man's scissoring left arm was raised while he bolted, switchback fashion, upslope. Mac heard the man squeal and saw him flip to the earth, rolling and failing, before coming to a tumbling stop back at the base of the slope where he began.

It came to Mac then, in the flash of an instant, that of course the poor fool whose life he'd just ended had been somebody's child. And of course the man had once done all the funny, foolish things kids did. Then, somewhere along the line, he'd grown up and somehow become numbed to the sadistic tendencies he'd seen blooming around him.

Somehow, Mac thought, *if they could blink away all the bigotry and hatred and unfounded stupidity in the world, there would be precious little need for folks such as himself and Boone.* There would be no need for anyone whose job it was to take on deadly tasks, no need for them to wound and kill fools over the constant quest for money and power.

That was all it really was. And one was interchangeable with the other in this world, that he knew for certain.

The second man to his left had taken cover behind a boulder when Mac shot his companion on the slope. Now he poked out his head and thought perhaps he might be able to make the run where his chum could not.

"Don't do it, fool," whispered Mac. "It won't end well."

But it was the man who had been cutting up on Mac's right side who moved next. He, too, had seen the squealing end of his fellow guard and had also taken refuge behind a low scrag of stunty pine. It was more the ghost of a tree than a tree, but it was enough to keep him hidden from Mac, or so he thought, for a few moments.

The man behind the pine decided on action and dug in his upslope boot, preparing to hurtle himself toward the cover of a boulder about twenty feet above. He made it two feet, his right arm holding a revolver and pinching off cover fire. But it was not aimed fire and it did him no good.

Mac swapped weapons again, snatching up one of the rifles he'd snagged from one of the men he'd shot minutes before. It was a big, beefy weapon and not something any man needed, unless he was hunting large game.

Mac had a flashing picture of a guard who had carried such a weapon, as if it were a daily labor that was going to earn him a pat on the head for extra effort from Kane or Shaky or Reg. It might well have been that man whose braces had been flopping as he came out around the cabin. *No matter,* thought Mac as he leveled on the next fool, the man crouched behind the pine to his right.

The man behind the stunty pine took a shot from Mac right in the knee, a particularly painful spot for anyone to get shot. This one punched in from the right and shattered the leg.

The man happened to be glancing down at that moment, looking to be certain he was going to avoid stepping in a hole he'd seen from below. That was when he saw his right leg bend as if jointed inward at the knee, or where his knee was a moment before.

It was a shocking thing to witness, and within an eyeblink of time, the pain set upon him like a fox on a broken-winged bird. He toppled, collapsing upon the shattered leg joint, grinding sand and scree into the raw wound.

As he rolled off it, screaming and clutching at his leg with both weapon-free hands, his fingers felt the slick, wet surface, and jagged ends of raw bone and shredded meat.

Blood sprayed, and within seconds the man's face and torso, arms and hands, were covered in bright red, slick, hot blood. The stink was immediate and revolting, and the man threw up on himself, screaming all the while. All this happened before Mac's second shot drove into his right shoulder and shut him up.

Mac gritted his teeth and regretted picking up the huge, ungainly weapon. Only an idiot would lug such a thing. It was unbalanced and crude and had made raw meat out of that poor fool's knee, and Mac had been aiming it not at the man's leg but at his chest.

With each shot Mac delivered that day, he knew he was adding another hour of sleep lost for each night of the rest of his life. If he kept on living like this, he would never again know the comforts of a restful, dreamless night. There would be far too many demons swimming in his head, plaguing him forever.

Mac shook off the grim thought and concentrated on the horrors the Chinese immigrants had endured at the hands of Kane and his men. It was enough to keep him raining lead down at the mass of sadistic guards. He only hoped his ammunition would hold out. He had two gun belts studded with shells. He needed to thin that herd of brutes down below and then continue on, up and over the ridgeline behind him, to get to the encampment.

He hoped Boone would be successful in freeing the line workers. There were plenty of them, but Hoke was no doubt up to the task. He knew his pard; Hoke would give it his all, and then some. He'd also die trying, even if there was but one man left to free.

"Hey you, up there!"

It was Reg; Mac would recognize that man's braying voice anywhere. And Reg was not a happy man. Mac smiled.

"Hey, Reg. What can I do for you?"

"You can die!"

Again, Mac smiled, because Reg knew he should have kept his temper in check. But he was unable to do so.

"What's gonna happen, MacCoole, is we're gonna surround you and shoot you plumb full of holes. So you just sit tight and wait for it to happen. That's what you can do for me!"

Mac said nothing but let his silence keep Reg guessing, as if Mac was in deep thought about Reg's proposal. Finally, Mac said, "Nah, I'm good. But I thank you for the kind offer."

Mac glanced around himself. He was in a decent position, with the ridgetop but a few yards behind him. As far as he could tell, no other of Reg's guards were worming their way around him.

The vile man's foul gang was stretched thin and growing wispier by the minute. It was Mac's job to keep them from sneaking up behind him and laying him low before he made his run for it. But every time he moved, someone unseen but definitely from the southwest of his position, fired toward him.

He had to do something, anything. No, no, he told himself. Such thinking only dulled the keen edges of his forming plans.

In the next couple of moments, a fresh-faced fella, likely at Reg's urging, cut even wider than the others had, and scrambled up the scree-riddled slope. He looked young to Mac, perhaps no older than his late teen years.

Mac didn't like to shoot anyone, much less a kid, but he was faced with an impossible choice: shoot the kid or be shot. The decision was a simple one when reduced to such stark terms. Trouble was the kid was cutting upward at the edge of his range. *Had to be a better way to go about this,* thought Mac. But nope, he could think of none.

He ran the tip of his tongue over his chapped, sun-cracked lips and, crouching lower behind the boulder, sighted in the fella's direction. It took him a few protracted moments to get what he hoped was a solid shot lined up. It was a distance shot, so he raised his barrel, and that was when he heard bootsteps sliding on scree coming from behind. They weren't wasting any time.

He touched the trigger and didn't wait to see if his shot was effective. He pivoted and snatched up a revolver he'd laid on the gravel before him. His hiding spot behind the boulder was only good for so long, he knew; then he would be exposed by whoever cut wide enough to gain distance and elevation on him.

He hadn't wasted any time spinning and picking up the other gun, but it might prove too late.

The man who'd come up behind him was no more than thirty feet away and had already stopped and, crouching, was sighting on him.

Mac aimed and squeezed the revolver's trigger. His gun barked and bucked in his big hand. His shot tore low into the man's gut, on his right side, just as the man's shot hit Mac's upper right arm. It peeled away a furrow of flesh and kept on going, into the hillside beyond Mac.

The man Mac had shot in the side did as all such men do—he howled and dropped his weapon and slopped sideways to the earth and spasmed, kicking his legs as if he was trying to remember how to walk while sprawled on his back on the slope. He would not be a further concern.

Mac growled, gnashing his teeth and sending spittle flying as he dropped the revolver and snatched at his right arm up high, close to the shoulder. He felt the wetness of blood seep through his clawed fingers, but he knew, just from feeling the wound, that it was not life-threatening, merely annoying.

It hurt like mad, but he'd received worse gunshot wounds and knew he could use it to keep alert and strive to make certain he didn't let anything like it happen again.

But in order to do that, he needed to get up and over the hilltop, and then he needed to put distance between himself and whoever else Reg had down there, waiting him out. He didn't think there were that many more of them, maybe four or five.

It was enough, but he knew Reg was no fool. He would have sensed something was amiss and might well be else-where in the vast work camp, perhaps at the diggings or along the line.

No, he'd have sent other men to check out those places.

Mac had to go. The sooner he helped free the folks at the encampment, the sooner he could proceed to the next phase of his plan to track down Kane.

He bent low and eyed the distance to his other side, where he'd made the long-range shot. There was the blue shirt of the young man, the young man who was now stretched out facedown on the earth, the graveled slope providing no comfort as he lay dead or dying.

Mac saw a blackness on that blue shirt, along the side nearest him. And he knew it was blood leeching into the cloth. The young man did not move.

Mac bit back another curse and, leaving the heavy rifle behind the boulder, he snatched up the revolver and the rifle, the two guns he had the most ammunition for. And doing his level best to ignore the screaming pain in his right shoulder, he bent low, with his cheek almost grazing the slope, and peered downslope around the base of the boulder.

He saw but one man, Reg, far below, beside the eastern end of the mess tent. Reg's hands were on his hips and he squinted looking up the slope, wondering, hoping, no doubt, that Mac had been wounded or killed in the latest snatch of this melee.

Mac was about to disappoint him. He stood and sent a bullet right down the slope at Reg.

As soon as he saw Mac spring up from behind the boulder like a child's toy, Reg jerked low and hurled himself behind the tent's corner.

Mac didn't much care if he hit Reg or not. He only wanted to buy himself time to scramble up the slope, and he took every advantage of the precious seconds he bought for himself.

He glanced behind himself three times as he switchbacked up the slope as quickly as he was able, given his wounded arm and the weight of the guns. But each time he saw no one, not even Reg way down below, peering up at him.

The lack of eyes on him only made Mac move faster. He crested the ridge and spied down the other side. He spotted no guards but was relieved to see, as he knew he would from his recollection of the terrain, plenty of boulders between him and the twisting lane that would lead him to the stockaded encampment.

Now was no time for slowing down, but he knew he would be fully exposed to anyone who might be trailing him from Reg's side, and though he could see no one ahead, that did not mean there weren't men hiding behind some of the tumbledowns and random boulders spread out below, as if they had been marbles scattered by a giant's hand long ago.

Speculating, he mused as he slid and switchbacked down the slope, was not useful. But forward movement was.

Mac plowed ahead, making for a cluster of rocks that might provide cover, if scant, from above and below.

He reached the spot and slid into a narrow declivity somewhat shaded between boulders.

His only concern in choosing such a temporary refuge was the presence of snakes.

This vile patch of land had been acrawl with them, and he did not relish having an encounter with such a creature.

He wished rattlesnakes no ill will, but neither did he seek them out. He wished they would leave him be and he would do the same.

But he realized that were he a snake and a big, two-footed bumbler such as himself stomped on in to his rocky home, he might well be inclined to sink fang first and quiz the brute later. He hoped for the best and half listened for the telltale sound of rattles and buzzing as he bent low, hopefully low enough not to get his head sniped from afar.

To the southeast, he heard gunfire, and hoped it was Boone winning out over his helping of guards in the only way Boone knew to do—by blasting away at them, a wry grin on his face.

Mac gingerly touched the thudding, throbbing wound, but his fingertips barely grazed the torn and chewed fabric of his chambray shirt before he winced. It was a corker of a wound, a furrow of some depth, he saw, as he lifted the wounded wing and peered at the bleeding mess.

It had happened mere minutes before, so there was no way the bleeding would have slowed, let alone stoppered itself yet. The pain did as he figured, however—it kept him alert, if flinching, at the constant, low-level agony of it.

Blood continued to pour down his arm and drip from his fingertips. He flexed the fingers of his right hand, and the action sent racers of hot pain up and down his arm. They lanced to the wound, then to the fingers, and back again, only to repeat. Yet he was gratified to feel the fingers worked without much more of a hitch.

Now, if he could just get the bleeding to slow and stop. "Time," he muttered. "Give it time, Mac." But he knew he had no time. Everything he still had to do should have been done already. He was operating at a loss, to put it in a business sense.

The sun was merciless, cooking him between the two smooth slabs of rock.

Far ahead, in the direction of the encampment toward which he was headed, he heard gunshots and had no idea what that might mean. His gut tightened at the thought of the innocents taking fire from Shaky or Kane, feeling cornered and desperate, perhaps, to cover any evidence of their obvious wrongs.

Mac wasted no more time there, hidden in the rocks. Keeping low, and with the rifle at the ready. Though holding it as he did pained the wound, he quickly wiped sweat from his eyes and swiveled his head left, right, then up and down the valley. He saw no one. His next bit of cover was a jumble of boulders once again, though smaller than this one. It lay fifty yards northeast, and in line with the trail he needed. He muttered one of Hoke's pet phrases, "In for a penny," and hit it hard, beelining for the boulders.

He was halfway there when a shot sizzled in, clipping his right boot's heel. It sent him sprawling forward, and the rifle flew from his grasp.

He'd barely hit the dusty earth when he was up again on his knees, scrambling forward, lunging, then regaining his feet. No shots dogged him just yet, but he knew they would.

The rifle lay a stride farther. He reached it, and as his fingertips brushed the stock, a second shot slammed the steel side plate and sent the gun spinning from his grasp. He glanced at it as instinct forced him to recoil, and he saw that the rifle was now a spoiled machine, unusable.

He did not try to grab it again but bolted for the cover of the next jumble of rocks, his heart slamming hard inside his chest, rising up his gasping throat. *This was it,* thought Mac. Shot in the back and left to feel his life juices leak out and leech into the dusty, sun-cooked earth of this hellish place.

By the time he reached the boulders, he had begun to think perhaps he might, somehow, for some freakish reason, be allowed to live. Who was shooting? And why hadn't he killed Mac outright when he had the chance?

It was a petrifying game of cat and mouse, and Mac did not like being the mouse. *But,* he thought, *he liked the notion of being dead even less.*

With four feet to go to reach the rock pile, Mac lunged and made it to safety, scrabbling the last few feet to get around the near side of the jumble.

He'd been going along at a steady clip when the shot whistled in. Now, mere seconds later, he was rifle free, exhausted, the slight scrim of dust atop the rock wafting up and over him. He did not care. He was alive; that was the only thing that mattered.

Mac fought hard to suck in a draft of fresh air and reconsider his situation. Here he was, pinned and beside boulders that had spent who knew how long baking away as well.

As if in response to his thoughts, another shot whistled in, buzzing a trough through the air before smacking and spanging off the boulder about a foot above his head.

"Dang it," Mac growled, hating the situation and unable to do a thing about it. Then, to make matters worse, from the southeast, across the narrow old boulder field, a distant but distinct sound of laughter came to him.

Somebody was having a grand old time at his expense. And then the person showed himself. Yes, it was a man, he guessed by the slowly approaching form skylined as he stood atop the ridgeline. Then the man strode down the decline, walking steadily toward the boulder pile Mac crouched behind.

The shooter strode with deliberate ease, a rifle carried low in both hands, before his belly. His laughter, sounding forced, continued to carry toward him.

Mac felt for the revolver, slid it out of the holster, and checked the thing for bullets. He filled it and watched as the man continued his approach.

It was possible this fool didn't know Mac had another weapon.

Mac thumbed back the hammer and waited to see how daring the man was.

When he had walked to within fifty feet, he heard: "MacCoole, you're a mess! MacCoole!" Again, the man laughed.

"That you, Reg? I thought I smelled dung."

The laughter pinched off.

Mac smiled slightly. He knew Reg was a vain man and considered himself a prize catch, particularly where the ladies were concerned. *Insulting him was a pleasure, and in a situation such as this,* thought Mac, thumbing sweat from his eyes, *one must surely take one's pleasures as they came.*

"You best watch yourself, MacCoole. I know you're a wounded man, a cur holed up, run aground, licking its wounds."

"You are right, Reg. I can't argue that. I'm about done in." Mac licked his lips. "In fact, I appear to have lost the use of my right arm . . . and my left heel is shot to hell."

Mac heard boots on gravel resume. "Is that a fact? Well, I will give you this, MacCoole. You're a tough one. I expect half the stories of you and your chum, Boone, are true enough, then."

"Oh? What are they?" asked Mac, doing his best to sound pathetic, wheezy, and ailing. He didn't have much experience in those traits, so it was a stretch. But it worked well enough.

Reg continued walking closer. "Oh, you know, that you and him are big-deal men, good with guns, saving towns, and getting women out of scrapes, all that sort of thing. But everybody has an end, MacCoole. And I expect you've reached yours."

Mac listened as Reg strode closer, slow and steady.

"I see you lost your rifle there, MacCoole." Reg made a clucking sound to indicate the shamefulness of the act. "Not wise for a hunted man to go around all gun free and shot up, now is it?"

He was close. Mac heard the steps gritting closer, closer. Then Reg's shadow inched up over the rocks. Mac continued to look up from his crouched, cramped position. And then there was Reg, leering down at him, not even holding his rifle in any useful pose, so confident of his superior position was he.

His wide, wide smile began to melt downward as he saw, nested in the shaded rocks below him, Mac MacCoole, grinning wide and looking up at him, his revolver aimed square at Reg's face.

"I . . . I . . ."

"Yes, Reg?" said Mac.

Reg jerked backward and tried to raise his rifle. But it was far too late for that.

Mac touched the trigger and the bullet hammered a death-dealing hole into the man's chest. Reg spun and staggered but remained standing as Mac sprang up and worked his hips around the rocks to stand before him.

The surly foreman looked at Mac with wide eyes and lips working soundlessly. A bubble of blood began to grow up and out of his big mouth.

"That was for all the innocent people you've harmed." Mac cocked the revolver.

"And this—" He shot him again, in nearly the same spot.

Reg whipped backward and slammed to the earth, dead as he hit.

"Is for shooting the heel off my boot!"

Mac hobbled over to Reg, noted that the small man had small feet and thus wore boots not worth wasting time trading. But the man did have a big head, and Mac nodded his thanks at the fresh corpse as he settled Reg's black topper on his own sweaty, sunbaked pate.

Next, he stripped Reg's gun belt and revolver from him. It came with a dandy hip knife, for which he was grateful as he almost always went about with a belt blade. Then he snatched up the dead man's rifle and moved onward, leaving Reginald Conley to bake in the sun.

A quick glance around showed him, as before, that nobody was in sight. Mac knew now, more than ever, that this was no guarantee he wouldn't be shot at any moment, but somehow he felt assured he was no longer being eyed from afar.

Where all Reg's men had gone Mac could only guess. He suspected some of them had skedaddled, hightailed it to unknown parts, anywhere away from this smoking, suddenly awful and incriminating slave-trade death ground.

But not all of them. And those were the ones Mac wanted next. The ones who dared to justify their means, the ones who sought to continue this hellish business. All in the name of money and power and greed.

Hobbling on the shot-up boot, Mac hustled as fast as he was able toward that trail that would take him to his next destination. He had a feeling that if Thurston Kane was still about the place, that rascal might be found at his cabin.

CHAPTER 27

"You remember what I told you, chum?" Boone glanced at the Chinaman, and though he received a look back, it was not one that instilled confidence. The man merely smiled. Boone decided a different tact was called for. "You ever shot a gun before?"

"Chan," said the man, still smiling and now nodding. "I call Chan."

"Oh, that's your name? Oh, well, okay, Chan it is, then. I'm Boone." He thumped his chest with a hand. "Boone. Or you can call me Hoke. Name's Hokum; given name anyways. But friends call me Hoke. Or just Boone."

The man's grin slipped and his eyebrows met in the middle.

"Oh, never mind. Call me Boone. That's the one we started with. I guess Mac's right. I talk too much when I'm in a tricky spot. There I go, doing it again. Okay, look, I got to get myself on over there. You understand? Me." He rapped his chest again.

"I'll go there, by them stacks of crossties. You stay here and lay down some covering fire. Not too much! You are shaping up to be a trigger fiend if I ever seen one. That's all well and good, but we'll run out of bullets before long and

I'll have nothing to try to savage those fools with but my folding Barlow."

Boone nodded, as if what he'd said made perfect sense to everyone beyond himself.

Chan stared at him again with that confused look.

"Okay, look, Chan. Me, Boone. I'll run over there. You, Chan." He pointed at each of them in turn. "Stay here." He drilled the point of a finger at the hard earth.

"Cover me while I run." He made as if his fingers were a little man running. "Okay?"

Then his eyebrows rose up and Chan grinned again and nodded. "Yes, I cover you. You run. Yes, yes."

"Excellent. Now we're getting somewhere. Look, I'm counting on you, elsewise my backside will be filled with lead and I'll be dead or dying out well before my dotage, and you'll be to blame, and then I'll have to come back and haunt you, and look, none of that is anything either of us wants, is it?" Boone smiled. Then realized he'd done it again.

Chan's eyebrows began to ascend.

"No, no, never mind. Cover me. Okay?" He nodded. "Cover me. Here I go." Boone tucked low and, glancing left, then right, he bolted for the broad stack of ties. He wished they were stacked a little higher, but four feet tall and six feet wide at the near end would have to do.

He darted forward, keeping the rifle tucked tight to his left side, ready to swing up but not wanting it to be an impediment. He wasn't lame all over from the beatings he received at the hands of the guards, but he was darn sure close.

A bullet drilled dirt tight behind his right heel, forcing a yelp from his mouth and a sneer to form on his lips. He did not want a foot wound. Or any wound, to be sure, but a foot wound would put a hitch in his gait that would never heal properly. He'd seen it before.

As Boone lunged, ignoring the hot, tearing pain of forcing himself to bolt hell-for-leather for those stacked crossties, the face came to him of an old-timer he'd seen all footshot and limpy for the rest of his days. That had been in the war.

Oddly, though, the old gent had sustained that crippling wound years and years before the war. He told Boone at the cookfire one night, when they were encamped outside of Gatlinburg, that he'd been shot by a jealous husband.

The old gent swore he wasn't the one who cuckolded the irate fellow. "But," the old guy said, "you try to tell a jealous husband such a thing, see how far it will carry you in conversation with the man. Bah!" He leaned forward and rubbed his foot.

The old man was seated cross-legged before the fire, his soiled wool socks looking like everyone else's in those days. He grimaced and groaned a little as he rubbed his sore feet.

The right foot was shot by that crazy, jealous husband as the old man was running from certain doom. Boone presumed, despite the old man's protestations, he'd been caught in the arms, or bosom, as he'd winked and all but admitted, of a buxom thing with red hair and a wide, inviting smile.

But that husband shot at him with the first weapon he could lay his hands on, a small-caliber rifle. The first shot sliced a clean nick in his left ear lobe. The old man lifted his straggly, scraggly matt of hanging gray hair, and sure enough, a neat gouge, as if his lobe had been bitten through by a tiny critter, hung there.

The next shot hit him in the heel and drove him face-first in the dirt.

This little episode came to Boone as he dove for cover. He cursed himself for not being in better condition. Was a time, he regretted thinking, when he could really give it heck and run with the best of them.

Why, he even outraced a bull grizz once. Course, it might

have had something to do with the fact that the critter got waylaid by the rank stink of a mangled, greening mountain sheep corpse.

It likely had gotten caught in the thundering spring river some ways upstream, then not been able to swim itself to safety on a riverbank, gotten carried downstream and been battered senseless on the rocks until it tumbled over the rapids and ended up legs akimbo, waiting for the grizz to thunder on by.

As Boone hoofed it past the dead thing, he'd muttered a word of thanks and regret, not in that order, and kept on running.

But those days of fleet-footedness were mostly gone. No matter, he told himself, gritting his teeth and rallying for the cause. In moments, he collapsed behind the stack of ties, leaning tight to it and sucking in breath he hadn't realized he'd held on the short but eventful run over.

Boone hoped Mac was able to tend to the folks in the encampment. At least get them to understand that he was there to help them, to get them on out of there. What they were going to do if they succeeded was another matter, one that neither Mac nor Boone knew how to wrangle.

There were dozens—several dozen, maybe more—Chinese folks who were, with each passing moment, becoming more worn down and losing what meager hope they held on to.

A fresh volley of gunshots peppered down at Boone, dancing like hot rain on the timber stack. "Hey!" growled Boone, showing his teeth.

He didn't think his shouts would alter much, but it felt good to let those demons know he wasn't someone to trifle with. He angled himself this way, then that, and finally, through a long, narrow gap in the logs, got a solid look at a guard, staring to his own left and right. And the fool had no clue Boone was watching him.

He could have picked him off, too; the distance did not pose a problem. But it was too much like shooting a sitting bird. No sport and no class, as his pap used to say. Still, life was life, and that evil guard would take his if given the chance. Heck, he might even be the one who tried to heel-shoot him.

Boone lined up and squeezed the trigger. Rock shattered, and a man screamed and howled and yowled and rolled around on the ground like he'd been hit, but Boone knew his shot was off.

Maybe he'd pulled it at the last sliver of a moment. But what his shot did do was drive hard into the rock face the man was hiding behind, sending outward a thousand tiny splinters of pain-inducing shards.

The man was really in a bad way, as Boone could see, because he'd thrown his rifle down and was still rolling on the ground, though his initial howls had abated. Instead, he was on one knee, holding his face in both hands as blood leeched between his fingers.

A man close by, looking flustered and uncertain what to do, looked left and right, then dashed from the cover of his boulder and made it over to the yowler.

He shouted, "Knock it off!" and with a free hand yanked on the bleeding man's right hand. He succeeded in pulling it away from the man's face for a moment, and through the gap in the timbers, Boone saw that mostly the man's cheeks had been severely peppered by rock shards.

"Good," he muttered, and lined up to deliver another dose to the newcomer. Anything to keep them out of the action and licking their wounds instead.

He squeezed the trigger just as the man shifted position. Boone was aiming for the man's calf, a meaty place to wound a fella but, with proper treatment, not a wound he'd die easily from.

But as the man shifted, he scooched his leg to his left,

shifting it enough that Boone's bullet drove straight into his kneecap. Boone winced as the man screamed and whipped backward, sprawling flat and howling holy terror into the blue sky.

He'd whacked his own kneecaps often enough over the years on rocks and such and knew it was a bad injury. Kneecap wounds didn't mend well, and were among the most painful a fella can endure. At best, if he survived the day's fighting, the man was going to be a limpy gimp.

Boone pulled on his matter-of-fact demeanor about it. "You sleep with dogs, you wake up with fleas," he muttered, another of his pap's choice phrases he'd grown up with.

"Hey, hey, Hokey Boom!"

It was Chan.

Boone was tempted to correct him on the hash he'd made of his name, but he dropped the notion once he saw what Chan was up to.

"I come!"

No sooner had the skinny, smiling, black-haired man said it than he ducked his head low, mimicking Boone's pose and, still clutching the rifle low but angled across his gaunt belly, he trotted toward Boone.

"No, no!"

The man ignored him and pounded closer, his worn sandals clip-clapping his progress and plumes of dust from bullets pocking all about him as he jackrabbited the whole way over to the timber pile.

As the little man came up beside him, panting, Boone reached for him and snatched a handful of his ragged shirt and yanked him closer. The shirt ripped clear down the front, but Boone's move succeeded in dragging Chan closer, getting his trailing leg out of the line of fire.

As if to seal the deal, another bullet ripped in low, furrowing a couple of inches away from Chan's leg. Wide-eyed, he pulled himself into an even tighter ball and hugged his knees up close to his chin, the rifle still held before him.

It was, Boone lamented, eyeing the sad state of affairs that was Chan, no way to defend oneself.

"Look, Chan," said Boone, glancing about on all sides, barely looking at his new companion. "If you're going to be of any use to me or to yourself, you have to tighten up. You hear me?"

Chan squinted and craned his head forward, as if he was hard of hearing. Boone realized the man's grasp of the English language was tricky at best.

But then again, he mused, his grasp of the Chinese language was nonexistent, so he had to give the man credit here. And even more for trying to learn as he went. That was the mark of courage, of someone not afraid to fall in the mud and get up and do it again.

"Well, never mind about all that just now, little pal," said Boone, trying to force a smile. "We have got to make it to that cache of, well, whatever it is they got cached in there, you *comprende*?"

Boone realized the man was still studying him, so he said, "Never mind that, too. Now, just stick close by me. That you have to understand. Or you're breathing your last, and that's not a thought to take lightly."

"Okay, Hokey!" The man nodded, smiling and whispering his response.

Another thing came to Boone, then. He turned back to Chan. "By cache, I mean that little building over there. You see it? They got something in there they don't want anyone else to have at. The guards come and go from there now and again, but I don't see them leave with weapons or much else.

"I expect it's where they keep smaller construction goods that might well walk off if they was left out. Or else items that can't be left to the weather."

But Boone was hoping the cache would contain his

favorite small yet eminently useful item in all the world, widow-making boom sticks. Dynamite.

In the war, he was a munitions expert. Mostly because the fella he trained under got himself blown up. Or rather blew himself up. Boone had taken care to learn all he could from the man who was, by most accounts, one heck of an explosives operative. Until he wasn't.

The trouble came when he got a little sloppy and mixed his off-hours boozing with his on-hours blasting. He exploded, and Boone learned one of the most valuable and shocking lessons of his life.

But in his time working under the man, he also learned to love the wonders of dynamite and of making big things become smaller things with but a single stick, a short fuse, and a match. The thought still made Boone a little giddy.

"Okay, while those two over there are moaning and whining, it'll be the same thing as last time. You understand? You cover me. That direction back there, behind where we come from, that's where there's still a single man shooting, got me?"

Surprisingly, Chan looked filled with the seriousness of the situation. Finally. He nodded a grave face at Boone, then pointed, holding his grubby, callused finger close by his face. "Shooting man there. I keep him busy. You run."

"To the cache, then."

"Cache, yes." Chan nodded, offered Boone a quick smile. "Okay."

"Good. Then, when I get there, you come along and I'll cover you. Got me?"

"Yes." Another nod. "You cover me. Good. Okay."

Boone nodded once himself, then, glancing in as many directions as he could, he held his rifle up and dashed for the little shanty with the closed door. It was built partially into the slope of a graveled hillside. And it hadn't been built long before, because the lumber still smelled of fresh-sawn wood and it curled and popped but was still light colored, not yet pocked and puckered and lined with cracks.

It was perhaps as big at the base as a couple of work wagons, and tall enough that an average-height man wouldn't bean himself walking in. *Mac would have trouble with that door,* thought Boone. But then again, Mac had trouble with every door. Even with his hat off. The galoot was just too big.

One, two gunshots dogged Boone's heels, and another that surprised him came whistling in from ahead, to his right, beyond the cache.

Well, now, that's interesting, he thought as he reached the side of the building and piled up with his back to the planking. He'd made certain there weren't any gaps in the wall through which he might be seen should anyone be in the shack. He didn't think there was anyone in there, but what did he know?

Turned out it was double planked, so there were no such gaps. But he wasn't going to sit here all day and take his chances that someone would pick him off anyway.

"Chan!"

The little man poked his head around, and Boone realized that though the man wanted to be useful, he really wasn't. He couldn't recall hearing Chan lay down any covering shots on this run or the last. *Ah, well,* thought Boone. *I made it, so what's the difference?*

"Let's go!" he shouted.

Chan didn't need any more prompting. With those damnable sandals clip-clopping beneath him, the man tucked into his low, awkward pose and dashed straight for Boone.

Boone half stood and threw lead up the berm behind where they'd been, below, but hidden by the timbers. He thought maybe he heard a yelp or a curse, but he couldn't be certain. He'd let loose two shots, aware that he didn't have an unlimited supply of cartridges.

Chan made it, but not before a shot zipped in from above them, from southeastward. That was a direction from on high that Boone hadn't expected to receive attention from. He spun, saw a fella skylined atop a jag of stone about thirty yards up the escarpment.

He trusted his canny knack for doling out accurate shots in tense situations, a skill honed in the hills around Hoddy's Gulch as a youngster, and further polished during the war, then refined in the ensuing years dealing with all manner of miscreants whilst on the trail with Mac.

He touched the trigger of the strange-to-him rifle and heard a yelp. A second later, the man above, who'd drawn back in time with the yelp, roved forward, farther, farther, then pitched, crumpling slowly, and dropped headfirst—it looked to Boone as if the poor fool fell—gripping his chest. His hat slipped from his head and sailed down in a much gentler fashion than did its owner.

His rifle slipped from his grasp as if time had slowed, and it clattered, beating him down the same trail, the last he'd ever take.

About a dozen feet below from where he began his descent, the man, still wailing, slammed headfirst onto a jutting ledge of stone. His head cracked like a smacked egg and blew apart at the sides, but held together enough that most of him continued his flopping drop to the graveled slope below.

"Good Lord," muttered Boone as he watched the man drop, then slop to a rolling stop.

The fallen man's head was a misshapen red clot of blood, bone, hair, and skin.

"If the shot didn't do the trick, the fall did." Then Boone shook himself free of the oddness of the moment and jerked Chan down to a squatting position. "We got to get in there." He nodded at the building they were hunkered beside. "Cover me. And this time, shoot your fool gun to do it!"

"Yes!" Chan smiled. "Cover you, okay!"

"Right," said Boone, feeling less confident with each passing second of his new pard's ability to comprehend what he was saying.

He eyed the spot before the building, the mixed terrain of it, part of which they had beelined from, and decided to risk the ten feet or so to get to the front door of the little building.

"Cover me now, Chan!" he growled, and with his rifle poised to shoot, he scrambled low around the front of the shack and made it to the door.

Boone reached up, knowing it was going to be locked, because why on earth would it be otherwise? Yet he was shocked into momentary stillness when the thumb latch showed no resistance.

Of course it wouldn't, he told himself, fool! It was a thumb latch. And as such, it was likely only to be locked from the inside. Which meant it was likely occupied, he thought. He shoved the door open, hunching so low he was almost belly to the ground; then he scrambled in. If there was someone inside, they weren't worried about folks coming in. Or they were dead. Or stupid. Or . . .

He whipped to one side and looked around. Or not there at all.

He took in the interior with a glance that worked from right to left. It was small, but one space, and stacked with crates. Crates with his favorite word on them—"Dynamite," he said, smiling and chuckling. *Hoo boy, it's like every good and special thing a child yearns for has come all at once and landed in his lap, eh, Hokum Boone? And I am that happy child!*

"Huh?"

Boone's gleeful smile froze on his face. Someone was in there, far in the back. He leaned forward and looked, back there, in the dark and shadows. But the half-open door emitted the only light available. It was not like they were going to encourage folks to strike a match and light up a lantern in here, now, was it?

"Who's there, now?"

"Huh?"

The voice said the same thing, and then whoever said it rustled and scuffed at the plank floor with a boot, then another.

"What's going on there?" said the voice.

Boone held the rifle up, stock to cheek, ready to fire. Wouldn't be long before someone out there saw the door to this munitions shed cracked open and crept up on him.

Still, Boone felt oddly safe, considering he was in a small structure with what looked to be enough explosive material to shred him six times over and have bits and pieces enough to put aside for another go.

The thought made Boone shudder. "Hey now, yourself, there!" He hoped he was addressing an unarmed drunk sleeping off a binge, cowering in the far back darkness of the shed.

He advanced, after giving the doorway one more glance. He hoped Chan was okay. He didn't hear a single shot. But he couldn't turn his back on whoever might be back there in the dark. He'd tend to Chan in a moment.

Boone advanced, then halfway into the depths of the shed, he cut to the left side of the space, and using crates to hide behind, he advanced slower, peering ahead as much as he was able.

The person in the back sounded as if he was just waking up. He was making all the noises men make after a nap— smacking his tongue and lips, yawning and stretching from the sound of it. And then it sounded as if he was doing one of those shakes after rubbing his face with his hands.

Boone's eyebrows rose. "Who's back there anyway?" He tried to sound as if he had plenty of right to be in there, not a smidge of which did he feel.

"Who do you think's back here, man? That you, Smitty?"

"Uh . . . yeah, yeah . . . man."

"Okay. Your turn, I guess?"

"Uh . . ." said Boone again, eyes wide. He had no idea what was happening, but it sounded odd. "Sure, yeah."

"Gimme a minute. Half dressed back here."

Boone's eyes stayed wide. What all was happening in here? And then clunking noises sounded from the dark corner in the back and a shape emerged, standing up and moving slowly forward, still in shadow but becoming clearer as it drew nearer.

"Man, I don't know what it is, but I sleep better in here than I do in my own cot. I was out like someone hit me with a hammer."

"You mean you slept through all that gunfire?" Boone said this before he realized the man wasn't someone he should be conversing with. Luckily, he still held up his rifle.

The man said, "Gunfire?" Then he took another step forward, but slower, and paused. He was half in the light now, and he was on the big side, with shaggy hair and beard. Boone recognized him as one of the guards, a large fellow, wide of shoulder and big of hand, hard to miss. He was also tucking in his shirt and tidying himself up.

"Who in the heck are you?" said the big fella.

"'Bout to ask you the same," said Boone, not wavering with his rifle. About six feet separated them. "You raise them hands up to your ears and hold them there or I'll pop you one. Got it?"

"Uh, yeah." The man did as he was bade. "I was just taking a nap. Hot in here, but at least it's shady. You know, no harm done. Cut my pay if you want to. No harm done."

"Hmm," said Boone, rolling with it. "I don't know about that, see? Mr. Kane, he's a stickler for keeping things moving, for paying men only when they work. If he finds he's being cheated, why, he's liable to make sure you're . . ."

"What? Oh no, what's he gonna do to me?"

For a big fella, thought Boone, *he sure turned into a whining little thing at the hint of a threat.*

"Well, I'll tell you. He might not take it kindly to know he was being robbed by the very men he put his trust in."

"Oh, look, I didn't mean no harm. The others, they do it, too. Hawkins and Jonesy, Clapper and that Polish fella, too. A bunch of us! Ain't just me!"

"Hmm. I need some time to think on this. Meantime, you get on over to that corner there. By the door, that's it, and keep them hands high. Where's your gun?"

"I left it over there. Behind you in that other corner by the door."

"Okay, I see it. Now, you stand in that corner like a good boy and I won't be a minute."

This was annoying. He'd been growing used to the notion that he had the room to himself, could pilfer a few sticks and then see what was what. Now he had to tend to this big goober. And Chan . . .

He leaned close to the door. "Chan! Get in here! Chan!"

Presently, that clip-clapping sound drew up, and the little man poked his head in through the half-open door. "Yes, Hokey Boom?"

"Look, that ain't my name—aw, get in here before you get shot!"

"Hey!" said the big man, looking over his right shoulder at them. "What's going on here?"

"I thought I told you to stand with your sniffer in the corner!"

"I recognize you now," said the big man. "You're one of those troublemakers Shaky warned us about!"

"Don't believe everything you're told in life, son, and you'll be all the better for it. Otherwise, this here's what you'll get!" Boone smacked the side of the big man's curly head with the gun butt. He aimed for the spot above the ear, where a solid blow will often fell a man like a sack of wet cornmeal.

This one proved no different. At first.

The big man slopped downward, his knees banging the floor planks first, then he flopped sideways. But he was still yammering, making odd sounds that weren't words.

I either hit him too hard and addled him up good or I didn't whack him hard enough! Boone shrugged. *Nothing for it.* He drew back and delivered another hit to the big man's bean. That one did the trick. Boone didn't know if the fool was dead or knocked cold. But one thing was for certain—if he was playing possum, he was a damn fine actor.

"Okay, now, Chan. Look, get away from that open door, man! Okay, now open up one of them crates. No, on second thought, you stand here, see?"

Chan nodded, smiling.

"You are the oddest fella, all happy and whatnot. Okay, now stand guard."

"Chan no like guards."

"No, no, I reckon not. Okay, then, be watchful."

The Chinaman squinted at him and shook his head.

Boone sighed. "Don't let anyone in."

"Ah! Okay, okay." Chan turned and faced the doorway, the rifle held out as if he just might know how to use the thing. Boone had his doubts, and as he rummaged in the crates, he kept a watchful eye on the door, just in case.

He was soon rewarded with what he hoped to find, laid in neat rows like waiting soldiers, slumbering, *not unlike the big dolt on the floor,* thought Boone, brown-paper-wrapped cylinders thicker than a man's thumb. Little beauties waiting for him, and him alone.

He wanted to lug off every single one of the two dozen crates. Just to have, because a fella rarely came upon such a horde. But he was limited as to what he could stuff in his tunic. Luckily, his buckskin shirt was cinched in the middle and had ample room in there.

He began stuffing in the lengths of dynamite. "Hell." He giggled, glancing at Chan and the door. "If a fat man can carry around all that extra weight, what's to stop little ol' Boone from lugging a few choice pounds, huh? Heck sight easier to get rid of than fat!" He followed up with a handful of coils of wick.

"What you do?" Chan nodded toward Boone's wondrous stash.

Boone smiled. "Anything I want to, now." He nodded toward the rifle in the corner behind Chan. "Grab that and come on. We have to get on out of here and make things go boom!"

He chuckled and bolted for the door, ducked low, peered out in both directions, and said, "Follow me close, Chan. And no lollygagging!"

"No! No gag!" Chan clung close to Boone, and they made for the left edge of the broad lay-down yard. Boone's plan was to switchback a route over to the low ridge to their southwest. From there, they could hopefully evade most of the scattered guards roving the entirety of the worksite.

He and Mac and the freed slaves had caused a slow, spreading ruckus, and whoever was not one of them was their enemy and had good cause, at least in their own stunty vision, to dole out a hatful of hurt on him and Chan.

Boone catwalked low and made for the nearest large thing behind which they might hide and gather themselves for the final push over the ridge. A sloppy mound of boulders and unearthed rubble gave way to a heap of snapped timbers and busted machinery—wagon axles, wheels, and a festering carcass on the far end of a bone-rack ox that couldn't keep up any longer.

"Poor beast," said Boone once they'd made it to the far

side of the rubble mound, not five yards from the rank, dead brute.

Chan couldn't seem to take his eyes from it. Finally, he said, "I know him. So sad." He shook his head. "So sad."

"Can't disagree with you, Chan. These savages have no kindness in their hearts if they do that to an innocent beast. But look." Boone swiveled his gaze in as many directions as he could. "We might have gotten lucky trotting over here. But it's a longer run to that ridge." He pointed behind them. "You see that? We're going there next. Up and over, to safety on the other side. Got me?"

"Up and over!" said Chan, his lost smile suddenly reappearing.

"Good. Okay now. We go together. Hand me that spare rifle. I'll lug it. You got all you can do to hold that other one and run at the same time. But needs must, as an old fella from England once told me."

Boone was proud of himself for recalling that phrase, though he couldn't place the man's face any longer. He sighed. "Make it speedy, Chan."

Again, the Chinaman looked confused.

"Oh for heaven's sake, stick close to me. Here, now!" And without further chatter, Boone bent low and joggling and jiggling the tunic full of sticks of dynamite, he ran low and fast, lugging a rifle in each hand.

He heard Chan's sandals flapping close behind. As he bolted, he looked left and right and prayed nobody behind them would send a shot their way.

None did, and they made it to the base of the ridge. He immediately began switchbacking on up the face of the graveled slope, knowing Chan would have trouble doing the same with that lousy footwear he had. But there was nothing for it.

Halfway up, as he cut to his left to begin ascending the

next-to-last run up the side of the ridge, a bullet sizzled in, pocking low and kicking up dust.

Whoever sent it had just noticed them, he thought, *and was testing the range.* He'd raise the barrel a bit and dole out another shot any second. And at that distance, they'd feel it before they heard it.

Sure enough, a second shot punched dirt about six feet before Boone. He jerked right and kept churning. "You with me, Chan?"

He did not hear the clip-clapping of those sandals, so he turned his head and saw his companion had halted and was aiming his rifle across the way, toward the far side of the natural bowl rimming the work area from which they'd just emerged. "Chan! Get up here! You'll get shot, sure as I'm a Boone!"

But the skinny, grimy little Chinaman held his ground and held that rifle, too, as though he were a marksman. He looked to be testing windage and eyeing the range. And then he touched the trigger, and an eyeblink later, Boone saw a low, dark shape jerk upward—a man who'd been crouching.

Chan had drilled the son of a gun. Not a killing shot, at least not right away, because the rascal was up on his knees, flailing his arms as if he were imitating a tree in a windstorm. Then he pitched backward and out of sight.

The little man wasted no time but spun and, smiling, made straight up the berm for Boone. Boone collected his shocked wits and resumed his trek. They were nearly there when another shot sizzled in, this time from west of them. Boone glanced that way and saw a man on horseback thundering toward them.

Without pausing to aim, Boone jerked a shot in the man's direction. Of course it did nothing but kick up dirt yards before the man, but it might have bought them a second or two.

He scampered up and over the top of the ridge, with Chan close behind.

Boone saw no one on the other side, but it was a jagged place of massive boulders and trails cut in, arroyos and gullies veining the scene below them, some man-made, some worn by time and storms.

He was set to tug Chan down and out of sight beside him, but Chan was at it again, sighting that rifle toward the rider. Boone heard the horse's hooves pounding on the hardpan, and he squinted, looking down that way. He could ready a stick and lob it down, but man, he hated to kill a horse if he didn't need to.

Within seconds, Chan made the decision a moot point because he repeated his shot. Boone saw it catch the rider square in the throat, jerking the man backward off and out of the saddle.

His rifle flew up, arced high as it left his upflung arm. The other had snatched at his shot throat. Turned out he hadn't left the saddle entirely. His left boot was snagged in the stirrup and the horse, harried by the shots and the commotion on its back, tore hell-for-leather on down the length of the narrow work valley below them.

The rider looked to be dead, but if the shot hadn't done the job, the beating he took from the scrambling horse would have. The man's leg slammed and whipped until Boone was certain it was going to rip clean off the fella's body.

The rest of him had jounced right up and over the saddle and now slammed and slopped with each thundering lurch the horse took. The man whopped against the hard-packed earth. In between those intermittent slams, the body turned this way and that, his head whanging off boulders and his arms looking as if he was trying to grab the earth as he thundered over it.

Boone knew the man was no longer among the living. He was a hoof-stomped, dirt-smacked brute with a blood-smeared neck and head. It was not a pretty sight. Fortunately, the horse passed by beneath them and slowed up only when it came close to the front of the little dynamite shack.

It kept galloping, but slower, nearing the stone-faced end of the work valley. At that end there was nowhere to go but back the way it came. Or up either side, scrambling and digging. But it did not do that. It slowed and slowed, dragging the sad mess that was the guard who had shot at them.

"Oh, so sad," said Chan, his mouth covered with a grubby hand.

"Don't worry," said Boone. "He'd have done the same to us. Damn fine shooting, son. Where did you learn the trade?"

Chan smiled and kept eyeing the terrain below. "My father teach me. Before we come here he say, 'Chan, that place crazy. You shoot men before they shoot you.'" He nodded, as if that said it all.

Boone returned the nod. "Right smart fella is your pap. I had me one of them myself. Something about a father to keep a fella on the good foot. Now, we got to get on down there and—" Boone had shifted and looked downslope behind them.

He saw a cluster of men: six, all armed and on foot and making their way up toward them. They hadn't yet seen Boone had caught sight of them, but it was obvious they were beginning to spread out and were bent on reaching Boone and Chan in silence. Boone poked Chan and nodded toward the men. Chan shifted and made to shoulder the rifle.

Boone stopped him. "Not this time," he whispered. "Too many."

"What we do?"

Boone grinned and touched the side of his nose. Chan gave him the confused look and shrugged.

Boone reached into his tunic and slid out a stick. He handed it to Chan, then freed his Barlow folder and quick as a wink sliced off a short length of wick and readied the stick. Then he thumbed a match he'd freed from another nest in his tunic and set it to the end of the wick. For a fraction of a second he grinned at it, and his eyes reflected the dancing, dazzling sight of the sparking, hissing wick. It had been a long time since he'd had the pleasure, and Boone savored the brief, sparking moment like a child savors the luscious taste of a boiled sweet.

Then he winked at Chan and lobbed the stick hard down the slope and to the left, toward the skulking, secretive group of killers.

It hit, and for a moment Boone thought all was lost. His eyes widened and then his growing look of dismay gave way to a broad smile. Screams trailed the resounding boom as shards of rock and boulders whipped every which way. A number of them hit Boone and Chan, and both men groaned and gasped, but they were alive.

As the dust cleared, they saw the remnants of the sneaking patrol as wounded men twitched and flailed on the rubble-strewn embankment. Others lay unmoving, their limbs bent in odd poses.

It was not a sight for the weak, but Boone was impressed that the one stick should render such a satisfying result. "Good batch, that," he said, patting his tunic. He was pleased and relieved to note that he had plenty more where that one came from.

The only downside of the event was that the sound might well attract other of Shaky's men, wondering who all was using dynamite when they were supposed to be stalking a handful of troublemakers.

"Come on, Chan," said Boone. "We got to make tracks while we can." He half slid down the ridge side, scree scattering below them. They traversed just below the ridgetop and made eastward. When they had ventured beyond the range of the dynamited spot and its gruesome remnants, Boone cut downslope.

"We're headed for that winding roadway there." He nodded dead ahead to a trail that looked well used and would lead them up over the other side of the next ridgeline. It petered out to the southwest, but he was not headed that way.

He had in mind to round up and come back on the encampment from the east, roughly the way he and Mac had when they rode in that day, when had it been? Less than a week before? Seemed like a lifetime and a half ago.

"Horses!" said Chan, just to his right. He pointed ahead, and as they neared a tumbledown of boulders, sure enough, a gaggle of horses, all tethered together, came into view.

Boone grinned. "We're riding with lady luck now, my friend!" He inspected the horses and chose two that looked to be solid and the least likely to spook.

The pair he selected were the only ones in the group to stand their ground and not fidget when he approached. He made certain not to leave any part of his body in close proximity to the mouths of the strange horses, however, no matter how calm they seemed. He'd been gnawed on by plenty of horses, and he never came away feeling as though the bites and nips were of use to him.

He mounted up on one and then looked over at Chan, who stood looking up at him. "What's the matter?" And then he knew. "You ever rode before, Chan?"

The man looked at the horse, then at the earth, and shook his head.

"Aw, now, that's nothing to be shamed over. I could tell you stories of the greenhorns I've seen who never admitted such a thing, and then my word, what a mockery they made of the situation. Here now." Boone slid out of the saddle.

He tugged the reins of his chosen mount and walked on

over to Chan, who still held his horse's reins and looked sheepish. "Okay, then, come over to this side of the horse. Always this side, unless you're in a situation where you need to make a quick escape!" He winked.

"Now, hoist that foot, no, the other one. Yep, your left, on up there to the stirrup and . . . man, we have to get you some other footwear. Those things'll trip you up before long, I don't doubt. You need moccasins. Finest sheaths you can ever cover your foot with. Good enough for my Indian friends, good enough for this sorry fellow." He thumbed his chest.

"Okay, now grab that thing there. It's the saddle horn, and pull, pull, and bounce yourself up into the saddle. You see?"

They dallied a few more moments, then Boone said, "Okay, now grab tight, and don't worry about that rifle. I'll deal with it. Okay, see? That's a scabbard for the gun. Slide it in there and don't worry about it. Now, we got to make tracks, Chan. Hang tight, hug the horse with your knees, and stick close. And if you get in trouble, just yelp and I'll help."

Boone mounted up again, and at first they made slow progress, winding up that narrow trail. But Chan was a quick study, and they were able to cover more ground quicker. Soon they were nearing the rise.

"Okay, we're out of cover of most of those lucky boulders down below. We have to keep a sharp eye and we don't want to linger at the top. We'll be skylined by some rascal with a fair eye and a good aim. Up and over, let's go!"

They made the last push fast, and as Boone glanced back, he saw Chan barely hanging on. He didn't dare slow their progress, though. Time for that once they were over. They crested the ridge and had no choice but to follow the trail several yards north, then south along the ridgetop until it cut eastward, switchbacking down the far side in the direction Boone wanted to go.

But the thing he saw below chilled him, and he halted, holding up his hand. Chan halted just behind. Boone didn't have to explain to the man why they had stopped. Both gazed down below, right where they wanted to ride, and saw something they did not want to see.

Three white men on horseback had their guns drawn, revolvers all, and had surrounded a handful of other folks, five from the looks of it, standing below them, their hands held up in the air.

"Oh no!" said Chan. And the wind, a slight breeze, was enough to carry that quick oath of surprise down the slope to the group. One, then two of the men shifted their gaze. And then one of them shouted and pointed upslope at Boone and Chan.

Boone raised a rifle and waved. "Hey! Got another one!"

The man down below who had pointed now waved his revolver high, as if in greeting. Boone took that as a good sign they were buying the ruse. It would only work for a short spell, though, because he figured they would soon recognize him.

He turned and aimed the rifle at Chan. "Chan, you play along with this. I'm going to make like you are my prisoner. Savvy?"

Chan's eyes were wide, then he nodded and smiled. "Ah, okay, Hokey Boom. You trick them!"

"Yep, that's about it. Now, you got to ride ahead of me. Follow the trail. That's it, and pretend to look sad and defeated. When we get close, I'm going to see about opening up on these fellows. Okay?"

Chan shrugged and nodded.

Boone took that to mean the man was in on the idea, and they proceeded, limited in their descent. "And remind me to tell you my real name later. I can't have Mac calling me Hokey Boom. That won't do."

The entire ride down the trail, Boone kept an eye on the

group below. They didn't shift their stances much, but he could tell he was being watched by at least two of the three men.

The closer they rode, the better he could see them, and he recognized the ones on horseback as guards. The ones standing on the ground he now saw were women. And then his heart sank.

They looked an awful lot like the ones he and Mac had saved from the slavers a few days before. So they hadn't stayed put like they'd told them to. Or else they'd been found. Either way, it didn't look like a good situation for them.

"Don't get too fidgety, Chan. I'm going to try to stay hidden behind you for as long as I can, then I'm going to give those three a blistering."

"Okay, Hokey Boom. I trust."

"Good. Good. When it's safe, you can shuck your rifle and make certain nobody else is coming around." *This would be tricky,* thought Boone. But not impossible. After all, he had two rifles and two arms.

They were able to ride down the slope, with Boone keeping tight behind Chan on three switchbacks. When they were roughly twenty yards from the group, Boone was able to see that the women were indeed the ones he and Mac had saved, no guessing there.

But they didn't appear to be harmed, yet. He also saw that the men were alternately peering up at him and Chan, and doubt was fixing itself on their features.

"Any second now, Chan. When I say so, you lean to your right, got me?"

"Yes, yes!" whispered Chan.

"Good. Hold. Hold . . ."

They rode down, down, and just as they leveled out after the last switchback but were still slightly higher in elevation than the group, it was just what Boone wanted. One, two steps more. "Okay, Chan!"

The Chinaman ducked down to his right side and at the same time scrabbled a free left hand at the rifle in the boot.

Boone sat stiff and upright, tugging the rifle to his shoulder, and leveled on the pointing man, the farthest of the three. All three riders had looked up by then, square at Boone and Chan, and there was no mistaking the shock, then the anger on their faces. All three swung their revolvers at Boone and Chan.

Boone took that as a sign of hostility, just what he needed to justify blazing away at the trio, and he sent a bullet at the first one.

It caught the man in the meat between his upper arm and his neck, just below the left shoulder. He squealed and jerked, falling to his left out of the saddle.

Boone cranked and leveled on the second just as two bullets whistled at him. One sizzled on by and the other slapped into the horse's flank. He felt the beast shiver and quiver.

One thing he hated was a man who shot a critter. It gave Boone even more reason, not that he felt he needed any more, to dispatch the three.

He sent his second bullet square into the middle rider's chest. The man's hands whipped upright, as if he had just found salvation at a tent revival.

To Boone's right, he sensed more than saw Chan had pulled the rifle from the boot and had it ready to go.

That left the third man, but that one was wilier, and he slid down out of his saddle and snatched at the nearest of the women, who had all tucked low and were scattering like frightened ducklings.

He nearly missed her but managed to snag her braided hair with a clawing free hand and jerked her to him, jamming the revolver into her cheek. She, like the other women, did not utter a sound, and showed, as the others, her only emotion—fear—through her wide eyes.

She was breathing hard and the man held her hair tight, pressing his face, leering and red with rage, tight to hers as he peered around his living shield.

"You coward!" growled Boone, not moving his own cheek from where he had it snugged to the stock of his rifle.

"Coward or not, you best drop that gun. Both of you! Or this fool woman will get a dose in the head. You hear me?"

The next couple of seconds were tense, with Boone squinting through drops of sweat running down his face. He felt the sun pucker his head and knew he'd have sunburn all over his head and ears and cheeks and neck. It would hurt and then itch.

But if he didn't do something soon, he would never have to worry about that because that man would shoot that woman and then he'd shoot them.

Boone hated stand-off situations such as this. He'd been in a few, and each had ended in no way he could have predicted. But he did recall Mac saying the obvious to one such fellow one time, when the rascal had held a gun to an old man's head.

"You go ahead and shoot him. Because as close as you are, that bullet will do you some damage, too. Not to mention getting all that blood and bone on your face."

"And while you are sputtering and trying to get away from the mess you've created, we'll gladly shoot you dead. Really, you have nothing to lose. So, go ahead. Be our pleasure to help you out in such a way, wouldn't it, Hoke?"

Boone recalled that situation, not but three years prior, in Illinois or Missouri or some such. He could never remember where all they were and when.

Mac, on the other hand, was a fellow with a mind for recalling useless details such as that.

Boone hoped Mac was making out fine with his half of the operation.

He squinched one eye closed, then opened it again. "You go ahead, mister, and shoot that poor woman. And as soon as you do, why, me and my friend here will open up on your sorry hide and—"

As soon as Boone got to that point in his little chat, Chan's rifle barked, and the man holding the woman jerked fast to his right, spinning in place as if he were dancing drunk.

Boone glanced at Chan, but the man was already lowering his rifle and leaning forward.

"Po?" he said in little more than a whisper.

"Chan?" said the woman who'd been held prisoner.

Chan jumped down from the horse and fell to one knee but kept his eyes on the woman. She still stood in the same spot, her hands to her face. She was not crying but she was drawn up tight, her shoulders narrowed. The other women moved toward her and surrounded her.

By the time Boone hopped out of the saddle, Chan was nearly to the women. They eyed him and he them. Then someone, one of the women, again said, "Chan?"

By then Chan was already to them. Boone noted that he'd dropped the rifle halfway there and even lost one of his confounded sandals. They apparently knew each other, which was dandy with Boone. But his first order of business was to check the shot men.

The first he'd hit was still writhing. Boone had not intended to leave him in pain, because now he'd have to deal with a prisoner. The second man he'd shot was either a damn good actor or as dead as he'd ever be. And the third . . . well,

Chan did for him with another of his trick shots, and the man was face blasted and done for.

Boone walked over to the first man and noted the fellow's right hand scrabbled in the dirt toward his revolver, still a few feet away, where it had landed when he flopped from his horse.

"Not so quick, there, little cowboy." Boone leaned down a bit and held the rifle barrel trained on the man's pain-wracked face. "Don't make me wish I shot you in the head to begin with."

"Hey! Hokey Boom!"

It was Chan, pointing past Boone toward the north.

Boone looked that way and caught a glimpse of a dark hat ducking back down behind the low ridgetop. "That's where we're headed. Or I am anyway." He turned back and pointed toward the ladies and Chan. "You grab up these weapons from the men here and get to cover."

They all retreated from the dead and dying. The one left alive moaned and scrabbled with a clawing hand at the dirt beside him, his revolver gone, now in the hands of one of the women.

From behind a scatter of knee-high boulders, they watched the ridge where they'd seen the hatted figure appear, then disappear again. "Chan," said Boone. "If you can, you and the ladies make for the camp with the kiddies and old folks. Free up as many of your kind as you can."

"What about you?" said Wan Li.

"I have to go find Mac, see if he needs help. I'll be making for Kane's cabin. I have a notion he's holed up there."

"Yes." Chan nodded. "He goes there."

"Okay, then. That's good enough for me. I'll head that-away. Isn't that trestle they're building past there?"

"Yes," said Chan, smiling brighter than ever. "Big, very big."

"Good," said Boone. He patted his tunic. "Maybe I can make it small, very small. Anything we can do to foil the progress of this vile operation."

He looked to the ridgeline. "I don't see anybody up there anymore, but I don't like sitting still. That's the direction I need, so I'm going, stranger or no."

He dashed forward, keeping low, and ducked behind another boulder. "Round up your friends and kin and meet me at the trestle!"

The last thing Boone heard as he pounded feet from cover to cover was Chan shouting behind him, "Okay, Hokey Boom! See you!"

Hokey Boom. I really have to have a talk with that boy.

Boone made his way up the east flank of the ridge, slower than he would have liked, but there was nothing for it. With a stranger up there—likely a guard—he didn't fancy having a hole put in him at this stage of the game.

He was about two thirds of the way to the top, east of the spot where he'd seen the ducking figure, when he heard the crack of a pistol shot. It sounded as if it came from where that fella had been.

That meant the man was in a fight with somebody, likely a Chinese worker newly freed. Or with Mac. Either way, Boone figured he should lend a hand.

He shucked his revolver and, keeping low, scrambled as quick as he could the rest of the way up the slope, eyeing upslope of him the entire time. Now was no time to let down his guard.

Then, from the direction the shot had sounded, he heard the muffled, slapping thuds of fists hitting flesh. Grunts and groans and quick, hot bursts of angry language rose up, coarse words of rage, then more fists.

He scrambled up, covering the last dozen feet with speed, and there, to his left, just below the berm of the ridge, two men were battling it out. One of them, whose back was to Boone, was a big man, wide of shoulder, swinging large, ham hands ending in brute fists.

For a moment, Boone thought it was Mac, but no, this man had a head of shaggy, dark hair. And then the man scooted to his right, and Boone saw his opponent. And *that* man was Mac.

Boone saw that neither man held a gun. Their holsters were empty and their revolvers were some yards away from them, where they'd been lost in the melee.

And for a sliver of a second, Boone thought his pard didn't look so good. His right arm hung as if it was a trial for him to lift it, and for good reason, Boone saw. The arm was a long, grim-looking limb covered in sticky, wet blood from a shoulder wound.

And when Mac tried to dance away, evading his big opponent's fists, he wasn't his usual, quick self. He was slow to move and so caught blows in the chest, and one on the side of his head that clearly rang his bells for a moment. Mac swayed, shaking his head as if to right himself and focus his blurred vision.

His big foe took the opportunity to look away from Mac and search the ground for something. Something he saw within moments, just as Boone did, too. It was the man's gun.

Yes, Mac MacCoole was most definitely the loser in this fight, and if Boone didn't do something quick, Mac would not make out at all, and in pretty short order, too.

Boone angled northward, holding up his own revolver, ready to fire should the brute catch sight of him. So far, so good. He had to shift position because if he shot the man, he'd risk shooting Mac accidentally, and that would not do.

And then the big man ducked low and snatched up his

revolver. As he spun, moments from shooting the still slightly dazed Mac, Boone dropped to his right knee and shouted, "Hey, you! Big goober!"

That was enough to confuse the large man, and he looked toward Boone. So did Mac.

As Boone cut loose with a shot, then a second right on the heels of the first, Mac dove low, to his left, away from his big opponent. He hit the ground with an "Oof!" and rolled.

The first shot caught the big man in the middle of his breadbasket. He was one of the guards. Boone recognized him in the moment between the first and second shots.

The first one did the trick, as the man, his eyes impossibly wide, and his mouth much the same, jerked his gaze from Boone skyward, as if he'd been told there was a wonderful bird up there he had to see.

He still held the revolver but loosely, by the walnut grips, as if it was something much too hot to hold.

The second one spun him and jerked his gaze back down. Gone was his wide-mouthed and wide-eyed wonder, replaced with a heavy-lidded gaze that leveled straight at Boone.

Of all the men Boone had ended in his life, this one, he knew in a finger snap of an instant, would be one he'd not forget. The look the big man gave him then seemed to speak to him.

If a look could talk, it would have said, *You devil. You have done the thing no one else could ever do. You have taken my life from me and I will not forget this. I will carry a hot coal of hatred for you into eternity.*

With a flick of his hand, the man dropped the loosely gripped revolver. Still staring at Boone, he began a slow, slow topple forward. Even as he fell, his black gaze stayed fixed on Boone's face, locked with his eyes.

Even after he crashed face-first to the dusty earth, like a mighty tree felled by a relentless ax man, Boone held his pose, on one knee, his revolver held out before him in a long, stiff-armed grip, his eyes wide, his breath snagged in his throat.

A voice to his right said, "Hoke, my word. Thank you. Once again, you've saved my skin."

The voice drew closer, and a hand lay on his shoulder. "Hoke. You okay?"

That broke the spell. "Huh?" Boone shook his head, as if to dispel an irksome fly. "Oh, hey, Mac. You . . . you okay?"

"Funny," said Mac, helping Boone up. "That's what I asked you."

"Oh, yeah." Boone dragged a hand down his face and slid his revolver into his holster. Then he knuckled his eyes. "I tell you, Mac, that big goober gave me a dose of the creepin' willies, I don't mind saying."

"You and me both," said Mac.

Then he looked past Boone toward a group of people, southward, armed from the looks of it, far below the ridge. It appeared they had been watching the proceedings, or as much as they could see from down there.

Boone eyed them. "My traveling friend and his people." He gave them a big, exaggerated wave and shouted, "Okay!"

In return, he received the same from a slight man with dark hair and a rifle, who shouted, "Hokey Boom!"

Boone smiled and shook his head.

"Did that fellow say what I thought he did?" Mac grinned, despite the soreness he felt all over his body.

"Huh? No idea what you're on about. You must be addled by all them blows that big fella laid onto you."

"Yeah," said Mac, retrieving his revolver and a black hat. "That must be it."

"I see your boot's been shot all to hell. You want his?"

They both looked down at the dead man's boots, but they looked, if anything, too large and far too worn.

"I'll stick with these," said Mac. "Let's head out."

"Kane's cabin?" said Boone.

"Yep."

CHAPTER 28

"So, what's the story with them?" Mac nodded past Boone at the departing bunch of Chinese.

Boone glanced back. "They're the ladies we saved. Nearly got themselves killed, they did. Good thing we come along."

"We?" said Mac. "You have a rat in your pocket?"

"Huh? Oh, no, no. Me and Chan."

"Who's Chan?"

"Oh, him?" said Boone, nodding toward the quickly moving group. "Oh, that's Chan. Picked him up along the way. He wouldn't leave me be, so I figured he'd be safer tagging along instead of getting caught and killed by one of Reg's boys."

"He hold his own? No time for games here, Hoke. I know you."

"Oh, now, you think you know me, you big goober? Truth is, you don't know much of what you claim to, and that's saying something." Boone nodded with finality. "But this here Chan fella," he said, nodding to his newfound friend, "he's a heck of a shot. Never seen the like. I can't be certain, but he says he ain't much experienced."

Boone leaned toward Mac. "He claims such, but it seems unlikely. And that means he might well be a fibber."

He shook his head. "Imagine fibbing on something like that. What is the world coming to, Mac?"

"That's rich, coming from you, Hoke." Mac grinned, relieved to be back in his pard's presence. It had been a long ol' day, and it showed no signs of letting up.

"Now look, you," said Boone, wagging a finger in Mac's face. "If I wasn't so worn down to a frazzled nub, I'd take a round or three out of your hide, big or no. But we got bigger fish to stuff on the flames."

Both men were cautious but pleased with how all this was playing out. They traded what scant information each had as they made their way toward Kane's cabin, or where they guessed it was located.

"Chan and the ladies are going to round up what others they can, see if anybody else needs a hand. I told them to meet up with us yonder, by that trestle. Seems like a good enough spot to keep out of harm's way, and we might be able to blow the thing, if that other crew Kane is eager to meet up with is more of the same as Reg and Shaky and the guards."

"Blow it?" said Mac. "Don't tell me those explosions I heard . . ."

Boone nodded, a wide smile on his face. "You betcha!" He patted his bulging tunic.

"Oh boy," said Mac. "If I know you, there won't be a structure left standing in a five-mile radius of this place."

Boone rubbed his hands together and cackled. "You know, if you hadn't got your boot all shot up, we'd make better time!"

"Well, pardon me," said Mac. Then, as they rounded a bend in the roadway, he stopped and gestured toward a fancy cabin anchoring a clearing ahead. They ducked to the roadside and took cover behind a boulder.

"Speaking of frying up a big fish," said Mac. "You about

ready to begin with Kane? From the buggy out front, it looks promising that he's inside."

"Good. I want to get my fingers on that rascal's neck. What's the plan?"

"Well, it's entirely possible he has already heard there's some sort of disruption to his business here."

"Oh, you mean what I added to the guards' chili?" Boone winked and slapped his buckskinned thigh. A small puff of dust rose up. "You didn't eat any, did you?"

"Nope," said Mac. "You hinted you might do something of the sort, so I stayed clear of anything but bread."

"Good thinking! Some days back, before they decided we was criminals, I sneaked in and dosed a big ol' pot of chili with something I fixed up. An old family recipe from Hoddy's."

Mac grinned and shook his head. "Well, that might well tip him off. That and the shooting and explosions. Hard not to hear such things."

"That's true. So, you think the rascal will be waiting for us?"

"Not for long. If my guess is correct—and I think it will be—he'll be leaving any time now. Probably to go round up the law he has paid for."

"What makes you think he'll leave?" Boone eyeballed the front of the cabin.

"Simple," said Mac. "That barouche is loaded with luggage."

Boone nodded. "I see that now. Oh, will you look at that! A fella just came out of the front of the cabin, then ducked back in."

Both men watched the shadows on the long, low shade porch.

"If Kane is still in there, which seems likely, he'll be guarded for sure," said Mac. "I can't see why any man who has done intentionally, willingly, the awful things he's guilty of would not take every precaution, especially if he sniffed revolt in the offing."

As if to verify his guess, two men wearing bandoliers of bullets stepped out onto the porch, their eyes sweeping left, then right, and back again.

"Either of them look familiar to you?" said Boone, swallowing back a lump. He knew Mac was thinking the same thing; they had overlooked putting much thought—or any at all—into how many guards had come with the new batch of Chinese workers.

"I hope Chan and the women are going to be all right," said Boone.

"Me too. You get the feeling we messed this one up from the start?"

"Yeah," said Boone. "But it's never too late to turn the tables on these goobers."

Mac smiled. "That's true. We're closer than ever to cutting off the head of this snake. We get Kane trussed up, we can go help the others."

"So the plan . . ."

"The plan," said Mac, stretching to his full height and rolling his sore shoulder, wincing at the creeping stiffness, "is . . . we get back behind the place, then separate. You take the left side, I'll go right."

"I always take the left."

"Fine, then I'll go left."

"Nah, I'm used to left by now. You want me to be at a disadvantage?"

Mac rolled his eyes as he bent once more and circled the clearing, making for the rear of the cabin. "Fine. You get left. And no complaining."

"Complain? Me? You have to be kidding, Mac MacCoole. I'm the least little complainer you ever are likely to meet."

As they bickered, in whispers, they crept along, keeping the clearing to their left. They both spotted the big boulder that would serve as their jumping-off point. Dead center behind the cabin.

They kept quiet until they were nested behind the boulder. "You have enough ammo?"

"Have to. No stores around," said Boone.

They loaded up and nodded once to each other. Then they each hunkered low and, catwalking, they crept to the edge of the clearing. There were two windows at the back of the place, but both had been shuttered and boarded up. One more nod to each other, then they proceeded on their separate routes.

Mac made for the right, keeping the rifle canted across his front, one hand on the rear stock, one on the forestock. He could jerk it up and fire from gut height if need be, perfectly suitable for close-in work. He made it to the back right corner of the cabin, a sizable structure, especially so from close up. And well-built, too.

Not for the first time did Mac think it odd that so much obvious money and effort was put into building seemingly permanent structures and the like here when the entire point of a railroad camp was to be temporary because it moved all the time.

Then again, perhaps the point here was to establish a permanent base from which to conduct the extensive operations that this massive undertaking surely required.

Before he'd turned renegade and gotten savaged by them, one of the friendlier guards had explained to him that there was another crew farther east, at a ravine, constructing a trestle bridge so the rail line could continue there.

Apparently, it wasn't all that far east from here. And then, once they reached that, this camp would be moved beyond, to the far side, and the entire project would continue in that direction, beyond where the easterly crew had already laid tracks. It was to join up some miles from there with a line already extant, owned by the Pacific Crest Railroad.

Mac stood at his full height and leaned the left side of his face against the planking, on the board and batten construction, but tighter and more meticulously crafted than the other buildings they'd erected. The pine still carried a warm tang, baking as it did all day in the dry, sunny weather.

He peered around the side and saw another pair of windows along the wall. They, too, appeared to have been shuttered. It was now even more obvious that Kane was planning to depart.

"Not if we can help it," he whispered and crept along the side of the cabin, keeping low and tight to the wall. As he moved along the wall, about a thirty-foot length, creeping closer toward the front, he heard two voices within. He paused and pressed his left ear to the wall.

One voice was louder than the other. The louder voice rose in pitch and then shouted. This time Mac could make out the words: "What are you paid for, then?"

Had to be Thurston Kane.

The other voice said something, but too low for Mac to make out. Then the first resumed. "I don't want excuses. That's all I've heard since I arrived this time. You have let me down, Shaky. And Thurston Kane does not like to be let down. You will pay for this, do you hear me?"

"Yes sir."

"Good, now there's still a chance to salvage this mess you've allowed to happen in our very midst. but we have to work fast. Do you understand that?"

"Yes sir."

"I can't hear you!"

"Yes sir!"

"Good. Now, carry my bags to the carriage and then drive me to the stable. My driver will be there. I'll return to

San Francisco and send the law here to deal with this mess you've created. Help them and you will be amply rewarded."

"Yes sir."

"But if it goes the other way, Shaky . . . there will be no place on earth you can hole up where I won't find you. Remember, soon I'll have the complete fortune and financial power of Blaswell's empire at my command, and you will still have your . . . your what? Hmm, that old horse and the half-empty bottle in your pocket. Face it, Shaky. You're a mess. You were a worm, nothing when I found you, but now look at you. You have money in your pocket, plenty of decent whiskey, and men under your command. And you want to throw all that away because of what? You and your men have a case of the runs? Pathetic! Tighten up or you're gone. There's still time, Shaky, but the door is closing on your future. Make the correct decision and have this situation under control, or else."

As he heard all this—anyone within fifty feet of the house would have heard it all through the plank wall—Mac crept right up to the front corner of the cabin. He peered around it and looked along the length of the front of it.

A long, deep porch ran the entire length, and the two guards they'd seen earlier still stood there, flanking the door, their rifles held across their chests as if they were in the military and not in some power-mad fool's private death force.

At the far end, opposite his corner, Mac saw slight movement, then caught Boone's eye. His pard nodded once, grinning, then looked up at the guards. They were closer to Boone than to Mac.

Mac knew what to do. While it would be a slight risk to expose himself to whoever was in the cabin, he would provide the distraction so Boone could lay into the two guards up close. He stepped out into the clearing, and at the same time the two guards did exactly as he and Boone knew they would—they swung around with wide eyes and drooped mouths.

Mac said nothing but nodded, smiling. His rifle was ready, and the men seemed to know that because they did not raise their guns.

And then Boone walked out toward the front steps from his side of the cabin.

The man nearest Boone said, "How many more of you are there?"

Before Boone could answer, from just inside the darkened doorway of the cabin, Mac heard a familiar voice say, "Oh, for Pete's sake!" Then Shaky stepped out of the dim interior and onto the porch.

He held no gun, though he wore his revolver on his hip. Instead, he tugged free the bottle riding in his jacket pocket and knocked back a big swig. He tamped the cork back in place.

"Drop 'em, boys." Boone walked out before the steps.

The two guards atop the three steps above didn't know what to do. On the one hand, their boss stood right behind them. But then that big ol' guard-turned-traitor, MacCoole, had them covered with his rifle from farther out.

And now here was the crazy, buckskin-wearing woodsman telling them to drop their rifles.

"You drop those guns and they won't hit the floor before you do," said Shaky.

"Bold talk, Shaky," said Mac, "considering you aren't even holding a gun."

"Ha!" said the drunken foreman. "I don't need a damn gun to best the likes of you, MacCoole and Boone!"

Another voice joined in, belonging to a man emerging from the shadows inside the cabin. "Are these the two you told me about?"

"Yes sir, Mr. Kane. That big one yonder is Mac MacCoole,

and the little one in the smelly suit of clothes is Hokum Boone."

"Smelly!" yipped Boone. "You have spoken your last, mister!"

"They don't look like much," said Kane. "If I had a gun, I would shoot those criminals. Oh wait, isn't that what you're paid to do, Shaky?"

The drunk sighed. "Yes sir, it is a fact that I am paid to shoot criminals."

"Oh, never mind," said Kane, his voice tight and some-how odd.

Mac tensed. He couldn't explain it, but it was one of those moments when everything shifted and soon became something else, usually something sinister. He'd felt it at various times in his life, beginning in the northern army, specifically during the war.

He recalled the first time, an otherwise mirthful moment during mess the evening before a battle, one of the first, one that the higher-ups, unfortunately, had been shouting about for weeks, calling it a big, make-or-break moment for the young army. And the largely green, inexperienced soldiers did not know how to take that.

Sure, many of them chuckled and joked about it, claimed it was all for the good of the cause, and tried to mask their raw, knock-kneed fear of dying on the morrow instead as joking bravado.

And then a rail-thin fella—not the youngest in the company by any means, but a man of perhaps thirty years, with a wife and three children back home on his farm in New Hampshire—excused himself from the table, folded his napkin, and walked outside.

It was not uncommon for men to visit the latrines at odd times, even in the midst of a meal, for the latrines were often busy places, and a modest fella could get some peaceful time, often during meals, when others were less interested in using them.

No one thought a thing about his departure from the table until they heard the snapping crack of a gunshot several minutes later.

The thin father and husband from New Hampshire, a man named Grimley, as Mac recalled, was found dead, a letter from his wife clutched in one hand, his revolver in the other, where it had flopped after he'd shot himself in the temple.

The letter did not include any incriminating news, nothing indicating there was anything but love and hopefulness awaiting him back home. And yet he'd taken his life.

That memory reminded Mac of the palpable feeling that presaged Grimley's death. Since then, he'd tried to pay attention to such odd moments in life, often with mixed results. And now here he was, in the midst of another.

"Hoke, tighten up!"

Boone flicked his eyes to Mac for the briefest of moments. He knew exactly what Mac was on about because he knew him so well. Mac MacCoole never wasted breath on such sentiments, and rarely spoke in the midst of the tensest of moments.

Something odd was in the offing and Mac sensed it, and that was good enough for Boone.

He tensed, willed himself into higher alert, and then it happened: Kane, still holding in the doorway, just in the shadows, dug something out of his jacket and dropped to one knee.

Shaky, standing before him, spun. In the act of pulling out his bottle yet again, he slid it back into his coat pocket as he moved, crouching at the same time.

This afforded Mac a clear view of what Kane was up to—and what he saw caused him to drop low to his left side, pivoting on his knee, and then continuing on and rolling with his momentum. There was a bullet in the offing and he didn't want to be anywhere near the line of sight of that scowling little snout on Kane's gun.

As he moved, keeping an eye on the man's weapon, Mac was also aware that the two guards, who had been caught in the middle of all this, were uncertain in that finger snap of a moment about just what to do. And so, as with anyone who dithers, they did nothing of use.

The guard closest to Mac should have moved farther than he had. The shot from Kane's hidden gun, if it had been intended for Mac, tore a path straight through the hot air and into the middle left side of the guard's back.

He'd been twisting to his left, and Mac saw the man's profile change from curious and confused to alarmed. But by then it was far too late.

The bullet drove like a lead fist into the man's back and he convulsed, snatching at his back and staggering with the force of the blow.

He dropped to his right knee and his rifle's stock slammed the floorboard of the porch. The jarring motion followed through as he continued toppling. His finger jerked down on the trigger and the gun fired, driving a bullet upward, but to the man's left—right into the bottom of the jaw of his fellow guard.

That man jerked backward, stretching his already tall height higher, stiffening as if he'd been lifted hard in the chin by an uppercut.

And Mac guessed he had, at that.

Shaky was a drunk, but he was an old gun hand, and finding himself in the midst of this exploding scene of madness, he shoved backward, slamming against the doorframe to the shocked Thurston Kane's left, and clawed for his revolver at the same time.

"No sir!" barked Boone, already making his way up the bottom step of the porch.

The jawshot guard, meanwhile, had pitched forward and

folded over the waist-high railing, then flopped neat as you please to the rocky earth below.

Mac advanced, aiming right at Kane, who still wavered, balanced on one knee, his little gun held before him in his right hand, but looking for all the world like a confused child. His eyebrows were high, his eyes wide, and his mouth an *O* of awe and confusion.

Mac kept the rifle trained on the man while he awkwardly folded his big frame beneath the porch rail and knee-walked forward until he cleared the rail with his head. He stood, keeping the still-twitching, backshot guard between them, on the floor by Mac's feet.

The man was no threat, gagging and mewling, whimpering and spastically clawing at his bloody side and back. A quick glance down told Mac all he needed to know. The poor fool had been hit in the vitals and would bleed to death, a long, slow process of terrible pain.

So far, Boone's threat was having little effect on Shaky, who kept up with his clawing at his holster. He slid down even lower against the doorframe and rolled inside the doorway, knocking Kane aside and, in the process, shoving him from Mac's line of sight.

Kane's pistol snapped again, and the angry bee that left it whizzed without interruption by Mac's body, but close enough that he heard it sizzle by.

He was already on the move, hugging the wall to his left and approaching the doorway.

Boone had gained the top of the steps, and he quick-stepped over to the right side of the open door.

Now they were facing each other, flanking that doorway. As far as Mac knew, all the windows were closed and shuttered, and he saw no other doors leading to the outside.

He gestured with his chin to Boone, who glanced quickly in and saw no one close by Mac's side of the door. Mac did the same for his pard.

Boone nodded one, two, three. At that, they both reached in and pinched off a shot.

Enough was definitely enough where the two hiding fools were concerned. Shaky should be dead, both men silently agreed on that. And Kane was the boss of the mess, the one who, according to what they had learned, had been the one to foul the once-noble enterprise with greed by resorting to slavery.

Shouts of fear from two voices boiled out the open doorway.

"Don't like it, eh?" cackled Boone. "Then come the heck on out here! We're through playing games with you two brutes!"

He looked at Mac and shrugged. Mac shook his head, reminded once again of how very humorous Boone could be in a sticky situation.

The wiry woodsman remained unflappable as always, but he seemed to take on an air of extra-righteous fluster when circumstances took a grim turn.

"I'm hit! Hit . . . don't shoot. . . ."

It was Shaky, and neither Mac nor Boone trusted the wrathful drinker. He was as straight as a handful of beetle legs.

"Drag your sorry self on out here, then!"

"Can't . . . can't move. You've crippled me with your lucky shot!"

"The only thing lucky about it would have been if it had nipped you in the head!"

Mac listened with caution and thought he heard low, swishy sounds, perhaps whisperings. He shook his head in a tight, quick motion, concern wrinkling his brow.

"No choice, then, but to lob this here dandy little stick of dynamite in on you two."

Again, there was silence from inside. Mac nodded and Boone grinned, tugging out a paper-covered stick of dynamite from his tunic, rigged it up, and said, "Okay, then, I'm fixing to light the fuse unless you two come on out of there."

There was no sound: no begging, no nothing. So Boone struck a match. "Hear that?"

"Kane!" barked Mac. "You alive, or did you do the world a favor?"

A moment passed in which Mac could have sworn he once more heard the low flurry of whispering. Then Shaky shouted, "He's hit, something's wrong with him. I think he's bleeding to death!"

"Uh-huh," said Boone, rolling his eyes. "And you can't seem to move your body, eh?"

"Yeah, yeah, that's it."

"Well, maybe this'll shift you!" He set the dwindling match to the tip of the wick, and for a moment nothing happened. Then, as if it had been conjured to life, the thin cord sizzled and snapped and popped.

"Ain't that purty?" said Boone, just loud enough for Mac to hear him.

"Yes, now would you please make a decision?" said Mac. "I don't fancy spending eternity in a hundred pieces scattered all over this foul place."

"Put it out! Put it out! I'm coming out, I swear it!"

It was Shaky, not Kane, who yelped in that begging voice. Boone's grin slid from his face and he sighed with regret, then licked his fingers and squelched out the sizzling, smoking fuse tip. "You folks ain't got no sporting blood, that's the trouble as I see it now."

By then, Shaky had begun to make good on his word and once more appeared close to the doorframe. His pasty, bristled face emerged from the shadows, his hands raised to midchest height.

"You are crazy."

"Yeah?" said Boone. "And you are a liar and a half. Never would make it in Hoddy's, I tell you true."

"Hoddy's this and Hoddy's that . . . oh, shut up about Hoddy's!" And before another word was spoken, Shaky lunged for Boone, covering the four or so feet between them in eyeblink speed.

He moved too fast for Mac, who moved backward a step. By then it was too late to get a shot at the drunken foreman. He couldn't risk hitting Hoke.

Boone, on the other hand, had no worries about hitting himself with gunfire. He knew what was happening even though he could not quite react the way he would have hoped. At least not initially.

Shaky slammed into him, landing atop him and lunging for his throat. The man, for a stringy drunk, was surprisingly wiry and fervent in his attack. He growled and snapped his teeth like a feral dog.

He'd pinned Boone's rifle crosswise between them and, with it, the woodsman's hands. But that didn't mean Boone was powerless. He brought a knee up hard into Shaky's groin and with the suddenness of a finger snap, the attacker's growls turned into mewling cries. Shaky began to curl up as Boone shoved away from him.

He was almost out from beneath the man when Shaky snatched at his leg and dragged himself back toward Boone.

But this time Boone was ready, and at the same time he slammed the rifle barrel atop Shaky's greasy pate. Mac, who had stepped backward toward the railing once more, in an effort to gain a clearer shot at his pard's attacker, had dropped to his right knee and squeezed off a shot.

It caught Shaky high on the left side of his chest and he screamed. The sound clipped off into a ragged gurgling as the bullet's trail filled with blood. Blood quickly welled up, spouting out the gasping man's mouth and nose.

He spasmed, and the man's right arm, which gripped Boone's left moccasin, grasped and scrabbled. Then his frenetic hold lessened and withered, a lifeless claw retracting, curling in on itself, never to flex again.

"Damn, son!" Boone shoved backward away from the freshly dead man. "I had him! I had him!"

Mac nodded and said, "Sure you did," looking toward the cabin door once more. "Kane! Come on out now. You've gotten plenty of innocent—and not-so-innocent—people killed, and the number's climbing higher with each moment! Give it up and let the courts decide if you're fit to walk amongst the rest of us again."

They heard nothing in response from inside. They both crept once more to their respective sides of the doorframe, flanking it and looking in.

This time, they were able to see more of the inside of the cabin, which the shuttered windows had prevented. They peered in, rifle barrels first sniffing the air.

"Why can I see light?" whispered Boone.

Mac wondered the same but bent low, peering, knowing he could receive a bullet for his troubles. He hoped Kane was one of those dandies who carried a loaded two-shot hideout gun, but no other bullets for it.

Usually, such guns were a citified affectation, with no other purpose than to make the owner look cute in his own mirror, barely dangerous at the games tables, and perhaps to impress a woman.

"Me left, you right," whispered Mac. Boone nodded, and they both whipped inside, fast, hoping to confuse and per-haps even overpower Kane within moments.

Now that there was a little more light illuminating the dim interior of the shuttered cabin, it was difficult not to notice it was a sumptuously appointed space. Once they ventured deeper in, it was also obvious where the newfound light was coming from. In the far-rear left corner of the front room, the dim glow rose up from the floor.

Boone hustled over to it and peered down. "Trapdoor!" He spun and pointed. "Mac, the buggy!"

From out front, they heard the telltale rumble and creak of buggy wheels grinding on gravel, of horses' hooves and the quick snap and crack of a whip, of a man's voice shouting, "Ha! Ha! Git! Git up there!"

They charged to the door and stepped over two bodies. One was Shaky and the other was the second guard to die. The first was still alive, emitting a whistling and groaning every few seconds, but otherwise immobile and lifeless.

Both Mac and Boone were down off the porch and had cleared the steps in a single stride, but the buggy was even faster. Soon it outpaced them, leaving them bolting toward the retreating boil of dust.

They did not slow their gait, but kept on, despite their aching bones and hides, the abrasions and cuts and scrapes and throbs of their various wounds. The buggy continued to outstrip their solid efforts, leaving them gasping in the dust and exhaustion and heat of that awful day.

"He's headed for the stables," said Mac.

"How do you know?"

"Heard him through the wall. Heard he's been known to say unpleasant things about his boss, Blaswell, the owner of this entire affair. And the man's daughter, too. Apparently, Kane is set to wed her."

"Good Lord, a nest of killers and thieves!"

"We can't be certain Blaswell and his daughter are in on this. Kane is in charge of it, after all." Mac straightened, having overcome his gasping at last.

"Bah!" spat Boone. "They're all rascals and thieves when they get that rich! Wouldn't be shocked to learn Blaswell himself issued the orders."

Mac said nothing to this, mostly because he was far too tuckered out to get into an argument with Hoke over people he did not know and probably never would.

And besides, he thought, wiping his face with a scrap of his shirt, *if he had to be honest about it, he didn't much care.* He was here to do one thing, and that was to free the Chinese laborers from misery and worse.

So far, they'd barely been successful. He hoped the laborers were working together to overcome the remaining guards. But right then, Mac knew he and Boone had to keep going.

"We'll need to scare up Lincoln and Chummy at the stable and take off after Thurston Kane. You up for it, pard?" Mac grinned, knowing it would be a fool's errand to try to keep Hoke away from the pursuit of this much evil.

They continued their trek toward the stable at a lope, with Mac hobbling slightly on his shot-up boot. In the distance to the southwest, where the current section of the rail camp had been set up, they heard one, then two rifle shots. Then nothing following.

Neither man spoke, for they knew shared speculation was a waste of breath and they had dire need of every sip of air they could pull in if they were going to run down Kane any time soon.

CHAPTER 29

"Papa."

"Yes, my dear?" Winterson Blaswell lowered the large kerchief he held before his face in an effort to keep the dust from the road from further incursion into his nose, mouth, eyes, and who knew where else.

But he could not keep from gawping at the wonderous countryside about them. He saw, too, that Philomena was enchanted, despite the dust.

They had had rare occasion to venture forth on excursions in recent years. It seemed the more success he achieved in business, which had been significant in the past decade or so, the truth of the matter was he had neglected his daughter, at least in spending time outside of their mansion, together.

Long gone were the days when they would take Sunday strolls in the park, or rides along the waterfront in a buggy, just for fun.

This trip west, first by ship, then by rail, then by private coach, had made him see what fun they could have been having together all these years had he not been consumed by making money and building the Blaswell empire.

"Papa, as much as I hate to bring this up, I really must say it before we meet up with Thurston."

"All right, my dear. You know you may say anything to me. What is it?"

"Papa, you have a blind spot where Thurston Kane is concerned. I hope you know that."

"What?"

"It's true. I've waited far too long to tell you this. I know you wish for us to marry, and while he is an agreeable sort . . ."

"Philly, dear, Thurston is much more than agreeable."

"There you go again, interrupting me with praise heaped upon Thurston. I tell you, Papa, there is something about the man that I find worrisome."

Blaswell kept silent for a moment and stared at the landscape. He had to admit that his daughter was a particularly shrewd person, one of the sharpest he'd ever known, in fact. This was notwithstanding that he held a particularly high opinion of himself.

Still, when he heeded her advice in the past, he never had cause to regret it. So Winterson Blaswell decided to keep his mouth shut and listen for once, instead of bowling over his daughter's words with his usual bluster and bravado.

He leaned forward. "Tell me your concerns, then, Philly."

"Really?"

He was tempted to take that sliver of doubt as an opening into which he might jam the toe of his now-dust-covered but bespoke, imported boot. Instead, he nodded.

"Well," said Philly, leaning forward as well.

He could not help but notice once again how many mannerisms they shared. Would that she were a man, she would be the perfect person to take over leadership of Blaswell and all its holdings.

"Don't you find it a little odd that the reports we've

received from Thurston regarding the progress of the rail line are glowing yet incredibly infrequent?"

"But—"

She held up a gloved hand and continued, "And how, precisely, was he saving, as he has put it time and again, the Blaswell empire so much money? I ask you, how is it possible to be both underbudget and ahead of schedule, and in the extraordinary amounts he claims, both in time and in money? To make money in this day and age of empire and expansion, it is necessary to spend money. And on a venture such as this, much money must be spent to ensure it is as robust as it needs to be to not merely exist but be profitable well into the future."

"Yes, well—"

Again, Blaswell was interrupted by his not-so-demure daughter's raised gloved hand. "And there was that journalist from Sacramento who managed to speak with some of the engineers and construction crew, and they were, as I recall, fearful and reticent."

"Well, now, Philly, I'm sure that—"

"No, Papa, please. Let me finish. The journalist went on to say that he tried to contact Thurston for an interview six times and yet was unsuccessful."

"That doesn't mean—"

"I know it doesn't mean much. In fact, we don't know the particulars of the journalist's bona fides, his intentions, or anything about him. But, well . . ." She let her hand drop into her lap.

Blaswell regarded her for a moment, then smiled. "That's why we've made this journey, Philly. I'm so pleased you suggested it. And it will have a twofold purpose: We'll surprise the young man and we'll be able to check up on his progress at the same time. And as a pleasant bonus, we have managed to spend ample time together. The most, I believe, since your dear mother passed on."

Philomena regarded her father. He looked tired but happy, genuinely happy. She could not continue to trample on his desires on this day. Instead, she returned the smile.

"Yes, I'm certain you're right, Papa. I do believe all will be revealed with Thurston, and we will be able to have a laugh—between us, mind you—once we arrive at the site."

She looked out once more at the passing scenery and willed herself to keep smiling. But inside, Philomena Blaswell was concerned, very concerned. And annoyed and frustrated. And downright irked.

Something, her usually trustworthy gut told her, screamed to her, was wrong, very, very wrong, and she needed to find out just what that was. And she knew Thurston Kane was the very man she had to speak with about it.

CHAPTER 30

Thurston Kane whipped hard on the horse towing his buggy and within a few hair-raising minutes had the stable in his sights. *There*, he thought. *There my driver will be waiting and I will finally be able to* . . . But a sight he had not expected to see greeted him.

It was something that up until that very moment, he had never thought to see. For until that very moment, Thurston Kane knew that deep within himself he had the ability to turn this debacle into something profitable and worthwhile again.

He knew it would not be easy, but he felt certain that if he could get back to San Francisco, he could hire new workers. To heck with the Chinese workers; they were expendable, he'd proven that. And he'd pulled in a tidy profit, too, and all without building those silly little villages for those undeserving lesser humans that Blaswell, the sentimental fool, had instructed him to do.

Kane had never had the intention to do that, but instead had nodded his head and said, "Yes sir," and then gone ahead and built a railroad on the cheap. Well, the beginnings of one anyway. He dismissed as unsuitable those firms that Blaswell arranged to work for him and hired his own people.

He'd hired the contractors and engineers and guards and gunmen he wanted to hire.

And it had worked, as he knew it would. His plans were flawless. And even when it all began to wobble, and the seams began to pop, it was still salvageable. Until those two intruding devils—MacCoole and Boone, were they called? Until they showed up.

And yet, even then, even when they had killed his guards and roused the cursed, ungrateful Chinese workers into a frenzy, even then Thurston Kane felt certain he could right the ship.

All this raced through Kane's frenzied mind, like a swarm of rats, one thought leaping over another, and another, boiling away in his brain.

And then, still a distance of several hundred yards from the stables and barns, he crested the last rise that would lead him there, where he had intended to meet his driver, and that mewling little worm of a man, Ralston, his assistant.

They would hitch up fresh horses and race for the coast and civilization. Back to the offices. If he could only get back to his meager yet pivotal office in San Francisco, there he could fix it all. He would arrange for new workers—whites, yes, he'd hire real workers—and an entire new construction crew. There were plenty of people hungry for money. It would all work out well.

But from that distance of several hundred yards, as he topped the rise, he saw the last thing he expected to see that day, the thing that changed everything. The thing that flipped the lever in his mind and made him think only one thing: turn and run. Run eastward and get distance between you and them.

"Oh no! Oh no no no no!" He jerked back hard on the lines, reining the foaming, lathered, panting team to a dusty halt and stared through the clouds of dust at the impossible. . . .

And yet there they were, the utterly unmistakable, girthy

form of Winterson Blaswell, and beside him, in a plain frock, his homely, suspicious daughter, Philomena. And beside them . . . that smarmy little assistant, Ralston, no doubt telling them everything that had gone awry in the past few days.

Blaswell, it looked to Kane, had his fists planted on his wide hips. And Philomena, beside him, looked to be staring in his direction with . . . a collapsible telescope? *My word!* They were spying on him! That was what they were here for—to spy on him!

"No!" shouted Thurston Kane, cursing a blue cloud loud enough for them to hear in the still, hot air of the blue-sky day. He growled and yanked and growled and yanked and turned the team right there in the roadway.

Despite their heaving flanks and lather, they responded to the harsh snapping of the buggy whip lashing their rumps and backs. And once more they pounded hard back along the same roadway they'd just run. Back toward the east, back toward his cabin.

Kane looked back toward the stables, and even through the dust he saw the big mound of the man, Blaswell, and beside him, Philomena, glassing him. Curse them! And they were waving their arms at him; waving for him, no doubt, to stop, to turn, to come back, to explain all!

No, no. Not yet. There was still time to fix all this, but he could not face them just now. He needed time, dang it! Time to think, which always saved his bacon in the end. Time and thought.

Time and thought, time to think . . . The rats in his brain tumbled and squealed and roiled and fought and squawked. And Thurston Kane whipped and lashed the straining rumps and flanks and backs of the lathered, lunging horses.

But no, he realized, he could not go back to the cabin. There were bodies there. And those foul men, MacCoole and Boone, lurking still, no doubt, looking for him.

Then where to?

And then he knew. It was a slim sliver of hope this last notion represented, but it was enough of a hope that he nearly smiled. The trestle! Yes, the trestle.

If he could cross the trestle, by God, he could gain time to think and then . . . But what if they followed? For surely they would seek him out; Winterson Blaswell had not become the tycoon he was by not following through on a thing. No, he would dog Kane to the ends of the earth to find out what had happened, why he had not followed his orders. And then he would have to explain what would be of utmost importance to Blaswell—what Kane had done with all of his money?

Thurston Kane growled once more and gritted his teeth as the clouds of road dust rose up about him. He would not give back all that money he had saved. Money he had made! He would die first.

CHAPTER 31

"Hoke, hold on a minute. Hold on."

Both men watched Kane's buggy, or rather the boil of dust it left behind, recede from sight. There was no way they were going to catch up with him.

"I think we're overlooking something, Boone."

"What's that?"

"How did Shaky and his men get to the cabin?"

Boone looked at Mac. "Are you saying what I think you're thinking?"

"No idea how to interpret that, Hoke, but it's likely they used horses." Mac looked back. The cabin was way back there, though still in sight.

"It would be a whole lot smarter to hoof it back to the cabin and look for their mounts than for us to run on foot all the way to the stable. If there are horses, they'll be in the trees, likely in that copse to the north of the cabin."

Boone nodded, and the two men began walking back toward the cabin, catching their breath and wiping dust and grime and sweat from their faces.

"That's the one direction we didn't cover when we circled around back of the cabin."

"Worth a try," said Mac. "It's not as if we've gone all that far anyway."

It took them a couple of minutes to trot back to the cabin. They were within sight of the cabin when they angled left, toward the north and the trees there.

The land sloped slightly, and tucked back in there they found a three-sided, open-to-the-shade shed for the horses. And inside, there stood three mounts, hipshot but saddled and ready to ride.

"Okay, choose one and let's go."

Mac chose the biggest, and Boone thought maybe he'd chosen Shaky's, because a quick rummage in the saddlebag turned up a mostly full bottle of decent whiskey. They mounted up, and Mac led the third horse with a lead line. They threaded their way up through the trees to the lane and Boone swigged from the bottle, then handed it to Mac.

It was just the thing to cut the grime and clear their heat-addled minds. Neither man wanted more than a couple of swigs, however, because any restorative effects the whiskey had would quickly head in the other direction, making them sluggish and dozy. Those were things they could not afford to feel.

Once on the lane proper, they tied the third horse's reins to the cabin's porch rail. Should something happen to them, they didn't want the beast forgotten. Then they made a hard ride straight for the stable. It was a simple enough direction; that roadway led right to it, and then led onward and away from it, westward, and so, eventually, to the coast.

They made it roughly halfway back to the stable when they heard a shouting ahead. Within seconds of this, from around a bend thundered two horses leading a buggy—the very buggy, they soon realized, they had been chasing.

And standing in the driver's well, with knees braced against the front, crouched, none other than Thurston Kane himself, howling and wielding the buggy whip as if he was punishing the very air itself.

He didn't appear to see them in the roadway before him,

or if he did, he didn't care a whit about a collision. Instead, he thundered straight for them, shouting brute sounds, cursing the horses, nearly screaming at times.

"We best let him pass, Mac. He's gone crazy!"

Mac nodded, and they split, each taking a side of the road. Within seconds, the team, the slamming buggy, and Kane's flailing form all passed by, not slowing, shouting louder than ever.

"Those horses are spent," said Boone. "Can't last at that pace."

They turned and followed Kane, keeping him in sight but far enough back that they wouldn't eat all his dust.

They shouted to each other as they rode.

"How far does the road lead?" said Boone.

"No idea, but I think it loops, arching southeastward. Which is about where that trestle sits, if I remember correctly what Reg told us."

"Something like that, yeah. At any rate, he won't get far with those horses, not the way he's driving them."

They followed along at a decent distance, always keeping him visible, but somehow Kane's horses didn't flag all that much. They kept him in sight, at times following the dust cloud he left in his wake. They passed the spur that led to the cabin, half expecting Kane to stop there. But he did not. Now they were traveling on a road they were unfamiliar with.

As they rode, Mac's guess about the road curving southeastward proved correct. The terrain was largely rock and gravel, but with a scattering of trees that thickened and thinned as Mac and Boone rode on through.

Then the landscape changed again as they found themselves angling southward. Boone's mount flailed and flagged, favoring her right rear hoof. "Mac! Hold up. She's lamed on me."

They slowed to a stop, and Boone slid down out of the

saddle. They knew they should have kept the third horse instead of leaving it at the cabin. But it was too late for that. Their only hope was that Kane would soon so exhaust his team that he would also be afoot. To wherever it was he was headed at such a clip.

Mac hauled Boone up behind him and they continued their journey, leaving the lame horse standing hipshot by the roadside and looking not a little sad.

With any luck, they could return that way and retrieve the lame beast.

They were riding slower now as Mac's mount had to lug the pair of them. And that was about when they heard horses behind them. Uncertain who that might be, they angled off the road, not wanting to be caught unawares by any of Shaky's men, for it would surely quickly become a gunfight.

Boone slid out of the saddle. They took no pains to hide themselves but waited with guns at the ready.

Presently, the sounds they heard showed themselves to be yet another buggy, a large barouche, open topped, and driven by none other than the man who kept the stable. He pulled up when he saw them.

"You two! You're alive! Well, that's something anyway."

"Alive?" said a large, well-dressed man in the buggy. Also seated in it, Boone and Mac saw, was a thin woman. Both appeared to have traveled a fair distance in the wagon because they were dusty faced and rumpled.

"Yeah," said the driver before Mac or Boone could respond. "Shaky and Reg and the men laid in for these two. Some of them placed wagers that these two wouldn't last the week. But it looks like they made it through."

"Enough of all that," said the fat man. He leaned forward and eyed Mac and Boone. "Have you seen a buggy ride by here with a . . . a madman driving?"

"So," said Boone, "you looking for Kane, too?"

The fat man nodded and the woman said, "We most certainly are looking for him!"

"Uh-huh," said Boone, shifting his rifle a little bit, more for show than for any other reason.

"Let me guess," said Mac. "You are Winterson Blaswell."

"How did you know that?"

"I didn't exactly. But I know it now."

"Are you two men seeking him as employees might an employer or for some other reason?"

Mac eyed the man and woman, then said, "We are as close as you are going to get in these parts to law enforcement officers who aren't on Kane's payroll."

"Then you aren't part of the shenanigans that man and the other one back at the stable—Ralston, was it?—have been telling us of?"

"Not hardly," said Boone. "Like Mac said, we're trying to stop him. He's been running a slavery ring, mistreating them Chinese something fierce."

He strode to the buggy. "We have to get to him before he escapes! You got room in there for me?" He didn't wait for an answer but hauled himself up into the buggy beside the driver. "Mac, lead the way! Kane won't get far anyway with that team of his. They're about played out."

"These, too," said the stableman, clucking the team into action once more and falling into line behind Mac.

"Not like Kane's," said Boone. "He's about killed them. It's a wonder they made it as far as they have." He looked back to the bewildered Blaswell and the woman. "He's treating those horses about like he has treated the Chinese workers. Working them to death!"

"My word," said the fat man.

"You said it, mister!" Boone eyed the road ahead, past

Mac, who, he saw, was slowing. The roadway widened and sloped downward slightly. They pulled up alongside Mac and looked at what he was eyeing.

A rough-cleared, unfinished railbed angled in from the southwest. But it was what it led to that attracted their gaze. A steep ravine, roughly several hundred yards across to the other side, sat before them, running north-south. And spanning it perched a massive trestle topped with newly laid steel rails. The rails ended at the near west side of the trestle and had come from the east side.

Off to the left side of the widened roadway sat Kane's barouche, leaning as if about ready to overturn down an embankment. Struggling to keep from sliding down there themselves stood his two horses, lathered, sides heaving and heads hanging low. Long strings of snot trailed from their noses and one horse looked about ready to collapse.

Of Thurston Kane there was no sign.

Boone leapt from Blaswell's buggy and ran to Kane's.

"Careful, Hoke!" shouted Mac. "They could topple over any second!"

"You bet!" shouted Boone without looking back. He pulled out a hip knife and sawed away at the traces, freeing the ragged, haggard team before they could succumb to exhaustion or gravity.

"Who are they?" shouted Blaswell.

They all looked at him and saw he was pointing toward where the unfinished railbed emerged from between boulders and scrub pines. Walking along it was a group of people dressed in grimy, loose-fitting clothes. They all had dark hair, and the person in the lead—a man, from the looks of him—carried a rifle held across his chest.

"That's my friend, Chan!" shouted Boone, making for the group. "And the women we saved, Mac, and other Chinese folk, too!"

Before Boone could get to them, they heard a shout.

Emerging from behind a boulder toward the advancing group of Chinese laborers was Thurston Kane.

He held a revolver and stepped quickly up to the member of the group nearest him. It was one of the women, and Mac knew by her features it was Wan Li, the leader of the five women.

For his part, Kane saw foul Chinese slaves creeping up on him from behind. The raw gall of these creatures! To try to deceive him! Thurston Kane, a man said to have promise, oh so much promise! Well, he would show them who they were tampering with. . . .

Kane moved quickly, hooking his free arm about the neck of the nearest Chinese laborer, a woman. He jammed the gun's barrel into the side of her head. Then he dragged her backward a few feet from the others in the group, careful to keep her writhing, fighting body before his own.

The others halted, startled, hands raised as if they had been nabbed themselves. Chan, fronting the group, stood frozen, the rifle forgotten in his grasp.

Kane continued to drag her, moving foot by foot toward a boulder close by the near end of the trestle's mouth, where the tracks from the other side ended. Not far from this end of the trestle, atop the new tracks, sat one of those small carts that moved by pumping the seesawlike handle in the middle of the cart.

"Hold there!" bellowed Mac.

Remarkably, Kane complied. He stood mesmerized, the gun's barrel digging hard into the woman's temple. He blinked once, twice, three times, and seemed to focus his gaze for the first time in long minutes.

He saw Blaswell and Philomena and stared hard at them, as if he'd just recognized them. Then he spoke. "Ah, yes, I see! Mr. Blaswell and Philomena, what a lovely surprise! I do wish you had mentioned your visit to me. I could have had a sumptuous meal laid out for you. You could have learned all you needed to from San Francisco and not out here in the wilds, among the savages."

Kane glanced around himself, a sneer on his face. "In fact, you could not have chosen a worse time for your surprise visit."

He looked about them once more, beyond the wide, plump shoulders of his boss and past the rail-thin, plain face of his intended. Then he looked left, squinting hard into the trees, then behind him at the dusty roadway.

Then Kane smiled expansively and opened wide his arms, the revolver still aimed at them all. Dust billowed from his caked, no longer dapper clothes. His once-tidy, oiled hair hung in strands in his face and his once-clean-shaven face was now begrimed and stubbled.

"What happened to you, man?" shouted Blaswell. "I see the West has been too much for you. You . . . you've gone native, for God's sake!"

For her part, Philomena merely stared hard at Kane with narrowed eyes, her brows pulled tight in concern. Her mouth, too, was a pinched thing, as if she had just sucked a lemon. She did not look at all concerned with how she appeared.

And in that moment, Thurston Kane knew he had ruined the entire careful plan, and a little part of him was relieved. He did not want to marry that woman and spend his life bowing to her, for he saw her now as he had never seen her before—a strong, intelligent woman who would keep him in check at all times.

There would never be an empire for him to run. He would be a figurehead, a foolish companion, the father of her brood. Oh dear no, not that.

Kane realized that Blaswell was still talking, getting himself all worked up, his fat face redder than ever. He was saying something about how Kane was a crook, a charlatan, and that he would be locked away for life and then some. If the state of California or wherever in God's name they were had anything to say about it, they might well have him put before a firing line!

"What?" said Kane, shaking his head. "What?"

"You heard me, you . . . you . . . you charlatan! You thief!"

And then Kane knew only one thing he could do, the one thing that needed doing: He needed to flee. And at his back was the trestle, and on it sat a handcart, waiting for him, a cart that would take him to freedom. It was a route they would have a devil of a time following—certainly not on horseback. And that was the direction he must go.

He backed farther and laughed. "You fat fool! And your horse-faced daughter! Do you honestly think I would let the likes of you hand me over to your so-called authorities? Ha, I say! Ha!"

With that, Thurston Kane half spun on his heel, the tails of his dust-caked frock coat twirling in a most impressive manner. All the while, he held the gun to the woman's head.

Now slightly frazzled and laughing maniacally, Kane zipped along, laughing, thinking he was going to get away. But the Chinese woman was not cowering, not helping him, not afraid of him.

And then a tremendous, snapping, cracking sound echoed up and down the ravine from far below them. Everyone froze and watched the only moving thing, Thurston Kane, resuming his frantic ramming up and down of the handcart's handle.

The cart rolled forward another six feet, then slowed, despite Kane's frantic efforts.

"Help me, damn you!" he growled at the Chinese woman. She looked the several hundred feet back up the rails toward the side of the ravine from which they'd come. Toward all the people who stood there, arms outstretched as if they might somehow help her, grab her, pull her back.

In that moment, she must have made a decision, for she moved with catlike speed and grace from the far end of the handcart to the end closest to the ravine's edge and the small crowd gathered there.

"Oh no you don't!" Kane lunged for her. The cart rolled, lurching several more feet, but it wasn't from his pumping efforts. A second cracking sound, louder and closer, rose up to them from below, followed by others, quick and tight, as if they were gunshots.

"They're shooting at me!" screamed Kane, and he turned back away from trying to grab the Chinese woman and snatched for the upraised handle in the middle of the cart.

But another cracking sound, this time from the timbers directly below the cart, rang out, filling the air with sound.

The Chinese woman wasted no time but bolted, abandoning the now-slumping cart and running like a cat, bounding forward on the balls of her poorly clad feet.

Two strides from the handcart, she stopped and turned, looking over her shoulder at Thurston Kane, whose eyes were wide, his mouth even wider, as he gripped the side of the cart, the slumping, leaning cart. He caught her eye and in a terrified whimper said, "Help me! Save me!"

"Where is my husband? Where is my son?" Wan Li's voice was never so strong. It was a solid, even steely thing, matched only by her steady gaze.

"You . . . you speak English?"

Wan Li offered a slight nod. "Of course. Many of us do. Where is my family? Tell me the truth."

In that instant, she saw in Kane's eyes that he not only did not remember her son or her husband, he looked upon her, and all her people, as something not human, something no better than cattle or dogs or rats. She also saw and knew, with a mother's instinct, that the man would dispose of her son, her husband, all of them, as one might the body of a reviled beast.

The massive, timbered bulk of the trestle bridge shifted again, slumping to the right, the very side Kane was on, and the gleaming rail began to come free of the timbers it was spiked to.

Kane's handcar rolled, then began to tip, so slowly that at first it appeared as if it were merely rolling once more. But no, it was lifting from the left side. Kane's weight on the right side did not help.

He screamed, shifted, and the thing tilted faster. He froze, his eyes impossibly wide, and he stared at her, beseeching her with his screams, with a clawing hand, and with his wide, wide eyes.

And Wan Li turned away from him and sprinted, from crosstie to crosstie, back toward the near end of the trestle. She ran toward the gathered crowd there, toward her friends, new and old, toward all those people shouting and holding out their arms and pointing at something behind her. Their eyes grew terribly wide, their faces long and open-mouthed.

Beneath her feet, Wan Li felt the crossties moving, as if they were melting, as if she weighed more than all the people in the world, and her tremendous weight was shoving them down below her.

She did not dare look back but ran even faster, clawing her way forward. Not far to go now, no more than fifty feet, then thirty, then less, the smaller of the two men who had saved them, Boone, the one in the animal-skin clothing, was moving forward onto the trestle, his arms outstretched before him. He was coming to help her once more, beckoning her with frantic gestures.

She could hear nothing but the tremendous cracking, snapping sounds. She did not dare look back, did not want to see that horrible man, Kane, right behind her, clawing for her, anger coloring everything about him. She did not want to see his gun spitting a bullet at her.

Then the sound increased and whooshed all around her, and the man named Boone grabbed her arms, and she was reaching for him. And the bridge beneath her disappeared.

Magic—it must have been magic. For it was there, beneath her as she ran, filled with vibrations, yes, but it had been there, the solid wood and steel of it all. And then it was gone.

And she was falling, falling.

She looked up, screaming, and then her arms screamed from the jerking pain of being held tight by the man Boone, who stared down at her, his eyes wide. But there he was, not far, a little more than an arm's length above her. But he, too, was hanging down.

Above him, Wan Li saw his partner, the big man, MacCoole. And the big man was looking down at her, too, but he was holding Boone's legs. MacCoole's face was hard, tight, his lips pulled back and his teeth, his big, white teeth were grinding hard together, his eyes nearly squeezed shut.

And then she felt herself jerking upward, with great speed, moving the last few feet upward, as if she was shoved up from below by unseen hands.

Then sounds such as she'd never heard before filled the air, and they seemed as if they would never stop—crunching, cracking, twisting, snapping. What was it?

And in the midst of it all, a long, lone, high-pitched scream sounded, as if it were a needle piercing that thick fabric of sound.

The next thing she knew, she was staring up at the clear blue sky far above. She was lying on her back. The big man, MacCoole, and the other man, Boone, were collapsed beside her in a pile, also staring upward. Nobody else seemed to be there.

And then Wan Li heard them, the others, shouting and

screaming. And she saw faces crowding down about her, instead of the crunching, snapping, brutal sounds of something collapsing and dying,

And then she was surrounded by smiling Chinese faces, her friends, scooping her up in hugs she hoped would go on forever.

CHAPTER 32

Later, Winterson Blaswell was still talking.

"In his zeal to save money, which he did in ample amounts, Thurston Kane ordered to be constructed the inferior structure that took his very life."

"It makes you wonder where he dug up the so-called engineers and other experts who are supposed to design and build these things for a living." Mac gingerly touched his right shoulder and grimaced as he shifted, stretching his back and arms.

In holding tight to Hoke's legs as Boone reached for the woman, Mac opened up the scant bit of healing the wound on his arm had managed in the past few, frantic hours. He closed his eyes and sighed. He felt as though he could sleep for a week.

Just then, standing to his right, Hoke said, "I am so knackered I could curl up in a ball like a kitten under one of them big-needle pines yonder and snore away for a month in the pine duff. I swear it." He capped the statement with a massive yawn.

Mac nodded. "Yep, me too. But there's a whole lot to do yet. We can't let all those rascals off the hook. And . . ."

"Mac?" said Boone.

"Yeah?"

Boone nodded past his big pard. "I think that woman is

already starting in on most of those items, and a whole lot of others. She's writing herself up a big ol' list. And haranguing that poor devil from the stable at the same time. And that Ralston fella, too. He showed up a few minutes ago in another buggy. He'll wish he stayed away, I'll wager."

"Good," said Mac. "It's her duty anyway, to deal with all this."

"Yes," said Winterson Blaswell, stepping over to stand beside them. "Indeed it is. I have been a fool, and after all this terror and mayhem and sadness, I am only now realizing it. My dear daughter, Philomena, is twice the person I could ever be."

Boone gently rapped the big man's gold-watch-chained belly and winked. "That's saying something." He smiled and chuckled.

Blaswell sputtered a moment, but then allowed a slight chuckle to pass his lips.

"You were saying, Mr. Blaswell?" said Mac, eyeing Boone.

"Yes, merely that my daughter, Philomena, is the most capable person I know, and the most logical person to take over the running of the Blaswell empire. I should have seen that years ago."

"Never too late," said Boone. "Unless you're Thurston Kane." He glanced over at the ragged timbers hanging in space over the ravine.

"Indeed," said Blaswell, also looking toward the place where a short while before, a massive, impressive-looking yet flimsily built trestle had dominated the scene. "Indeed."

They were all silent for a few moments more, then Blaswell continued. "On our arrival at the site, I was confused, startled by what I was seeing. Yes indeed, there were rail lines being laid down, and the bed looked appropriately robust. And it appeared to be running through the terrain to and fro in the directions it needed to go. But I saw few workers, and those I did see were haggard and wandering, thin and ghostlike." He shook his head in misery, his eyes moistening with welling tears.

"Then we saw men: white men, not thin, but some with guns, and most of them were running as if for their lives. Others of them were not upright, however. They had been clubbed, tied, shot, oh. . . . Only one of them stopped when I bellowed at him to do so. He recognized my name, thankfully, and looked suitably impressed."

Mac had the measure of this man now. Even in a moment of crisis, Winterson Blaswell wanted it known that he was to be respected. And who could argue with that? Anything he'd ever heard of or read about Winterson Blaswell was by and large praiseworthy, a self-made multimillionaire.

Blaswell went on, "I . . . I don't understand any of this. But fortunately, the man who stopped was an engineer and he—rather quickly, I might add—explained enough for us to learn the truth of the situation. And I am here to tell you!"

Blaswell stood his full height, his red face glaring, his muttonchops quivering with rage. He pointed at the ravine where Kane's paltry trestle had been. "Thurston Kane was a charlatan of the first order! I should have had him imprisoned, at the very least!"

He looked skyward, his big shoulders slumped. "I never thought I needed to check up on him. I had no idea how vile Kane was. I merely thought he was a gifted, shrewd businessman."

The fat man looked at Mac and Boone and his daughter and the stableman and the Chinese workers. All of them. "I trusted him. Oh but I have been a fool. And at what cost? While he lied to me, all along that monster was pocketing freakish profits at the cost of human lives!" He gestured toward the haggard Chinese workers. "How can I ever hope to make reparation?"

Philomena Blaswell walked over and laid a hand on her

father's arm. "There is no way to bring back lost lives, but we can do all we are able for the living. And we shall begin right now."

"And to think I almost took him into our family, as my son-in-law."

The snort and quick bray of laughter from the woman beside him brought all eyes to her. "Do you really think, Papa, that I would marry that fool? If so, you are deluded. I love you, Papa, but you are deluded. We have much to discuss, but this is not the place, and most certainly it is not the time."

"I'll say," said Boone.

CHAPTER 33

Some days later, after helping to sort matters at the rail camp—and with the cringing help of Ralston and a few other of Kane's employees who either didn't have the foresight or the ability to leave while the leaving was good—Mac and Boone were paid handsomely by a grateful Winterson Blaswell.

He vowed to personally see to it that each Chinese family was reunited to whatever extent they were able. He hired the Pinkerton Agency to find the missing and sold and had the paltry unmarked graves of those who died exhumed and relocated to a proper burial site. And he offered homes and land to the survivors and vowed to fund the establishment of a town—a railroad town—as per his original vision.

As Mac and Boone rode out, somewhat rested and most definitely ready to resume their former lives, they felt that, with Philomena Blaswell riding point on the operation, the Blaswell empire would do its level best to make right the monumental wrongs perpetrated in its name.

Within minutes on the trail, Boone commenced his chatter, as Mac knew he would.

"I tell you what, Mac, that thing looked as if it was made of matchsticks and kindling wood! It just plain old collapsed. I ain't never seen the like." Boone shook his head.

"You bet," said the big man. "I don't think anyone who witnessed that has ever, or will ever, seen its like. I can still hear it in my head, that gargantuan whooshing sound."

"Two dollars says it's because that rascal Kane cut so many corners building the thing that it was as weak as water."

"Careful, Boone. You know what they say about speaking ill of the dead."

"Bah! You think he gave a fig to anybody but himself? What could happen anyway? I ain't the only one to think and speak ill of Thurston Kane. You heard Blaswell and his daughter."

Mac shrugged. "Who knows? Maybe his ghost will come back, float right up out of that ravine, all the way down there at the dusty, jagged bottom hundreds of feet down, and . . ."

"Don't say it! Oh, Lordy, don't say it at all. You know I can't entertain such notions! Now I'll never sleep tonight. I ever tell you about the time the ghostly figure of the big silver buck deer nearly killed my pappy?

"Oh yes sir." Boone nodded. "It all but peeled the hide off him. Pappy swore it was the spirit of all the deer he ever shot for the table to feed our humble brood. All them spirits balled up in one huge, angry, stomping, fire-breathing, silver-colored buck!"

"It breathed fire?" said Mac, then lit his stinky black cigarillo and blew a huge blue-gray cloud of smoke at Boone. "Like this?"

Boone tried to howl his righteous rage at Mac and snatch at him at the same time, but he was coughing so hard he could barely stay in the saddle. After the coughing jag passed, he shot a long, knobby finger at his pard. "You just wait, Mac MacCoole! I ain't through with you yet! One of these days you'll wake up and wonder. . . ."

"Wonder what?"

Boone smiled and held his chin high. "Well, now, that's for me to know, ain't it? You just think on it."

"Hmm," said Mac. "I do my best thinking when I'm puffing on a cigarillo. I guess I better get to it."

Sometime later, as they rode the dusty trail southeastward home, toward Denver City, Boone said, "That daughter, Philomena, she ain't much of a looker, but I do believe she took a shine to me. Kept asking me about my buckskins."

Mac laughed. "That's because you had her cornered, and she's too cultured to tell you they smell bad."

"Aw, a little thing like that shouldn't matter none where love is concerned," said Boone. "All that money could go a long way to making a fella smell good."

"Most fellas, yes. But not you, Hoke," said Mac. "You, my friend, are singular in that regard."

"I'll take that as a compliment."

"Never said it was one."

They bickered, sore and battered but lucky to be alive, as they rode on back to Denver City to rest up, heal up . . . and wait for another telegram.

TURN THE PAGE FOR AN EXCITING PREVIEW!

When innocent people are threatened,
Preacher punishes the guilty,
dispensing his own brand of justice—
one bullet at a time. . . .

JOHNSTONE COUNTRY.
WHERE EVIL DWELLS . . .
AND JUSTICE AWAITS.

In a North American British province, a group of
Norwegian settlers have carved a life for themselves
in a lakeshore village called Skarkavik.
Hunters and fishermen, they raise their families in peace
under the natural cover of the surrounding forest.

Decker Galloway believes the land's natural resources
are being wasted on the few when so many have a greater
need. Having made his fortune logging the wilderness
of the eastern provinces, he wants to turn his axes
and saws loose on the untouched western region.
And no villagers are going to stand in his way.

But then there's Preacher.
He doesn't mind standing in Galloway's way.

Together, Preacher and his friend, the warrior Tall Dog,
will remind the Norwegians of their Viking ancestry
and declare war on Galloway's gang of murderous
gunslingers—with Preacher leading the charge.

**National bestselling authors
William W. Johnstone and J. A. Johnstone**

THE FIRST MOUNTAIN MAN
PREACHER'S BLOODY RAMPAGE

On sale wherever Pinnacle Books are sold.

LIVE FREE. READ HARD.

www.williamjohnstone.net
Visit us at www.kensingtonbooks.com.

CHAPTER 1

"Look out!" Preacher said as he lunged forward, grabbed his companion's arm, and jerked the tall young man back.

The big wagon, loaded heavily with barrels, rumbled past. The team of massive draft horses never slowed as the driver slapped their rumps with the reins.

"Watch where you're goin', you blasted red heathen!" the man yelled at the tall, buckskin-clad youngster standing beside Preacher. The young man had gotten distracted by his crowded surroundings and strayed too far into the street.

"If this is civilization, I'm not sure I like it," he said as he watched the wagon careen on down the cobblestones. "It is too dangerous here."

Preacher laughed and slapped him on the back. "Civilization ain't that much worse than the frontier, Tall Dog. It's just got a different set of dangers to look out for, that's all."

The young man called Tall Dog asked, "What was in those barrels the wagon was carrying?"

"Not much tellin'. Beer, whiskey, sugar, flour, gunpowder . . . could've been just about anything you can fit in a barrel. It don't matter. If those horses had knocked you down, chances are they'd have trampled you to death before the wagon ever ran over you."

Tall Dog gave the mountain man a solemn nod. "Then

you've saved my life yet again. I will never be able to repay all the debts I owe you, Preacher."

"Don't be so sure about that. You've pulled my fat outta the fire more'n once, remember?"

Tall Dog nodded. They set off along the street once more, trailed by a big, shaggy cur that appeared to be as much wolf as dog.

The two of them made a pretty impressive pair. Tall, broad shouldered, and muscular, Preacher was in his forties but looked younger.

Years in the mountains had left him with a deeply tanned face that didn't really show his age. Only scattered strands of silver threaded through his thick, dark hair, mustache, and beard.

The broad leather belt around his waist supported a pair of holstered Colt Patersons, the newfangled repeating revolvers that had been given to Preacher a while back by a company of rangers down in Texas. He also carried a sheathed hunting knife and had a tomahawk tucked behind the belt.

Tall Dog towered over Preacher by several inches but was built whipcord lean. The reddish tint to his skin testified to his Crow heritage, but the dark blond hair, shaved on the sides and left long on top to work into a braid that hung down his back, revealed the other side of his lineage.

His father was Olaf Gunnarson, a Norwegian who had immigrated to America and become a fur trapper and mountain man. Once in the mountains, Gunnarson had met, fallen in love with, and married a young Crow woman who had seen quite a bit of the western half of the continent during her various captivities and wanderings.

The Maker of All Things Above had blessed their union with only one child, a boy who had grown tall and strapping and strong. Olaf had called him Bjorn, but he usually went by his Crow name, Tall Dog.

Today he was armed with a couple of flintlock pistols and, in a scabbard that hung down his back from a strap around his shoulder, a Spanish conquistador's sword with a curved hilt around the handle. His mother had picked up the weapon, an *espada ancha*, during her travels as a young woman down in the Southwest.

During the year since their first meeting, Preacher and Tall Dog had become staunch friends and shared several adventures. They had worked together during the fur trapping season and amassed one of the best loads of pelts Preacher had taken in quite a while.

Now they were in St. Louis. That load of pelts was sold and had been stored in a fur trader's warehouse, and Preacher had money in his pocket.

He figured on spending some of it at Red Mike's.

No trip to St. Louis was complete without a visit to the tavern not far from the riverfront. Preacher had been stopping in there for years, every time he was in town, for a few drinks, some chin-wagging with the burly Irishman who ran the place, and occasionally some companionship from one of the buxom wenches who served drinks.

If Tall Dog was going to live the life of a mountain man, going to Red Mike's was a vital part of his education.

The youngster seemed to be having second thoughts about it. He said, "Perhaps it might be better if I went back to the stable where we left our horses and gear."

"Don't you want to see Red Mike's for yourself, after hearin' me talk about the place?"

"Is it noisy and crowded and smell bad like the rest of this city?"

"Well . . ." Preacher grinned. "Some might say that's a pretty fittin' description."

"You go ahead, Preacher," Tall Dog said. "I will await your return at the stable."

Preacher wasn't going to argue with him, although to be

honest, he was a little disappointed. He'd wanted to see what sort of reaction Tall Dog would provoke from the other customers in the tavern.

After all, it wasn't every day a fella laid eyes on a half-Viking, half-Crow warrior carrying around a conquistador's sword.

But the decision was Tall Dog's to make, so Preacher was about to say that he'd see him back at the stable when Tall Dog suddenly stood up a little straighter and frowned. That made him tower over his surroundings even more than before.

"Something wrong?" Preacher asked.

"That woman. I have never seen anyone such as her before."

Preacher looked where Tall Dog was looking, across the street to where a young woman was hurrying along. She wore a gray dress and a dark blue cloak with the hood thrown back to reveal tumbling waves of auburn hair.

From this distance and angle, Preacher couldn't see her eyes, but he was willing to bet that they were green and that she had a scattering of freckles across her face. He knew an Irish colleen when he saw one.

"Do you know her?" Tall Dog asked.

"You reckon I know everybody in St. Louis? I never saw her before, but I agree, she's mighty easy on the eyes."

"Her hair . . . it's so bright. Like the late afternoon, when the sun is low and the air begins to thicken with the approach of dusk."

"You know where she's going?"

Tall Dog's gaze snapped around to Preacher. "Of course not. Do you?"

"Not for sure, but I can tell she's an Irish lass, so she's probably on her way to Red Mike's."

She might not be headed anywhere near the tavern, Preacher thought, *but Tall Dog didn't know that.*

"Perhaps I should go there after all."

"Maybe you should. And even if that gal ain't there, some other good-lookin' wenches will be."

Tall Dog shook his head. "None to compare with that one." He looked over the heads of the crowd in the busy street and went on with a note of alarm entering his voice, "I don't see her anymore."

"Let's see if we can find her."

Tall Dog didn't say anything else about skipping Red Mike's. He strode along beside Preacher with a determined expression on his face.

The auburn-haired girl had disappeared into the throng of people. Preacher and Tall Dog didn't spot her again as they made their way toward Red Mike's.

Preacher honestly believed that they might find her at the tavern, but if they didn't, that would be all right. Looking for her was just an excuse to get Tall Dog to come along without being stubborn about it.

After leaving Dog outside with a command from Preacher to stay, they paused just inside the tavern's doorway. Tall Dog looked around, his keen eyes searching intently for the object of his interest.

"I do not see her, Preacher."

"The place is pretty busy. Maybe you just didn't notice her. Come on over to the bar with me. We'll ask Mike if she's been here."

Several customers called out Preacher's name by way of greeting. He grinned and nodded to them.

"It seems as if everyone here knows who you are," Tall Dog commented.

"Well, I been comin' here a long time, and sometimes you just want to be—"

Preacher stopped short as a young woman hurried up to him. The neckline of the dress she wore scooped low enough to reveal generous portions of her creamy, ample breasts.

Blond curls tumbled around her face to her shoulders, which were also left partially bare by the garment. She carried a currently empty round tray in her left hand.

"Preacher!" she said. She reached up, wrapped both arms around his neck, and pulled his face down to hers. Her lips pressed against his in a long, urgent kiss.

Whoops of approval erupted from some of the men in the tavern.

When Preacher finally broke the kiss and lifted his head, he saw that Tall Dog was staring at him with one eyebrow cocked quizzically.

"Um, this here is Molly," Preacher said. "And dang it, girl, I've told you before, I'm old enough to be your pa."

Molly still had her arms around his neck and her body pressed close to his. She grinned and said, "Yeah, but you ain't my pa."

Abruptly, her forehead creased in a frown as she went on, "You aren't my pa, are you, Preacher? I mean, you've been coming to St. Louis for a long time, and my ma worked in a place like this. . . ." The frown went away and the grin came back. "Oh, well, I don't care. I'm just glad to see you again, Preacher."

"Yeah, I, uh, got that idea." Preacher nodded toward his companion. "Molly, this here is Tall Dog, a good friend o' mine."

Molly finally let go of Preacher and boldly surveyed Tall Dog from head to foot. Judging by her expression, she liked what she saw.

"I don't reckon I've ever seen an Indian like you before," she said.

"That's because he's half Norwegian."

Tall Dog said, "Have you seen a young woman with hair

like the late afternoon sun? She was wearing a gray dress and a blue cloak and was headed in this direction."

The frown reappeared on Molly's face. "Don't you know better than to ask a girl about some other girl?"

"He's lived in the mountains all his life, with his ma's people," Preacher said.

Molly let out a disgusted snort. "That's no excuse. Would he ask some Indian girl if she'd seen some other Indian girl?"

"I doubt that it would cause offense if I did . . ." Tall Dog said with a tentative note in his voice.

"Oh, I'll bet it would. You'd probably just be too thick-headed to see it, you big—"

From behind the bar, the burly, mustachioed Red Mike called, "If you're through welcomin' Preacher and his friend, Molly, I've got drinks here that need to be delivered."

"I have to get back to work," the blonde said, "so I suppose I'll just have to forgive you, Tall Dog. That was what Preacher called you, isn't it?"

"Yes, I—"

She came up on her toes, kissed him on the mouth, and then twirled around to head for the bar and pick up those drinks.

Tall Dog gazed after her with a somewhat stunned expression on his face. After a moment, he said, "Does she always act like that?"

"Fussin' at you one second and kissin' you the next?" Preacher laughed. "You really don't know much about gals, do you?"

"I still say it is different back home."

"I ain't gonna waste time arguin' with you. Come on, let's talk to Mike."

On the way to the bar, Preacher paused a few times to greet old friends, although thankfully, none of the whiskery, buckskin-clad frontiersmen planted kisses on him as Molly had.

Red Mike's customers were split about evenly between fur trappers who were just visiting St. Louis but spent most of their time in the mountains or out on the plains and rivermen who lived in town and worked on the docks or the vessels that plied up and down the Mississippi.

Preacher got along all right with the rivermen, for the most part, but he didn't feel the same kinship with them that he did with other mountain men.

The fur business was in a serious decline. Preacher knew that within a few years it would be difficult for a man to make a living by trapping.

He wasn't sure what he'd do then, but his wants had always been simple and he'd never had any desire to be rich.

The river, on the other hand, would always be there and would always need men to work on and along it.

Not Preacher, though. He couldn't stand being tied down even that much.

"Howdy, boys," Red Mike said as Preacher and Tall Dog reached the bar. "Who's your friend, Preacher?"

"This is Tall Dog. We've been trailin' together for a spell. His ma's a Crow and his pa's a fella named Olaf Gunnarson who came over here from Norway."

Mike nodded and said, "I thought you had a bit of a Scandihoovian look about you, son." The tavernkeeper smiled. "I reckon your ancestors and mine fought each other tooth and nail about a thousand years ago, but you're sure as blazes welcome here in my tavern today."

Mike extended a big paw across the bar, and the two men shook. Tall Dog said, "I've heard stories from my father about the days when the Vikings went to war against the Irish. Those were epic battles."

"Aye, so they say. Those days are long past. What can I get you fellows?"

"Beer for the both of us," Preacher said, "but I'll have a shot o' whiskey with mine."

Mike hesitated and looked at Tall Dog. "No offense, lad, but I know that some members of your blessed mother's tribe have a difficult time with spiritous drinks."

"My father has also told me stories about the mead halls and the prodigious amounts of mead my ancestors could consume. I believe I will be all right to have one mug of beer."

"Comin' right up, then," Mike said as he reached under the bar for a pair of pewter beer steins. He filled them from a keg, set them on the bar in front of Preacher and Tall Dog, and then snagged a bottle of whiskey and an empty glass from a shelf.

Preacher and Tall Dog took hold of the steins and lifted them, but before they could drink, a harsh male voice spoke behind them.

"What the hell is this, Mike?" the man demanded. "Since when do you allow filthy, heathen redskins to drink in your tavern?"

CHAPTER 2

Preacher stopped with his beer stein halfway to his lips. He looked over his shoulder and saw a big, broad-shouldered man standing behind him and Tall Dog.

Preacher could tell by the rough work clothes that the man labored on the docks. He glared at Tall Dog with intense dislike on his beard-stubbled face. Thick, black hair fell down over his low brow.

"Back off there, Dechert," Mike said. "I'll be havin' no trouble in here, you know that."

"If you don't want trouble, you shouldn't let savages in here."

"Take it easy, friend," Preacher said. His words were civil enough, but his voice held a hard edge.

The riverman called Dechert turned the glare on him. "I know who you are. You don't scare me, Preacher."

"Not tryin' to scare anybody, just don't want to ruin a peaceful visit to my favorite tavern."

"It's my favorite tavern, too, or at least it was until it started stinkin' of Injun."

Tall Dog had been looking over his shoulder at the stranger, too, but now he pointedly turned back to the bar in a dismissive gesture.

"I would like to ask you a question," he said to Mike. "We are looking for a young woman—"

Dechert said, "Keep your dirty redskin hands off the gals around here, you damn—"

As he spoke, he grabbed Tall Dog's shoulder. Dechert was pretty big, but he had to reach up to do that.

Preacher didn't wait any longer in the hope that trouble could be averted. It was too late for that now.

He crashed the beer stein in his hand against the left side of Dechert's head.

The stunning blow was enough to drive the riverman to his knees. Preacher dropped the beer stein and pivoted to throw a left-hand punch into Dechert's face.

The clout drove the man over backward and left him sprawled senseless on the tavern's sawdust-littered floor. A couple of men sitting at a nearby table had had to jump up and back to keep him from crashing into them.

"Blast it, Preacher!" Red Mike burst out. "Why'd you—"

"Didn't figure you'd want one of your customers gutted right here in the tavern," Preacher interrupted to say. "That's what would've happened mighty quick-like if he'd kept on tryin' to manhandle Tall Dog."

With a solemn nod, Tall Dog said, "I would have been forced to defend myself."

"Well, it ain't over yet. Look out!"

Preacher heeded Mike's warning and jerked his head around in time to see a flung chair sailing through the air at him. He didn't have time to duck, so he threw up an arm and deflected the chair so that it clattered against the bar.

However, that wasn't the end of it. Four men who had been sitting at a table had surged to their feet. One of them had thrown the chair. Because their clothing marked them as rivermen, too, Preacher assumed they were Dechert's friends.

One of them confirmed that by shouting, "We can't let

him get away with what he did to Otto! Get the cowardly *schwein*!"

They charged at Preacher and Tall Dog. A few men who happened to be in the way scrambled to get clear.

Red Mike yelled curses and told the men to stop, but they ignored him. Preacher and Tall Dog turned to meet the charge.

Tall Dog reached up and closed his hand around the grips of the sheathed sword on his back, but Preacher snapped, "Leave that blade where it is. We don't want to kill these idiots."

Tall Dog glanced at him, shrugged, and let go of the sword.

The way the attackers were clumped together, Preacher and Tall Dog couldn't separate them and tackle two apiece. They all came together in a knot of slugging, flailing fists.

Preacher didn't bother much with trying to fend off any blows. He just absorbed the punishment and dished out some in return.

The battle continued in that furious fashion for a moment, until one of the rivermen worked his way around behind Tall Dog and jumped on his back. He wrapped his arms around Tall Dog's neck and his legs around the warrior's waist and yelled, "I got him! I got him!"

Tall Dog reached back with both hands, grabbed the man's ears, and twisted them as he bent forward at the waist. The man howled in pain and his arms and legs loosened.

Quick as a flash, Tall Dog shifted his grip and caught hold of the man under the arms. With a powerful heave, he sent the man flying over his head to crash into another of the attackers.

A few feet away, Preacher caught one of his opponents with a straight, hard right to the face and felt the satisfying crunch as the man's nose flattened under the impact. Hot blood spurted across the mountain man's knuckles. The man reeled back, clutching his nose and groaning as crimson streamed from it.

That exchange gave the other riverman just enough time to set himself and hammer a punch into Preacher's midsection. Preacher's belly was ridged with muscle and hard as a washboard, but the man who hit him was large and powerfully built. The blow was enough to drive Preacher back against the bar.

With little room to maneuver, Preacher wasn't able to avoid the man's lunge. The punch also knocked most of the breath out of him, so he didn't react quite as quickly as he normally would have.

As a result, the riverman was able to clamp both hands around Preacher's neck and bend him back even more. He aimed a knee at Preacher's groin in a vicious thrust.

Preacher expected that and twisted the lower half of his body just in time to avoid the worst of it. The riverman's knee caught him on the thigh. That made Preacher's leg go numb for a moment, but the choking hands held him up so he didn't collapse.

Bright red rockets began to go off behind Preacher's eyes. He knew the lack of air would make him lose consciousness in another minute or so, and that would end the fight.

Even though his muscles didn't want to obey his commands, he brought his arms up and hacked down with the edges of both hands, driving them against the spots where his opponent's shoulders met his neck.

That paralyzing double blow made the man let go of Preacher's neck. He stumbled as he tried to stay on his feet. Preacher lifted a right uppercut from his knees.

It landed under the man's chin. His feet came off the floor, his legs flew up, and he slammed down on his back.

Blood leaked from his mouth. Preacher spotted something lying in the sawdust next to the man that might be the bitten-off tip of his tongue.

Keep your tongue behind your teeth during a fight. That could be a painful lesson to learn, Preacher thought as he leaned on the bar and tried to catch his breath.

All four of their attackers were down, either unconscious or bloody and moaning. Dechert, who had started the fight by harassing Tall Dog, still lay senseless in a puddle of spilled beer. But at least it was over.

Then Preacher realized that wasn't the case at all. Half a dozen more rivermen were on their feet and advancing deliberately toward the bar. Three of them held large knives, while the other three gripped makeshift clubs that were actually chair legs wrenched free.

Preacher glanced at a nearby table where several frontiersmen sat. He knew one of them and asked, "You boys plan on takin' cards in this game, Cullers?"

The man grinned back at him. "Why would we do that?" he wanted to know. "We're havin' too much fun watchin' you hand these river rats their needin's!"

"These men are armed, Preacher," Tall Dog said. He reached up, closed his hand around the sword again, and cocked an eyebrow.

"Go ahead," Preacher said.

Steel whispered against leather as Tall Dog drew the *espada ancha*.

The sight of the sword's broad blade made the gang of rivermen hesitate for a second. The weapon gave Tall Dog greater reach . . . but there were six of them.

Besides, they had made it obvious to everyone in the tavern that they were entering the fray. They couldn't back down now, not without injuring their pride.

With sudden, harsh yells, they charged the tall warrior.

Preacher stepped back, figuring he might as well watch the show, too.

The man with the longest club leapt over a fallen combatant and reached Tall Dog first. He gripped the bludgeon in both hands and swung it with speed and power.

Tall Dog swatted it aside with a flick of the blade that seemed effortless. He could have backhanded the sword across the man's throat and opened it up with the razor-keen edge, but instead, he slapped the flat of the blade against the man's head.

That made the man stumble, fall, and pitch forward to ram his head against the bar. He dropped senseless to the floor.

Tall Dog shifted to the side so he wouldn't trip over the man he'd just put out of the fight. Again, he didn't seem to hurry, but he was standing there in one place and then he wasn't, in less than the blink of an eye.

That caused the man who tried to rip him open with a downward knife stroke to miss badly. Tall Dog lifted the sword and slammed the heavy brass pommel at the end of the grip into the man's head.

He fell next to the man with the club, who was also out cold.

Tall Dog whirled out of the way of the next man, whose club struck the bar with enough force that he lost his grip on it. With his free hand, Tall Dog grabbed the back of the man's neck and shoved his head down.

The man's face bounced off the bar, and his knees buckled. He crumpled next to the other two.

That accounted for half of the fresh wave of attackers.

The trio still on their feet had learned from watching how the fight worked out for their companions. Instead of coming within reach of the sword, one of the men drew back his arm and threw the knife he held at Tall Dog.

The *espada ancha* flickered in the lamplight as Tall Dog whirled it in an arc. Metal clanged against metal as the sword struck the flung knife and knocked it away.

While Tall Dog was doing that, the remaining man holding a club sprang close enough to him that he was able to ram the chair leg into the warrior's side.

Tall Dog grunted in pain but didn't give ground. He swung his left forearm in a sweeping blow that caught the man on the side of the head and drove him against the bar.

The next instant, Tall Dog was behind him, his left arm looped around the man's neck and the sword at his throat. Utter silence gripped the tavern because everyone in there knew that it would take only a slight motion of Tall Dog's wrist to cut the man's throat from ear to ear.

Only one of the rivermen who'd wanted trouble was left. He held a knife, but he threw it on the floor with a quick motion.

"It's over!" he said. "Don't kill him, mister."

"I never kill anyone unless I have no choice," Tall Dog said. He added into the ear of the man he held on the brink of death, "Is the fight over?"

The man started to swallow but stopped as he realized that would put more pressure on the blade pressed to his neck. He licked his lips instead and said, "Y-yeah. No more t-trouble."

"Very well." Tall Dog took the sword away from the man's throat but kept the grip on his neck. "Gather up your friends and leave."

"We . . . we sure will!"

From where Preacher leaned casually against the bar, the mountain man said, "Don't get no ideas about lurkin' around outside and jumpin' us later, neither. Won't be no askin' polite-like next time. Just killin'."

Tall Dog finally released the man he held and gave him

a little shove. He stepped back and with another of those economical movements sheathed the sword on his back.

Preacher straightened and stepped over beside him. They watched as the two rivermen began hauling their companions to their feet. Several other men who worked on the docks came forward to help.

Some of the men who'd been knocked out regained enough consciousness to stumble from the tavern under their own power. Others had to be carried out. But within minutes they were all gone.

"Sorry about the ruckus, Mike," Preacher said as he and Tall Dog turned again to the bar.

"You fellas didn't start it," Red Mike replied with a shrug, "and for a change, there's not any blood on the floor to clean up. A few chairs got broken, but I reckon I can repair them. As brawls that you're mixed up in go, it wasn't too bad, Preacher."

That brought a laugh from the mountain man. "Maybe we'll try harder next time. And I pretty much steered clear of this one."

"I noticed." Mike looked at Tall Dog. "I believe you were about to ask me something when the trouble broke out, son."

"Yes, I was, sir. We came here looking for a woman."

Mike lifted a bushy eyebrow. "Well, I suppose something can be arranged, as long as the gal is agreeable—"

"Not like that, Mike," Preacher said. "Tall Dog's talkin' about a particular woman we saw on the street headed in this direction. Mighty pretty gal with dark red hair. We didn't get a real good look at her, but she appeared to be Irish to me."

Mike surprised them by responding, "Wears a blue cloak with a hood on it?"

"That is her," Tall Dog said with a note of excitement in his voice. He looked around. "She is here?"

"Not right now. She was here earlier today, though." Mike stroked his chin and frowned, evidently in thought. "You know, this is a mite strange."

"What is?" Preacher asked.

"The fact that you fellas came in here lookin' for her just now, because when she stopped in before, *she* was lookin' for *you*, Preacher."